Like a
Love
Song

Center Point
Large Print

Also by Camille Eide and available from
Center Point Large Print:

The Memoir of Johnny Devine
Like There's No Tomorrow

**This Large Print Book carries the
Seal of Approval of N.A.V.H.**

Like a
Love
Song

Camille Eide

CENTER POINT LARGE PRINT
THORNDIKE, MAINE

ISBN: 978-1-68324-988-7

Library of Congress Cataloging-in-Publication Data

Names: Eide, Camille, author.
Title: Like a love song / Camille Eide.
Description: Center Point Large Print edition. | Thorndike, Maine :
    Center Point Large Print, 2018.
Identifiers: LCCN 2018036581 | ISBN 9781683249887
    (hardcover : alk. paper)
Subjects: LCSH: Large type books. | GSAFD: Love stories.
Classification: LCC PS3605.I36 L54 2018 | DDC 813/.6—dc23
LC record available at https://lccn.loc.gov/2018036581

Dedicated to Dad,
whose patient love and persistence,
in spite of a step-daughter's resistance,
taught her to trust in a Father's love
that will never fail.

"Father to the fatherless, defender of widows—
this is God, whose dwelling is holy.
God places the lonely in families;
he sets the prisoners free and gives them joy."

PSALM 68:5-6

CHAPTER ONE

Adoption disrupted . . . undisclosed behaviors . . . inability to bond . . .

Susan Quinn squinted at the new girl's bio as the words on the page swirled in a taunting blur. She rubbed her eyes and refocused on the document. She was in no frame of mind for processing the information about Juniper Ranch's newest resident. Not after the unsettling confrontation she'd just had with her handyman. Or rather, *former* handyman.

"Sue?" Bertie padded into Sue's office, footsteps muted by Birkenstocks. In spite of her hunched frame, the old woman got around like a flower-powered ninja. "She's here." Bertie peered out the window. "The new girl. But . . . I think you'd better come take a look."

Sue dropped the sheet on her desk, adding it to the mounds of paperwork and overdue bills. What limbs she wouldn't give for this transfer to go smoothly. But experience had taught her to hope for the best and prepare for the worst. With a sigh, she headed for the office's outer door. "Wish me luck, Bert."

Bertie offered her a waiver form. "Holler if you need me."

Sue frowned at the paper. "Why do I need this? We'll take care of everything in the office."

"Wouldn't bet on it." Bertie nodded toward the window. "Look."

Sue opened the door and peered outside.

A late-model Escalade sat in the drive beyond the front lawn, engine still running. A man, barely visible behind tinted windows, remained in the car while an athletic-looking woman in designer warm-ups dropped two pink suitcases on the front porch of the main entrance. A black-haired girl stood beside the bags, shoulders cinched up so tight they nearly touched her ears.

Jasmine—the new girl.

Sue's heart tripped.

The woman hurried back to the SUV. Halfway across the lawn she turned, said something to the girl, and then pointed to the front door.

Sue's breath caught and stung. *No. Please don't. Not like that. Don't just dump her and go.* She rushed outside, down the steps, and across the lawn. "Hi, Mrs. Walker?"

The woman turned with a start. "Is this Juniper Ranch group home?"

"Yes." As Sue approached, she glanced at Jasmine. The preteen was as stiff as a fence post.

"We got lost trying to find the place." Mrs.

Walker crossed her arms like a shield. "Where do I sign?"

Sue couldn't answer. Bertie was right—the woman was ready to sign away her child on the hood of a car. Sue stole another look at Jasmine, who stared at the hot pink bags in silence.

Beyond the girl, curtains twitched in the den window, partially revealing the curious faces of Cori, Edgar, and Tatiana.

While Mrs. Walker signed the papers, the man remained at the wheel, shoulder belt still fastened. It took the woman all of six minutes to complete the paperwork.

A new Juniper Ranch record.

Then the couple drove away. The Escalade's brake lights didn't blink once.

Sue joined Jasmine on the porch, feeling oddly connected to the girl who hadn't uttered a sound. Sue had done this countless times and still didn't have the words. What could she possibly say to a kid who had just been dumped off on a total stranger?

I'm sorry, sweetheart. I know the feeling. But you're among friends here.

Sue inhaled the dry, sage-scented air and made a quick study of the new girl.

Wafer thin. Cambodian, maybe Vietnamese. About eleven or twelve. Jasmine's paperwork was a jumbled maze of inconsistencies and missing information—which was not uncommon—so Sue would have to best-guess her age.

"Well, Jasmine." Sue summoned a bright smile for a moment that was anything but. "You hungry? We're not serving dinner for a while, but I bet I can find you a snack."

The girl turned her gaze toward the long driveway leading away from Juniper Ranch. The ribbon of dust disturbed by the Escalade rose and spread slowly, drifting in the afternoon sun, bound to settle in some other place.

The pair of suitcases flanked Jasmine's feet, price tags still attached. A couple of bags that held everything. And nothing. Much like the beat-up green Samsonite that had, long ago, followed Sue to more foster homes than she could count.

Sue's stomach growled as she grabbed a suitcase. "All right, kiddo. Let's get your stuff inside. We'll get you set up in your new room."

Jasmine turned then, her eyes almost level with Sue's.

No shocker there. At five-two, Sue was used to meeting preteens eye to eye.

The girl's face had no remarkable features. Wide nose, small eyes. No abnormalities, no physical handicap that Sue could see. No sign of the kinds of imperfections that often made Mr. and Mrs. Disenchanted back out of an international adoption.

What fears haunt you, little friend? What coping quirks couldn't they handle?

"I no need room." A frown creased the girl's brow. "I no—I *not* staying here."

"Well, we can discuss that. Just not here on the front porch. Okay?" She softened the question with a gentle smile.

Jasmine's frown deepened. Thick tears pooled, glittering in her dark eyes.

Oh, honey, no, please don't do that . . . A quiet ache squeezed Sue's heart. It wasn't the first time she'd stood on these weathered steps, a silent witness to the aftermath of a "disrupted" adoption. It came with the job. But no matter how many times she'd done this, she still couldn't get used to watching a young heart break in the middle of her front porch.

Sue shifted the girl's bag to her other hand and motioned with her head. "C'mon, kiddo. This way." She opened the front door and went inside. If she hesitated or looked back, it wouldn't work. "It's not Disneyland," Sue called over her shoulder, "but at least it's a place where you can fit in."

The door hung open, letting in cool October air.

Sue headed for the stairs. "Fitting in" might be aiming a bit high. But she would do whatever it took to make Jasmine feel like there was one place in the world where she wouldn't be an outsider. Sue reached the staircase and paused.

No sounds of footsteps came from the porch.

Dragging a girl inside and forcing her to stay

wasn't high on her list of favorite things to do. *Come on, Jasmine. I'm offering you some dignity here. Please take it.* Fighting the temptation to look, Sue headed up the staircase, straining to hear sounds of Jasmine following.

Fourth step. Sixth.

Take it from me, little one. The sooner you learn to stop longing, the sooner the pain will go away.

Ninth step.

The urge to look back reached a cresting point.

Then, shuffling footsteps and the click of the front door.

Sue turned and gave the skinny girl with the pink suitcase a smile. "C'mon, slowpoke. Follow me."

While Miss Elena introduced Jasmine to the kitchen crew, Sue dashed to her office and grabbed the new paperwork. Maybe she could learn something else about Jasmine while the kids were occupied with dinner duties.

"Hey, boss." Bertie came from the dining hall, trailed by the scent of toasting garlic bread. "Bowman clocked on, but he's not—hey, you okay? I didn't want to mention it earlier, but you look like something not even Ringo would drag home, and that dog's not picky."

"Thanks, Bert." Sue tugged the band from her frazzled braid and combed fingers through her blonde waves. "You know, you ought to try

14

saying what you really think instead of bottling it all up like that. It's not healthy."

Bertie snorted. "You think you're joking, but you have no idea what I hold back."

"Ha." Sue returned her attention to the paper. Actually, after the day she'd had, she probably looked like she'd been thrown under a tractor and dragged across one of the neighbors' alfalfa fields. She needed no reminder that her professional look had taken a long departure from her social services days of pantsuits and heels. But for running a place like this, a braid, sturdy boots, and a pair of well-worn jeans *was* her professional look, and the only one that made any sense.

Besides, who was there to get all dolled up for? Juniper Valley, little more than a speck of dust in the wide expanse of Oregon's outback, wasn't exactly swarming with eligible guys. Not that she had the time—or the need—for any of that.

Sue massaged her throbbing temples. "About Bowman—"

"He clocked on at three, but I haven't seen him. I think he might have left."

"He did."

Bertie froze, her look instantly wary. "What's going on?"

Sue scanned the file once again. "Mr. Bowman no longer works here." When Bertie didn't comment, Sue looked up.

The thin line of the dorm supervisor's mouth made her look like a Muppet.

"Something you want to tell me?"

Bertie's gaze darted away.

"Have you seen him hung over at work after he was warned?"

With a shrug, Bertie took the paper from Sue and read it, frowning. "Hard to say what someone's been doing on their day off, boss."

Sue stared at Bertie. "You're kidding, right? You know the rules."

"Yep."

"I made it clear he'd be gone if he ever showed up like that again. And today he's not only hungover, he's half hammered." Sue glanced out the window toward the shop. If only she could go back to the first time she'd talked to him about the issue and follow her gut. "I can't believe I gave him a second chance."

Bertie glanced up. Sympathy radiated from behind her round lenses.

But in Sue's mind, another face came into view.

He won't do it again, Suzy. He just had a li'l too much. You know how he is . . .

No, Mom, ten-year-old Sue had finally gotten up the nerve to say. *How should I know how he is or how any of them are? Most of the time, I don't even know their names . . .*

"Well, if he was warned," Bertie said, shutting

down Sue's ancient memory, "then he had it coming."

If anyone had earned the right to question Sue, Roberta "Bertie" Hayes had. "He knew the rules and signed the ranch's conduct agreement like everyone else."

"You're right. Absolutely." Bertie's forehead pleated into a frown.

It wasn't like Bertie to hold back. "What?"

Bertie tossed the paper onto the desk with a long sigh. "It's just, what are we going to do? We got a mile-long list of repairs, and being short on care staff, we were already pulling doubles, and now—"

"Now we get creative and figure something out, just like we always do." Sue rubbed her temples. "I won't compromise safety just because we need a body. I'd work myself to the grave before I'd keep a guy like that on staff."

Bertie locked Sue in a hard stare. "Trouble is you're working the rest of us into the ground right along with you."

The pasty gray patches beneath Bertie's eyes matched the ones Sue had noticed on her own face. The work had been harder lately, no doubt. She and the remaining core staff had to shoulder the load with the constant turnover of college interns, and worse, the loss of Emily, her best dorm counselor. Had it already been a year since Emily left?

"Listen, Sue, I'm not trying to add to our troubles. But in case you haven't noticed, Elena and I are nearly shot from running short-handed. And now we're down another staffer."

Our troubles? Sue studied Bertie. The care staff at Juniper Ranch shared Sue's heart for outcast kids but did they have the same vested interest that she had in making this home work?

"Now Elena and I will have to split the boys' dorm shifts," Bertie said. "And I'm not even going to bring up adult-to-child ratios." Arms crossed against her faded tie-dyed shirt, she pinned Sue with a steady look. "We need help."

Sue nodded. "You're right, I'm sorry. I'll get us some help. Right away."

On her way out to the work shop, Sue mulled over the day's events. She did not regret her decision to fire Bowman—the kids' safety came first. And the ranch would bounce back. It would take more than a staff shortage to topple the system she'd spent two years building. Discipline and routine not only kept Juniper Ranch running smoothly, it gave the kids a sense of stability, of normalcy. And these kids needed to feel normal and stable even more than they needed food and shelter.

But Bertie was right. Losing Bowman was a blow.

Sue straightened the cardboard over a busted-out shop window, then made the call to Layne

Stevenson. Getting through to a DHS district manager was a lot harder now than it was when Sue and Layne worked family cases for the county.

Layne answered with a cheerful "hello," then listened as Sue asked about college interns.

"We didn't get many interns this term, but I'll see if I can figure out something."

Sue slipped inside the shop and flicked on the fluorescents. "Thanks, Layne. I owe you."

"Speaking of help, I was going to call you."

"Really? You're finally coming to work for me?"

"Tempting, but no." Layne chuckled. "I'm a newlywed, remember? I like going home every night to a warm body. You oughta try it."

Sue shook her head. Layne's "warm body" was a former NFL linebacker who made King Kong look like a Happy Meal toy. She shivered. "I'm plenty warm, thanks." She picked her way around the mess.

Her Suburban sat in the center of the shop under a film of high desert dust. Her old Harley stood behind the Suburban, streaks of sunset glinting off the chrome, and her Honda dual sport was parked next to it. In one corner, the riding mower lay in pieces. In another, discarded car parts were piled in a heap like a dismantled carcass, and most of her tools littered the shop as if three-year-olds had been playing tune-up.

"Sue, I hate to mention it, but your last licensing inspection—"

"I know." Sue heaved a sigh. "I'm on it."

Layne's end went silent for several seconds. "Really? You'll have all the repairs done in time for the follow-up?"

Sue leaned against the Suburban. The latest list of repairs the state required to keep her license was the toughest she'd ever received. With Bowman gone, Sue had no idea how she was going to get the repairs finished in time. She groaned.

"I'll take that as a no," Layne said. "Listen, I've got the perfect solution for you. My brother's boss from Alaska is in the area, and he's looking for temporary work until the first of the year. Dan said he's absolutely the best guy—"

"Boss of what?"

"Um, well . . . an offshore oil rig. But he's—"

"An *oil rigger?*" Sue hacked out a laugh. "A roughneck? Great. Who are you going to send next, a lumberjack and a couple of bikers? Maybe they can pull night watch in the girls' hall." Sue yanked open the driver's door of her Suburban, climbed in, and cranked the key.

A few feeble chugs, then nothing. Big surprise.

"I'm serious, Sue. Joe is an all-around handyman and knows how to manage a crew."

"I'm sure he's charming, Layne. On an oil rig. But I need someone with experience handling kids with special needs. You know that."

"Yes, in the long run, in optimal circumstances, absolutely. But you're going to give old Bertie a stroke if you don't get some help. You have to hire someone."

Sue rested her aching head on the steering wheel. Pain and fatigue rolled over her in a cold fog. Why couldn't Emily have stuck around instead of running off to Scotland?

"Sue?"

She slipped out of the Suburban. "Sorry, Layne, but Juniper Ranch isn't hiring oil drillers. If you want to help, find me some experienced temps or at least a couple of interns. Just make sure the interns know they'll be living in the desert a hundred miles from the nearest club. Thanks." She let herself out of the shop and trudged the path back to the porch.

From somewhere inside the house, a metallic crash rang out, followed by shouts.

CHAPTER TWO

Joe Paterson wiped the men's room mirror with the towel, then grabbed his razor and leaned closer for a better look. He smoothed a hand over his head, already fuzzy with a day's worth of dark growth. He'd kept up the shaved-head routine even after Dave's funeral, but there was no point shaving it any more.

By now, his best friend probably had a full head of hair and was discovering that everything Joe had told him about heaven was true. No more pain, no more chemo.

Father, thanks for letting me be there when Dave gave his life to You. Glad I got to be a part of that. Clearing the sudden knot in his throat, Joe stowed the memory, returned to the mirror, and gave his dark jaw a shave. Then he stuffed the towel in the stained laundry bag marked "Gordy's," grabbed his duffel, and left the men's room.

In spite of the bustle in the crowded truck stop diner, the waitress at the register beamed a dimpled smile as Joe passed her.

"Thanks for the shower." He made a mental

note to remember this truck stop in case he ever made another road trip through Oregon.

Blushing, the waitress glanced around. "Actually, only truckers are supposed to use it, so it'll just be our little secret."

The older lady who'd served him breakfast strolled up and cocked her bleach-blonde head. "Well, big guy, did you finally get enough to eat?"

"I did, thanks." He checked the time. Going on noon. He could still get to Bend and search the public records before the courthouse closed for the weekend. The three-hour drive would give him plenty of time to rehearse what he wanted to say to his ex-adoptive dad.

Not that he needed practice. In the fourteen years since Joe had aged out of the system, not a day passed that he hadn't thought about finding John Jacobs and making him hear the truth about his family.

"Sure we can't bring you out a few more Gordy's Grinders?" Blondie nodded toward the kitchen. "That is, if we got anything left back there."

"I'm good, thanks."

She winked at him. "Aw, hon, I'm just kidding. Strapping guy like you—" She tapped his bicep with her order pad. "Bet it takes a lot of protein to maintain all that muscle, huh?"

Joe answered with a smile. If he were still

seated, he'd have to add a couple more bucks to her tip. He stepped outside and climbed into his pickup truck.

Next order of business was getting directions to the Bend courthouse. He reached under the seat for his laptop, but his fingers groped at empty air. He looked around the cab and under the seat again.

His laptop, coat, and extra duffel of clothes—gone.

He jumped out and checked the truck bed.

His tent, sleeping bag, and fishing poles were gone too.

Adrenaline surging, he scoured the lot, feet pounding the blacktop, searching for signs of his stuff.

A man pumping gas said he'd seen someone near the truck but couldn't remember any details.

Blasting out a breath that didn't unload his frustration, Joe returned to the diner.

Blondie met him inside the door.

"I need the number for the local police," he said. "Someone stole all my stuff from my truck while I was in here."

"I'm so sorry, hon." She scrawled the number and handed it over. "Might as well have a seat while you wait for the deputy. Lemme get you some more coffee."

Temples pounding, he strode to a window seat at the far end of the diner, made the call, and sat back to wait. Idiot. In Alaska, he'd always left his rig unlocked. He'd forgotten how different things were in the Lower Forty-Eight.

Joe closed his eyes. *Father, I need to get that laptop back. That information will be hard to replace. I don't care about the rest of the stuff. I can get new camping gear. And clothes. And my*— "Oh man." Joe dragged a hand down hard over his face.

"What, hon?" Blondie was back, pouring steaming coffee into a clean mug.

Joe groaned. "My guitar."

"Well, that sure stinks. What kind of person has the nerve to steal a man's stuff in broad daylight?" Blondie shook her head as she walked away.

Joe watched the highway, still kicking himself for leaving his stuff free for the taking. Minutes stretched into half an hour. Not only was his stuff gone, now he was losing time. He checked his watch. His chances of making it to Bend in time to do any searching today were dwindling. If he got that ranch job Dan had told him about, no telling how long he'd have to wait before being able to search again.

After a long stretch of cars, a Multnomah County sheriff's cruiser finally entered the lot.

Joe drained his cup and stood.

Within a minute, Blondie's voice rang out above the dining clatter. "Oh, you can't miss him, hon. He's that big bruiser right back there."

The officer approached.

Joe didn't miss how the deputy sized him up. Pretty much everyone did. Cops were less obvious about it, but they still took note of his six-four frame and two-forty build.

The deputy took down Joe's basic information, then asked about witnesses and his belongings, taking careful notes.

Joe listed everything he was missing. Fishing gear, clothes, laptop, sleeping bag, tent, some pictures, a few personal things, his Bible. And the smoothest sounding Martin D-28 he'd ever heard.

The officer scrutinized Joe's license. "What brings you to Oregon?"

"The rig I worked on in Alaska was dismantled. I start a new job down in the Gulf of Mexico in a couple of months."

The officer nodded. "You visiting Troutdale or just passing through?" He handed back the driver's license.

"Passing through. I'm hoping to stay in the Bend area until the Gulf job starts."

"Got family there?"

If you could call it that. "Uh, sort of. I'm trying to find some relatives that I . . . lost touch with." Joe wiped moist palms on his jeans. *No names, please. I don't want them to know I'm looking.*

The officer wrote more notes. "We can put you

in touch with the county's victim assistance to get you some clothes, maybe some gear."

"Thanks, but I'll be fine. Should have a job lined up soon."

The deputy gave him a business card and said he'd contact him with any news.

When he'd gone, Blondie returned and set a coffee carafe down. "You staying around here?"

"I'm headed for Bend, or thereabouts." With any luck, he could get on at the ranch in Juniper Valley. A farm wouldn't pay anywhere near what an oil rig paid, but he didn't really need the money. He needed a place to blend in just long enough to settle his business.

"Well, leave your number and we'll let you know if we hear anything."

Joe rose, pulled out his wallet, and offered her a ten. "Sure appreciate that, ma'am."

"Aw, hon, you're a doll!" Blondie winked and tucked the bill inside her blouse. "You be sure to come back and see us again."

Not likely. Once he found a place to stay, he'd be laying low for a while.

Sue broke into a run. The sound of kids yelling swelled as she dashed up the steps, into the house, and rounded the corner to the dining hall.

Thirteen-year-old Edgar lay facedown in a landing strip of spaghetti sauce, still clutching an empty serving pan.

"Edgar?" Pulse racing, she dropped to his side and touched his shoulder. "Where are you hurt?"

The boy mumbled, "I'm okay." But he continued to lie in the pasta, torso heaving.

Sue shot a glance at Elena.

The older woman shook her head. "There is maybe a little more sauce, Miss Susan, but that was pretty much all of tonight's dinner."

She nodded. Fabulous.

Bertie shuffled in and surveyed the damage. Some of the kids gathered around the pasta, others around Edgar. Plastered to the far wall, Jasmine scanned the scene, dark eyes wide.

One teenage voice rose above the rest. "Look at my new shoes! You *idiot*—they're totally ruined!"

"Brandi!" Sue spun and stared the older girl down—as best she could. With seven inches and forty pounds on Sue, Brandi often tried to turn their conflicts into a physical challenge.

Ignoring Sue, Brandi leaned close to the prone boy and hissed, "Thanks, Twinkie. It's all yours now. Eat up. You probably like eating off the floor anyway, fatty."

"Hey!" Anger sent pain rippling through Sue's already thumping head. She willed the girl to make eye contact. "That is *not*—"

"Sue . . ." Bertie shook her head and held up three fingers.

"Third strike today?" Sue turned back to the

28

girl. "Okay, Brandi, looks like you're doing a whole lot of dishes tonight."

"No." Brandi shook her head. "I'll take the push-ups."

Battling with the troubled sixteen-year-old required a level of energy that Sue could usually summon, but double shifts and little sleep had left her running on a thin ribbon of fumes. "Make it forty. And when you're done, you'll help clean this up."

Brandi opened her mouth.

Sue cut her off with a flat palm. "We can make it ninety."

The girl jutted her chin at Sue, then backed off and dropped to the floor.

Sue took Edgar's saucy arm and helped him up.

Chin quivering, he kept a straight face despite the tomato chunks and basil bits clinging to his chubby cheeks. Tears had already cut white stripes through the red sauce.

Poor kid. Sue grabbed some napkins and handed them over quickly before he broke down in front of the others. "Sure you're not hurt?"

He nodded and swept a glance around the room, as though looking for his accusers. No one said a word. "Sorry, dudes," he whispered.

Sue wiped a blob from Edgar's chin. "It's okay, buddy. Stuff spills."

"But . . ." Brandi puffed between push-ups.

"Not usually . . . everyone's entire . . . dinner."

"That's twenty more, Brandi." Sue turned to Bertie. "Elena is probably in there hunting for something else to serve, so I'll take some of the kids in to help with that. You and the others can work on getting this cleaned up." On her way to the kitchen, Sue nodded at Jasmine. "And please keep an eye on her."

"Sure, boss. No problem."

Something in Bertie's tone broke through the haze of Sue's now full-scale headache. "You sure?"

Bertie was already shuffling toward the cleaning closet. "Yep. Piece a cake."

The kitchen crew scrounged up an odd assortment of leftover pastas and cooked up the motley batch. Elena concocted a grayish-white sauce that vaguely resembled Alfredo and almost didn't taste like powdered milk. It took some work, but the staff and all twelve kids finally ate.

Sue left the kitchen in the hands of the cleanup crew and scanned the dining hall for Jasmine. In the scuffle of kids tidying the room, it took a minute to spot the girl.

She stood at the dining hall window with her back to everyone.

Sue weaved her way toward the girl, dodging a speeding mop bucket and kids with tubs of dirty dishes.

The kitchen door opened and slammed against the wall.

Jasmine jumped and spun like a startled jackrabbit. She cast a hopeful look toward the front foyer, but when she saw Sue approaching, she scowled and turned back to the window.

"Hey." Sue came alongside the girl. "Pretty cool view, huh?"

The only thing visible in the growing dusk was the dark, flat-topped silhouette of Table Rock to the east, rising just beyond Juniper Ridge Canyon.

The kid's steady vigil probably had nothing to do with the view. Sue leaned against the windowsill. "That's Table Rock."

Jasmine offered a sideways frown. "Table?"

"Yep. There's an old Indian legend about it."

The girl stared in silence at the lone mass.

"Want to hear it?"

Jasmine shrugged.

"The people who lived in this valley long ago believed a giant used the flat mountain as his table. One day, a young native woman wandered far from home in search of food and the giant caught her. He told her he was hungry and, if she didn't give him food, she would be his dinner. She had nothing to give him, so she knew she was in trouble."

The girl didn't speak, but her eyes turned to Sue as if asking for more.

31

"She knew she was no match for the giant's strength, but she was quick and very smart. She had a long stick for digging roots and she poked him in the eye with it. While he was blinded and bellowing in pain, she escaped. He reached out to catch her, but he couldn't see where she went. Then, using her stick, she vaulted from the top of the rock. They say she landed in the east, in the land of her mother's people."

A question burned in Jasmine's eyes. "That true story?"

Sue opened her mouth but hesitated. How could she explain whimsy to a girl like her? "Most native legends were stories from long ago that people told to understand how and why things are. They passed the stories down to their kids."

Jasmine's forehead puckered in a frown. "So . . . parents lie to kids."

A dozen thoughts raced. "Jasmine, sometimes parents aren't—"

"I so tired. I sleep now?"

Sue glanced at the time.

Bedtime wasn't for another hour. But few would gripe if Sue decided to make an exception for a newcomer. The only one likely to make a stink about it was probably busy getting the spaghetti sauce out of her new shoes.

"Kids are not allowed in the rooms until eight-thirty. But for today, you don't have to follow that rule. Miss Roberta is on bed watch tonight, so I'll have her take you to your room."

"I not need. I know where."

Sue smiled. "Good girl. You learn quick. But just this once, I'd like Miss Roberta to go upstairs with you to make sure you have everything you need. Okay?"

Jasmine nodded.

"Okay, kiddo, go get some rest. Things will look much better tomorrow. You'll see."

The girl took one last look out the window and straightened her narrow shoulders, which somehow only made her seem smaller. "Better tomorrow," the girl whispered.

CHAPTER THREE

Sue couldn't shake the unease that had gnawed at her all day. Something about Jasmine was off. Something aside from the fact that she'd just been dumped at a house full of mismatched strangers three months after being hauled halfway across the world.

The girl's pre-adoptive life had been even worse. According to her file, Jasmine Walker was the product of prostitution. She'd started out life eating from garbage cans and fending for herself on the streets of Cambodia before being placed in a convent orphanage. The poor kid had a boatload of problems and some behavioral issues. And that was only what had been documented. There was no telling what hidden scars Jasmine carried.

Sue had seen it before. It would take time and patience to help Jasmine gain some healthy coping skills. But that wasn't what kept Sue tossing and turning. No, it was something else.

"So . . . parents lie to kids."

Sorry, little one. Hate to break it to you, but yeah. Parents lie. They let you down. Some even hurt you.

Bowman's thick-lidded eyes and warm, whiskey-tinged breath crept into her thoughts. Sue punched her pillow, rolled over, and closed her eyes.

The stink of male sweat mixed with whiskey fumes lingered. It wasn't overpowering—the others might not have noticed it on him.

But for Sue, one whiff was all it had taken to send a tremor of revulsion through her body. A violation of her senses that wouldn't leave.

"Suzy Q . . . where are you? Come on out now . . ."

She pressed her eyes with the heels of her hands until the ghosts of ogres long past disappeared in a kaleidoscope of blinding light, sending flashes of pain through her skull.

Trying to sleep was pointless. Because on top of everything else, something else about Jasmine's attitude was really bugging her.

She put on shoes and a hoodie, then left her room in the staff quarters and jogged across the backyard. She entered the main house through the kitchen door and headed up the stairs, tamping down a ripple of apprehension.

On the second floor, Bertie looked up from her seat in the hall. "Something wrong?"

"I want to check on Jasmine."

"Your new chickadee is sound asleep. Has been for hours."

"Good." Sue nodded and cracked open the

door to the room Jasmine shared with Haley. She glanced at the bed, then froze.

The shape in the bed wasn't right.

The pulse in her temples kept time with her mental *no* . . . *No* . . . *NO* . . . as she dashed to the bed and touched the bump of a leg. "No! I knew it!" Sue whipped the cover off the bed, sending a pillow dummy flying.

Haley sat up with a groan.

Sue rushed out the bedroom door and squeezed past Bertie. "Call the sheriff—we've got a runaway!"

Bertie followed as Sue thundered down the steps.

"And wake Elena. Tell her to take the Suburban and head south. I'll take the dualie and cover the ground east, toward the ridge." She dashed down the stairs, spurred by an odd certainty—Jasmine would head for Table Rock. In the foyer, she zipped her sweatshirt and grabbed a flashlight, then barreled out the front door.

Bertie's voice called out from the front porch. "Hate to break it to you, Sue, but the Suburban's still broke down."

Sue stopped with a groan. Of course it was. She'd meant to call the guy who claimed he'd fixed her vehicle. He'd charged plenty for whatever he'd done, which was obviously nothing. The Suburban was like everything else around here. Ever since Emily left and the college kids kept bailing without notice, too many things had been falling through the cracks.

A scared, hurting kid shouldn't be one of those things.

She ran on, calling over her shoulder, "Then Elena will need to borrow your veedub." Sue sprinted to the shop and raised the big door.

She jammed on her helmet, then straddled the bike and fired it up. When she tapped the choke down partway, the bike stalled. "Come on! I know it's cold, but you gotta work with me!" She fired it up again and revved the throttle while she rolled out of the shop.

Ringo came running from the barn.

"Sorry, boy, not this time."

Wagging, the greyhound feigned ignorance of plain English and circled the bike as if preparing to spring.

"You can follow, but you're not riding. You have to help me look for Jasmine." She kept the throttle high and took off. She scanned the brushy terrain on both sides of the driveway, going just fast enough to keep from stalling. When she reached the highway, she stopped and squinted at the shadowy slope rising toward Juniper Ridge.

The bike's engine sputtered out.

In the deep silence, Sue held her breath and listened, amazed as always at the unmarred stillness of this vast, empty desert. "Jasmine," she whispered. "Where are you?" She peered up at the ridge.

Though the sky was clear, there wasn't enough moonlight to see much.

She fired up the bike and crossed the road, then continued east through brush and dry cheatgrass, heading up toward the ridge.

Ringo followed.

As her eyes adjusted to the dark, she looked back over the valley floor. *Let 'em go, sweetheart. They didn't want you. You don't need them. Just let 'em go.*

The track widened into a trail that wound around sagebrush, juniper trees, and boulders, then took a snaking ascent up the ridge.

The Honda nearly stalled, so she gunned it. The acceleration launched her toward a cluster of brush. She swerved and almost lost control yet continued to climb.

The buzz of the bike's motor carried across the still valley as she searched the hillside. No sign of the girl.

The trail grew steeper until it reached the crest. A black expanse of ravine yawned to the right.

As she worked her way along the ridge, the odors of a hot bike and too-rich exhaust revived her headache. From up here, she could see more of the valley below but nothing that looked like a girl.

A determined, ill-equipped little girl.

A bright reflection from the bike's headlight pulled her attention to the juniper tree in front of her. Sue swerved but the bike fishtailed. She braked hard.

The wheel locked up and the bike spun, catapulting Sue over the ridge.

She grasped for brush, branches—anything— as she plummeted into the ravine. She tumbled through trees and bushes and over jagged rock. Sharp stone gouged into her back and forced out a yelp. A blow to her elbow sent a burst of pain up her arm. Prickly branches clawed at her neck and arms. Her right foot caught and twisted her leg, causing a thunderous pop. Her shoulder slammed against something cold and hard and brought her to a dizzying stop.

White pain tore through her shoulder, and a searing shot of lightning exploded in her leg. Sue screamed.

A piercing echo rippled through the canyon and blended with the faint sound of a high-pitched bark as everything went black.

CHAPTER FOUR

Sue woke in a narrow bed with shiny bedrails. Her mouth felt as if she'd eaten a pound of dust. Her entire body ached, some parts worse than others.

A vague memory of riding a bumpy hammock toward a starry night sky flashed in her mind.

She tried to move, but her body had turned into a hundred and nine pounds of cast iron, and her right leg burned like a hot cannon. Was she paralyzed? Panic seized her. She reached for the rail, but the move shot pain through her right arm and shoulder. She yelped.

A nurse came to her side.

"How bad is it?" Sue croaked.

"They've examined the knee but will need to do an MRI to know for sure." The nurse brought a cup of water to Sue. "Feel like you can answer some questions?"

Sue nodded and gulped down the contents of the cup.

The nurse rolled a monitor and keyboard cart to the bed and typed as she asked about the accident.

Sue closed her eyes and tried to remember what had happened. Slowly, like a choppy, old home movie, she saw herself falling, reaching for branches, tumbling through brush. Crashing into a rock. The twist and pop of her leg. Losing control of the bike. Searching for—

"I need to go—it's urgent—" Sue reached for the bedrails but a jolt of pain in her shoulder made her cry out. She drew a few calming breaths. With her left hand, she felt her head and face, then ran fingers down and met crusty, stinging scratches that crisscrossed her neck and collarbone. "There's a missing girl."

The nurse looked up from her keyboard. "What girl?"

"A foster girl at the home I run. I have to find her."

A nurse's aide in a flowered tunic came in and handed something to the nurse.

Sue's right arm and shoulder hurt like fury, but the burning tightness in her knee was far worse. The unnatural weight of her right leg meant she probably wouldn't be walking out of here anytime soon. Panic rose again but she held her breath and fought it.

"Okay, looks like we're all set," the aide said, turning to Sue. "I'm here to take you down the hall for an MRI." She released something beneath the hospital bed and wheeled it toward the hall.

"Please wait. I need to call someone. I was

41

looking for a runaway when this happened. I need to see if she's been found."

"Oh, I'm sorry." The girl rolled Sue down the corridor. "Is there someone I can call for you?"

"Yes." Sue gave her Bertie's and Layne's numbers.

"Just relax for the procedure, and I'll make sure your friends get the message."

After the MRI, another aide wheeled her back to the room. Sue must have dozed off for a while because she woke with a jerk when the nurse returned.

Layne Stevenson followed, decked out in swishy navy warmups and a long, blonde pony-tail.

Even in Sue's hazy state, seeing her friend in anything but a jacket and skirt was a shock. And no makeup on her Naomi Watts face—a double shock.

"Sue? Are you okay?" Layne bent close, wincing. "Have they given you anything for pain?"

"Layne," Sue said, voice raspy, "I've got a runaway."

Layne nodded. "They found Jasmine, and she's back at the ranch now. She's okay."

Sue closed her eyes. "Thank goodness."

"I told Bertie we'll know more soon." Layne studied her, then shook her head. "You're really lucky, you know that? This could have been so much worse." She reached into her bag, took out a blue-wrapped ball, and peeled it. "You really scared me!" She held up a truffle. "Open up. Doc's orders."

Sue reached for the candy with her good arm and nibbled at the smooth dark chocolate. She let the silky, rich bittersweetness melt in her mouth and slip down her throat, her taste buds singing. She couldn't remember the last time she'd had chocolate and not had to share it with a handful of kids. "Where was Jasmine? Was she scared?"

"Elena found her. Jasmine was hiding up in a tree somewhere on the property, clutching a big, long stick."

A stick? *Way to go, Sooz. Great bedtime story for a skittish kid on her first day at the ranch.*

"I called the agency and arranged for a couple of respite-care temps to come out," Layne said. "They'll start today. But that's all they are— temporary. What you need is regular, dependable help. And I'm sorry to be the bearer of bad news, but you've got a far more serious problem than a staff shortage."

The only real problem Sue could see was that she was out of chocolate. Sue licked her lips. Was there none left in Layne's bag? Some friend. She should know better than to tempt an addict.

"I'm sorry. I know the timing stinks, but—"

A doctor came in, greeted Sue, and said he had her test results. "Two ligaments in your right knee are damaged. The MCL is torn, which could possibly heal on its own. Unfortunately, your ACL was severely damaged and requires reconstructive surgery."

"Surgery?" Sue gasped. "But . . . not with anesthesia, right?" *Please say no . . . please . . .*

He signed off on a clipboard and handed it back to the nurse. "Most likely."

Oh no . . . Sue's skin went clammy. They could hack on her with a pickax as long as they didn't put her under.

"But we need the swelling to go down first, which could take days or a week. The bruised shoulder and lacerations, we'll treat now. And we'll fit you with a knee brace and crutches before you leave."

Crutches—that had to be a good sign. "So I can walk?"

"To get the swelling down, you need to stay completely off that knee. After ligament replacement, you'll need physical therapy. The more effort you put into it, the better your chances are of regaining full, pain-free mobility."

"How long?"

"About twelve weeks, more or less. Again, that depends on you."

"You mean home therapy, right?"

"In a clinic. Three times a week."

"*Three* times a week?" She did the math. "For three *months?*" Sue shook her head, making it throb. "I run a youth home in the desert ninety miles from the nearest clinic. There's no way I can leave the ranch for a whole day three times a week. I'll learn the stretches or whatever and do them myself."

"Sue." Layne leaned close. "You've never had PT before, have you? There's a reason it's known as Pure Torture." A sympathetic smile stretched her mouth wide. "If you want to walk and play volleyball with the kids and ride that beast of a motorcycle again, you have to do this right."

The doctor gave her a list of clinics.

Once he was gone, Sue turned to Layne, blinking back tears of frustration. "Please tell me I'm just hallucinating from the wreck."

Layne drew a deep breath. "I'm sorry, Sue. You know I'll help you in any way I can." She looked like she had more to say but was holding back.

Sue waited.

Layne reached in her bag, pulled out another blue Lindor ball, and unwrapped it as she spoke. "Remember your failed inspection last month? The one that left you with a list of repairs and thirty days to do it?" Layne gave her a steady look. "Sue, if those repairs aren't done to code by the first week of November, they'll yank your license and shut you down. So unless you want to scatter those kids to the wind and lose everything you've worked for . . ."

Sue eyed the chocolate. A burning knot tightened her belly, flat-lining her appetite. "Things have been hectic lately. We've done some of the repairs. I just haven't had time to finish it all. Bowman was making progress, but . . . I had to let him go."

"Bertie told me. But time's running out. Follow up inspection is in less than two weeks."

"Can you get me a delay?"

Layne shook her head. "Sorry, there's nothing I can do. At least, not about the inspection." Her arched brows perched higher and waited.

Ignoring her friend's baited expression, Sue made a mental list of all the opposition her home had faced in the last two years. Income had always been sporadic. Even more so lately, thanks to some major tax troubles for the Beaumont estate, her biggest private donor. Letters from the bank had become routine. State licensing regulations, county housing codes, food and funding shortages—she and the kids had worked together every time and found a way to solve each problem. She wasn't about to lose her home now over a couple of broken windows and some leaky plumbing.

Layne folded her arms along the bedrail and leaned close. "Remember what I said about my brother's boss in Alaska? He's here until January and needs the work. It's the perfect solution for now, Sue. I'm sure he can fix everything. He could get all your repairs done *and* solve your male dorm counselor problem."

"*Dorm* counselor?" Sue huffed out a laugh. "My care staff has special training in handling troubled kids. Working at Juniper Ranch isn't like running a crew of men." Especially big, burly men with girlie tattoos and who knew what else.

Layne leaned back. "Okay, so he might not be ideal counselor material. But he can definitely help you out of a really tough spot. And it's just for a few months. If it makes any difference to you, it would help him out too. Besides, it's a steal of a deal. Joe is probably worth far more than whatever you were paying Bowman."

The sensation of being trapped in a corner and bullied into submission soured the lingering taste of chocolate. "I don't like this, Layne. I don't like being forced."

"I know, Sue. I'm sorry. But I don't think you have any other choice."

See, it's that no choice *part I really dislike.*

People shuffled about their business on the other side of the curtain, while Sue lay trapped, a victim of rotten circumstances outside her control. A familiar feeling of powerlessness crept over her, but she refused to let it take hold. She was no longer a small, defenseless child. Swallowing her dread, Sue said quietly, "Since this *Joe* is already on his way, what am I supposed to do? Hire him sight unseen?"

"You interview him like you would anyone else."

An interview. Where I drill this total stranger and pretend I actually have a choice. "Okay, let's say he passes the interview. Until I get a full background check and references—which *you* are going to provide me, by the way—he's only working on repairs under supervision, and he's not coming anywhere near my kids. He lives off-site until everything clears."

Layne's eyes widened. "*You're* going to supervise him?"

"Of course."

A slow smile spread across Layne's face. "So that's a yes?"

Sue turned toward the assortment of hoses and medical panels on the wall. Sometimes Sue secretly admired Layne's subtle powers of persuasion.

This was not one of those times.

CHAPTER FIVE

At her desk Monday morning, Sue listened to the kids doing schoolwork in the den—a passable distraction from the pain. The interview with the oil rigger was set for ten o'clock. It would have been better if it wasn't so soon, but the repairs weren't getting done by themselves, and the deadline was fast approaching.

Layne had put a rush on the guy's background check, but there would still be a wait. Since Sue didn't have his full file, she prepared a list of questions for him.

Her knee throbbed. Of course, she was supposed to be icing it. With the Ice Machine. The contraption was little more than a flat pad attached to hoses dangling out of a picnic cooler. It looked more like a science fair project gone berserk. And evidently, she was supposed to strap it to her leg. All day.

The sounds of laughter filtered into the office.

Sue pulled herself to standing, wincing at the stabbing pain in her knee and arm, and crutched her way to the study.

Miss Graves, the ranch's part-time tutor, had her first shift of students hard at work.

Chaz spun from the computer screen and frowned. "Hey, Miss Susan. You can't be in here. You're supposed to have that knee elevated and on ice."

His lilting lisp reminded her of Linus from Charlie Brown. Except a Linus with a proficiency in robotics, aerodynamics, explosives, and a half dozen other things Sue was sure she'd rather not know. "Chaz, I don't think it'll hurt to come in here and see how you guys are doing."

The kid shook his head. "You can't have surgery unless you get the swelling down, and you can't get the swelling down unless you elevate and ice your knee. You'll never get better if you're in here every five minutes bugging us."

Sue smiled. "Thanks, buddy. I'm touched by your heartfelt concern." She ruffled his hair and hop-thunked back to her office.

Smart aleck. He was probably right.

She entered her office and gasped.

A huge man stood just inside the outer door of her office, blocking the exit. He was built like a linebacker, a skin-tight, green T-shirt straining across his chest.

"Who are you?" A steely pain in her shoulder sucked the breath from her lungs.

The man only stared.

Sweating from ricocheting pain, Sue shifted her

weight on the crutches, but one slipped out and clattered to the floor. She struggled to balance on the remaining crutch with her bad arm, sending a fresh surge of lightning-sharp pain. Dizzy, she tried to focus on the guy, but everything swirled and the floor began to tilt. Darkness swallowed her as the man lurched toward her, arms stretched out.

Falling . . .

Floating up . . .

Up and away . . .

In the dark, voices murmured.

Sue forced her eyes open and blinked against the light streaming in the window. A pair of dark eyes fringed with long lashes met her gaze. Not Bertie's faded blue ones, but rich, mocha brown. And close. Chocolate eyes, muscular jaw, woodsy aftershave, and male—all extremely close.

"You okay?"

The voice, deep but quiet, rumbled through her. It seemed she was in the green giant's arms. Her pulse sped. "Yeah, and I'd really appreciate it if you'd put me down."

He lowered her carefully, then grabbed the other crutch and offered it to her. "You must be Susan Quinn."

Heart pounding, she stood as steady as she could. "That's right."

With a pained smile, he held out a hand, then must have thought better of it, because he let it drop. "Joe Paterson. I'm here to see you about a job."

Joe glanced around, noting the newer walls and flooring. This office wasn't part of the original structure. He still couldn't believe *this* was the ranch Dan had told him about. If he got the job, he couldn't wait to poke around, see how else his old group home had changed. Plus, a job at Juniper Ranch would allow him to be close to Bend but out of sight. He'd struck out at the courthouse on Friday, but here he could still work on tracking down the Jacobs family without any of them knowing he was around.

It took Susan Quinn a while to get her brace-encased leg situated on a chair, but she didn't seem the least bit open to help.

"Should I . . . go get someone? I mean, since you passed out?"

"No, I'm fine, thank you. Please have a seat."

Whatever was wrong with her leg, it looked painful. And her face was pale, which didn't make her any less attractive.

He lowered his gaze to the pile of papers between them on the desk, being careful not to stare at her, something he'd caught himself doing more than once.

She had a natural, clean kind of pretty about her, like a girl from a soap ad. Her big brown eyes had grabbed him immediately—something about the way they contrasted with her blonde hair. She had a little upturned nose and small, full lips that reminded him of a tiny rose.

Lips that, at the moment, were pressed tight. Blood-draining tight.

Finally settled in, she drew a shaky breath and met his eyes. "My apologies, Mr. Paterson, for the . . . um, fainting spell."

"No problem. And call me Joe, please."

She cut straight to her first question, asking him about his experience with maintenance and structural repair work.

When he stopped talking, the only sound was Susan's pen scratching notes on paper.

She went on to explain the rules and work details. Then she showed him a list of repairs and asked if he could get them done by the end of next week.

As he read the list, he sensed her scrutiny of him. When he looked up, her expression remained even, but a hint of wariness lingered in her eyes. He resisted the urge to wipe his palms on his jeans. Something about this woman got right under his skin. And stung.

Father, I don't know what's bothering her, but You do. Help her with it, whatever it is.

Sue shifted her hips to relieve some of the pain and stiffness in her back. If only she had more time, more information. More options.

Joe set the list down and nodded. "I can have this stuff done to code by the end of next week, as long as I have the tools and supplies I need."

"Great." She gave him an application. While he filled it out, Sue studied the man. Good looking, no denying that. And he seemed polite, but his size made her nervous. He had to be six-four with a logger's physique and arms the size of tree trunks. She felt like a wounded field mouse next to a water buffalo. He appeared to have an easy friendliness about him, but Sue had learned long ago not to be fooled by the way people seemed. Plus, he acted oddly nervous, putting her radar on high alert. A guy his size had no reason to be intimidated by a small woman on crutches.

And he didn't seem worried about being able to do the work. Something else had him off kilter.

And what's with the shaved head and tight T-shirt? Who does he think he is—Vin Diesel? Sue cleared her throat. "Just so you know, even though there's no official dress code for staff, if you work here, you'll need to rethink your choice of clothing."

Joe glanced down at his clothes, then met her with a questioning look.

"There are teenage girls living here. The . . . skin-tight T-shirt look isn't appropriate."

"Sorry. My clothes were stolen at a truck stop. I grabbed a couple of shirts at a feed store in La Pine and this was the largest size they had. As soon as I can get to a regular clothing store, I'll take care of it." He gave a slightly pained smile. "Trust me, I'd rather have my own stuff."

She replayed his words and the inflection of his voice, giving her warning instincts a chance to kick in.

Nothing.

She needed to keep him talking. "Layne said you have family in the area. Were you planning to stay with them?"

Joe stopped writing. "I don't know where they are right now, and I'm not . . ." He looked up. "To tell you the truth, I thought I'd be staying here. I guess I'm so used to living on a rig I sort of expected that."

Think again, mister. Not until I get every last scrap of your history. But . . . the High Desert Inn in Juniper Valley was closed for renovation. He couldn't very well camp out with near freezing temperatures at night. She'd have to either turn him down for the job or let him stay at the ranch.

And time was running out.

The feeling of being forced into a corner by this guy's existence swelled again. How had the survival of her ranch come down to taking in a total stranger built like Paul Bunyan? If he *were* to stay, she needed some kind of reassurance. How could she be sure she could trust him with her kids? Or with her staff? Or with herself, for that matter?

A guy like him could do pretty much anything he wanted to anybody.

A shudder swept through her. She needed to dig deeper, to know more. "Why do you want to work with kids?"

Joe rubbed his palms along his thighs. "I'm not really looking to work with kids. I do have experience in a group home setting, but I'm mainly here to help with whatever repair work you need before I head to the Gulf." He avoided her eyes. Not a good sign.

"Tell me about your group home experience."

He took a long look at his surroundings. "I lived in one for about six years," he said, deep voice softening. "This one, actually."

"What? Are you saying you lived *here?*" *In my house?*

Joe nodded.

Of all the assumptions about Joe Paterson forming in Sue's mind, this was not one of them. Had foster childhood scarred him as it had her?

He folded his arms on the desk and leaned forward, looking around. "It was called My Father's House back then."

He was awfully close. His long-lashed eyes gave the muscular cut of his face a boyish look, especially with that dimpled smile.

Which he knew, of course. Total player, most likely.

Sue leaned back, trying to gain a little distance.

"Yes, I've heard. The Realtor told me the place used to be a religious group home."

His eyes met hers. Even his half smile produced a dimple. "It was a Christian home."

Whatever. Same thing. "How did you like group home life? What did it teach you?"

Joe didn't answer right away but gazed at some point beyond her. "I think you and I both know group home life has its moments, but for me it was still home. Even with all the oddball personalities and differences, it felt like a big family. You learn a lot about getting along when you live in tight quarters, twenty-four seven, with people you probably never would've chosen as friends."

Again, not the kind of answer she expected. She tried to imagine him as a boy, like Edgar or Chaz. "How old were you when you came to live here?"

"About twelve. I stayed until I turned eighteen and went to work in Alaska."

"Really?" Her curiosity ignited like a match to gas. "You aged out?"

He nodded.

In her experience, few group homes had the staff or resources to adequately equip their young residents for successful, independent adulthood after leaving the facility. But it could be done. In fact, it should be top priority.

She herself, along with too many others, had

been drop-kicked into the unknown at eighteen, unskilled and unprepared, without any of the tools needed to succeed in a confusing adult world. She had learned to survive the hard way. She wasn't about to let her kids drift in and out of the system or struggle to get a leg up as she had.

"How did aging out go for you? I mean, if you don't mind, I'm always curious to hear from people who grew to adulthood in a group home. Did it prepare you to live on your own?"

Joe examined his interlaced fingers. "I came to My Father's House after spending most of my childhood in foster homes. And there are great ones, but let's just say mine weren't among them. Those weren't good years. I was always on the outside. Had no clue who I was. By the time I came here, I . . ." With a shrug, he shook his head. "I had no hopes for my life. I couldn't imagine growing up and amounting to anything, or even . . ." The quiet pain in his face was unmistakable.

"Surviving?"

He nodded.

A flash of understanding struck her. She'd seen it in many of the boys she'd taken in. They'd come to her completely stripped of self-worth—tuning everyone out, often displaying anger, depression, impulse issues, and sometimes suicidal behavior. It had taken poor Edgar a long time to believe he even had any business breathing. She could easily picture Joe as a kid Edgar's age, feeling hopeless and unwanted, desperate to know if he even mattered. That picture tugged at something deep inside. In spite of her wariness, Sue felt a keen sense of pity for this man.

"But all that changed. At My Father's House, they taught me basic skills—like how to take care of myself, how to keep a bank account, that kind of stuff. But they also taught me how to work hard, have integrity. Take responsibility for myself. Be a man. They didn't just *tell* me I had worth; they taught me to *be* a man of worth."

This was exactly what Sue wanted to teach her kids. "So there is hope," she said softly.

"There is, if the counsel you're following is . . ." He studied her for a moment as if she were the one being interviewed.

The idea made her stiffen.

Whatever he was going to say, he didn't finish.

"Now that you've had some time on your own as an adult, how do you feel about being raised in a group home instead of a traditional home?"

Joe's look pierced her. "Thankful. Living here changed my life." His face struggled to conceal some sudden emotion. "I'm pretty sure it saved me."

Surprise lifted Sue's brows, but instead of asking him to explain, she clamped her lips.

He'd probably tell her how he'd found God here or something. If that were the case, he'd be disappointed. Things were different at Juniper Ranch. No deadbeat, absentee dads were allowed here. Especially the giant, invisible kind.

Her gut had better be right on this. "Mr. Paterson, I need the help, as you can see."

"Please, call me Joe."

"I'll be honest, Joe. I'm reluctant to have you living here until your background check comes through. But with your situation, I don't see any other option. So I'll hire you, but on the condition that you will sleep in the staff quarters out back and only work around kids when other staff members are present. You can store your things in the work shop. As you saw by the conduct agreement, we have strict rules here. No alcohol at any time, on *or* off premises. And you are never to be alone with a child."

He nodded, but an uncomfortable look passed over his face.

If it hurt his feelings that she couldn't fully trust him, it couldn't be helped. Hopefully, he understood. She would do whatever it took to protect her kids and staff. "So if that's agreeable to you, welcome to Juniper Ranch. Do you have any questions?"

Joe shook his head. "None for now." He smiled. "Thanks for taking me on, Ms. Quinn."

Sue nodded. "And just so you know, we refer to

each other as 'Miss Susan' or 'Mister Joe' around the kids, and we expect the kids to address the adults the same way."

"Miss Susan. Got it."

Good. Now let's see how you are at following the rest of the rules.

CHAPTER SIX

When evening came, Joe lowered himself onto the splintered step at the door of his new room behind the main house and listened to the hush of night, silent except for the steady thrum of crickets.

He'd spent most of the day getting familiar with the place again. From what he'd seen, the kids kept the staff on their toes from morning to night. But now, the stillness worked like a sedative. The air here smelled of sage, just as he remembered. And it was cold. He'd need to find a thicker work coat. He'd forgotten how chilly nights were in Oregon's high desert.

Almost as chilly as his pretty, new boss.

What was eating at her? Every time they crossed paths, *Miss Susan* seemed to stiffen. As if she could get any stiffer. Her watchful eyes and the tilt of her chin clearly showed her distrust. As if she knew something. But she couldn't have seen or heard anything of his past. None of that stuff would be included on a background check, as far as he knew. None of the people he'd listed as job references knew how his time with the Jacobs family had come to a traumatizing end or how shame had left a stain on his soul. Yet it felt as if Sue Quinn had traveled back in time and sat in on the family court proceedings, heard the condemning testimony and terrible words his ex-mother had used. Heard the horrible accusations.

One of which, unfortunately, had been true.

Regardless of what Sue knew about him, she clearly didn't trust him. The way she looked at him took him back to that time, bringing up guilt he'd spent years trying to forget. Perhaps the more he stayed out of her way, the better.

Tuesday morning began with a kiddie-sized breakfast and a single cup of coffee.

Miss Roberta, the old hippie lady, must have seen him trying to score a refill from the empty pot because she brought him a big mug at mid-morning.

He thanked her and kept working. Replacing leaking plumbing and Sheetrock helped him ignore his rattling stomach. A little.

"You gonna throw this away?"

Crouched near the utility room wall, Joe pivoted.

A dishwater-blond kid with Harry Potter glasses, a lisp, and a face full of zits inspected the warped plasterboard Joe had removed to get to the leaking pipe.

"I'm going to hang on to it, just until I pick

up some new Sheetrock to replace it with." Joe stood and held out a hand. "I'm Joe. Uh—Mister Joe. What's your name?"

"Charles P. Montgomery." The kid's chin jutted up a notch. "But nobody calls me that."

It was either a statement of fact or a command. "So, what do you like to be called?"

"Just Chaz."

For the next hour, Chaz followed Joe around the compound as he worked, talking nonstop. Apparently there was a flight training school somewhere nearby. In between the kid's stories about stealth fighter drills and his theories on what kind of testing the government was *really* doing, he asked Joe what he was doing and why.

Curiosity was a great teacher.

He sealed the leak in the utility room, then set a fan to dry the area, so he could check later for more leaks, before moving on to the next item on his list—smoke alarms. Oddly, many of them were missing.

"I know where they are. Come with me." Chaz headed for the front door.

"All right. Hey, aren't you supposed to be in school?" A girl named Brandi had complained at breakfast about spending weekday mornings in the schoolroom, but Chaz had been following him most of the morning.

The kid snorted. "I'm always finished before breakfast. C'mon, out here." Chaz led him outside and along the sloped trail to the shop. Inside, Chaz took Joe to the workbench and pointed to a heap of mangled smoke detectors.

"Huh." Joe tilted his head to get a better look. "I wonder why these are all dismantled."

Chaz started picking through the pile. "I think this piece goes with that one."

Didn't really appear to be a match. Joe would have to sit down with the whole mess and try to see what went together, if any of it did. "How'd you know these were out here?"

"I put 'em here."

Ah. "Did you also take them apart?"

"Pretty much. I can see how the different types work now. It's simple, really. See this battery?" Chaz explained the route of the detector's electrical current and how the alarm sound was triggered. He actually got it right.

"So you take things apart and figure out how they work?"

"Yep."

"And then . . . you put them back together?" It was a long shot.

Chaz spotted something behind Joe and dodged around him to a pile of parts on another workbench.

Joe followed. This next pile contained pieces of light fixtures and assorted small appliances.

Guess that would be a no.

Chaz shuffled through the pile without pausing.

Joe had known kids with compulsive tendencies. This kid needed something to focus on. Something complicated enough to keep him challenged. "Hey, Chaz. How would you like a job?"

The kid whipped around so fast Joe thought his glasses would sail clean off his head.

Screams pierced the quiet mid-afternoon like a siren, shooting darts of fear through Sue. She grabbed her crutches and struggled to her feet. Ignoring the pain in her arm and leg, she hurried to the office door and went outside.

Another scream came from the barn.

Heart thumping, she moved toward it as fast as she could, horrible pictures springing to mind. *Idiot! Why did you hire a strange man, and why did you let him stay here?* As Sue reached the barn, Vince, Deeg, and Tatiana joined her, trailed by Karla, one of the new temps.

More screams made Karla jump. Deeg swung the big door wide open for Sue.

Adrenaline coursing, Sue entered the dark barn, moving through a cluster of teens.

Inside, Jasmine pressed her back against a support beam, her wide eyes directed at the other end of the barn where Ringo paced in front of the goat stalls, looking for an escape.

Sue heaved a sigh. Poor dog. Screaming girls were beyond the scope of the greyhound's therapeutic abilities, even with his easy-going nature. "All right, everyone, show's over, it's just Ringo. Time to move along."

Karla, still shaken, gathered her crew and disappeared.

Sue approached the girl slowly. "Jasmine? Are you hurt?"

Jasmine didn't take her eyes from the lanky dog, who was now making a wide berth around the girl. As Ringo shot past them, Jasmine let off another ear-piercing scream.

Sue touched the girl's shoulder.

Jasmine turned and chomped her teeth into the fleshy base of Sue's thumb.

"Ahh!" Sue jerked her hand away.

The girl made a move to run.

Sue grasped Jasmine's tiny shoulders, losing her crutches in the process.

Jasmine screamed again, thrashing and twisting to escape Sue's grasp, kicking at Sue's shins.

Sue couldn't let the girl loose in this state. She clutched more tightly, sweating at the sharp pains in her knee and now in her shin and hand. "Jasmine, stop! No one's going to hurt you!"

A snarl, starting deep and low, came from Jasmine's throat and turned to high-pitched shrieks.

Ah. The coping quirk.

As the girl writhed, her head whipping back and forth, Sue's balance slipped. She wrapped herself around the girl in a restraining hold and pitched them both against the barn post.

Grunting, Jasmine tried to bite Sue's shoulder.

Sweat running down her temples, Sue held Jasmine against the wooden beam. "Jasmine, I'm not—going to hurt you," Sue said between breaths. "But you—need to stop—fighting me."

Jasmine went limp, and they both crumpled to the ground.

Sue's braced leg threw her into a weird angle, pinning Jasmine half beneath her. "Jasmine? Are you okay? I'm going to let go, but you need to sit tight and calm down. Do you hear me?" Sue slightly loosened her grasp on the girl and looked at her face.

Jasmine's eyes were closed, her body limp.

"Jasmine?" Was she hurt, or just faking for a chance to get away?

The girl's breathing slowed to a steadier rate. Though her eyes were still closed, her taut look showed she was conscious.

Sue took a deep breath. "Jasmine, I'm going to let you go. Don't try to run, okay?"

The girl didn't move or make a sound.

Slowly, Sue released her grip on the girl and rolled back.

Jasmine scrambled into a sitting position and cradled herself in a tight ball, rocking in a short, rapid rhythm. She tucked her face deep into her knees.

And coping quirk number two. Poor kid. Sorrow seeped through Sue's chest, heightening the tension of the moment and the pain screaming through her body. It took everything she had to keep tears from forming. "Jasmine?"

The girl kept rocking.

Sue propped herself into an awkward sitting position and waited in silence.

Bertie poked her head around the doorway, but Sue gave her the all-clear nod. Bertie flashed a thumbs-up and left.

Jasmine's head lifted. She peeked at Sue, then she squashed her face into her knees again.

"You okay?"

Silence.

Sue looked around for Ringo. Poor dog. He'd probably never set paw in here again. "Did the dog scare you?"

Jasmine mumbled into her legs. "I not scared."

Sue smiled. "Well, maybe you weren't, but I sure was. I could hear you screaming from inside the house."

Jasmine glanced up and checked the doorway. "I not like dogs. They mean."

"Oh, honey, not Ringo. He's the sweetest dog you'll ever meet."

"Ringo?" The girl cocked her head. "Not wild dog?"

"No. He lives here. I rescued him from a shelter."

Jasmine relaxed a bit. "*Your* dog?"

"Yep. Well, he's everyone's, actually." Sue shifted her leg, wincing. "Ringo used to be a racing dog. When greyhounds start getting older, they aren't fast enough for racing anymore, so they are retired or sent away. Sometimes, if a dog is lucky, he gets to go to a good home where he can run and play and be part of a family."

Jasmine kept eyeing the doorway. "Walkers have cats. I no like. They bite and—" Her face scrunched in a wicked hiss. She made a claw and swiped at the air near Sue's face.

Sue forced herself not to flinch.

Apparently Jasmine had forgotten about biting Sue's hand—or had blocked it out. Fear had a way of making people react in all manner of strange ways.

"Jasmine, if I had cats like that, I wouldn't like 'em either." She shifted her weight again, relieving the awkward angle of her leg. "But Ringo would never hurt you. He likes to play ball and go for long walks. Want to know what else he likes to do?"

Curiosity lifted Jasmine's face.

"Ringo *loves* to ride motorcycles."

The girl's eyes widened. "How?"

"When I ride, he curls up on the tank in front of me. I don't know how he does it, but he stays on. He has amazing balance. And he *loves* going fast."

Jasmine stared out the door for a long time, thoughts working her small face. "Ringo fast race dog?"

"Yeah. He's still crazy fast, even though he's older now."

"You race too?"

"Me? What do you mean?"

Jasmine gave the universal teenage eyeball roll. "On *motorcycle*. You go 'crazy' fast?"

As fast as that throttle will let me go, kiddo. "When it's safe, yes. Sometimes."

With two fingers, Jasmine plowed long, parallel tracks in the dust. "Dog smart. He find new way to race. Faster way."

Sue grinned. Smart little cookie. "I guess you're right. I never thought about it like that."

Peering over Sue's shoulder at the doorway, Jasmine moistened her lips. "I find Miss Karla now, finish work." She stood but lingered near the post.

It took some effort, but Sue got her crutches beneath her and pulled herself to standing.

Matching Sue's slow pace to the door, Jasmine hung close. Outside, she stopped and swept a glance around the compound.

A wagging Ringo trailed Edgar and the rest of his crew.

Jasmine's body went rigid.

Edgar turned and stroked the dog's head, then crouched down to ruffle his neck fur.

Eyes fixed on the dog, Jasmine muttered, "Ringo lucky. He find home where even dog fit in."

With an hour or two of good daylight left, Joe had time to start a new project but needed a few supplies. He entered Sue's office and froze.

Sue was sitting on a folding lounge chair with her back to him and her leg hooked to an ice machine. Beside her, an older girl in a wheelchair spoke, her sing-song speech soft, her head tipped slightly to one side.

Fiona . . .

A jab of something long buried stung his gut. Quietly, he turned to leave.

Sue's voice stopped him. "Can I help you, Mister Joe?"

The girl turned her head to see him. "Hi, Mis-ter Joe. I'm Dai-sy."

He suppressed a wince. "I can come back later."

"Now is fine. Daisy doesn't mind."

It don't matter, Joey . . . she don't know nothin' . . . she's—

He had to fight to avoid visibly shaking the memory from his head. Different girl. Different home. Different life. Joe exhaled. "I need some hardware supplies. Do you want me to get that in Juniper Valley?"

Daisy laughed, long and low.

Sue smiled at the girl. "Depends. There's

usually not a lot to choose from out here. You'll probably have to get it in Bend. But if Valley Hardware and Feed has what you need, you can put it on my account." With a grimace, she shifted in the chair. "That is, if they let you."

"I'll check it out, thanks." He started to leave but remembered Chaz. Better clear the idea with Sue. He didn't need any wrong ideas forming in her head. "There's a boy—Chaz. I think I might be able to help him with his . . . habit."

"So you found Chaz's handiwork," Sue said. "What did you have in mind?"

"I could give him some projects to keep him busy. Maybe teach him to study how things work without taking them apart." He met her gaze. "He could work with me when he's not doing schoolwork. If that's okay with you."

The intense scrutiny of those pretty brown eyes rattled him. No, it wasn't just her eyes. Her golden-blonde hair was down and loose, framing her face in soft waves that lay gently around her shoulders, partially covering the deep scratches on her neck and collarbone. He'd never seen her hair any way but pulled back in a tight braid. Probably felt as soft as it looked.

Stare check, man.

Joe inspected the flooring. Decent grade. Hemlock. Maybe oak.

"Okay," Sue said. "You can give it a try. As long as the two of you are never alone."

Another jab nudged his gut. With a nod, he ducked out and went into town.

By dinnertime, Joe had checked a couple more items off the list, but the rest of the repairs needed wiring and plumbing supplies that required a trip into Bend. But for his first day on the job, he'd accomplished quite a bit, and that felt good.

With a smile, Joe hummed his way into the dining hall. Something smelled delicious, like potatoes and gravy. He added the lyrics to the tune stuck in his head.

Jasmine stopped at his side with a stack of plates in her arms. "I know song." Jasmine's mouth curled slightly. "Sing more."

Joe grinned and launched into the chorus.

Jasmine set the plates down and bobbed her head in time with his thigh drumming. "Likaway you walk . . ."

Joe dove into a rooster walk and sang the next line.

Jasmine answered with a chicken wing flap.

This kid was all right.

A couple of teens burst into the hall and stopped, watching Joe and Jasmine strut around the table, singing.

Jasmine joined him again, off-key, for the last line. "Likaway you walk, Suzy Q."

As more kids filed in, Joe went back to humming the tune. Probably just made a total fool of himself, but everyone was grinning.

Except for the woman on crutches in the office doorway. She resembled a kid in size but apparently not in humor.

Crud. Must have missed the no singing rule. Lord, if I didn't know better, I'd think my boss was allergic to fun.

A group of kids formed a line against one wall, but no other staff was there, besides Sue, who was still shooting him a blistering look.

He crammed his hands in his pockets, stomach groaning loud enough to scatter a pack of coyotes.

Another bunch of kids brought out steaming pans of mashed potatoes, gravy, and green beans from the kitchen and set them on a long sideboard.

As the kids arranged the food, Sue crutched her way closer to Joe. The effort seemed to wear on her. Her head tilted up and she offered a thin smile. "Funny. And so original."

"What?"

When she didn't answer, Joe scrambled back over the last few moments. The song. "Oh. Suzy Quinn. Actually, no. That wasn't—"

The corners of her mouth tucked back in a way that said *I'm not stupid.*

"I wasn't singing about you. Really. It's just something I like to sing."

Head cocked to one side, Sue studied him. In the depths of those eyes, something intense yet guarded tugged at him, pulled him right in.

Sadness, a flash of pain. Whatever it was, she had a tight clamp on it.

"It's not one of my favorites." She pivoted on her crutch and went back to her office.

Joe got in line for chow, winking in answer to the kids' curious stares. He glanced over his shoulder at the office doorway.

Father, she may be gorgeous, but she's pricklier than a juniper. Help her let go of whatever has her wound so tight. Help her know You. And help me have grace. Thanks.

CHAPTER SEVEN

By the time surgery day arrived, Sue had been forced to yield yet again. Bertie suggested Joe drive her, since his absence wouldn't leave them short-handed with care staff. Sue wanted to argue, but it was true.

At first light Friday morning, Sue hobbled out to Joe's truck. *Just me and Giganto. Fabulous.* The early morning chill stung her cheeks. She grimaced. If healing from knee surgery took too long, she might miss the last of any decent riding weather.

Bertie helped Sue clamber up onto the seat.

A week after the accident, her shoulder didn't hurt much, but pulling herself up was still a pain. And since she was likely to be in far more pain after surgery, it was a good thing the kids either hadn't noticed that today was Halloween or had decided not to make a big deal out of it. If she was as drugged up as she suspected she might be, trying to duplicate last year's bonfire and ghost stories might turn out more frightful than any of them were prepared for.

Wearing a green John Deere stocking hat, Joe

climbed in and they headed out. He took the rutted dirt roads slowly, making an effort to avoid the potholes. For the first several miles, neither one spoke.

In the silence, Sue concentrated on relaxing. From the moment surgery became a future reality, she'd tried to forget about the impending anesthesia. Thinking about it now cinched every nerve and muscle in her body. Each procedure she'd had involving anesthesia had ended badly. Each one, a full-on panic attack.

The truck ate up the distance to town.

By this time tomorrow, she'd be home recovering, on the road back to normal. She could do this. The reward for her amazingly fast recovery would be a long, full-throttle ride. She didn't care how cold it was.

But disturbing images of past surgeries, waking up in an uncontrollable panic, disoriented, vulnerable, and totally out of control kept playing and replaying in her mind, driving her blood pressure higher. Her insides knotted.

"Hey, you okay? Are you in pain?"

Joe glanced at her, the *V* between his brows deepening.

"I'm fine." *Liar.*

"Okay. Just checking."

She took a deep breath and focused on the road ahead, a long, gray ribbon cutting a path through the sparse forest of slender, red-barked pines.

Maybe if she stared at the passing trees long enough, she could zone out and get her mind off the nightmare to come.

It didn't work.

She pulled in another breath and eased it out through her nose, since forcing it out between clenched jaws wasn't happening. Maybe she'd watch the woods on both sides of the road for deer—always a good idea on this highway, and especially during dusk and dawn. When she checked the other side, Joe was watching her again. Intently.

"Hey, so, uh . . ." His rumbling voice trailed off. He scanned the woods beyond her as though searching for something. "Bet you didn't know I'm a local real estate tycoon, did you?" He smiled. "Twelve lush acres of dust and tumbleweed just outside La Pine. My tenants love it."

Sue lifted a brow. "Tenants?"

"Yeah. Sage rats, jackrabbits, and coyotes."

She leaned back and rested her head against the seat. "So what are you going to do with it?"

"Let the coyotes have it, I guess. I have no idea why I bought it, other than it was cheaper than dirt—literally. When I left Oregon, I didn't think I'd be back. Ever." He frowned. "I'll probably sell it. I forget I even have it until the tax bill comes."

Sue nodded. Yearly property taxes on the ranch were due soon. Another migraine.

"But I don't have any bills, so even with the taxes creeping up, it's not that big of a deal."

"No bills?" Sue huffed. "Must be nice. How do you manage that?"

"Working on a rig, you don't have much chance to run up bills. And since it's just me, I don't have many expenses. Truck insurance, fishing license, food—that's about it. On my off weeks, I rented a room in a lodge at Monashka Bay. Run by a nice lady. She always cooked a ton of food." He shook his head. "Oh man. She made the *best* chicken-fried steak and gravy." He clapped a hand to his belly with a wistful sigh.

Sue hadn't thought about the amount of calories it must take to keep a guy of his build functioning. Was he getting enough to eat at the ranch? Probably not. Consistent food supplies were another constant source of headache.

Joe talked about Alaska all the way to Bend, and by the time they arrived at the outskirts of town, she hadn't once thought about the surgery. She eyed Joe's relaxed profile. Had he sensed her anxiety and talked her ear off to distract her?

No, he was probably just a chatty guy.

But as she directed him through town to the clinic, the idea kept coming back.

When they arrived, Joe pulled to the curb and got out, then came around to her side and opened the door.

She swung her braced leg out first, then used her crutches and climbed down. "Thanks for driving me. You probably have a lot of errands to do. I'll call you when I'm done." She pivoted and hobbled toward the glass door.

Joe beat her to it and held it open, ignoring the automatic door button. Then he dove ahead of her and got the inner lobby door too. Once Sue was inside, he slipped out without a word.

Sue made her way to the front desk and gave the red-haired nurse her information.

"Where do you want this?" Joe's voice from behind her.

She turned.

Joe carried her bag.

The receptionist directed him to a cart in the hallway.

Joe deposited the stuff and returned to Sue's side. "After my errands, I'll come back and wait here till you're done."

Right. Like you're not going to shoot pool or down a few beers while on the clock, like any other guy would.

He just stood there.

Why? Was he expecting a tip? "Okay, thanks."

Joe flashed a dimpled smile and ducked out.

Sue watched him through the glass doors until his truck pulled away from the curb.

Okay, so maybe not all roughnecks are rough.

• • •

Someone is holding me down . . . I can't fight . . . can't run and hide . . .

The sound of screams yanked Sue into a heart-pounding panic.

Who's screaming? Where am I? Who's holding me down?

Terror rushed over her in rippling waves, and the screaming—her own—surged, swirling around her head like converging sirens. "Get away from me!" Her words came out thick, muddy. She tried to fight but couldn't move. "Let me go! Help!"

She wanted to run, but nothing worked. Icy fear raced through her veins. She was slipping away. The ground dissolved beneath her. She screamed for help, grasping for something to break the fall.

Claws clamped around her wrists.

She screamed until something dark and over-powering pushed her down, forcing her deeper into the soft, white ground.

So dark . . .

Sue floated up to the light, toward the sound of people talking softly. Everything was blurry. She felt loose. And so light. Like a balloon drifting away. She opened her eyes.

A woman who smelled like licorice appeared wearing a paper hat. "Susan? Can you hear me?"

She nodded slowly. The motion made her brain

spin. *Whoa there, Nellie . . . something's not right . . .*

"You had a little trouble with the anesthesia. We gave you something to help you relax."

Oh yeah, I'll have a little more of that. A giggle tickled her throat. Sue couldn't remember the last time she'd giggled. Yep, something was definitely fishy. "Am I good to go now?" Sue's words were sludge in her ears. She lifted her head, but a wave of dizziness dropped her back against a pillow. *You drunk? That's against the rules, missy.*

The nurse came close and smiled. "It will take a few hours for the sedative to clear your system, but you should be feeling better very soon."

"Ohhh, I don't know about that. I'm feeling purdy good right now."

Darkness peeked in around the edges of the window blinds.

Sue blinked against the overhead lights.

"Your boyfriend is in the lobby. Are you ready to see him?"

Sue squinted at the smiling lady. "My *what?*"

The nurse's smile faded. "Big guy in a green stocking cap? He's been waiting for you for hours."

Sue took a deep breath and huffed it out to clear the fog. "Oh yeah. He's my giant. I mean my handy." *MAN, Sooz. HandyMAN.* She giggled again.

"Since you've had a sedative, the surgeon gave your friend the instructions for home care. He's also got your equipment and your pain prescription. You need to come back on Monday for a follow-up. Looks like you're all set to go."

Everything the woman said whooshed up and down like a rollercoaster. Sue wrinkled her nose and her whole face scrunched. "Can I stay here? This place is nice. And reeeeally quiet."

The woman smiled apologetically. "I'm sorry, the clinic is closing soon. Don't worry, in a few hours you'll feel much more like yourself."

"Okeedoke, I got this." She grasped the bedrails and pulled herself upright.

The room twirled off-kilter like a bloated ballerina.

"Hold on. Let's get you a wheelchair. You're not quite ready to walk to your car."

Two aides helped her into a funky wheelchair that made her leg stick out in front like a torpedo. Were they the same people who held her down earlier? For some reason, she didn't care. But something was *really* messed up with that leg. It was twice as big as the left one. And though it was super heavy, she couldn't feel it. Sweet.

The lady wheeled her to another room.

Sue's tongue stuck to the roof of her mouth. "I'm thirsty." Hadn't she already said that?

Joe put down a book and stood, stretching.

"Heeeyyy, big fella," Sue said. A string of giggles bubbled out.

"All right, here you are." The nurse smiled up at Joe. "She's all yours."

Joe's eyes went wide, like the nurse said he'd be delivering an open crate of rattlesnakes. But when he bent down, the bug-eyed look disappeared. "Ready to go home?"

She nodded once. "Yep."

An aide wheeled her through glass doors and out to the truck.

Joe opened the passenger door, towering over her like a giant oak in his brown work coat and green stocking hat. "Think you can stand up?"

Sue tipped her head all the way back so she could see his face. "Nope." She grinned. Her cheeks felt all rubbery.

Joe pressed his lips flat like a Muppet. Just like Bertie. He messed with the truck seat, then spun around and stood there looking as bewildered as a jackrabbit in the middle of the road. "So, do you, uh, want me to help you get in?"

"Surrre."

Joe puffed his cheeks and blew out a big blast, then reached down and lifted her from the wheelchair.

He smelled like leather and summertime. His face was close and he looked really cute in that green hat. It made his dark lashes look long. Maybe Joe and Bertie could do a puppet show for the kids. Flapping their mouths and arguing over how to spell a word, like on Sesame Street. Like Bert and . . .

"Ernie." Sue giggle-snorted.

One of Joe's eyebrows shot up and the other went down.

Cool trick. She tried to copy him, but her eyes got all blurry, and she saw two of him. Two was better than one. "Ha!"

Shaking his head, he put her on the seat, which took a while because her torpedo leg didn't bend.

After he shut the door, Sue leaned back and closed her heavy eyelids.

By the time Joe pulled into the Walgreens drive-thru, Sue was out cold. Whatever they'd given her had her completely toasted. He picked up her prescriptions, then headed southeast for Juniper Valley.

His afternoon of scouring public records for Jacobs had turned up nothing. What he needed was reliable Internet access, but with only a dumb phone and no laptop, he would have to borrow a computer from Sue or a library. He just needed one good lead.

When they reached the ranch, he parked as close to the house as he could get, but a couple dozen yards of sloped lawn lay between the truck and the house.

He glanced at Sue. Light from the porch made her skin glow. She looked peaceful. Angelic.

Yeah, when she's unconscious.

Joe braced himself. "Sue?"

"Hmm?"

"We're home."

"O-kay."

Joe went around and opened her door. He looked at her leg, then at the crutches. This was going to be tricky.

Sue chuckled and Joe looked up. She wore a wide, sleepy smile that made her eyes twinkle.

Wow. First time he'd ever seen her smile like that. Too bad it was temporary. And drug induced. Her full-on smile would probably knock a guy's socks off if she ever cut loose.

"Hey, Ernie." Her speech still had a little slur. "Where's the wheelchair?"

Ernie again? "Sorry, that belonged to the clinic. Think you can walk yet?"

"Surrrrre." She took hold of the door frame and started to slither out, torso first. He was pretty sure she didn't know the lower half needed to come out, too.

"Whoa." Joe winced. "Let's rethink this."

"Joe?"

"Yeah?"

"I'm reeeally thirsty."

He nodded. "I'm just going to, uh . . . carry you inside." She'd probably scream her head off if he touched her, but no way was he letting her take a nosedive on the lawn. "That okay?"

Sue's chin dropped in a single nod. "Yep."

Yeah, you just remember you said that. Carefully, he swiveled her legs out first, then scooped her up. Even with layers of bandages and a bulky brace on her leg, she felt light—way too light for an adult. He headed for the porch.

She pointed at her toes. "Watch the torpedo, Ernie."

"Ernie?"

"Mm-hmm." Sue nodded. "Bert and Ernie."

This was definitely a side of Sue he never would've believed if he hadn't seen it himself. Whatever they'd given her, maybe they could send some more. A bunch more.

As he carried her to the house, Sue rested against him and closed her eyes. He slowed his steps.

She snuggled up to him and mumbled something into his jacket.

"What's that?"

"I'm just gonna rest here a while, okay? This place is good. Safe."

His arms tightened around her.

She snuggled closer and pressed her cheek to his chest.

Slowing even more, he watched her, afraid to breathe. When he could finally exhale, his breath moved a golden curl across her forehead.

Her rosebud mouth turned up at the corners in a broad, sweet smile.

Something in his chest stood still. *This is nice. Except she thinks I'm from Sesame Street.* He spoke softly. "So I'm a Muppet, huh?"

"Yeah," she breathed, eyes still closed. "Only waaaaay better looking."

Joe nearly tripped on the porch step. "Is that right?" He grinned, hoping he didn't sound as pleased as he felt. At the door, he had to turn her bandaged leg around and then back her in.

Bertie met him in the foyer. The old woman's eyebrows nearly shot off her head when she saw Sue in his arms. She led him to the office where a cot was set up.

He deposited Sue onto it.

Bertie helped get her situated while Joe went out to the truck for Sue's things.

When he returned, Sue was murmuring to Bertie, ". . . feelin' purdy good."

"Great. So you think you'll sleep okay tonight?"

"Yep. Hey, Bertie, are all my kids here?"

"All tucked in, safe and sound." Bertie glanced at the clock above the desk.

Sue let off a noisy sigh. "Aww, Bert. You're sooo good. You'rrre the best."

Bertie threw Joe a look. "They gave her drugs, didn't they?"

Joe bit back a smile and leaned down close to

Sue. "Looks like you're iced up and all set now. I'll stop by in the morning and give you the rest of the instructions for your knee. You let me know if you need anything else." He stood to go.

Sue reached out a floppy hand and touched his. "Joe?"

He held his breath.

She smiled at him through sleepy eyes.

Man, but she's pretty.

"Thanks, Joe."

"Anytime." He nodded to Bertie, headed through the kitchen, and went out the back door to his quarters. His stay here would come to an end in a couple months, but for the first time, he didn't find the idea of going to the new job quite so appealing.

You're here to find old man Jacobs. Make yourself useful while you're here, but don't go getting attached to this place. Or anyone in it.

CHAPTER EIGHT

Over the next two days, Sue's post-op life alternated between bouts of broken sleep, pain, and pure aggravation. The broken sleep wouldn't have been so bad if it weren't for the goofy Sesame Street dreams. And no one warned her about the increased pain. As soon as her meds wore off, her knee throbbed like a gun barrel full of hot, crushed glass. But sitting in one position for hours at a time was enough to make her want to set her toenails on fire.

By Sunday afternoon, the sound of teens down at the volleyball court was a welcome distraction.

Maybe she could get Bertie to help her down to the pit, so she could watch the kids play. If Sue asked, Bertie could probably figure out a way to carry her down—

The thought of Joe Paterson sprang to mind, crowding out every other thought. Joe in a green stocking cap and work coat, carrying her in his massive arms.

Now *that* was random.

Sue closed her eyes and strained to hear the

game. Which kids were playing? She could guess. She could also guess which ones were only watching because she wasn't there to coax them into the game.

But the idea of being in Joe's arms kept invading her thoughts. She had a distinct impression of him cradling her against his broad chest. And although the thought of being that close to him rattled her, another sensation prevailed.

A sense of safety. Peace.

You're delusional, Sooz. Nobody's safe. You have to find your own safe place. Make your own peace.

Bertie's face appeared at the office door window. She stomped sand from her Birks and popped inside. "You're up. You've got a couple days' mail here. Need anything?" She set the mail on Sue's lap.

"Yeah. I need to get back to work. I need to pass that inspection. And I need to know what's going on around here."

Bertie shook her gray head. "Everything's running like clockwork, boss."

"Liar." Sue drilled her with a look. "Tell me everything."

With a sigh, Bertie pulled the desk chair close to the cot. "Well, Brandi and Jasmine got into it. That was a cat fight waiting to happen."

"Oh no! How bad?"

"Could have been worse. A lot of screeching,

mostly Brandi. She cornered Jasmine and accused her of taking her stuff. Called her a 'freak pack rat.' " Bertie's lips pursed to one side. "I checked it out. Jasmine's got a good little stash started."

Sue's brows rose. "Like—?"

"Weird stuff. Wrappers. Spoons. Pencils. Shoes belonging to Brandi and Sonja and some of the others. And food." Bertie folded her arms. "Looks like we've got another hoarder."

No surprise, given Jasmine's history. "Did you get them to make up?"

"I think so, but I'll keep an eye on 'em. Brandi got her stuff back and that seemed to do the trick. She lobbed a few parting cracks at Jas, though. I think Jasmine was more embarrassed than anything else." Bertie shook her head. "I tell you what, that kid has no fear in her. You should've seen her standing toe-to-toe with Brandi. Jasmine's half her size."

"I can picture it. She's a survivor."

The older woman lifted her chin and peered at Sue through the bottom of her glasses. "Reminds me of another headstrong girl I know."

Sue leaned back and stretched to relieve the muscle spasms that came from sitting so long. "What else? How are the new girls doing?"

"The new *girls* are doing fine. Especially the tall, dark, hunky one."

Sue's jaw dropped. Bertie had no business checking out a guy half her age. "I was getting to that. How are the repairs coming? Have you seen any of his work?"

"Joe's doing a fine job, Sue. And fast, too. He can do pretty much any job you give him. Too bad he won't be around long."

"Yeah, too bad." She had meant it as sarcasm, but it hadn't come out sounding that way.

"Although—and I hate to say it—I can already see one problem with having him here."

"What?" Apprehension tingled up her spine. The older girls were taking an interest in him? Or worse—the other way around?

Bertie glanced over her shoulder toward the dining hall. "That fella eats like a football team. We've gone through two extra cases of canned food just since he's been here. And the bread! That last donation of day-old from the Valley Market didn't even last two days. I don't know, Sue. Might have to ask him to provide his own meals."

Sue frowned. She hated to ask anyone to do that, considering how little she paid the staff. But food was not plentiful at the ranch, never had been. Receiving regular donations of food and supplies from local businesses, families, and churches was never Sue's idea, but for the kids' sake, she'd come to appreciate the help. And even more, she'd grown to depend on the extra food to fill in the gaps when funds came up short. "Let's not worry about that now. We'll figure something out after we pass inspection."

Bertie nodded, but her gaze darted away.

"What?" Sue said. "Something else wrong?"

Bertie's face creased with worry. "Elena's got family trouble back home. I think she's gonna leave."

"Back home? You mean Mexico?"

Bertie smoothed a wrinkle in Sue's blanket. "Her mom's gotten worse, and Elena is the only family she has. Don't think it'll be long before she has to go."

"We have to have a full-time boys' dorm counselor."

"Well, as it happens, there's a guy here now—"

"No. Joe's not trained to work with kids."

"How'd his background check and references turn out?"

Fingering the mail, Sue said, "Fine. Glowing, actually. But that's not the point. You know what it takes, Bert. Not just anyone can handle these kids."

A slow smile spread across Bertie's face. "From what I've seen, Joe's not just anyone."

Actually, he did have a way with Chaz. Still, he was barely more than a stranger.

"I don't know if you've noticed," Bertie said, "but the kids really like him. I had a group down at the volleyball pit, and we could hear him singing." Bertie glanced in the direction of the rise north of the house. "Up in that old boarded-up chapel. They stopped the game and wanted to go see what he was doing."

Sue frowned. "What's he doing in there?"

Bertie shrugged. "Clearing the clutter maybe. Wasn't that on the inspection list?"

It *was* on the list, but Sue had meant to do it herself. Somehow, the ranch's first few inspections had overlooked the old chapel perched on the north slope. Since the small building was boarded up and not in use, she saw no reason for it to meet fire code. But the state sent a new inspector who didn't care that the one-time chapel was now nothing more than a storage shed.

"What's in there?" Bertie asked. "Your stuff or the previous owners'?"

"Furniture, I think. We stored the leftover donations in there after our last fundraiser." And another fundraiser was needed, if the bank letter topping the stack of mail was what she suspected.

Bertie followed her gaze and nodded at the envelope. "Problems?"

Sue laughed. "What, this? No. The state is threatening to take away my license. I wrecked my knee, making me not only maimed but also *more* in debt. Plus we're ridiculously short-staffed, and, thanks to the Beaumont estate's Chapter Eleven bankruptcy, we've officially lost a huge chunk of monthly income. I don't see how a bank letter could possibly be more bad news, do you?"

Bertie sighed. "Pain meds wearing off, huh?"

Sue leaned back. "Sorry you got stuck with crab-sitting duty."

Rising, Bertie grinned. "No sweat. What's one more behaviorally challenged kid?" She trudged toward the dining hall, calling over her shoulder, "There's one piece of mail in that stack you might not want to torch along with the rest of the bills."

Sue gathered the pile of mail Bertie had tossed in her lap.

One lumpy, square envelope coated with tape and sparkly bits stood out. "TO MISS SUSAN" decorated one side in red glitter-glue.

She peeled away strips of tape, slipped out the folded construction paper, opened it gently, and smoothed the poster.

It was a collage of drawings, cropped snapshots, poems, magazine pictures, and stickers. And a couple math equations penned in the shape of a heart next to the scrawled signature of Charles P. Montgomery.

With a smile she couldn't contain, Sue turned the poster and read every contribution, noting each name or set of initials and the simple, sweet wishes for her speedy recovery. Tears blurred her vision. She scrubbed them away and studied the poster again.

The kids were the reason she was here, and the reason she would fight tooth and nail to keep their home.

With a sigh, she shuffled through the rest of the mail, sorting it into piles.

Junk, bills, and important stuff. The letter from the bank kept falling out of its stack, as if it didn't think it belonged in the junk pile.

Hissing out a breath, Sue opened the letter.

Notice of default with foreclosure proceedings underway.

She leaned back and closed her eyes. When funds got tight, Sue paid what she could on the loan, but staff wages always came first. To avoid auction, she needed to come up with the massive past-due amount. But she also needed to find a way to generate more monthly income. When she'd started the ranch, her operating budget was met through a variety of sources. Some sources made her nervous, but her passion to create a home for unwanted kids drove her to bend a little, to let go of the need to be in full control. Layne had reminded her that other group homes operated on a blend of funds from the state for some of the kids, private funds from some of the adoptive families, and private donors. It was the dependence on donors—something outside her control—that had always unnerved Sue, but in order to realize her dream, she'd taken Layne's suggestion and allowed others to help. That decision was one she now regretted, one that had come back to bite her just as she'd feared.

Before the accident, she'd been planning

another fundraiser. Now there was no time to waste. She needed to get that project going. She hoped it would bring in enough money.

Because at this point, hope was all she had, and even that was running out.

When Sue needed a ride to her checkup on Monday, the job fell to Joe again, which worked to his advantage. He needed to get electrical supplies in Bend.

By Monday, Miss No-Nonsense had clearly returned.

Another advantage. Some late-night thinking had reminded him that he had no need for entanglements. He was here to resolve relational issues, not pile on more. But as Sue crutched her way to his truck unassisted, Joe couldn't shake the memory of her snuggling against him, or his suspicions about her need to feel safe. And it felt good to be needed, which also didn't help.

As they drove to Bend, Sue asked about his progress on the repairs.

"If I get what I need in town today, I should have everything finished tomorrow."

"Great. Thank you."

He glanced at her. After spending years proving he could be trusted, he wasn't about to screw up now. And besides, the future of Sue's home was on the line.

At the outskirts of town, Sue got a call on her

cell. She listened for several seconds, wincing. "Thanks, Layne," she said in low tones, "but you really didn't have to sing." As the caller went on, Sue fingered the tips of her braid. "No, I mean it. What's the big deal? It's just a number." Picking at fuzz on the edge of her knee brace, she heaved a sigh. "Okay, I will. Thanks."

Joe watched the color creep through Sue's face as she stowed her phone.

"It's your birthday?"

She flung a stunned look at him.

"Just a guess. The big three-oh?"

With an eyeball roll, she nodded.

He pulled up to a stoplight. "Happy birthday! How are you going to celebrate?"

"I'm not."

"Aw, come on. You have to do *some*thing."

Sue shook her head. "I never really was into birthdays."

Would the *other* Sue feel the same way? He grinned "Come on. Hot fudge sundae, at least? My treat."

She gave a sideways look. "Thanks, really, but no. I'd rather forget it."

The light changed, and he accelerated. He gave it one last shot. "You still have to eat, birthday or not. We can call it lunch." His eyebrows went up. "So what do you like—Chuck E. Cheese?"

She quirked a brow.

"Mexican? Texas barbeque?"

She didn't answer, but he could tell he was getting warmer.

"Steak and ribs? Seafood? I know—surf and turf. I'm in the mood for a juicy steak and some jumbo garlic shrimp." He glanced over just in time to see her tongue poke out to wet her lips. He grinned. "All right. Steak and seafood it is. Right after your appointment. Deal?"

She shook her head. "I don't think I can manage a restaurant with this leg."

I think you mean 'torpedo.' Joe suppressed a smile. "What about takeout?"

Sue sighed. "I appreciate the thought, Joe, really, but I'd better not."

"Don't tell me you're on a diet." No way. With her slender frame? He still couldn't believe how light she had been when he carried her into the house after surgery.

Or how cute . . .

He cleared his throat. "Well, I'm hungry, so if you don't want to eat, that's fine, but I hope you don't mind if I do. I can celebrate your birthday enough for the both of us."

"No doubt," she said under her breath.

He glanced over and found Sue's lips curved in the faintest of smiles. Miss Susan had better watch herself. Mocking was almost teasing, which, in some circles, was considered fun.

While Sue was at her appointment, Joe went to the electrical supply store, which ended up not having the panel he needed. The clerk offered to order it, but it would take a week to get—a week Joe didn't have. When Joe told the guy he needed it today, the clerk offered to call around town and let Joe know if he'd found one.

He headed back to the clinic, praying for the sake of Sue's inspection that the panel would turn up today. When Sue emerged from her doctor appointment, Joe broke the news. "Looks like we have some time to kill. I guess you can't get out of lunch now."

"All right, you win."

Joe found a drive-thru burger joint boasting the best milkshakes in the state. "What will you have?"

"A kid's burger is fine."

Joe turned to the speaker. "Four of your biggest burgers, a couple biggie fries, and three old-fashioned shakes—chocolate, strawberry, and banana."

Sue guffawed.

By the time the girl at the window handed over the last bag, Joe's stomach sounded like a grumbly, old dog. He parked at the edge of the lot and nudged a loaded bacon cheeseburger toward Sue. Let her diet stand up to *that*.

Soon, the smell of melted cheese, sweet onions, pickles, and hot, salted fries won out. Sue took the burger and chowed down, hardly slowing.

The scratches on her neck had faded a bit.

His gaze traveled to the deep hollows above her collarbone. He tried not to stare, but couldn't help wondering why she was so thin.

Between bites of burger, Sue nibbled fries and kept eyeballing the chocolate shake.

He swallowed a mouthful of burger. "Take the chocolate one if you want it. I got dibs on the strawberry."

She bit her lip, then grabbed the shake and went to town on it. After slurping awhile, she set it down and pressed a palm against her belly with a painful groan.

Joe chuckled. "I thought you'd be one of those girls with a sparrow appetite. But man, you can really put it away. I think you just outdid me."

With a glare, she reached for the shake and took another couple of slurps.

"I always thought girls ate less on a date, not more."

Sue sputtered. "What? First off, this is in *no* way a date. And second, with the mountain of food you bought, I don't need to make sure there's enough for everyone." She bit her lip.

Joe frowned. "What do you mean 'enough for everyone'?"

"Nothing." She fiddled with her straw.

Was she having trouble supplying food for the kids? "Do you need food? I can help."

She studied him as if debating whether or not to admit he'd guessed right. "Sometimes we come up short and have to make things stretch." She sighed. "But we manage if we're careful."

He couldn't help taking another look at her pronounced cheekbones. His chest went suddenly numb. Did she go without food to make sure the kids had enough? No wonder she was so light. And so uptight. Hunger had a way of stealing one's joy.

Though decades had passed, Joe remembered exactly what constant hunger felt like. "I lived with a big family once. Food was scarce. Making it stretch for the foster kids wasn't exactly . . . a priority." Joe spoke gently. "But it's obvious you do whatever it takes to make sure everyone in this family is well taken care of."

Sue made circles with her cup, swirling its melting contents. "That's the first time I've heard anyone else refer to Juniper Ranch as a 'family.'"

He shrugged. "Why not? Families come in all types. Like on a rig. When you work miles from shore, there's a strong sense of family. Only on a rig, everyone earns their spot. If a new guy— let's call him 'John Smith'—proves himself, he goes from being called 'Smith' to 'Cousin John.' If he goes on to gain the crew's respect, he might move up to 'Uncle John.'"

Sue poked around in her shake with the straw. "We don't encourage nicknames at the ranch. They're not usually based on a person's positive qualities." She thunked her cup down on the console. "Usually, it's just mean. Some of the kids came up with Chaz the Spaz. I hate that. Everyone has some flaw that makes them less than perfect."

"Maybe they don't know any other way to bond."

"Maybe. I overlook a lot of stuff, but I don't tolerate put-downs. Everyone needs to feel safe and fully accepted, especially in his or her own home. Most of these kids are here because they have some quirks. They need to feel like they're an equal part of the family, not an outsider. I can't control what happens after they leave, but I *can* teach them not to put each other down and not to let anyone tell them there's something wrong with them."

Her passion for outcasts hit Joe like a boxer's punch. If only the people he'd depended on as a kid had defended him a fraction as much. If only he'd had someone like Sue on his side when he was being accused of horrible things. Of being a freak.

Sue turned to him. "But maybe things were different for you."

"What do you mean?"

"On the rig."

"Oh. Right."

"So what was your nickname?"

Joe felt his face go warm. "Well . . . the rig boss is usually considered the father figure."

Her brows shot up. "Father Paterson?"

He chuckled at the picture that conjured. "Papa Joe."

"Really?"

He nodded.

Sue gave a slow shake of her head. "Disturbing."

"How's that?"

She took a noisy slurp of her milkshake and wiped her mouth. "*Dad* is the last thing I'd ever call someone I actually respect." She spoke with such a quiet calm—almost calm enough to disguise the scorched edge to her words.

"I take it your dad wasn't exactly Father of the Year."

She stuffed her cup into one of the sacks, then crimped the opening closed with crisp, even folds until the bag was locked down tighter than Fort Knox. "No. I'm pretty sure none of the guys my mom brought home qualified for that."

Aw, man. Joe lowered his voice to match her tone. "How many were there?"

If she was feeling any emotion, it was hidden behind an empty smile. "Not a clue. You could ask my mom, but I'm pretty sure she wasn't counting."

Man, what a past.

Slowly, Joe stuffed his wrappers into a sack to hide his amazement that she was actually opening up, then stowed the sack behind the seat. "I'm sorry, Sue. Sounds like you had it pretty rough."

Sue gazed out across the parking lot. "Rough? I don't know. I learned a lot. Like how to confuse a drunk by switching my hiding places. Or how my mom would rather accuse me of lying about her boyfriend than give up the creep."

Anger and pity burned through him at the reminder that some parents were capable of such terrible betrayal. "I'm sorry, Sue."

"No." She shook her head. "I shouldn't have brought it up. What's past is past."

Heart sinking, he held back. Since a "religious group home" was of no value to her, she clearly had no use for God. So how *had* she gotten past it? Because without the healing love of Christ, Joe knew without a doubt he'd still be one angry man, poisoned by bitterness over the things he'd endured.

Sue gathered the rest of the bags. "Thanks for lunch. I'll repay you."

"For a birthday lunch? Yeah, right." He shook his head. "That's against the rules."

A half smile quirked up a corner of her mouth. "See, another reason I don't like birthdays. Rules."

Joe chuckled and fired up the truck. When he took out his phone and saw he'd missed a call, he listened to the message and chuckled again. The electrical panel he needed was available at a store across town.

Thank you, Father.

As he headed to the supply store, Joe found a radio station playing oldies rock and roll and kept the volume low.

Sue dozed, face relaxed, both hands resting on her stuffed belly.

CHAPTER NINE

Standing at her bathroom mirror, Sue shifted her weight and checked the strain on her leg. Not too bad, but she hadn't gotten permission to lose the crutches yet. And she'd have to wear the brace for the first few weeks of physical therapy, but with a little luck and hard work, maybe it would come off early and she could go for a ride. A much needed ride.

The state inspector still hadn't come, and the wait was making her nerves feel like violin strings stretched miles past their limit.

She brushed her hair. How had it gotten so long? Of course, she hadn't had time for a trim in ages. The layers reached well past her shoulders now, the curls falling long and loose.

Such a pretty girl.

She'd heard it enough times to know it wasn't just the creeps who thought so. Though working for the county had meant wearing a more polished look, she'd always avoided anything that drew attention to her figure. For as long as she could remember, she'd had a way of bringing out the worst in men. But a clean face and baggy clothes only did so much. It had taken growing a cold shoulder and brisk demeanor to make the *hands-off* message perfectly clear.

Her reflection showed her hair in a shining cascade over one shoulder. The hair and her small, full lips made her look like one of those sultry movie stars from the '40s.

Was that what people saw when they looked at her?

What did Joe see?

Sue quickly wove her hair into a tight braid, then headed for the main house. Inside, she checked on the kids working in the study.

Cori and Tatiana were helping Linda, another temp, make fliers about the fundraiser sale to put up in town and mail to neighboring communities.

"Hey, Miss Susan," Chaz said. "I got an idea. Invite the flight school to send pilots to do aerial stunts. That'll draw a ginormous crowd."

"I'm sure it would," Sue said, smiling. She wheeled Donovan and Daisy into the dining hall and read to them for an hour, then went outside. Vince and Deeg were cleaning out the chicken coop while Sonja and Haley worked on sorting recycling. Sue met Edgar hauling a large box out of the shop, trailed by Ringo. Sue crutched into the building.

Elena had Brandi toting bags of stuff from the shop to the burn barrel out back, while Jasmine swept the floor. Someone was under the hood of the Suburban.

Sue moved around to the front.

Joe was up to his elbows in motor. When he should have been taking the day off.

"Hi. What are you doing?"

Joe wiped his hands on a rag and straightened. "Seeing what it'll take to get your rig running." As he turned to her, his eyes roamed over her face and hair. "I meant to tell you I was going to work on it. Hope that's okay."

"Yes, of course. I meant why are you working on stuff today? You've finished the inspection list, and it's your day off."

He shrugged. "Just looking for something to do." A dark grease smudge across his forehead added a comical look to his raised brow.

Sue felt an insane urge to wipe away the smudge but held back. Joe seemed different somehow. Maybe it was the crop of thick, dark hair coming in. Why was he letting it grow back? He and Vin Diesel on the outs?

She met his gaze. "Thanks, but you really don't have to work off the clock."

His grin faded a tad. "I know that, but I like to keep busy." His voice deepened. "If it's all the same to you."

There were plenty of reasons he shouldn't work for free. And she didn't like the idea of owing him any favors, but what could she say?

Beyond him, the workbench was clean, the big tools hung up, the smaller ones in labeled boxes.

She turned back to Joe, a twinge of shame tugging at her. "I don't think I've told you how much I appreciate everything you've done and how quickly you finished the list. Thank you."

Joe's gaze held hers for several long seconds, then he gave a slight nod. "My pleasure."

"Pleasure?" Sue laughed. The job he'd accepted could hardly be anyone's idea of pleasure.

His eyes fell to her mouth and lingered. Then, in an abrupt move, he turned back to inspect the engine. "How's the knee?"

"Better, but the recovery pace is killing me. I start physical therapy on Friday." Sue squared her shoulders. "I'll need someone who's not care staff to drive me there. Do you mind?"

He lifted a black rubber cap and tugged on some wires. "Sure," he said finally, his tone quiet. "No problem."

Sue glanced behind the Suburban at her old Sportster. A thin coat of dust dulled the red tank and black seat and fogged the chrome. She crutched closer and took a rag to it.

Joe shut the hood, then came around and stood beside her. "That yours?"

"Yeah." Sue rubbed a scratch on the seat. "I bet it's the first Harley you've ever seen custom lowered to fit a five-foot-two woman."

Joe gave the bike an approving nod. "Sweet. Not the bike you wrecked on, I take it."

"No. That was my old Honda XL100."

"Was? Where is it now?"

"Probably lying in a twisted heap somewhere at the bottom of the ravine."

"Whoa." Joe shook his head. "Must have been a scary ride."

Forcing back images of tumbling through the brush-filled, stony ravine, she suppressed a shudder. "Yeah, it wasn't much fun."

"Which ravine?"

"Come outside and I'll show you."

Joe followed Sue out the door and down the drive until the ridge was in sight.

She pointed. "Just over that hill. There's a canyon between Juniper Ridge and Table Rock." She let out a wry chuckle. "I know, not the most ideal place to ride."

Joe squinted at the ridge top. "Oh, I don't know. I've ridden worse." A slow grin softened the muscular contours of his face. "A lot worse."

She could easily picture him straddling a massive cruiser. "In Alaska?"

"Yeah. My friend David and I rode whenever we could."

What would cruising full throttle on an open stretch of Alaskan road feel like? She sighed. "I bet that was a blast."

"Some of the best times I've ever had."

"But . . . you probably didn't ride as a kid, if your life in foster care was anything like mine."

Joe turned to her with that drilling look of his. "No, I didn't do anything like that until later. As soon as I turned eighteen, I sort of started over. In more ways than one."

His answer reminded Sue of a question that Layne had brought to her attention the day before. "Joe, something turned up in your background check that confuses me."

Although his gaze didn't flinch, something in his eyes turned slightly wary.

"There seem to be records of you under two different names. One is Joseph Paterson, and the other is Joseph Jacobs. Is that correct? Or was there a mistake?"

Joe's jaw tensed. "It's right."

A tingle of apprehension crept up her spine. "Why two names?"

Joe stuffed his hands into his pockets. "My little brother and I were adopted by the Jacobs family when I was eight." He glanced down and toed at a scruff of cheatgrass in the driveway. "I'd taken care of Ben since he was a baby, so I was glad they took us both. But the adoption didn't work out, and I went back to foster care." He kicked at the clump of grass until it came loose. "After I turned eighteen, I went back to using my biological name."

It took a moment for the meaning of his words to sink in. Joe had been the victim of a terminated adoption. Rejected and abandoned, just like the kids Sue cared for. The weight of the news pressed against her heart. "I'm so sorry, Joe. How old were you when the Jacobs family sent you away?"

"Ten."

"What about your little brother?"

His gaze shifted to some point in the desert beyond her. "I heard they sent him away too, later."

"Were you two ever reunited?"

"No, I never saw him again. I've tried to find him, but . . ." Lips pursed, Joe shook his head, then gazed across the desert in silence.

How long had it taken him, just a child, to get over being ripped from his family, and worse, torn from his only brother? Poor little guys. Sue blinked back tears.

Joe turned to her and stilled. A vulnerable look softened his features.

Of course, he'd probably never fully gotten over it. No one really did. "Joe, I'm so sorry. How anyone could do that . . ." Sue stopped herself before the emotion choking her voice gave way to something else. Something childish and embarrassing.

As she held her breath to quell it, Joe's gaze remained locked on hers.

The air between them suddenly went still. Her sympathy melted into another kind of emotion that seemed to radiate from her in waves.

"Hello?" A male voice called out from behind her.

Sue turned.

A man in a button-down work shirt and jeans, clipboard in hand, descended the porch steps and headed toward them.

"Looks like inspection time," Joe said quietly. "I'll be in the shop if you need me."

The man approached her with his state inspector's badge in hand.

Sue stole a peek at Joe's tall frame and broad shoulders as he headed toward the shop. Joseph, a young boy sent away from his family to live among strangers, scared and alone.

All of the sudden, Joe Paterson didn't seem so big after all.

Bertie clocked on and joined Sue in the office while the inspector finished writing up his report. He made a couple of *X*s, then turned the clipboard to Sue and asked her to sign.

With a trembling hand, Sue took the pen. She had to look twice to see that the box next to *Compliant* was checked. She exhaled and signed on the line, smiling. As Bertie showed him out, Sue sank into her desk chair.

Bertie spun around, grinning like a cartoon

cat—wearing purple tie-dye and John Lennon glasses. "You did it!"

"*We* did it." Sue grinned. "No. You know what? Joe did it."

Bertie's eyebrows danced. "Told you he was good."

Sue stood, her heart singing. "I'm going to go tell him."

"Sorry, boss, no can do. He's gone."

"What?" Her pulse kicked up. "What do you mean 'gone'?"

"He took off in his truck. Said he needed to go into town."

So he wasn't *gone* gone. "Did he say when he'd be back?"

Bertie shook her head. "Nope."

Of course Joe needed some time away from the ranch and the kids after all the work he'd done. It was just too bad he wasn't around to hear the good news.

She pulled out her phone and found his number.

But then again, maybe she shouldn't bother him on his day off. Passing the inspection probably wasn't as important to him as it was to her. He had no personal stake in the ranch. Why should he? He was leaving soon.

With a sinking heart, she gave Bertie a brisk nod. "Well, good. That's out of the way. The next mountain to tackle is the fundraiser."

"You sure don't waste a second, do you?

Well, congratulations, anyway." She shuffled out, muttering, "Party's over, everyone. Back to work."

They needed to pay off the past-due mortgage and get the bank off her back. *Then* they could party.

Sue headed toward the dining hall and collided with a breathless Jasmine. "Whoa, kiddo. Where's the fire?"

Wide-eyed, Jasmine tugged on Sue's sleeve. "Come! Now!"

"What's wrong?"

"Brandi!" She ran for the stairs.

"What is it?" Sue followed the girl. "Did she do something to you?"

"No." Jasmine grasped Sue's wrist and tugged her up the steps. "To Brandi!"

"What do you mean?"

Jasmine turned, her face a mask of panic. She thrust an upturned wrist in Sue's face and made a slashing motion across it with her other hand. "Brandi has knife!"

Sue climbed the stairs as fast as she could.

CHAPTER TEN

"Open the door, Brandi!" Sue tried to force the bathroom door open, but it wouldn't budge.

From behind the door came rustling and hurried movement.

Fear of what the girl was doing to herself shot through Sue's veins like ice. "Brandi! Let me in!"

Jasmine froze, eyes wide.

Cori and Haley came running from the stairs, and Haley covered her mouth. "Did she cut again? Is she going to get sent away?"

"No!" Brandi's voice was a growl. The door cracked open half an inch.

Sue shoved a foot in the crack and threw her weight against the door, forcing it open.

Inside, Brandi backed away. "I didn't cut, Miss Susan, I swear." Her pleading look hardened to a glare as she spied Jasmine in the hall. "Little freak snitch!"

Eyes fixed on Brandi, Sue said quietly, "Haley, go with Jasmine and Cori down to the kitchen and join Miss Elena's crew." Sue closed the door behind her and called Bertie on her cell for reinforcement. Then she turned to Brandi. "Tell me where the knife is, Brandi. Don't move, just tell me."

The girl shook her head. "I wasn't going to do it."

Sue gave her a dead level eye-to-eye. "Where is it?"

Brandi shrugged.

"Okay. Against the wall, please, and show me your arms."

Rolling her eyes, the girl backed against the wall, pushed up her sweatshirt sleeves, and raised both arms.

No visible marks.

But when the girl moved again, Sue caught a whiff of something that nearly gagged her. "Where'd you get the beer, Brandi?"

"Aw, man. It wasn't me, I swear. I fell in the mud at soccer practice and I had to borrow another girl's jersey. The beer spill was already there." Her voice rose. "I wasn't drinking!"

Sue made a mental note of every word Brandi said so she could document the incident later. "Miss Roberta will check you for marks. You'll need to remove your street clothes."

A knock at the door came, then Bertie's voice. "Sue?"

Sue called her in, never taking her eyes from the girl in case she had the knife on her.

Bertie entered the bathroom and inspected Brandi. "She's clear."

"See? I told you I didn't cut."

Sue nodded. "Miss Roberta, please search the gym bag for a knife. And anything else that doesn't belong there."

As Bertie checked the bag, Brandi chewed on her lip. Her eyes weren't tracking right.

Sue stepped closer and sniffed.

"I wasn't drinking, Miss Susan, I swear. Smell my breath. You can have me tested or whatever. I wouldn't do that. You know I don't want to go back to that juvie hospital. Please don't send me away—I have to stay here. Please!"

"Found it." Bertie held up a Swiss army knife, then pocketed it.

Brandi swore beneath her breath.

"Okay. Give her back her clothes, but not the jersey. I need to see that."

As Brandi got dressed, Sue inspected the soccer jersey. Brandi was right—it wasn't hers. It had a stain on the front and carried the faint but unmistakable smell of beer. "Where's your jersey?"

Brandi wiped tears from her eyes. "I hung it up to let the mud drip off. I guess I left it there."

"Which high school girls were you hanging out with at practice?"

Bertie wrote down the names as Brandi spoke. The girl wasn't usually prone to crying nor this compliant. Something was off. It was hard to tell if this was the effect of alcohol or genuine fear of being sent away.

The teen's last cutting offense had ended with a warning that if it ever happened again, she'd be sent to a juvenile facility until she turned eighteen.

Frustration burned in Sue's heart, but she kept herself from showing it. If Brandi were sent away now, it would go on her record and might land her in a place where her life would never be the same. Her semi-normal life here, filled with privileges, sports, and a measure of independence, would be stripped away. Any hope Sue had of seeing Brandi make something of herself could be ruined with one phone call.

And yet Sue had a rule to uphold, a decision to make. "Brandi, you were already on probation from last time. What were you doing with a knife? Where did you get it?"

Scowling, Brandi wiped her nose on her sleeve. "I got it from Megan's little brother. I was . . . only thinking about it." She lifted her face, chin quivering. "The girls were bragging about how their families were all at the tournament last weekend and how even their grandparents came, and I felt like a piece of dirt, you know? I had to listen to that and all I could think of was how nobody cares squat about me. Nobody. I just . . . felt so alone." A fresh wave of tears streamed down her face. "Part of me wanted to do it. But I didn't."

Bertie cleared her throat.

Sue glanced at the older woman. Her expression was hard to read, but she didn't seem too moved by the girl's story.

Brandi ignored Bertie and pleaded with Sue. "I only wanted to hold it, just for a while. Having the knife made me feel like I was in control, you know? But I wasn't going to use it." Her eyes begged. "I don't want to get sent away and lose everything I've worked for."

Bertie gave a faint headshake.

"Please, don't send me away, Miss Susan." Brandi's rising voice choked on her tears. "I promise I won't ever touch a knife or do anything like that again. I need to learn to believe in myself. I know this place is my only chance to do that. Please?"

Folding the jersey slowly, Sue mentally tallied the facts. Brandi knew the consequences.

She also knew alcohol was grounds for immediate removal and that Sue could give her a drug test, as well as talk to the high school about the other girls involved. As far as blowing her probation, she hadn't actually cut herself.

Sue leveled her gaze on the girl, forcing Brandi to look her in the eye. "First off, no more soccer. That was a privilege and an opportunity for earning trust, which you've chosen to break. And second, if you *ever* come in contact with alcohol or have a cutting instrument of any kind in your

123

possession again, you will be sent away without discussion. Do you understand?"

Wiping her blotchy face, Brandi nodded. "I won't. I promise. Thank you, Miss Susan."

Sue stepped into the hall, Brandi on her heels, Bertie following.

Jasmine waited near the stairs.

As Sue and Brandi passed Jasmine, Sue sensed a wordless exchange between the two girls. She stopped and looked at them. "And you two need to get along."

"I know." Brandi aimed a flat smile at Jasmine. "Little J here was just looking out for me. We're cool."

Brandi descended the stairs with Bertie, but Sue waited until they were out of earshot and then turned to Jasmine. "It'll take some work, but can you try to be friends with her?"

Jasmine glanced down the stairwell, then back at Sue. "Miss Susan not see all," she said, face grim. "Brandi not anyone's friend."

Dusk crept across the valley, deepening the sky. Nearing the road to the ranch, Joe downshifted for the turn. Not only had they passed inspection—news he'd gotten via text from Bertie—but, thanks to a couple hours on a Juniper Valley Library computer, he'd found old man Jacobs. John and his disabled adult daughter, Fiona, were living in Bend. Minus the ex-mom. Apparently

Leia Jacobs had left the family and moved out of state. Their son, Ruben, was in prison—also no surprise. Joe would soon pay the old man a visit and tell him the things he'd long wanted to say.

But not today. Passing inspection called for a celebration.

As the truck climbed the drive, a nagging reminder dampened Joe's mood. He still hadn't found his brother, Ben. Finding *him* would call for the biggest party of all.

Pole lights blazed across the compound, reminding him of a homing beacon, and a wave of nostalgia swept over him. My Father's House was the only place from his childhood where he'd felt like anyone cared. Like he had any hope of a future.

Unlike what he'd received in the Jacobs home.

"Thank you, God," he said as he climbed out of the truck cab. "For showing me Your Father's heart. For making me feel like a son." Heading to the porch, Joe imagined Chaz and Edgar and the others going on with their lives from here. What they needed was a caring, steady, male role model, like the ones he'd had.

How hard would it be to provide that himself? Not hard at all. He could see himself working with these kids and giving them some much needed stability. The image stirred a surprising sense of joy—until he remembered he was only here temporarily. Joe stowed the thoughts and entered the house.

The foyer was empty. In the den, a couple of kids lounged on couches, reading. Chaz sat at a computer, his big glasses throwing off a bluish glare from the screen.

"Hey, guys," Joe said. "I got some stuff to bring inside. Want to give me a hand?"

Eyes fixed on the screen, Chaz pushed his glasses higher on his nose. "Just a sec. I'm IMing with the chopper pilot who flies drills over the ranch." Grinning, he launched into a burst of key-tapping. "I'm tricking him into telling me his flight schedule."

"No problem. I've got a truckload of melting ice cream and hot fudge sauce, but if you guys don't want a party, I'm sure I could eat it all my—"

"What? Ice cream and *fudge?* J-man, you coulda said that!" The boy's chair toppled over as he and the other kids scrambled for the door.

Edgar and Haley grabbed boxes of groceries, while Joe hauled in a couple of bags. He went to work setting up the dining hall, putting out plastic bowls and cups, and lining up soda bottles and tubs of ice cream.

Sonja, Tatiana, and Cori came in and squealed when they saw all the stuff.

Grinning like a kid at his own birthday, Joe handed out balloons to blow up. He set out syrups, whipped cream cans, and candy toppings on the sideboard.

Chaz counted eight buckets of ice cream aloud and read off the flavors, the pitch of his voice rising higher with each one. A chorus of excitement filled the dining hall.

"Oh man—cookie dough? I *love* cookie dough!"

"Whipped cream in a can!"

"M&Ms!"

Edgar toted in a box of groceries. "Dude, this stuff don't look like party food. It's like . . . regular food."

Jasmine watched the activity, eyes wide. She followed Edgar and pulled a gallon jug of maple syrup from his box. "This for party too?"

"No, that's for pancakes—"

The door to the kitchen swung open. Sue entered the dining hall but came to a standstill when she saw the commotion. She stared at all the food, her eyes huge.

Joe smiled.

"What's going on? Who—"

"Hey! Miss Susan, check this out!" Chaz grabbed a pair of whipped cream cans and shook them like maracas. "Ice cream par-TAY!"

Sue's gaze swept around the tables laden with party ware and frosty tubs of ice cream. Her eyes widened even more when Cori danced around with two squeeze bottles of hot fudge.

Which reminded Joe of the special bag he'd stowed under the driver's seat. He dashed outside to the truck and retrieved it. When he returned, Elena and Linda were in the dining hall, watching the jostling teenagers.

Sue turned her attention to Joe and the room quieted.

Oh, right. She probably didn't like ice cream parties any more than she liked birthdays.

"Mister Joe," she said quietly, eyebrows on the rise. "What is all this?"

"It's a party." He tried for his most disarming smile. "We passed inspection."

Bertie nudged Sue with an elbow. "See? *Some* people know how to stop and smell the chocolate-covered roses." She grinned at Joe. "You got hot fudge over there? Nuts?"

"I got it all, Miss B." He raised a brow at Sue. "Say the word, boss. Ice cream's melting."

Sue shook her head as if to clear a fog. "Okay, yeah. Everyone, please thank Mister Joe for the—" She glanced around the room, still taking it all in. As the kids hollered their thanks and stormed the goods, Sue moved toward the boxes of groceries deposited near the kitchen.

"Hey!" Bertie hollered. "What are we—a herd of wild hogs? Make a line! Manners go for parties too."

With a grin he couldn't contain, Joe watched

the kids scoop ice cream and slosh soda and squirt whipped cream in bowls.

Jasmine stood back and stared at all the food, palms pressed to her cheeks.

Sue wove her way through the buzzing mob. "Joe, I . . ." She stood there looking as if she wanted to speak but had forgotten how.

Joe grinned. Seeing her speechless was the cherry that topped his day. "Hang on, I have something else." Joe slipped the package of chocolates out of the grocery sack and offered it to her. "Congratulations."

She looked at the package and then at him, her expression deeply puzzled.

He nudged it into her hands. "Hope you like chocolate. It was a guess."

"A *guess?* Dark Lindor balls?" She kept looking at the bag as if she'd never seen chocolate balls wrapped in shiny blue wrappers. Sue turned and watched the kids licking fudgy spoons and squirting whipped cream into each other's bowls.

Ah, crud, here she comes. Miss Thou-Shalt-Have-No-Fun.

"Joe, this is really nice of you." A frown creased her brow. "But I wish you would have asked me first. The kids are actually . . . better off without this kind of stuff."

Better off? "Oh, right. Sugar high, I get it. But really, would it hurt just this once?"

A pair of luminous brown eyes met his. "What

hurts is the hope this kind of thing stirs up. They probably won't get a treat like this ever again. It's a lot easier on them—on us all—if they don't have it to begin with."

Something in him deflated. He spoke lightly. "It's just ice cream, Sue."

She inhaled as if gearing up for a speech. "I know, and it really was nice of you to do this. It's just that next time they want it, I'll have to say no, and then they'll be disappointed. These kids don't need any more disappointment."

His heart sank. "So you'd rather keep them used to going without?" He tried to stop himself but couldn't. Her logic was killing his joy. "Do you really think denying them treats will keep them from wanting them?" A thought crashed over him like an icy wave. *She's the one who's afraid of wanting.* Sorrow tugged at his chest.

Sue studied the shiny blue package in her hands, touching the cellophane window that offered a glimpse of the wrapped candies inside. "I wouldn't call it denying them. More like avoiding disappointment. And needless longing." She met his gaze. "I'd think you of all people could understand that, Joe."

The quiet resignation of her tone caught him by surprise. Clearly, her need to protect them from disappointment came from something much deeper and far more personal than balloons and hot fudge. "I understand life can be cruel, Sue.

Bad things happen. I also know how tough it can be for a kid to bounce back when life repeatedly knocks them down. But this isn't one of those times."

Some of the kids were already wound up and showing signs of sugar overload. Jasmine licked her spoon, giggling at Haley.

Sue looked back at Joe, her expression torn. "I don't know. Maybe you're right. I've been trying so hard to guard them from broken promises that I . . ." Glancing at the bubbling teens, she eased out a sigh. "You're right. It's just ice cream." She kept watching the kids as if wrestling to believe her own words, then glanced at the boxes of groceries. "I don't know how to thank you for all this. I hate to think of what all this cost, especially considering how little you're getting paid to work here."

"It's no problem. Don't worry about it."

"Hey." Edgar sauntered by carrying a bowl heaped with ice cream and offered Joe a fist bump. "You rock, J-man."

Sue gave him a look.

He sobered. "I mean, Mister Joe."

Joe smiled. "You're welcome, Edgar."

Edgar ambled off, shoveling a giant mound of dripping goo into his mouth.

"That's an awful lot of groceries," Sue said quietly.

She probably wouldn't like the reasoning

behind it, especially since she seemed to have trouble accepting his help. "Well, I'm living here and eating your food. I just want to keep eating while I'm here, if that's okay with you."

Her shoulders relaxed. "Yes, it's okay if you eat, especially since no one would dare try to stop you." Then she examined the chocolates again, another frown forming. "Who told you?"

"Told me what?"

She stared at the bag as if deciding what to do with it. "Nothing. Thank you."

When she looked up again, her hesitant smile melted him in a way that spread through his limbs and threatened to take him out at the knees.

She limped away, bag close to her chest.

Whatever had just happened, a serious crack was forming in Miss Susan's wall.

CHAPTER ELEVEN

Joe glanced at the silent passenger seat, expecting to see her asleep, and found Sue staring out the window instead. Probably had a lot on her mind. He wasn't in the mood for talking either. The folded map in his back pocket pulsed with every heartbeat, beats that quickened as the truck edged closer to Bend.

Today he would face them. Whether old man Jacobs wanted to or not, today he would hear the truth about what had really happened and the damaging choices his family had made.

Once Sue was inside the therapy clinic, Joe pulled the Google map out of his pocket and read the directions to Goshen Road. Seemed clear enough.

What wasn't so clear was what Joe would do once he got there. Would the old man let him in or would Joe have to force his way inside? Would he get a chance to speak his piece? Would Fiona remember him? And if so, how much did she remember?

And though he'd heard Leia Jacobs was no longer in the picture, who knew? Maybe John's wife had come back. Joe had thought plenty about what he'd say to the woman who, in order to save her own skin, had heaped lies and accusations on Joe like burning filth. He'd ask her how she slept at night after abandoning a scared kid at a time when he needed his family the most.

Joe pulled out onto the main road and headed north. Regardless of the reception he'd get from the Jacobs family, he had only one goal: to make them hear the truth. And while he was at it, to let them know that, despite their accusations, he'd turned out to be a decent, responsible man. What they did with the information was their business. He wanted nothing from them. Clearing the air was something he needed to do.

Fueled by a fresh blast of determination, he drove to the north end of town, navigating through sparse stretches of commercial neighbor-hoods.

This area didn't match the clean, upscale look of downtown Bend. Graffiti and gang-tagging covered buildings. Steel bars guarded doors, and beater cars littered vacant lots. At a bus stop, a guy bundled in ratty coats slept next to a shopping cart loaded down with junk.

Joe found the address and stopped across from a sagging apartment building.

Garbage surrounded the building. Litter stuck to patches of dirt and weeds like faded postage stamps. Four skinny punks sat on the front step of an apartment that had cardboard stuffed into broken windows. A cussing brawl between a man and a woman, punctuated by sharp screams, carried through Joe's closed truck window. Somewhere else, an infant squalled. The ragged siding and peeling roof were worse than anything he'd seen, and he'd seen plenty of dumps.

Number seventeen was the last apartment on the lower level.

The baby's cries weakened to a listless whimper. The punks leveled glares at Joe.

He ignored them and took a closer look at the apartment.

No one went in or out, and no one seemed to be moving around inside. What kind of life did they live?

He stepped out of the truck. The smell of decay roiled his stomach as he crossed the street, keeping an eye on the guys at the other end who continued to stare.

If John Jacobs lived in this place, he must have hit rock bottom.

Doesn't matter how they live. They're going to hear what I have to say. He aimed for the door and marched across the "yard." An accidental strike from his boot sent a baby bottle with congealing contents skidding across the dirt. He could picture a grimy toddler picking it up and sticking it in his mouth. *Don't look. Doesn't matter.* But his footsteps slowed in spite of the mental pep talk, and he stopped a couple of yards from the door.

A wooden ramp, splintered and sunken in the center, hung askew on the front step. No sound came from inside. No TV, no conversation. No lanky old man downing a case of Bud on the front porch.

The odor of rotten trash assailed him, coating his nostrils and throat with the stench. He focused on the door.

The baby's wailing resumed, the weary, monotone cry of a child who knew no one is coming.

What am I doing here?

He'd come a long way, spent a lot of time preparing for this. He needed to do it.

So why did he feel like trash?

Someone was crying, this time a woman. Crying and moaning. He couldn't tell if it came from the brawling couple or from apartment seventeen. Could be Fiona, a mentally and physically disabled woman with the mind of a child, who lived in filth and saw drug deals, neglect, and who knew what else outside her front window.

What had forced Jacobs to live here? Because no one would willingly choose this.

Maybe he was reaping what he'd sown. Had God brought Jacobs low because of his family's sins? It didn't get much lower than this.

And now Joe was going to march in there and

tell them off. Lay down a list of all the wrongs they did to him.

A wave of nausea rolled through Joe's gut, dousing the fire that had driven him hundreds of miles to this door. *Father, what am I doing?* Forcing down the queasiness, he marched back to the truck and started it, then jammed the stick into gear and floored it.

Pure Torture, as Layne had called it, was a painfully accurate nickname for what Sue had just endured. Why would anyone choose a career as a physical therapist? It had to take a certain kind of person. The sadistic kind, obviously.

Sue spotted Joe pacing near the clinic entryway and crutched toward him, gritting her teeth to keep from hissing at the shards of pain. They'd told her to take something before coming in, but, like an idiot, she'd ignored the advice.

Joe opened the door for her and followed her out.

She climbed into the truck, all the while vowing that next time, she'd swallow her pathetic need to prove she wasn't a wimp and take the meds. By the time she settled into the passenger seat, a film of perspiration coated her face and neck. As she reached for her buckle, Joe barreled out of the lot, knocking her off balance. She grabbed the armrest on the door and shot him a look. "Good grief, where's the fire?"

He turned south on the main highway without a word.

Why was he in such a hurry to get back to the ranch? His new duties as daily work-crew boss had been divided among the other staff today, and the kids would be finished with their chores by the time she and Joe returned.

Sue closed her eyes and leaned back. Since Joe didn't seem too chatty, she could catch a cat nap. Lately, sleep had come in precious short supply. But after several minutes, the silence in the truck rattled her. It wasn't like Joe to be so quiet. She peeked at his profile.

Wearing a grim look, he breathed deeply of the air rushing in his window.

"What's wrong?"

His hand jerked on the wheel.

"Sorry—I didn't mean to startle you. Guess you were kinda lost in thought there." *And maybe it's none of my business.*

But Joe didn't seem to hear her.

Sue fished a water bottle from her tote bag and took a long drink. Something had upset him; she could feel it. Did he resent spending the day bringing her to town?

No, not likely.

She took another sip and gave in to the nudging in her gut. "Joe, are you okay?"

He checked the rear-view mirror as they neared a passing lane, veered to the right, and let a four-by-four pass them like they weren't moving. "I'm good."

Sue studied the unusually stony look of his jaw and chuckled lightly. "Sorry to break it to you, but you're a terrible liar."

"I know."

A few more miles of silence made it clear he didn't want to talk. And why should he? The man had a right to his privacy.

She leaned back and closed her eyes, but her leg throbbed too much to let her sleep, and Joe's dark mood filled the cab like a coastal fog. The urge to ask tugged at her again, but before she could speak, Joe cleared his throat.

"Remember me telling you about the family who adopted me?"

"Yes. Jacobs, wasn't it?"

Nodding, he checked the mirror again. "I've been looking for them for a long time. Turns out they live in Bend. While you were at therapy, I went to see them."

What would have possessed him to do that? The ache she'd felt when he'd told her about being separated from his brother burned through her again.

Clearly, his visit with them hadn't been a jolly reunion.

"So how did it go?" she asked.

"It didn't. I mean, when I saw where they live . . ." His hands strangled the wheel. "I couldn't do it." A silent struggle played out on his face.

She could only guess what demons had driven him to find them in the first place. "What couldn't you do?"

Eyes fixed on the road, he said, "I thought they needed to hear the truth. I've been planning this for a long time. But when I saw where they live, telling them off seemed . . . pointless."

Out of all the people she could see confronting someone in anger, Joe wasn't one of them. She had dreamed—fantasized, actually—about visiting one particular foster family from her past and unleashing a verbal hurricane on them. And bulldozing their house to dust while she was at it. But there was no point, nothing to be gained by it. She'd survived. She had no need for revenge or retaliation. She'd moved on. "So you went to confront them but then changed your mind?"

He nodded.

"Why?"

Slowly, he shook his head. "Not a clue."

"Maybe you felt sorry for them?"

His lips formed a line. He nodded.

If sympathy had rendered Joe unable to follow through with a confrontation, then he had more compassion than anyone she knew, including herself. How ironic, and how unfair. It proved to Sue, once again, that so-called family had more power to inflict damage than anyone else.

Her mom's voice broke through her thoughts. *You're coming home with me, Suzy—isn't that cool? We'll be together again! We'll have a blast, sweetie. I promise. Hey, let's go to the beach and have a party! Just you and me. We'll stuff ourselves with shrimp cocktails and chocolate and build sandcastles—*

Sue shifted in her seat and focused on the dusty, dry desert outside her window, but memories of that cold, gritty weekend at the beach swept across her thoughts like frigid sea foam. The chocolate and castle-making and silly laughter as she and her mom chased each other in the waves was short lived, coming to a silent halt by her mother's sudden absence. But by age twelve, Sue knew her mom well enough not to be surprised. To Mom's credit, she'd hung around longer than usual before sneaking off to the nearest bar.

It wasn't until Mom returned after midnight with some guy and "accidentally" locked Sue out of the musty cabin, leaving her to spend a wet night alone on a dark beach, frozen by the wind and pelted by gritty sand, that Sue had finally faced the truth. Love was a joke, a fantasy, nothing more than a castle of sand dissolved by the incoming tide.

The memory of her mom's betrayal had also dissolved over time, but the scar had not. It served as a practical reminder that longing for love was too painful. It left her feeling even emptier than if she'd never known it.

When you don't need love, no one can hurt you.

Joe, still focused on the highway, seemed lost in memories of his own.

Hearing about his struggles with his adoptive family made Sue even more convinced that the best kind of family was the kind she now had. The Juniper Ranch kids didn't let her down, because she expected nothing from them; they had enough struggles of their own. She could provide shelter, encourage and equip them, and give them what they needed without needing anything in return. She could handle a family like that.

Sue looked out her window at the white-capped peaks of the Three Sisters. Faith, Hope, and Love. Too bad those qualities weren't as solid as the mountains bearing those names.

Joe slowed for the junction and downshifted, then headed east.

"Joe, are you having second thoughts about leaving without talking to that family?"

"No," he said, his voice oddly quiet. "It was the right thing to do."

Her pulse quickened at his solemn tone. What was it about him that continually threw her off?

"You're a good man, Joe." *Where did* that *come from?* "I mean, for a roughneck."

With a weak laugh, he met her gaze for a moment before turning back to watch the road. "Not that good. I get a lot of help from God. But even with His help, it's taken me a long time to forgive them."

Forgive? No. She couldn't have heard that right. Forget—maybe. Dig a mental hole, toss them in, and bury them until their faces eventually faded from her mind, sure. But forgive? Sue massaged her aching knee. "Have they even bothered to apologize?"

"Not that I've heard."

"Then why waste energy on them? You're a hardworking, responsible man. You came out on top with no help from them. You don't owe them anything."

He uncapped the water in his cup holder and took a drink, then wiped his lips with a sleeve. "Forgiveness is rarely deserved. It's more like a gift. And you're right—I don't owe them. But I do owe my Heavenly Father."

With a snort, Sue turned to watch the blur of slender pines along the roadside. "Every father I've ever known either bailed or wielded the title like a club." She swallowed her rising bitterness. "The idea of being beholden to a father of any kind makes me want to vomit."

Joe kept his eyes on the road, but his grim look melted into something she couldn't stand.

Pity.

His hands loosened their stranglehold on the wheel. "Want to talk about it?"

"Nope. Nothing to talk about."

Fascinating topic, Sooz. Next time, just go with the nap.

CHAPTER TWELVE

After a second round with the *Psychotic Torturist* on Monday, Sue had a little better handle on the pain and was ready to do some therapy at home. And her reward—she could lose the crutches. Sue's neighbor, Mrs. Stewart, had driven her this time, which must have come as a relief to poor Joe after the last trip to town. One minute she was marveling at the man's scruples, and the next she was spewing long-forgotten stuff he didn't need to hear. Maybe the less said about fathers, the better.

Getting back into routine on Tuesday felt good. As she sorted through junk mail and some envelopes addressed to Joe, everything came to a halt.

Letters from both the tax assessor and the bank.

Sue rested on the edge of her desk and read the bank letter again and again, the pounding in her temples increasing each time. She'd gotten late notices before, but nothing that threatened the loss of her ranch with this kind of in-your-face finality. Combined with the tax bill, the amount due was staggering. Even if she solved her monthly income problem, the fundraiser needed to do insanely well, or the property would go to auction and she would lose her home.

Jasmine and Haley passed by outside the office window, engrossed in lively conversation.

No. She wasn't just losing her home—she was losing *their* home.

"Sue?"

She spun around.

Joe's broad shoulders nearly filled the doorway. His hair had filled in, dark, like his eyebrows, and was gelled into a nice-looking style. He smelled really good—warm and woodsy. Must have gotten cleaned up for his errands in town. "Your Suburban is running. I took it for a test drive. Should run fine for you now."

Her jaw dropped. "You fixed it?"

"Just needed the fuel injectors cleaned, lines flushed. A quick tune up, that's about it."

Her mouth gaped. "The guy who worked on it before said it needed about nineteen-hundred dollars' worth of repairs."

Joe shrugged.

"Are you kidding? That's amazing, Joe. Thank you. How much do I owe you?"

Joe chuckled. "Nothing. You pay me to do maintenance, remember? Chaz helped too." His smile fading, he spoke quietly. "Listen, I want to help with the fundraiser."

The way he said it sent a little thrill through

her. "Thank you. We can use all the help we can get."

"No. I mean with money. I have some saved, and I'd like to help."

Stunned, all Sue could do was stare. He seemed genuine, which was no surprise. What rankled was the idea of Joe offering his personal funds to help the ranch. *She* was the one who had lost income, the one who had foolishly depended on others. She could never let him part with his personal savings. "That's very generous, but I can't take your money, Joe."

He frowned. "You take donations, right?"

From strangers, when I have to. But not from a man who I—Panic fluttered in her chest. "I really appreciate the offer, but to do any good at all, it would take far more than you can spare. Unless they get the full amount due, the property goes to auction, and everything you gave would be wasted. All down the drain."

Joe stepped closer, the look in his eyes unyielding.

His nearness made her heart skitter, which he could probably hear.

"What if I could get you the whole amount you need?"

She had to replay his words to make sure she'd heard right. "I could never pay that back."

"It's not a loan."

On impulse, she sniffed him. Maybe what she'd

smelled when he came in wasn't aftershave. Because, for a sober guy, he wasn't making any sense. "That's very generous, but—"

"But what?"

"But it's ludicrous. Because no matter what happens to the ranch, you would never see that money again. I can't take your savings knowing that." *And I can't believe we're having this conversation.*

Joe folded his massive arms and studied her.

A girl could just about drown in those eyes.

"Do you always have this much trouble with gifts, Sue? Or just the ones from me?"

Her mouth opened, but she had no answer. The way his eyes fell to her mouth and lingered there sent a tingle across the surface of her lips.

"The offer stands if you change your mind."

She still couldn't speak.

Joe turned and left.

CHAPTER THIRTEEN

From the driver's seat, Joe peered at the front doors of the clinic. Why did Sue's Friday therapy sessions take so long? What were they doing to her? He'd considered waiting in the lobby, but being in town weighed on him like a half-ton drill pipe, so he hung out in the vehicle instead, reading a Louis L'Amour paperback, waiting for the steely heaviness to lift.

It didn't.

He closed his eyes. The Jacobs family had hurt him, but that didn't matter anymore. The fact that they had apparently fallen on such hard times had been gnawing at him since the day he had seen their place.

He needed to go back.

Joe checked his cell. He probably had enough time. He started the Suburban and drove to the apartments on Goshen Road. As he pulled to a stop across the street, he checked out the building, then watched number seventeen.

No movement.

He went up to the apartment, stepping around

the broken wheelchair ramp to get to the front door.

What am I doing, Father? I sure hope You know, because I have no idea.

He knocked.

After some bumping and shuffling sounds inside, the door opened and a thin, whiskered man in a wheelchair glared up at him. "What do you want?"

"John Jacobs?"

"Yeah?"

Joe didn't answer. The voice was similar to John's, but this was definitely not the tall, slump-shouldered man Joe remembered. "I'm Joe Paterson. But you used to know me as Joey Jacobs. A long time ago."

This guy couldn't be his former dad.

This guy was a pasty, withered scarecrow.

The old man took in Joe's height and breadth, his brow creasing in a deep furrow, eyes narrowed.

From somewhere inside, a woman's voice whined, "Close the door."

John coughed twice, then suddenly lapsed into a deep coughing fit, doubling over in his chair. It sounded like he was ripping out a lung. Beads of sweat popped out on his balding head.

When the fit subsided, Joe said, "Are you okay?"

John wheezed several times, then tipped his

ashen face skyward. "Does it look like I'm okay?"

Joe peered beyond him into the apartment. From what he could see, nearly every inch was buried in clutter. "Can I come in? I won't stay long. I just wanted to visit with you a minute."

John muttered something about what everybody wanted, then pivoted his chair and wheeled inside.

Joe followed.

The combined living room/dining room was heaped with boxes, newspapers, and all kinds of junk. A thick, foul stink filled the air. To his left, a half wall separated the tiny kitchen. A mountain of crusted dishes filled the sink and counter, spilling over to the floor. In the living room, one torn upholstered chair sat in the shadowy corner, piled with rumpled bedding and stuff Joe couldn't distinguish. A wooden chair in the other corner held a small portable TV topped with teetering stacks of cartoon videos. A small table in the dining area was heaped with papers, pots, pans, and a carton of generic canned beans. With all the clutter in the room, there was a path just wide enough for a wheelchair to pass from the door to the table to the kitchen and down a hall where he guessed the bedrooms were.

A frail woman in a wheelchair emerged from the hall. "Who's that, Dad? Who's here?"

Though Joe's former sister hadn't changed

as much as John had, something had aged her, altered her features. "Fiona?"

"*I'm* Fiona," she said, frowning. "Who are you?"

More foul smells he didn't want to identify assailed him, smells he suspected came from one or both of them. Joe fought off a shudder. "I'm Joe. Remember me? Ben and I used to play soldiers with you when we were boys."

"No," Fiona said in her sing-song voice, shaking her lolling head. "That was Joey. My little brother. No, he—he wasn't a big man. He was just a little boy. Joey went away. Mama went away too."

Joe nodded, but the movement left him feeling dazed. He turned to John. "How long have you lived here?"

The old man eyed Joe before he answered. "Too long." Turning away, he waved toward the buried chair. "Have a seat—if you can find it."

Joe looked around and decided against it. "Why the wheelchair, John? What happened?"

"Car wreck. Busted my back. Can't walk. Can't work, can't do nothing but rot in this hole, getting sicker every day." John rattled out another cough. "Yeah, I remember you. Scrawny kid. You sure packed it on, didn't ya?" He hacked out another coughing fit that lasted nearly as long as the first one. He spat and swore.

"Here, Dad, drink your water." Fiona wheeled to him and offered a grimy travel mug.

Joe winced. "Does anyone else live with you?"

John shook his head. "My wife ran off about ten years ago with some trucker. Rube's up at the state pen. Diana's gone to Texas. The others— they're gone too. All of 'em."

The walls and ceiling of the apartment sported overlapping water and mildew stains, dark and jagged from repeated moisture and leakage. No wonder the old man was sick. The place was probably crawling with every kind of mold there was.

He could just about taste it in the air. He held his breath. *I don't want to breathe in this place, and yet they live here* . . . "So it's just you two taking care of each other?"

"Yeah." He sized Joe up and down. "What do you do?"

"I've been working on an oil rig in Alaska for the last fourteen years. I'm heading down to work in the Gulf of Mexico."

The old man nodded. "Hope you got good medical. You don't want to wind up like me. I didn't have insurance when it happened."

"What about auto insurance? That had to cover something."

John shook his head. "Didn't have any. I was laid up so long I lost my house."

"What are you living on?"

153

The old man nodded toward Fiona. "She gets SSI. I've been trying to get it but don't know if I ever will. We get a food card."

Joe studied Fiona again. Was her fragility from premature aging, or was she malnourished? How did people starve in a country where tons of food was thrown away every day?

Joe took another look around the place. Rodent droppings littered the kitchen. He could just walk back to the Suburban and drive away. Put this place out of mind, make his visit with them a quickly fading memory.

So long, Dad, nice visiting with you. Hope things turn around for you soon.

He didn't owe them anything. John and Leia Jacobs had turned their backs on him and abandoned him like trash.

"She'll go to a state place when I'm gone. You ever been to one of those?"

Joe shook his head. "What do you mean, gone?"

John turned a glassy stare at Joe. "I'm dying. It's my heart."

"Joey?" Fiona's cheeks were wet. "Is that you, Joey?"

Her tear-stained face launched a barrage of disturbing images through his mind like a too-graphic movie, bringing with them a rush of guilt and shame.

She don't care, Joey. Hit her. She can't feel nothin'...

Joe strode to the kitchen sink and stood amidst crusted plates and garbage, steeling himself against the memory. But he couldn't escape it. The tears streaming down Fiona's bewildered young face, his handprint on her cheek turning an angry red. Rube's cruel laugh. The sadistic teenager's threats to hurt Joe and Ben if he didn't do what he said. A sick, cold-blooded punk left in charge every day to terrorize the younger and weaker ones.

"Joey?" Fiona called out from the other room.

"Just . . . getting a drink," Joe answered, voice crackling.

"No," John said. "Don't drink the water. You better go. You shouldn't be here."

Joe turned at the sound of wheels in the kitchen.

John's glassy yellow eyes found his. His thin lips trembled. "I always thought you'd be better off someplace else, Joey." His eyes darted away. "I hoped, anyway."

Joe's heartbeat kicked up a gear. "So you knew your wife was lying? You knew I didn't do the things she accused me of?"

John didn't answer, but nodded toward Fiona. "Look at her. She tries to take care of me now, but she's the one who needs care. Got the mind of a little kid. She don't understand why everyone's gone. Why we can't drive to the store for corn flakes and milk. She don't know I'm dying. But she remembers happy times." John looked up at Joe. "And she still asks for you."

Me? After what I did?

Fiona bumped into her father's chair. Her head drooped to one side. "I miss Joey. Where'd he go, Dad? Is he okay?"

"He grew up, Fee. Joey's a man now."

"He's a man now?"

"Yeah." John glanced at Joe and nodded. "He turned out a real fine man."

Joe mumbled something about coming back to visit soon and let himself out.

And all but ran to the Suburban.

Sue chuckled at the sight of Joe asleep at the wheel and tapped on the passenger window.

He jerked, then fumbled with the lock button.

Before he could get out, she opened her door and hoisted herself up. Good thing she'd taken pain meds before therapy this time. "Sorry it took so long. At least you got a nap out of it." She grinned. "Good news—I can lose the brace."

He fired up the Suburban, but instead of driving, he just sat there staring at the instrument panel, white-knuckling the wheel.

"What's wrong?" *And what's that horrid smell?*

"Nothing." He put the gearshift in reverse.

She laid a hand on his arm. "Hold on."

Joe glanced at her hand, the muscles in his jaw rippling. "I saw them."

Realizing she was still touching him, Sue slid her hand away. "Want to talk about it?"

He met her gaze. "I couldn't wait to get away."

She nodded. Seeing people from the past had a way of slapping a person in the face with useless memories. She'd done all the therapy, read the books, and concluded it was simply best not to go there. No looking back, just living in the present. Where the ghosts can't hurt you.

"I told them I'd be back."

"What? Why?"

Joe's big hands kneaded the rubbery steering wheel. "He's dying. They're starving. They live in . . ." He tilted his head back and examined the roof of the cab.

"Bad?"

Joe nodded. "Worse than bad."

Whoa. Most people would cheer at seeing those who had hurt them finally get what they deserved. But apparently not Joe.

Without another word, he drove out of the lot and headed home.

Why did he care? After the way they treated him? "Sure you don't want to talk about it?"

Joe's eyes were black with emotion. Whatever was going through his mind was tearing him apart. He shook his head. "Talking won't do squat. I have to do something."

"Like what?"

He welded his eyes to the road. "I don't know.

All I know is I can't go off and live my life and just leave them like that."

He didn't owe them. And he couldn't buy their love or acceptance or whatever this was about. Yet as much as she wanted to voice her suspicions, she knew it wouldn't do any good.

"They need to move. Somewhere safer. Healthier. They need someone to help them bathe and cook and clean so they're not living like that."

"Like who? *You* can't do it."

"I know." He sighed. "I don't know what to do."

"I don't mean to be callous, but why you, Joe? Aren't there county or state agencies that can help?"

"He's been denied for SSI so many times he's given up. They get help with food, but it's not enough. They can't even take care of themselves, Sue. You should have seen—" He shook his head. "No. I wouldn't want you to see that."

An image of her mom came to mind. On-again-off-again Mom. Unpredictable, unreliable, either missing or holed up for weeks with the curtains drawn. Little Suzy hiding out alone and not bathing for weeks. With a shudder, she remembered the fear, the hunger, the waiting for someone to come take care of her. And the dull realization that no one would.

"Sorry, Sue. I didn't mean to drag you into this.

You have enough problems of your own. You don't need to hear this stuff."

"I lived like that," Sue said quietly. "We went for weeks without food and electricity. Sometimes my mom would leave me with people—usually strangers—when she was sober enough to realize I wasn't eating. Once, we lived with a halfway decent guy who tried to help by paying her bills and taking care of us, but she got some crazy idea he was stealing from her, so she yanked me out of bed in the middle of the night and we took off."

Why had she told Joe that?

Maybe to relieve him of any worry that he'd exposed her to things too horrible to imagine.

As if he could. That stuff was only the tip of the iceberg.

Joe nodded. "Yeah, that's it."

"What?"

"Something I can do." He turned to her. "Before I leave for the Gulf, I'll find them another place to live. I'll be making more than enough on the next job to cover their rent and utilities. I'll hire someone a couple days a week to help. Clean, cook, bring food, get medicine, take them to the doctor. That's what I'll do."

Sue's mouth fell open.

"You probably think I'm crazy." His voice was barely audible. "Maybe I am. All I know is I'll go crazy if I *don't* do something."

She couldn't tear her gaze from the man beside her. *You confuse the daylights out of me. Who are you?*

Joe turned to her. "What? Spill it. What are you thinking?"

She scanned the barren terrain beyond him. "I'm thinking . . . I wish we'd known someone like you when my mom and I were struggling to make it."

He focused on the long, empty highway ahead, his profile impossible to read. "So do I, Sue. So do I."

CHAPTER FOURTEEN

"We got a problem, boss."

Sue's eyes burned from number-crunching and the headache that threatened to turn into a migraine. "What is it?"

"Come see for yourself."

Sue followed Bertie outside to the barn and past the goats to the long stalls in the back where the fundraiser items were being stored.

Bertie swung one gate wide and motioned Sue inside.

Stereo equipment, computer towers, bicycles, and other unidentifiable things had been disassembled and heaped into a jumbled pile.

"Chaz . . ." Sue spun and limped toward the house, Bertie trailing. But on the way, her steps slowed. It wouldn't do any good to talk to the boy now. Even if he *could* put the stuff back together, he couldn't possibly do it in time for the sale. She stopped and turned to Bertie. "Do you know where Joe is?"

"It's Sunday." Bertie tossed a nod in the direction of the chapel on the hill. "I'm decades older than you, so don't tell me you can't hear that."

Faint strains of baritone drifted across the compound.

She headed up to the chapel. With any luck, Joe could put the jumbled things back together. And maybe while he was at it, he could keep Chaz too busy to take anything else apart.

As she reached for the door handle, a rustling came from the sagebrush and she stiffened. What could that be?

Ringo bounded out of the brush, his whole body wagging, coat matted with crinkly sage and cheatgrass husks.

Goofball. Sue chuckled and rubbed his ears. More movement in the brush stilled her hand on the dog's head. "Who's there?"

Jasmine poked out from behind the small building, also speckled with twigs and bits of sagebrush.

"Jas? What are you doing?" *And with the dog that sent you into a panic fit?* "Are you okay?"

She nodded. "Me and Ringo listen to J-man sing." Jasmine tilted her head and watched the dog, who now appeared to be sniffing out the trail of a critter.

Sue was at a loss as to which bit of information to process first. "So . . . you and Ringo are tight now, huh?"

Jasmine nodded. "He like music too."

"Music?" Sue's brows rose. "Really. I did not know that." She smiled. "I need to talk to J—

162

I mean, Mister Joe. Maybe you and Ringo could go see if Miss Roberta needs help?"

As the sound of singing drifted from the chapel, Jasmine smiled the broadest smile Sue had ever seen on the girl.

The sound of Joe's rich voice grew in a steadily rising melody.

Instead of going back to the house, Jasmine took Sue's hand and towed her to the chapel door. They tiptoed inside.

The building had been transformed. Where heaps of furniture once filled the small room, six short wooden benches, cleaned and polished, sat in three rows with a center aisle between them. A cross hung in the middle of the far wall, with two tall, narrow windows on either side letting in warm rays of midday sun.

And there was Joe, his back to them, kneeling at the foot of the cross.

Sue stilled.

Jasmine held a finger to her lips and eased herself onto a bench.

Sue had little choice but to join her.

Joe lifted wide, outstretched arms as if he was getting ready to give someone a big hug. His mellow voice filled the room in a deep, solemn refrain. "Nothing compares to You . . . to Your unfailing love."

Oh. Private moment. Awkward.

"My heart cries out . . . All I need is You."

She held her breath, though she had no idea why.

Jasmine closed her eyes.

"My life belongs to You . . . I give You everything."

The depth of emotion in his voice gathered in her center like a sucker punch, set her heart pounding. She had never heard anyone sing like that. Ever.

How could anyone—especially a big, strong guy like Joe—sing of his need for God with such abandon, such passion?

In two swift moves, she slipped past Jasmine and hurried out. When she was a couple yards down the path, the chapel door banged against the outer wall, startling her.

"Miss Susan!" Jasmine hollered. "You want to talk to J-man?"

Sue winced and turned. Joe had to have heard that. "No, it's okay, he's busy. I can talk to him later—"

Joe appeared behind Jasmine and stepped out. "Hey. I was just, uh—want to come in?"

Sue couldn't find her voice. Or remember why she'd come. All she knew was that she needed to get some distance from . . . whatever that was.

Jasmine spied Ringo and took off after him, calling his name.

"I'm glad you're here, Sue," Joe said. "I want to show you something."

"You know, it's your day off, I shouldn't be bothering you. I'll just catch you later."

Joe rubbed his clean-shaven jaw. Along with new jeans and boots, he was wearing a pale blue button-down shirt that contrasted very nicely with his dark eyes and hair.

Joe Paterson cleaned up nice. Real nice.

"Unless you're in a hurry, I'd really like you to see this. It'll just take a sec. Wait here." Joe went inside the chapel and returned a minute later carrying a large, flat board about three feet high by eight feet long in the shape of an arch. He turned it around and held it up in front of him.

My Father's House was written in wide, white lettering on a dark green background.

"Cool, huh? It's still here." Joe lowered the sign and flashed a dimpled grin.

"Yeah. The old owners left a few things behind. They keep turning up."

Joe rested the sign at his feet. "It was in the attic above the chapel. I know it's just plywood, but I got a little choked up when I saw it. Brings back good memories."

Sue smiled. "I'm glad your memories here were good, Joe."

"They were. I was wondering . . ." Joe rubbed his jaw again. "If you're not using the chapel, I'd like to use it on Sundays. Do a service each week. Would that be all right?"

Her mind raced to recall what she knew about

church services, which wasn't much. She'd visited a church with a friend once, but the idea of God hovering nearby when people prayed, eavesdropping on their thoughts, had creeped her out, and she never went back. "Depends. What do you mean by 'service'?"

His eyes lit. "For the kids and staff. And you, if you'll come." He bent and wiped dust from the sign.

"Kids?" Sue pictured her dysfunctional, vulnerable teens in here singing his songs with the same abandon, telling God they needed Him.

No. What they *needed* was to learn how to survive on their own in a cruel, complicated world. Same way she had.

"I don't think that's a good idea."

"Yeah, maybe you're right." He straightened, brushed dust from his hands, and looked her in the eye. "Going to church might teach them some bad habits."

The man really enjoyed mocking her. "All right. What do you do in there, anyway?"

Joe shrugged. "Sing, pray, read the Bible. Spend time listening to God. That's about it."

She eyed him. How did he know it was really God he was hearing? And more importantly, what kinds of things did God *say?*

Joe's face stayed relaxed, calm. Yet eager.

Why was *she* always the one playing the party pooper? "Let me think about it, okay? I mean, you're welcome to use the chapel, but the kids . . ." How should she phrase her fears to Joe? "I don't want them getting confused." She checked to see if Jasmine was out of earshot and lowered her voice. "I don't want to get their hopes up in one more person who won't be there for them."

Like the time I was locked in my room for days with half a box of corn flakes and a coffee can for a toilet and I'd heard on TV that Jesus saves so I wrote a note and slipped it under the door asking Jesus to save me, but He didn't come.

No one came. It wasn't until a bus driver saw the bruises a week later that two ladies from social services came and took me away.

The memory hit her like a cannonball.

Joe was watching her intently, the My Father's House sign propped against his legs.

No thanks. Lifting her chin, she said, "Use the chapel if you want. But you can scrap that sign. Use it to start a bonfire or something. I have no use for it." She spun and headed for the house.

"Sue?"

She stopped.

Joe was already at her side. "You okay?"

Far too aware of his nearness, she forced her voice steady. "I'm fine."

"Did you want me?"

Those words in that deep tone set off a weird flutter in her chest. *Want you? What have you*

167

been smokin'? Where'd you get an idea like that?

Oh yeah, Chaz. Fundraiser.

"Yes, I almost forgot." She explained the problem with Chaz and the dismantled sale items and her need for things to be in working order as soon as possible.

He wore a pained look. "Wow. I'm really sorry for not paying closer attention to the boy. Yeah, I'll fix it right away."

"And I don't know how, but could you keep him busy? So he doesn't find anything else to take apart? At least until we get through the fundraiser."

Joe didn't answer. Instead, the crease in his brow softened, and his eyes wore a strange expression. Like his wheels were turning. "Sure," he said slowly. "There's just one thing." His eyes locked with hers. "A condition."

That did not sound good. "Which is?"

Joe rubbed his chin. "I'll keep Chaz busy if you agree to take a day off. Away from the ranch. You don't have to plan anything. I'll take care of it."

"*You'll* take care of it? What is that supposed to mean?"

He didn't answer.

Her voice rose. "You want me to do something with *you?*"

Joe nodded.

"Like a *date?*"

"No, no. Just . . . an outing. Just for fun. When was the last time you took a day off?"

"Last week. Three times. You were there for two of them, remember? I've left the ranch more times in the last two weeks than I have in the last two years."

He shook his head. "Physical therapy doesn't count. It has to be *fun*."

"Hey, I have fun."

"You?" Joe belted out a laugh. "Name the last fun thing you did."

Her headache spiked. "Well, it's not like I can just—"

"I know, when you're not running yourself into the ground, you're all fun, all the time." His eyes narrowed. "Name one fun thing you've done in the last year."

Sue snorted. "This is lame."

"A one-day outing, with me along to make sure you have fun, or no deal."

She let out a huff that could probably be heard all over the compound. "You'd hold a poor, compulsive kid over my head for a *date?*"

"It's not a date. Just . . . a friendly little outing. And like I said, I'll plan it. All you have to do is go along for the ride and relax."

Relax? "This is not exactly the best time for me to be taking a day away. I've got the fundraiser to pull off, the kids, the temps . . ." *Not to mention hanging on to my sanity, keeping every-*

169

thing together, trying to figure out your twisted game . . .

"After the fundraiser, then." Joe crossed his python arms and waited.

There had to be a whole warehouse of laws somewhere against being forced into spending time with a guy who looked like he could shred a semi with his bare hands. Hands she needed now or there wouldn't be much of a fundraiser. "Two hours, tops. *After* the fundraiser. And Chaz is your shadow from now on."

He crammed his hands in his pockets. "Half a day."

A growl escaped her clenched teeth. "Fine."

Joe smiled. "Deal."

Sue headed for the main house. What in the world had she just agreed to?

After breakfast Monday morning, Joe went to the study to use the Internet, but some kids were doing schoolwork there. Instead, he hung out in the dining hall and called the deputy who was working on recovering Joe's stolen stuff.

Same news as always—no word. And this time, the deputy added he didn't expect to see any of Joe's stuff recovered at this point.

As soon as the room cleared of kids, Joe pulled up a chair to the computer and searched for an apartment in a good neighborhood for John and Fiona. One that was clean and wheelchair accessible and not too expensive. The sooner he got them moved, the better he'd feel. Unfortunately, it would be a while before he started pulling in oil rig pay. An apartment, utilities, and a housekeeper-caregiver was going to eat through his savings pretty quick.

He spent an hour searching through every rental in Bend until he found a ground-level, handicap-accessible apartment near the bus line and markets. The rent was steeper than he'd budgeted for, but it would have to do. He also got a lead on a woman who could come twice a week to cook and clean, but he didn't want to send her until he got John and Fiona out of that toxic dump they were in. He would see John after work and make sure the old man knew he wasn't taking no for an answer. Joe could get them moved within a couple of weeks.

With the fundraiser coming up on Saturday, Joe's next order of business was getting Chaz's handiwork put back together, with the kid's help. Joe's end of the bargain with Sue.

His "just for fun" bargain.

What on earth had he been thinking?

Show her My love.

Yeah, that had to be it, because there was nothing earthly about the scheme. It had been one of those impulses that came on the breath of divine inspiration. It *wasn't* a date. He had enough sense to know that it was a God thing—

171

it had nothing to do with himself. Surely God wanted to pursue Susan Quinn, draw her close, and shower her with His amazing love and faithfulness. Joe was just . . . helping.

Right. Like God needed Joe Paterson's help wooing a woman.

CHAPTER FIFTEEN

Monday evening, Sue spent hours on the phone drumming up more donations for the sale. On Tuesday, a windfall landed in the form of an old four-wheeler and other items from a local estate sale. Sue caught herself smiling. A seed of hope had settled in her heart and put down tiny roots.

Wednesday, Joe went to see one of the farmers in Juniper Valley. When he came back, the sound of kids whooping pulled Sue out of the barn where she was stripping paint from an antique dresser. Joe's pickup had a long flatbed trailer attached, a stack of lumber piled on it.

Kids climbed into the truck bed and trailer and bounced until the whole truck-trailer combo rocked like a carnival fun house.

Joe laughed. "Whoa, guys, easy. The trailer's on loan." He gave Jasmine a piggyback ride down from the flatbed.

Sue made a mental note to remind Joe about not interacting physically with the kids, especially the girls. She took a closer look at the trailer. "Where'd you get it?"

"Borrowed it from the alfalfa farmer next to us.

Max Stewart. Great guy. He said to keep it till we're done with the fundraiser. Said we could use it to deliver stuff from the sale too, to help get people buying the big items. And he donated this lumber for the sale."

Stunned, Sue looked at the lumber, then back at Joe. "Wow, that was really nice of him. And you." Gratitude swelled in a confusing rush. She couldn't contain her smile. "Thanks."

He stared at her for several seconds, then looked away. "No problem. So I guess we can start hauling stuff down to the grange whenever you're ready."

"Great. And I got some more stuff pledged. If you and some of the guys could pick it up and take it to the grange, that would be a huge help."

Chaz hopped down from the flatbed. "Yeah, us men are all over that. You girls can go back in there and keep making cookies. Me and J-man got the heavy stuff." He gave Joe a complicated series of handshakes and fist bumps.

J-man. A mysterious twinge skittered across Sue's chest.

Thursday, Joe and four of the boys spent a full day picking up and dropping off more pledged items. While they were gone, Linda had Cori and Tatiana pricing clothing and cleaning up smaller appliances and household goods. Elena spent the day with Sonja, Haley, Donovan, and Daisy, baking mountains of cookies and packaging them in dozens. Sue, Jasmine, and Brandi worked on refinishing the antique chest of drawers.

During the work, Jasmine talked nonstop about Cambodia and the day the police took her to the orphanage.

Sue just listened, enjoying the sound of the girl's sweetly lilting, broken English.

"*You* got busted?" Brandi snickered. "Wait, don't tell me. You stole a car."

Jasmine wiped her glistening forehead with a wrist. "Not car. Motorbike."

Brandi's mouth flopped open. "Dude, I was totally joking. You stole a motorcycle? What are you—like ten? How'd you even ride it?"

That earned Brandi a glare. "I nine then. Almost fourteen now."

Sue's hand paused. "You're fourteen?"

Jasmine nodded and kept sanding.

Guess I could've just asked her.

The girl's tiny frame, her slight bone structure . . . starvation had a way of stunting growth. How long had she lived on the streets?

Jasmine had acquired survival instincts entirely on her own. And in so few years. Years that should have been spent being a kid.

Sue resisted a sudden urge to hug the girl. There was nothing to be done about her lost childhood now.

"So how'd you steal it?" Brandi asked.

Sue threw Brandi a warning look. "I think it's time we talk about something else."

With a shrug, Jasmine focused on her drawer. "Motorbikes everywhere in Cambodia. I only borrow for little while. To look for my—" Frowning, she bent closer and scrubbed furiously at a dark spot on the wood.

Wiping dust from the thick, oak dresser top, Sue eyed Jasmine. Would she volunteer the rest?

Brandi stood and brushed off her knees. "Look for your what?"

Jasmine blew the dust from the spot she was sanding. "Nobody." She took a quick peek at Sue. "I not need anyone."

A picture of Jasmine scraping by on the streets tugged at Sue again. "Sounds like you managed pretty well on your own."

Jasmine shrugged.

They worked in silence. But when Sue reached for the solvent, she caught a sparkle of tears in Jasmine's eyes. Sue shoved down a new wave of sorrow. She wouldn't wish Jasmine's life on anyone. But at least the girl had learned to survive, gained something useful from it.

Yeah. Just keep telling yourself that, Sooz.

By Friday, both the buzz of activity and the volume levels at the ranch had reached head-splitting heights. Joe and a few kids continued to haul goods to the grange. Everyone else finished pricing and boxing up the last of the items. Ringo sniffed and circled the boxes, as if giving his final approval.

Sue phoned a woman at the bank about the payment she planned to make the day after the sale.

The woman was about as understanding as a speed bump.

Didn't matter. Sue had never seen this many good items in any of the ranch's previous sales. With a decent turnout, they just might pull it off.

There was one item she'd avoided including in the sale. Her Harley. The thought of selling it had occurred to her more than once over the past several months, but a 1974 Sportster wasn't worth enough to make a difference in the month-to-month operation. What she needed was a large, dependable increase in monthly income. So she'd clung tightly to that one piece of herself, the only possession she'd ever really cared about. But now, avoiding foreclosure was the immediate issue, and thoughts of selling her bike nagged at her more and more as the sale approached. She tried not to think about it, but the choice between saving the ranch and riding was a no-brainer.

With any luck, maybe it wouldn't come to that.

Sue and her crew finished stacking the last items on the porch just after noon, about the time Bertie and her gang went inside to make lunch.

Joe and his trio returned from hauling stuff to the grange. "Is that the last of it?" Joe stood in the yard inspecting the neatly stacked boxes.

"Yeah." Sonja hopped off the porch. "We worked our tushies off!"

Edgar, Jasmine, and Cori climbed the lawn toward the house. "Check it out, we got some killer stuff," Edgar said. "We're going to be millionaires."

Sue hung a cleaning rag on the porch rail and chuckled. "I like how you think, Edgar."

"Hey." Joe nodded at Sue. "It's looking like a mini-mall down at the grange now. You should come see it."

The pleased way Joe said it sent a little thrill through her.

His humble pride, the joy of accomplishment . . . it almost seemed like he cared about this place. Like he wasn't just a temporary handyman, here for a short time before shoving off for bigger and better things.

Sue brushed the thrill aside. "I'll head over to the grange after lunch and start setting up tables and stuff."

"Nope, Miss Susan, it's all done." Cori jumped up and high-fived Joe, sending her black corkscrew curls dancing. "J-man ran us like dogs. We got it all set up."

"You did?" Sue's mouth gaped. How had he pulled that off? But then, she shouldn't be surprised. Joe was used to running a crew.

Jasmine took Joe's hand and towed him toward

178

the porch steps. "Papa Joe need food, Miss Susan. His belly angry." Jasmine growled with a ferocious face.

Joe burst out laughing.

"Papa Joe need food right now or he faint."

The others went inside, but Sue stood rooted to the porch, heat crawling up her neck.

Papa Joe?

Oh no. Absolutely not. These kids did *not* need to be reminded of their own absent dads, not when they were doing so well. And more importantly, they didn't need to go getting attached to a guy who was leaving in a month.

Still laughing, Joe caught Sue's eye. His smile faded, and his laughter fizzled out. He stopped at the top step, looking hesitant.

Jasmine tugged at him. "Come on, Papa Joe. You not hungry now?"

"Uh, yeah." His gaze never left Sue's. "Save me a spot, Jas. I'll be there in a sec."

Jasmine raced into the house, belting out a Beach Boys tune in her little sing-song voice.

"Something wrong?" Joe planted fists on his hips.

Sue drew a steady breath. "Did you tell her to call you that?"

Joe studied her for several seconds, then slowly shook his head. "No, Sue, of course not. She must have overheard me and Edgar talking about nicknames."

Cheeks cooking, Sue nodded. "Okay. So I can count on you to discourage that if you ever hear it again?"

Joe just stood there, searching her in a way that rattled her. "Yeah." His palms went up in surrender. "Whatever you say."

She went inside, awash with jumbled emotions. In the dining hall, she found Jasmine at the end of the line and asked her to come to the office.

Jasmine hollered at the kids to save a spot in line for Papa Joe and then joined her.

Sue closed the door and turned to the girl.

Jasmine's brow cinched with worry. "You mad, Miss Susan?"

Shaking her head, Sue searched for the right words. "No. It's . . . there's something you need to know about Mister Joe. He came here to help us, but only for a little while." She watched for a reaction.

Nothing.

"He has another job. He's going to work somewhere else." Not sure if Jasmine understood, Sue pressed on. "So he'll be leaving Juniper Ranch soon."

Jasmine's face sagged, taking the corners of her mouth down with it. "Leaving?" The worry deepened to a frown. "When?"

"Next month. Around Christmas, I think."

With a scowl, Jasmine folded her wiry arms. "Where he going?"

And then again, maybe she was making a huge mistake. "His new job is in Louisiana. Far away."

"But he have job here. He do good job."

"Yes, he does a very good job, but he has to go. It's a better job. More money."

Jasmine didn't move, only searched Sue's face, a wounded look on her own.

Sue reached for Jasmine's shoulder, but the girl jerked away.

"Everything about money here," Jasmine said. "When *you* go to new job?"

Sue shook her head. "I'm not going anywhere, Jas." *At least, I hope not.*

Jasmine's chin jutted up, bringing her dark gaze level with Sue's. "But parents lie. *You* tell me that."

Sue opened her mouth, but nothing came out.

"I missing lunch." Jasmine turned toward the door.

"Okay. I just wanted to make sure you—"

But the girl was already gone.

After lunch, everyone worked until the rest of the stacked goods were loaded and strapped onto the flatbed. Sue announced they would take this last load in the morning and thanked everyone for working so hard. As the kids went inside to get ready for dinner, Sue couldn't help but notice there was still a bit more room on the trailer. Just enough room for a custom-lowered, faithful, old cruiser.

Bertie secured a corner with a bungee cord and turned to Sue. "Well, boss. Looks like we might have this storm beat." She patted the trailer.

"I sure hope so." Sue turned toward the shop, prodded by a nagging urge to ride.

Why not? She didn't have to wear the knee brace anymore. It had been ages since she'd ridden.

She went into the shop and fired up the Harley, then sighed as she straddled the worn, familiar seat. She'd missed this.

As Sue strapped on her helmet, Bertie hurried past the shop, hollering and beckoning her to come outside. Leaving the bike idling, Sue took off her helmet and followed.

Squeals and barks echoed from the volleyball pit.

Sue hurried down the path behind Bertie.

Two girls were grappling near the net, arms tangled, hair whipping, scuffling feet kicking up clouds of dust.

Brandi and Jasmine.

"Hey! Stop that!" Bertie yelled and hurried toward them.

Ringo barked and lunged at the girls, dodging blows as Jasmine snarled and kicked. Brandi had a grip on the younger girl's biceps and was mostly trying to hold her off. Jasmine screeched and swung a foot, connecting with Brandi's knee.

"Ow! You little snot!" She swung a knee at Jasmine's belly. "I'll kick your teeth in!"

"Jasmine! Brandi!" Sue yelled.

Bertie grabbed Jasmine and pulled her off, locking her arms in a restraining hold.

The grunting girl kept kicking, her feet flailing in the air.

Brandi wiped a bloody scratch on her neck and swore. "What is wrong with her?"

Jasmine let out a string of ear-piercing screams and jerked her body and head side to side like a caged animal.

"See?" Brandi held up her bloodied hand. "I told you she's a freak!"

"What happened?" Sue asked.

Bertie kept a tight hold on the thrashing girl.

"How should I know?" Brandi threw up both hands. "One minute we're talking about the big sale tomorrow, and the next thing I know, she's scratching me and screaming like a freakin' tiger. I didn't even touch her."

"All right, that's enough. You shouldn't be down here anyway. Go inside now, Brandi. We'll take care of it."

Brandi marched off in a huff.

Jasmine's feet stopped and her body sagged.

Bertie tried to keep her on her feet.

Sue shook her head. "It's okay, let her down, Bert."

With a hesitant look, Bertie relinquished her hold on the girl.

Jasmine crumpled to the ground and hugged herself into a tight ball, rocking in rapid rhythm.

Sue crouched near the girl, ignoring the burn it caused in her knee. She stroked Jasmine's ponytailed hair.

The girl didn't flinch, didn't acknowledge the touch.

"What am I going to do with you, huh?"

No response.

Sue had no idea how long the self-calming process would take, so she sent Bertie back to the house and waited, murmuring soothing words. "What's up, Jas? What got you so upset?"

Jasmine didn't answer.

Patience, Sooz. Jasmine's adoptive parents probably didn't have the patience or preparation for this kind of stuff. Too bad. When she wasn't kicking and clawing and retreating into her safe little ball, Jasmine was an intelligent, engaging girl.

The rocking continued, followed by a low humming sound. A sound like—

Her motorcycle.

An idea struck.

"Hey, Jasmine, want to go for a ride?"

The rocking slowed. With her face still planted between her knees, Jasmine's voice was muffled. "Ride?"

Sue hauled herself up to standing. "Yeah, on my motorcycle. With me. Want to go?"

Jasmine lifted her head, but her hands covered her face. She took a couple deep breaths, then nodded.

Inside the shop, Sue made Jasmine put on a spare riding jacket and helmet and then mounted the bike. Jasmine settled behind Sue, arms around her middle, and they slowly took off down the dirt drive.

At the end of the road, Sue turned south and gradually brought the bike up to speed. "You doing okay, Jasmine?"

"Super fast!" Jasmine hollered.

That was all Sue needed to hear. Grinning, she hit the last gear, rolled the throttle back, and let her faithful, old buddy fly.

Jasmine gripped Sue's waist as they headed south toward the dry expanse of Summer Lake. The setting sun cast a warm, dancing glow atop the range of hills to the west.

The force and chill of the November wind struck Sue hard, numbing and invigorating her at the same time. She hadn't felt this kind of freedom in far too long.

As they made the long loop around the dry, grass-filled lakebed, Sue kept an eye out for darting rabbits and sage rats.

Jasmine's arms tightened around Sue.

As they rounded a curve, a pair of pronghorn

185

antelope raised their heads from across the grassy lakebed. Sue pointed them out to Jasmine.

A minute later, the girl tapped Sue and pointed east to a large eagle rising from the trees in the distance, its broad wingspan magnificent against the deep, multihued sky. Bald eagle migration had begun.

Just before they finished circling the dry lake, the phone in Sue's pocket vibrated. She circled the lake and headed for the junction back to the ranch.

The phone buzzed again.

She pulled over and checked her phone. Three missed calls from Bertie.

Wincing, Sue put the kick stand down and killed the bike. She let Jasmine off to stretch while she returned the call.

"Hate to have to ask you this," Bertie said slowly, "but do you know where Jasmine is?"

Sue winced. "She's with me."

Silence. "You didn't tell anyone."

"You're right, Bert, I'm sorry." She drew in a lungful of ponderosa pine-scented air. "Blonde moment. Won't happen again."

"Blonde?" Bertie snorted. "That's a new one. So did it work? Taking her for a ride?"

A few feet away, Jasmine fingered a leathery-green bush beside the road.

"I think so."

Bertie muttered something about rethinking her

methods for stress management and ended the call.

Sue dismounted and joined Jasmine. Helmet in hand, she stood beside the girl, who was watching a beetle. "You okay, Jas?"

She nodded, gaze following the insect's path.

"Want to talk about what happened with you and Brandi?"

Jasmine shrugged. "Brandi say kids have to leave ranch if we not get enough money. I tell her shut up. She laugh. Say I stupid." Jasmine tilted her head, still watching the insect. "My English stink, but I not stupid."

"No, you're not stupid. But you did attack a girl twice your size, Jas. Not the smartest move. She could've really hurt you. And it's not a healthy way to deal with anger."

The girl shrugged again. "What then—tell Miss Roberta? You say be strong girl and take care myself." She tilted her head, watching the beetle. "That what you do?"

"It's great to have friends and people in your life, but I've learned . . ." *Needing people only leads to hurt.* "The sooner you can take care of yourself without depending on anyone, the happier you'll be."

Jasmine bent closer to inspect the bug. "Happy like you."

Could there possibly be a more complicated topic to discuss with a fourteen-year-old kid who had hang-ups no one really understood?

Carefully, Jasmine coaxed the beetle onto her finger. "If bug has broken wing and can't fly, and I put in safe place away from mean birds, she okay because I help. Right?" She deposited the insect onto a lower branch.

The kid had a knack for logic. She'd make a great lawyer. "I'm not saying we don't need help sometimes. But we have to be strong on our own. If you protect that beetle all the time, she won't get strong enough to survive by herself. Then, the minute you leave, she's bird food. She's better off learning how to escape from predators now, without your help."

"Maybe I stay with bug and help, always watch. Keep mean birds away." Jasmine's eyes lit, guarded yet earnest. "Maybe someone always with me. Always help me."

At Jasmine's hesitant, hopeful look, a queasy feeling formed in Sue's gut. She'd probably regret this, but . . . "Like who?"

"Papa Joe say he has big Papa in heaven. God. He not see Him, but He always there. Always love and take care of him."

"He told you that, huh?" Her lips smashed together so hard they hurt.

"Yes. But why Papa Joe need help? He stronger than anyone." She hunted for the insect, then slipped carefully around the bush to follow its movements.

Sue couldn't explain Joe Paterson any more than she could sprout wings and fly to the top of Table Rock. "Mister Joe has his own ways. Whatever makes him happy, I guess."

Jasmine nodded. "He most happy when he sing to Papa God."

Sue wanted to scream. Because that was probably the only way she could shake the sensation making a knot of her insides. Instead, she stood and brushed off her jeans. "Well, since Mister Joe is leaving soon and taking his invisible 'Papa' with him, you and I will just have to keep watch for the mean birds ourselves, right, kiddo?" She climbed on the Harley and motioned for Jasmine.

Time to give *Papa Joe* a new rule about filling the kids' heads with fairy tales and empty promises.

CHAPTER SIXTEEN

After the last delivery of sold goods, Joe returned the trailer to the Stewart farm and headed back. He rubbed the knots in his neck. The sun had finally set on what felt like the longest day since he'd arrived at Juniper Ranch.

Everyone had worked hard at the fundraiser sale. The kids had done an amazing job working the tables and dishing up food while Sue manned the silent auction and kept everything running. With the turnout of buyers and the amount of stuff flying out of that grange hall, maybe they'd brought in enough to make the payment on the property.

And maybe his prayers had been answered.

He parked in the staff lot and trudged up to the main house. As he crossed the porch, he saw lights on in the office. He went to the office door, knocked, and let himself in.

Bertie nodded at him from where she stood near Sue, who sat at her desk looking exhausted.

"Seems like it went well."

"Yeah, it went okay." Bertie shrugged.

Sue was bent forward, massaging her temples.

Her braid was coming loose. She kept trying to brush a lock out of her face. With an exasperated sigh, she tugged off the band and combed fingers through her hair. Her cheeks glowed with a rosy tint from a long day's work. She looked tired and dusty.

And beautiful.

Joe cleared his throat. "So, how'd we do?"

Sue leaned back in her chair. "The kids were amazing. I'm really proud of them. And all of you. I know how hard you've worked." She looked up at him. "Thank you for everything you've done, Joe."

His heart did a drum solo, right on cue.

Her voice waned. "But we didn't get enough." Sue fiddled with a pen on her desk, clicking it over and over.

Bertie excused herself and padded out of the room.

Sue met Joe's gaze, her brow etched with more than just fatigue. Worry had seeped in.

Do something, Paterson. Fix this. "What's next?"

Tucking the curtain of blonde behind one ear, Sue turned her attention to a page of figures on her desk. "When I go to town for therapy on Monday, I'll go to the bank and make what payment I can." She sighed. "And I'll ask again for an extension."

"Do you think they'll give it to you?"

"I don't know. The problem is we still have a huge shortfall in our monthly income. I've gotten too many default notices already. So even if I can somehow scrape up the full amount past due, I can't default again or the property automatically goes into foreclosure. I need more income. Like a donor who's willing to start major monthly support immediately." Sue closed her eyes and squeezed the back of her neck.

An overwhelming urge to rub her neck and shoulders tugged at him. He stuffed fists into his folded arms. "Are there any expenses you could cut?"

Sue opened one eye at him, then closed it again. "If I let the temps go, I'd be down to four staffers—three care staff and you—and that's nowhere near the correct adult-to-child ratios. I can't operate like that. And I can't keep running the staff into the ground."

"I could help with the payment."

She turned wide eyes on him. "I appreciate the offer, really, but I can't take your money, Joe. I'd still have a month-to-month income problem, and one more missed payment will send us right to auction. Then your well-intended help would be down the drain, no use to you or me. Besides, you have that family to take care of now." She straightened, as if grateful to have something else to talk about besides money. "What's going on with them?"

"I found them another place in Bend. I'm going to move them next weekend, if that's okay with you." He eased himself onto a seat across from her.

Her face softened. "I'm glad you can help them. But I suspect the reason you can do that is because you'll have a high-paying, steady income coming in soon. All the more reason I won't let you give this ranch a dime. Not only are you using up your savings on that family, but you get very little income from working here. In fact, I'm afraid I won't be able to keep you on after the end of November."

Joe shrugged. "I still need a place to stay until I leave." He looked into her eyes. "I'd be willing to work in exchange for room and board. You'd actually be helping me. And if it helps you buy another month, that's thirty more days to come up with some more income."

"You'd work here for just room and board?"

Before she could fire off the *why* he saw in her eyes, Bertie came in and offered a plate of food to Joe, then one to Sue.

Sue waved it away. "Thanks, Bert, but I can't. Maybe later."

A pang hit Joe's gut. She wasn't eating. In fact, Joe hadn't seen her eat anything all day. With a sigh, Joe set his plate down. "From now until Christmas, I work for food. Deal?" He smiled.

Her gaze lingered on his smile for a half-dozen

heartbeats, then she turned away. "I'll think about it. I can't even promise we'll *be* here for Christmas."

"Well, let's just take things one day at a time." Joe lowered his voice. "Anything else I can do?"

Sue stared out the window toward the shop for a long time, then let out a tired sigh. "Yeah. You can find a buyer for my Harley." Defeat settled on her slumped shoulders.

It tore him up to see her looking so beat.

"Good night, Joe," she said quietly. "And thanks again for all your help."

"No problem." Joe let himself out. *If only I could* help.

After a few adjustments, the Harley grumbled like an old, fat tomcat. Joe left it running in the driveway as he finished buffing out the chrome, making the most of late November's fleeting afternoon sun. As he applied leather conditioner to the seat, something moved on the porch.

Bertie. And she was headed straight for him.

Joe killed the bike's motor and stepped into her line of sight to block her view. Hopefully, her business was with him and not in the shop. It was better if she didn't see what he had stashed in there. The less anyone knew about it, the easier to keep it a surprise. "Hey."

"Whatcha doing with the Harley?"

"Just tightening it down, cleaning it up. Sue wants to sell it."

"I know, and it's a shame." Bertie shook her head at the bike. "Gonna break her heart. But if it'll help her keep the place, she'll let it go in a heartbeat." She peered beyond him toward the shop doorway.

Joe moved to his right. He should've closed that door. "What can I do for you?"

"Actually, I came to give you a heads-up. I don't know if you heard what went down in the kitchen a little while ago, but things are about to get real—hey, what's that?" Craning her neck, Bertie shuffled around him and went into the shop.

Shoot. Joe winced. The old bird didn't miss a thing.

"Hey—isn't that Sue's old Honda, the one she wrecked?" Bertie's hunched frame forced her to turn her entire torso in order to look at him. "Where'd that come from?"

"I found it yesterday." He nodded in the direction of the ridge. "In the ravine."

Bertie cocked her head and peered at him like he'd just recited the Girl Scout pledge in Swedish. "You *found* it? What—you went out for a Sunday stroll down a steep canyon and just came across it lying there?"

"Something like that." He gathered the cleaning rags and put them away.

"How on earth did you get it back here?"

"Wasn't that hard. It's pretty banged up, but it rolls. Getting it up and over the ridge was the hardest part. Then it was downhill to the road. I loaded it in my truck from there and hauled it up here."

"Wow. You gonna fix it?"

"I'm going to try." He sorted through the metric tools, looking for a wrench.

Bertie chuckled, shaking her head. "Man, oh man, she's gonna flip out when she gets home. Can't wait to see the look on her face."

Joe stopped what he was doing and turned to her. "Actually, I was hoping to surprise her. I'd like to keep it a secret for now."

Bertie put up flat palms in compliance. "Hey, don't worry about me." She gave the bike a long, thoughtful look, then turned to Joe and peered up at him through her little, round hippie glasses. "I'll keep your secret, Joe. And if you want," she said, lowering her voice to conspiratory tones, "I'll keep your secret about the *bike* too."

He snapped a piercing look at her.

A slow, knowing smile spread over her face.

Aw, man. He grabbed the first wrench his fingers touched without checking the size and strode to the battered Honda, numbed by the reality that someone else had noticed something he barely acknowledged to himself. "Is it that obvious?"

Bertie chuckled. "Well, *now* it is."

A vehicle approached.

Joe stepped outside.

Sue's white Suburban climbed the long drive, pulling a thin train of dust behind it.

He spun toward the shop.

Bertie was already tugging on the big bay door, trying to close it.

"I'll get that." He shut the door just as Sue's car rounded the curve.

Bertie whistled through her teeth. "Sue's gonna blow a gasket when she hears the news."

"What news?" Joe said. "What's going on?"

Sue climbed out and came toward Joe and Bertie, her limp more pronounced, the way it always was after therapy.

Jasmine flew down the porch steps and met Sue with a stack of mail. "One mail for Papa Joe." The girl handed him a long envelope. Ringo, Jasmine's new shadow, circled the girl's feet with his happy, dumb-dog grin.

Joe glanced at the letter and pocketed it. More junk, as usual. "How'd it go at the bank?"

"Fabulous. They very kindly took my hefty payment and said they'd like another one just like it next week. And another the next week, and the week after that."

Ringo bumped Sue's hand with his snout.

She gave the dog's head a scratch and frowned at Bertie and Joe. "Come on, it's hard enough without you guys looking like someone died."

Bertie darted a glance at Joe. "Um, boss, actually, I know the timing stinks, but I have some bad news. Elena's mom is dying."

"Oh no! Is Elena okay?"

Bertie shook her head. "She's gone."

"Gone?" Sue's eyes widened. "She's *gone?*"

"Yeah."

"To Mexico?"

Bertie nodded. "She got the call, then packed up and left. One of the farmers came and took her to the bus station in La Pine."

Shaking her head slowly, Sue stared across the valley.

Father, she's worked too hard and cares too much about these kids to see it fall apart. "Can I help?"

She didn't answer, didn't seem to hear. Her gaze fell on the Harley in the driveway. She turned to Joe, eyes flickering with something he'd never seen, something wild. "Sure, why not." She stuffed the stack of mail into his hand. "Looks like you're the new boys' dorm counselor."

"Uh, okay, but . . ."

Sue mounted the Harley, fired it up, and gave it a couple window-rattling revs.

Jasmine patted her thighs, beckoning Ringo to her, then knelt down and hugged him tight. The dog licked her ear, but she seemed more interested in keeping a firm grip on him.

"Boss?" Bertie leaned in front of Sue to get her attention above the noise.

Ringo wiggled free from Jasmine's grasp, leaped, and plastered himself to the top of the bike's gas tank.

Sue turned to Bertie and shouted above the rumble. "Don't worry, Bert. I'll be back." She gave the throttle a couple more throaty revs. "I *have* to come back, right? The captain always goes down with the ship."

"But—"

The bike sped off around the curve, headed down the sloped drive, and disappeared from sight beyond the brushy knoll.

A moment later, the engine paused—probably when it reached the end of the drive. Then the bike hammered down the highway, the bursts of rising throttle and shift breaks carrying easily through the stillness. The growl of accelerating motorcycle echoed across the valley floor.

Bertie turned to Joe, face taut. "She's not wearing a helmet."

"Yeah, I know." Unease nagged at his gut over Sue's total disregard for her safety and the law. She was an experienced rider, but she was also upset and, therefore, not totally focused. Not focused *and* on two wheels—a bad mix. If the other bike was running, he would have followed her in a heartbeat.

Jasmine watched the valley as the motorcycle

sounds faded, then turned to Joe and Bertie. "When Miss Susan crazy-mad like me, she race. Fast as she can till angry talk far behind." Jasmine looked toward the valley again. "Don't worry. She always win race."

Joe strained to hear, but the bike sounds had been swallowed by the desert. No point telling Jasmine there wasn't a bike fast enough to beat what Sue was trying to outrun.

CHAPTER SEVENTEEN

After dinner on Tuesday, Sue squared her shoulders and faced the pantry. Based on what she and her teenaged helpers had found on the shelves, the next few weeks' menus looked like pasta with sauce, pasta with tuna, or applesauce with rice. Sue grimaced. Growing up, she'd gotten by on far less. And far worse. But these kids shouldn't be subjected to that kind of hunger, not in this house.

Temples pulsing, she read her shopping list.

Jasmine stopped rearranging cans. "You write tots and nuggets on list?" Her eyes brightened. "Papa Joe say he make for dinner sometime. He say it soooo good."

"Yeah, I'll bet." Sue snorted. Tater tots and chicken nuggets. Probably followed by candy bars and Kool-Aid. Or maybe just straight shots of pure sugar. What she needed to put on the list was a plan. With Elena gone, not only had she been forced to put Joe in charge of the boys, but now the job of planning meals had fallen to her—a job that wasn't exactly her strongest suit. Somehow, she not only needed to figure out how to get the most for her dwindling bucks, but also how to come up with nutritious meals that didn't taste like a shoebox.

She scanned the shelves again. "Okay, girls. Let's move these cans to the island and sort them into food groups."

Jasmine scooted a chair into the pantry and climbed up to reach the top shelf.

Sue turned and smacked into Joe.

His arms went around her as if by reflex, steadying her. "Sorry, I—didn't know you were in here," he said.

Jasmine and Tatiana giggled.

Joe let her go.

Sue drew a shaky breath. "What do you need?"

"I hate to drop this on you, but we have a busted hot water heater in the boys' dorm."

Stifling a groan, Sue turned and grabbed an armload of cans. She took them to the center island. "Can you fix it?"

Joe joined her. Frowning, he read the cans. "I could try replacing the elements, but the heater is pretty much shot. Best to replace the whole unit."

Fabulous. Sue bunched the fruit cans into a group. "How much is that going to cost?"

"Not sure." Joe palmed a ten-pound can of applesauce as if it were a softball. "I'll have to go to Bend to get one. I'll pray I find a good deal."

"You'll *pray* for a *water* heater?" Tatiana asked.

Joe chuckled. "Sure. It never hurts to ask God

for help, even with small stuff. I've been asking God every day to help me get my guitar back."

Sue pushed a lock of hair from her face. "What guitar?"

"The one that was stolen from my truck just before I came to work here."

"I'm sorry to hear that," Sue said. Joe sang *and* played guitar?

"Papa God hear you pray?" Jasmine's eyes went wide.

Joe nodded. "You bet. He hears you too."

"Me?" Jasmine stole a look at Sue and lowered her voice. "But my English not good."

Joe smiled at the girl. "I'm pretty sure God is multilingual, Jas. Besides, it's not your words. It's your heart. God's the best listener. You can talk to Him anytime, anyplace, about anything."

"So, Joe." His name burst from Sue's lips with more force than she'd intended. Time to get back to reality. "How soon do we need the new heater?"

"It's up to you, but the longer us guys go without hot water, the longer you girls will have to share your bathrooms with us."

Grimacing, she scanned her shopping list again, an idea forming. "Actually, we need food supplies. If you don't mind picking them up while you're in town, maybe you could get both? It would save time and gas. Tomorrow okay?"

"Hey, that's right—Thanksgiving's the day

after tomorrow." Patting his belly, he grinned. "Gotta stock up for that."

"Actually . . ." A turkey dinner and all the trimmings for the kids and crew was way beyond her budget, but she wasn't going to bring that up in front of the girls. She shot him a look she hoped was perfectly clear. "Just what's on the list, okay?"

He opened his mouth, but Jasmine patted his arm. "Did police find bad man who stole guitar?"

"No, they didn't catch him. But I hope they do. Then maybe I'll find out what happened to my Martin." He grabbed the broom leaning on the island and plucked invisible strings.

Tatiana giggled.

Joe handed her the broom. "Man, that was one sweet-sounding guitar."

The disappointment in his voice quieted the room.

That he could miss a guitar so much didn't surprise Sue. But then, few things about Joe Paterson surprised her anymore.

When Joe returned Wednesday afternoon, Sue sent a group of kids outside to help him unload supplies. Then she headed for the door to inspect what he'd bought.

Bertie stopped her and pulled her into the office. She wore a cat-that-ate-the-canary look.

Sue wasn't in the mood for games. She needed to get outside and see just how far Joe had strayed from her grocery list. "What?"

Without a word, Bertie handed her a fat wad of cash.

Sue unrolled the bundle and looked up at Bertie. "What's this?"

"You wanted Joe to find a buyer for your Harley, so he did. It's sold."

"Sold? It's gone?"

Bertie nodded at the cash. "Count it."

Sold? That bike had been like an old friend. A cloud of sadness passed over her, casting a shadow over what satisfaction she might have felt from making the sale.

But it was the right thing to do. She'd been selfish to keep it this long.

Sue thumbed through the bills and frowned. "Eighteen hundred?" She fanned out the cash on her desk, double-checked the amount, then turned to Bertie. "I told him it *might* be worth that much, cleaned up and during summer. I didn't think we'd get anywhere near that much, especially this time of year."

The old woman shrugged. "If that's what you told him to get, then that's what he got." Her voice lowered. "That guy would do pretty much anything you ask."

What had prompted *that* remark? Sue stuffed the bills into a money pouch and shoved it in her desk. "Most days he does what he's asked." Looking through the office windows, she craned her neck to see the bags the kids were toting into the house. "I have a feeling today's not one of them." She went to the door. Time to prove her suspicions correct.

Bertie's hand gripped her arm. "Maybe you should count it one more time."

Sue nearly laughed at Bertie's lame attempt to look innocent. The woman couldn't act her way out of a tub of tofu. "Seriously? You'd go to that much trouble to cover for him?" Sue sighed. "Okay, I give up. Go ahead. Spend every last dime we have on turkeys and pumpkin pie. I don't care." She started to leave, then turned back. "If you need me, I'll be in my room *packing* so I'll be ready to go when the bank kicks us out. Just tell me when the party's unloaded and out of sight, okay?"

Bertie grinned. "Whatever you say. You're the boss."

"Yeah, right," Sue muttered. She headed for her room out back, but halfway across the yard, a thought stopped her dead cold. Of course she got eighteen hundred for the Harley.

Because *Joe* bought it.

With a growl, Sue tromped to her studio and stood in the middle of the room, frustration mounting. Why did the man insist on doing stuff like that? The Harley, the extra food—she hadn't asked him to do any of those things. Why? What did he want?

The question and its possible answers sent a shiver up her spine.

She sat on her bed, suspicion growing. What were his motives?

He must have some. No guy was that nice just to be *nice*.

She surveyed the room, hammering her brain for a way to avoid getting tangled up in a long column of debt she couldn't repay on her own terms.

A guitar case sat in the closet. Her old Ovation guitar.

Perfect.

She dug out the case and marched across the lawn to the house, then propped the guitar near the bottom step and went inside.

In the kitchen, kids and staff were putting away groceries in the fridge and pantry. Bertie saw her first, then Joe. One by one, everyone stopped and stared at Sue. Edgar's left eyelid twitched.

"Hey, Sue," Joe said, voice dropping to an uncertain tone. "I can explain—"

Sue waved him off. "Yeah, I know, you bought enough turkey and stuffing for all of Lake County. I get it. It's fine." She gave him a steady look. "Joe, can I show you something? It's out back." She headed for the door but didn't hear him following.

When she turned to see why, no one had moved, including Joe. All eyes were on her.

"Wow." Chaz pushed his glasses up higher on his nose and peered at Cori. "See, I told you she wouldn't flip out. I *knew* I should've put money on that."

Heat rose up her neck as she stood there absorbing their stares like a taunted kid on the playground. Did everyone think she was a tyrant? She'd had to save every dime, plan everything in careful detail, find creative ways to make things stretch. Did they think she did those things just to be mean? Didn't they know how hard she tried to feed them and give them a good home?

No, they didn't. They were just kids. But still— it wasn't fair.

Sue inspected a super-sized box of pancake mix on the counter, blinking back the sting in her eyes.

Joe came to her side. "So what did you want to show me? Lead the way." His mass shielded her from the stares as he escorted her to the back door.

Wiping her eyes, Sue led him outside and down the steps, then grabbed the guitar case and offered it to him. "It's nothing like a Martin, but it'll play."

Joe took it, confusion crossing his face. He opened it slowly and eased out the acoustic guitar. He didn't say anything, just turned it over and smoothed fingers over the glossy black finish. Running a thumb over the strings, he looked up at her. "Is it yours?"

She nodded. "Go ahead. Give it a try."

Joe planted a foot on a step and rested the guitar on his knee. He plucked a few strings, gave them a quick tune, and then ran through a mellow, bluesy lick, his long fingers flying. He handled the instrument like a pro.

"It's a bit dusty," she said quietly, "but you can use it as long as you want."

His head snapped up, the light in his eyes unmistakable. "I'd hate to see you go without."

She shook her head. "I don't ever play it. Besides, I never was any good. You use it."

He lowered himself to sit on the step and ran through a riff that flowed off his fingers like bubbling waterfalls. Then he played a ballad, picking through a series of ornamental chords in a breathtakingly beautiful, classical style.

Oh yeah. The man could definitely play.

He laid the guitar on his lap and stared at it. "I don't know what to say, Sue. This is . . . really nice." His eyes met hers and his voice deepened. "Thank you."

She shrugged, forcing down a childish rush of joy. "It's no big deal. I just thought it should be played by someone who actually knows how."

Face softening, Joe gazed at her.

The tender look in his eyes gripped her. She

209

turned away. Enough of that. She had work to do.

"You remind me of my little brother, Ben," Joe said, putting the guitar back in its case.

An unfamiliar jab hit her gut. She laughed to smother it. "Yeah, I get that a lot. But passing for a boy actually comes in handy. You have *no* idea how hard it is to keep all the supermodel scouts off my back."

"I didn't mean the way you look, Sue."

Heat flooded her face. Of course he didn't.

"You're selfless. And loyal to the bone."

She scrambled for a joke, a quick way to deflect this sudden, too-probing focus on her, but she had nothing. Cheeks cooking, she turned toward the steps. "It's really no big deal. It was just sitting in a closet collecting dust."

Joe stood and touched her wrist lightly. "Sue, wait. I . . ."

At his gentle touch, she turned. From where she stood on the top step, she met him at eye level. The question in his eyes tangled her insides with crazy ribbons of warmth. With a gasp, she turned and fled into the main house.

Even if Joe admired something about her, it didn't matter—he had no part in this home, this teetering dream of hers. He was leaving and wasn't coming back.

She sped through the busy kitchen and kept moving.

But that tender look on his face followed her

like a full moon on a long, straight stretch of midnight highway.

There was one sure way to get rid of that.

She stormed out the front door, down the steps, and headed for the shop. A cold gust of wind stung her cheeks and whipped through her sweatshirt as she raised the shop door. Maybe that guitar didn't square everything, but it was a start. No matter what it took, Sue would even the score with Joe Paterson before he could even think about calling in any dues.

As she suspected, the Harley was still there. It wasn't hers anymore, but since Joe had taken liberties with her shopping list, maybe he wouldn't mind if she took it out for one last ride.

She reached for her helmet and froze.

Beside the Harley, her wrecked Honda sat in its usual resting place, the paint scraped in spots, but straight, upright, and shining like new.

CHAPTER EIGHTEEN

Eyes closed, Sue inhaled deeply at the door of the dining hall. Her stomach rumbled at the miraculous aroma of turkey and candied sweet potatoes and seasoned stuffing that filled every corner of the house. She opened her eyes. She wasn't dreaming—the food *was* real.

Jasmine stood at the long dining hall window watching the horizon. In fact, she'd been at that window or pressed against the one in the front den several times that day.

"Hey, whatcha looking at?"

Jasmine spun around. A sheepish grin pulled her mouth wide.

"You about ready for your first all-American Thanksgiving dinner?"

Jasmine took another long look out the window, nodded, and followed Sue to the kitchen.

Joe had his crew busy chopping salad, making gravy, and mixing up a giant batch of sparkling cider out of apple juice concentrate and club soda.

By the time the meal was ready to serve, Sue could hardly wait to dig in. Whatever kind of cooking they did on off-shore oil rigs, somewhere along the line Joe had learned to cook a turkey into the picture of mouth-watering perfection. Hopefully, it tasted as good as it looked.

When everyone was seated, Joe turned to Sue. "Mind if I ask the blessing?"

How could she refuse after all the trouble he'd gone to? "Sure, go ahead." Sue scanned the eager faces around the table.

Jasmine's seat was empty.

Joe cleared his throat and everyone around the table quieted.

"Father, we thank You for providing this meal and all the ways You care for us. We have so much to be thankful for, but nothing compares to knowing You. So we thank You for this meal, but even more, we thank You for the gift of Your Son, for Your unfailing love that makes a way for us to belong to Your forever family, as Your cherished sons and daughters."

Sue opened her eyes and focused on Jasmine's empty seat. She glanced one seat over and met Brandi's gaze.

Brandi snickered.

Whether or not Brandi or anyone else believed in God, Joe clearly believed every word he said.

"In Christ's name, amen." Joe smiled at the kids, then grabbed the tongs and started serving turkey.

Sue excused herself and went to the den.

Jasmine's gaze was again plastered to the drive. "Jasmine? What are you doing?"

"Nothing."

Nothing, my foot. "Okay, well, dinner's ready. Come and eat."

After one last search out the window, Jasmine went with Sue to the table.

Everything looked amazing, even down to the lumpy gravy, thanks to the combined efforts of Vince, Deeg, and Chaz.

Sue looked around the table. Most of the kids were smiling. Daisy laughed and Edgar stared in amazement at the food.

And then there were Joe's twinkling eyes, a slow smile spreading across his mouth.

Something about this felt right. Natural. Because even with the other staff away for the holiday, this didn't seem like a skeleton crew managing a dozen needy kids. This seemed more like—

Family.

Joy seeped through her like a slow trickle of honey, soothing her in a way she hadn't felt in a long time.

The sound of an approaching vehicle halted Sue in mid-scoop of mashed potatoes.

Jasmine twisted in her seat, eyes widening.

A car door slammed.

Jasmine bolted from the room and out the front door.

What in the world? Hurrying to the front porch, Sue nearly slammed into Jasmine, who stood rooted to the top step.

Mr. Stewart climbed the sloped lawn with a smile and two pumpkin pies.

As Sue greeted the farmer, Jasmine made an odd sound and darted back inside. Sue took the pies. "Thank you very much. And will you please thank Mrs. Stewart for us?"

When Sue returned inside, Joe met her in the foyer.

"Everything okay?"

"I don't know."

Jasmine was at the window again, eyes glued to the driveway.

"But I'm going to find out." Sue handed the pies to Joe. "Could you take these, please? Thanks."

She joined Jasmine at the window. "All right, kiddo, what's going on? Who are you waiting for?"

"You no need pretend, Miss Susan. I know about big surprise."

"What surprise?"

Jasmine rolled her eyes. "Walkers coming see me today. For holiday."

The *Walkers?* Sue hadn't heard from them since they dumped Jasmine on her front step a month ago. Where had the girl gotten an idea like that?

The raw hope on Jasmine's face sent Sue's heart plummeting to her stomach. "Why do you think they're coming today?"

The girl's widening eyes locked on hers. "Brandi tell me secret. She—" Jasmine spotted something behind Sue and tensed, rigid as a post.

Sue turned.

Brandi leaned against the doorway, a lazy smirk lifting one side of her mouth.

A guttural sound came from Jasmine. With a growl, she lunged toward the bigger girl.

Sue caught her shoulders and held her back. "Brandi! Why did you tell her that?"

Brandi made a lame attempt to smother a grin. "It was just a joke."

Jasmine screamed.

Sue tightened her grasp on the girl just in time to keep her from attacking. Jasmine's head thrashed from side to side, her incoherent screams nearly shattering Sue's eardrums. Over the noise, Sue ordered Brandi to her room.

Joe and some of the teens appeared in the doorway. Joe took one look at the scene and quietly sent the kids back to the dining hall, but he hung back, watching.

Jasmine's feet scissored in a kicking frenzy.

Sue steeled herself to keep a firm hold until the rage storm subsided.

The girl went limp, but Sue held on in case

Jasmine made any more sudden moves. "Take it easy, Jas. Just try to calm down."

Jasmine shuddered.

Sue carefully loosened her grip. Jasmine sank to her knees and Sue joined her on the hardwood floor.

Jasmine rocked herself, but instead of hiding her face, she turned to Sue, mouth bunched into a tiny knot like she was fighting to keep from crying.

Heart wrenching, Sue focused on how badly she wanted to rake Brandi over the coals.

Thick tears pooled in Jasmine's eyes. "No one want me," she said in a choked whisper. "I nothing. Only joke."

The pain in her words tore a gash straight through Sue's heart. "No. No, honey, that's not true. You're not a joke. You're an amazing girl. That was just Brandi's way of paying you back for telling on her about the knife. You're a very special girl."

"No! I just freak everyone send away. I belong to no one!" She burst out sobbing.

A rush of tears blinded Sue. Instinctively, her arms tightened around the child. How many times had Sue felt the same way? How many crushing blows had it taken for her to toughen up and block out the pain and terror of feeling utterly alone?

What's wrong with me? Am I so unlovable?

Swallowing the ache in her throat, Sue pulled the sobbing girl close and rocked her gently, whispering soothing words. She ordered her tears to stay back.

Jasmine plastered herself to Sue's chest as she sobbed, her wet face soaking Sue's blouse.

Sue kept rocking, stroking the girl's hair, whispering, "It's okay—shh, baby, it's okay."

Joe watched them from the doorway. He met Sue's gaze.

Shake it off, Sooz. Getting emotional will do no good.

Jasmine would get through this. Both Sue and Jasmine had survived lonely, painful times. They'd gotten through a tough childhood. It was possible. Kids were far stronger than adults gave them credit for.

But the sobbing child clinging to her now just blew that theory out the door. Jasmine had a hole in her heart bigger than Sue had any clue how to fill.

What am I doing? I can't . . . let her get that close. She can't need this. I *can't need this.*

Joe hung back where he could see both Sue and the other kids, hands crammed in his pockets, concern evident on his face.

Sue kept rocking, shushing the sobs, stroking the girl's hair until she felt Jasmine finally begin to relax. After a while Joe left, but Sue stayed with Jasmine for a long time.

· · ·

Under the velvety night sky, Joe sat on the edge of the front porch and closed his eyes. Brandi was behind whatever had caused Jasmine's meltdown, and that angered him. But what really worked him into a knot was the way Sue had embraced that brokenhearted girl. She seemed shaken by Jasmine's grief yet determined to comfort her. The image of her rocking the girl while fighting back her own tears tore through him.

Her silent but fierce love for those discarded kids smuggled right into Joe's heart in a way that got to him. Big time.

Father, I believe You brought me here to help her know You, but I don't know if the plan to spend one-on-one time with her was such a good idea.

"Hey." Sue came to the edge of the porch and lowered herself to the step a couple feet away, as if oblivious to what her nearness did to him.

Good one, God.

She massaged her eyelids, then rested her forehead in her hands. She didn't say anything, just drew a deep breath and let it out slowly. Apparently, she didn't come out here needing anything from him. Big surprise.

He leaned back on his elbows and gazed at the stars. High desert nights had a hushed, bottomless depth to them. Like Alaskan nights out on the water, far from city lights and sounds. Unmarred by people and all their noise.

"I may have been wrong about Jasmine," she said.

"How?"

Shrugging, Sue picked at a piece of cheatgrass stuck in the weathered wooden step until she had it free. Then she poked it into the crack again, as if realizing she had disturbed something meant to be left alone. "One of the families I lived with as a kid locked me in my room a lot. I remember thinking my real dad was in some other country on a dangerous secret mission, but he'd come back soon. And when he did, he'd find me and take me away from there." She shook her head. "I have no idea where I got an idea like that."

As much as he longed to sit up and see her unguarded expression, he resisted the urge. She'd talk more readily if he stayed right where he was.

"I must've been about eight. I'd been locked in my room for a couple days. I decided my dad was looking for me and the only reason he hadn't rescued me was because he didn't know where I was. So I wrote a message on the window in the condensation. 'Help me, Daddy! It's me, Suzy.'" She puffed a feeble laugh. "I even remembered to write it backward."

Her quiet words tightened his chest. He closed his eyes, longing to undo all the things that had hurt her.

Sue picked at the weathered step. "I'm not really sure why I'm telling you all this—I've never told this story to anyone."

"I don't mind. I'd like to hear it."

She sighed. "I waited at that window all day. Waiting and hoping, thinking if I wished hard enough, he would come." She lifted her face to the stars.

"But he didn't."

"Shocker, huh?" She offered a half smile. "I figured out my dad's big secret eventually. He was just a flake who left a trail of kids behind him without ever bothering to look back. There was nothing keeping him away, like being locked up or obsessed with a career. He was just some spineless, self-absorbed guy. I eventually realized he wasn't anybody worth pining over and forgot him. But for that little stretch of time, I kept waiting, hoping."

It took everything in Joe not to reach an arm around her and draw her close. Instead, he listened carefully to what she wasn't saying.

"I forgot all about that window message until today." Sue leaned forward, elbows braced on her knees. "I thought Jasmine was like me, you know? Not waiting around for someone who wasn't coming, no more looking back. But I guess I was wrong." Moonlight bathed her cheek in a soft, milky glow, tracing the curve of her jaw and cheekbone in shades of light and shadow.

Joe tore his gaze away and focused on the stars. "She's a *lot* like you. Maybe that's why she's here. You can reach her like no one else can." In the silence, he could sense her drilling him with a look. He turned and met her gaze. "You did the right thing, Sue. That girl needs someone who loves and accepts her just the way she is. Someone who'll hold her and let her cry and tell her it's gonna be okay."

Sue shook her head. "But it's not okay. And it won't be okay until . . ."

Joe sat up and watched her. "Until what?"

"Until she stops longing for someone who won't be there."

"How can you say that? Kids need to know they're loved by someone who always has their back, no matter what." He lowered his voice. "Everybody does."

She stared at him.

He launched off the porch and paced the lawn. Did the woman actually believe these kids were better off going through life alone? After a few more strides across the lawn, Joe turned and went back to tell her what these kids really needed.

But seeing Sue with her head hung low deflated his speech.

Fear was a powerful obstacle.

Perfect love casts out fear.

He went back to the porch and sat beside her. "I

saw you. Don't try to tell me your heart doesn't break for that girl." He lowered his voice. "She's desperate for a mother's love. Tell me you don't feel that."

She searched his face, a growing struggle evident on hers. "I do. I just don't think it's going to work. Not with me. I can't . . ."

Tears glittered and spilled. She twisted away and swiped her cheeks with both hands.

He ached to pull her close. *Yes, you can, Sue. I know you can.*

"Besides, I don't even know where any of us will be in a month," she whispered into the night. "What happens if I start playing the loving mom now and then have to ship her off to who knows where? She already thinks she's a freak nobody wants. I can't do that to her again."

"She needs to know someone cares." He plowed a hand through his hair. Gave the tone he felt coming on a chance to ease up. "It may seem pointless to you, but knowing someone cared about me even for a short time made a life-and-death difference for me."

Her gaze fell to the ground. "I hear what you're saying, Joe. But I think distance is best in this case. Especially now."

Father, she's making a huge mistake. Please help Sue and Jasmine find the love and peace in You they so desperately need. Show her—

Show her My love.

Aw man, not that again. "Do me a favor, Sue. Will you at least think about it?"

Sue didn't move, just aimed a long look across the desert. "Okay," she said softly, almost to herself. She lowered her gaze. "It's not like I have a choice. I won't be getting that scene out of my mind for a while."

That's right, open up that fierce heart of yours, just a little. "You'll do the right thing. I know it."

She searched his face. "That's quite a supply of faith you've got there, Mister Joe."

Joe smiled. "It's *all* I've got. Literally. By the way, I arranged for Linda and Karla to cover for you Sunday afternoon. For that outing we talked about."

Her brows rose. "Everything is falling apart, and you're still stuck on that?"

"We had a deal, remember?"

Sue dropped her head back. "So what exactly are we doing?"

He considered answering, then shook his head. "Nah. All you need to know is to wear hiking boots and a warm coat. I got the rest covered."

She stood and stretched, lengthening her figure and revealing soft curves usually hidden by her baggy clothing.

A rush of adrenaline reminded him to tear his gaze away. He sure didn't need to get caught looking.

"One time. That's it." She went inside the house and closed the door.

He had no idea what good a hike up Table Rock would do, if any. Maybe this outing would show her it was possible to have a little simple fun with a guy who didn't want anything from her. And hopefully it would help her begin to understand there was Someone who would never hurt or fail her.

Sure, no problem. A freezing hike and a thermos of cocoa should do it.

Sue's silhouette moved around in her office.

He could do this. He could spend time with her as a casual friend, help her lighten up. She'd be amazed at how fun a purely platonic outing with a guy could be.

A guy who felt things that were neither casual nor platonic.

CHAPTER NINETEEN

Sunday afternoon, Sue trudged up the path to the chapel, kicking up sand with her boots and kicking herself inwardly. Exactly how had she let Joe talk her into this "not date"?

As she approached the small building, bits of a song and soft, sweet strains of guitar filled the air. The melody line and bass notes wove together with his voice, blending beautifully into a smooth, lyrical sound, like a love song.

Sue closed her eyes. Though she had agreed to this "outing," she was in no hurry to put an end to that music. She strained to hear the softly sung words, but it was hard to make them out. She cracked the door slightly.

"Your love never changes."

His voice resonated with such depth, such sincerity, that she longed to hear more. Maybe he could bring the guitar along.

With what sounded like more fingers than he had, he picked a graduating run. "You know my heart, my every thought."

She staggered back a step. It was that "reading her thoughts" part about God that got under her skin. Didn't He have anything better to do? Hurricanes to re-route? Did He need to lurk in people's heads too?

The music stopped.

She was about to open the door when Joe started a new tune, this one simple, purposeful.

"You're everything I need . . ." Joe's voice came across much quieter than before, but still deep and clear. "My strength, my breath, my shield . . ."

The strumming continued, but the singing faltered.

Sue's breath quickened. His words both disturbed and fascinated her, like passing a car wreck. Afraid to look yet inexplicably drawn to do so.

The strumming slowed to single picked notes as he cleared his throat. "You take my sorrow and my pain . . . wash away all my shame . . ." His voice fell, hushed and husky. "Till all that's left . . . is Your unfailing love, deeper than the sea."

Oh no. No.

She turned and slipped down the trail toward the house, then hurried to a limp-jog. Idiot. What had she expected to hear from him in the chapel on a Sunday—Elvis? As she reached the porch steps, he called for her to stop. She continued up the steps and crossed the porch toward the door.

"Sue?" He sounded concerned.

She froze, hand on the doorknob.

Joe bounded up the steps, sending thunderous tremors across the porch. "Where are you going? Were you just up at the chapel?"

"I don't think I want to do this today, Joe."

His face drooped. "Why?"

She shrugged.

His dark brows rose. "Not even for a hike up Table Rock?"

Sue lifted her gaze to the flat mass beyond the ranch. That did sound like fun, actually. She'd taken the kids once and had always wanted to do it again.

"You did agree, you know."

True. She should just do this, especially since it meant getting it over with. "A quick hike, then."

"All right." With a smile, Joe zipped up his work jacket, then pulled a green John Deere beanie out of one of the pockets and slipped it on over his short, dark hair.

A sudden sensation of snuggling up to Joe danced across her chest.

Odd. Very odd, to say the least.

At the base of the plateau, he pulled his truck off the road and parked. "Race you to the top?"

Sue quirked a brow. "Challenging a crippled woman who has half your stride? That desperate for a win, are you?"

"Hey, I'll take any win I can get." A dimple punctuated his smile.

"How noble of you."

They hiked up the road a while, then ventured up the northeast slope, her knee loosening more with each step.

It wasn't too hard to keep up with Joe's longer strides—he wasn't moving like he was in any hurry to get to the top. He kept his eyes on the ground, stopping once in a while to inspect a pointed rock or flat stone.

Sharp gusts of wind stung Sue's ears. She pulled on her hood and cinched it tightly around her face.

"Hey, Sue, check this out." Joe crouched near a scattering of stones. When she was close enough to see, he took a pocketknife and carefully moved the sand from around a dark point, unearthing a triangular, flat stone. He picked it up and blew the sand off, turning it over in his hand. It had a deep notching on either side of the wide base, obviously a crafted piece, not just a pointy rock. "Side notcher. Nice one." He held it out to her. "Check it out. The tip is totally intact."

Sue noted the narrowed, sharper edges. "Looks like an arrowhead. What kind of stone is it, do you know?"

"Obsidian, most likely. The volcano produced a lot of it. The tribes in this area had a ready supply of it for all their hunting and tool needs."

"Volcano?" Sue frowned at the flat top of the hill.

"Not here—Fort Rock." He eyed her, one dark brow raised. "Don't tell me you live twenty miles from a historic landmark and didn't know it was once a volcano?"

She winced. "Sorry."

Joe shook his head and replaced the arrowhead.

"You're putting it back?"

"It's illegal to remove artifacts from here." He stood and brushed dirt from his hands. "All right, your turn. Let's see if you can find something."

They searched the ground as they continued to climb. After about ten minutes of hiking, she spotted something white and too evenly rounded on one end to be natural. She called Joe over.

He took his knife and carefully pushed some of the sand and debris away, exposing more of the piece. "Looks like a hand tool."

Gingerly, Sue lifted the stone away from its resting place. It was much longer than Joe's find, but definitely a hand-hewn piece, its edges sharpened.

"I'm pretty sure that's a scraper. Good find, Sue." He nodded. "Bet you didn't know you had an archeologist in you just waiting to burrow out, huh?"

"Actually, I did know. I was just hoping to keep it a secret a little while longer. Didn't want to make you look bad."

"Ah, sparing my ego. Nice."

By the time they reached the top of Table Rock, the cold wind had sapped the feeling from her legs and made her knee ache. She went to a level place near the drop-off and surveyed the view.

Low, brown hills in the distance hemmed the valley, which was a blend of green fields and sagebrush-dotted desert. A lone highway zigzagged through alfalfa farms, turning into a thin ribbon that eventually tapered off west toward the Cascade Mountains. Biting wind, far stronger up here than below, whipped across her cheeks.

Joe watched her from several yards away. On top of that flat expanse of rock, against the distant blur of hills on the horizon, he looked more massive than ever, an imposing figure against the silent, distant valley. Where no one else was around for miles.

Sue's belly tightened.

As he approached, Sue hugged her arms around her middle, squeezing her coat tighter. "About ready to hike back down?"

"I don't know about you, but hiking makes me hungry. How about a snack and a hot drink first?"

Sue felt her brows creep up. "Right. I'll just pop into the kitchen behind that sagebrush and fix you right up."

"Okay. Or we could just use what I brought." He pointed.

A cooler, camp chairs, and a box of stuff lay beyond a small rise a few dozen yards away near a rock-lined fire pit.

He'd come here earlier in the day and dropped off a full-blown picnic? What next—karaoke and cocktails?

"I'll get a fire going." Joe grabbed a dry chunk of juniper. "Got a couple camp chairs. You want to set those up?"

While Joe built a fire in the pit, Sue set up the chairs and placed them a safe distance from the flames, then dragged the cooler between them.

Joe hunted through a box and pulled out a thermos and a couple mugs. He sat down and offered one to her. "Cocoa?"

She took the mug, but . . . why had he gone to such lengths for a little hike? Something was fishy about all this.

When the fire was well ablaze, Joe removed some foil packages from the cooler. Leftover turkey and potatoes. A box of graham crackers. Marshmallows. Chocolate bars.

Did he know about her chocolate obsession and how rarely she indulged? The whole setup was beginning to feel like more than a simple hike. Him bringing stuff up early. Food. Chocolate.

Miles from another living soul.

What's going on?

Her heartbeat shifted up a gear.

Stay calm.

"So why are you doing this?"

Stoking the fire, he glanced over his shoulder at her. "What do you mean?"

"I mean all this stuff—a fire and food and chocolate and . . ."

"And what?"

Tons of things. Things guys just don't do unless they want something. She jutted her chin. "Buying my Harley for more than it's worth. Finding my dualie and secretly fixing it up."

A flush crept into his face. Like he was busted and he knew it.

Her breath quickened. Sue looked around. In the box was a bundle she hadn't noticed. A blanket.

A *blanket?* What part of the "outing" was *that* for? What had he really been planning? "What's going on, Joe? Are you hitting on me?" The pitch of her voice rose and carried. She scanned the empty terrain and distant valley beyond.

Where no one can see or hear us . . .

Adrenaline kicked her pulse into double-time. "Or did you bring me up here all alone in the middle of nowhere so you could—"

Icy fear shot through her veins.

She bolted from her seat.

So I could what? Joe rose and stepped toward her. "No way, Sue. I just wanted—"

She retreated farther.

"Sue." He took a step toward her.

She backed away faster, stumbling on rocks as she got closer to the edge of the plateau—to the drop-off.

"Whoa—hold on!" Joe rushed toward her, dread tightening every muscle. He had to stop her, but he didn't want to move even closer to the edge and reinforce her fear.

Fear of what? I could never . . .

He halted, palms up. "I'm not going to hurt you."

She checked behind her, then studied him, her face stark white.

God, You gotta do something. "I just wanted you to get away and take a break. After everything that's been going on. That's it. And the food was just leftovers." *Mostly.*

Arms folded taut across her stomach, she watched him as he spoke, as if measuring every word for lies or truth.

What else could he say? All he'd wanted was for her to have a good time, eat her fill, and relax for a change. To discover she could trust a man. Apparently, that was asking too much.

Sue lifted her chin. "What about the blanket?"

The *blanket?* What did she think—that he had *planned* to attack her? "The blanket was just in case you got cold." His tone fell flat under the full weight of her suspicion and fear. "I didn't mean to freak you out."

She didn't seem convinced. She glanced behind her at the edge of the cliff, as if tumbling down a steep embankment was preferable to being near him.

How could she even think that? Does she really believe I could hurt her? Joe dragged a hand over his face.

Had those past accusations lingered on him like a visible stain?

He pivoted away, stung from being under such vile suspicion. He stood with his back to her, hands on his hips.

"No." Sue's voice was a raspy whisper. "Oh no . . ."

No *what?* He wasn't even near her. He turned and faced her, wary of what he would see.

Distress filled her eyes and tightened her features. She looked small, alone. She didn't meet his eyes, but instead fixed her gaze on the fire pit. "Joe, I'm sorry. I guess it's too easy for me to go there sometimes."

With everyone? Or just me? He sucked in a breath. Held it. *Let it go, man.* "It's okay." He forced himself to say the words. "I'm sorry I scared you."

She said nothing, just stared at the fire, its crackling flames snapping echoes in the stillness.

"Do you want to hang by the fire for a few minutes?" *Or however long it takes to melt that fear lingering in your eyes?*

Without making eye contact, she nodded.

Joe led the way. He stirred up the fire while Sue pulled a chair closer to the heat. She sat down and stretched out trembling hands, warming them.

Still afraid? His heart twisted. Willing his fists to unclench, he took his seat.

"It's not you, Joe," she whispered, anguish trailing each word.

You sure about that? "Do you want to tell me what it is, then?"

Something painful churned beneath the surface of her strained expression. "It's not really a campfire-and-hot-cocoa kind of topic."

"Let me be the judge of that."

She unscrewed the thermos and poured steaming liquid into a mug, then held it out to him, but he shook his head. Sue clasped her hands around the mug as if trying to capture some of the heat. "Men have always been . . . interested in me." Her voice was small.

"Like physically?"

Nodding, she stared into the fire again, her eyes dark reservoirs of silent pain. "As far back as I can remember. Even as a kid."

The hollowness of her voice constricted his heart. *Just once, God. I'd love to get my hands on every last one of those pieces of trash. Just once.* "Sue." His voice rumbled across the stillness. "The ones who treated you that way were sick.

Not everyone is like that." *I'm not like that.* "You know that, right?"

She met his eyes for the briefest moment, as if it cost her dearly to let him see inside her. "I'm afraid I get signals mixed up sometimes."

He looked at her, willing her to see into his heart. "I'm not like that, Sue. I would never hurt you. Ever."

Tears sparkled in her eyes. "I know that. I'm really sorry."

"Don't worry about it."

She nodded, then turned away and wiped furiously at her cheeks.

Aw, Sue . . . He grabbed the foil packs of food warming at the edge of the fire and offered her one. He'd have to watch his every word and move from now on. Make sure nothing he did or said could be seen as putting the moves on her. Double sure.

After a good-sized helping of turkey, mashed potatoes, and casual conversation, Sue seemed to ease up a little.

He polished off the last of the food, then stoked the fire with a few more hunks of juniper. Dusky gray darkened the eastern horizon. Joe returned to his seat, while Sue got the blanket and pulled it around her. He caught the hint of a smile on her lips. "What?"

Sue nodded at the empty food containers. "Did you get enough to eat there?"

"I'm good." He patted his belly. "For now."

She leaned back and yawned. "Good. Because I was afraid I'd have to tell Jasmine the legend of the hungry Table Rock giant is a true story after all."

"Isn't it?" Chuckling, he opened the bag of marshmallows and grabbed a roasting skewer. "The way I always heard it, the hungry giant is a slobbering troll with jagged fangs and foul breath. But from hearing Jasmine tell it, your version sounds pretty tame."

"Tame?" Sue briefed him on her version of the legend, then listened to his. They were both chuckling by the time he finished.

"Somehow, I don't think Jasmine would be scared of either giant," Sue said.

They talked about the other kids for a while, comparing notes.

Joe slid a hot, roasted marshmallow off the stick and smooshed it between chocolate and graham crackers before offering the sticky treat to Sue. He told her about Chaz and his newest obsession with the helicopters and planes that flew drills over the ranch. "Chaz showed me his plan for shooting down one of the helicopters. He's got a schematic drawn out showing all the variable trajectories." Joe stabbed another marshmallow. "It's pretty good, actually."

"What?" The word came out muffled around a mouthful of marshmallow.

"He wants to shoot it down with a car. You know, like on *Die Hard 4*?"

She shook her head.

"You haven't seen that? Oh man. Bruce Willis is a cop who's getting boxed in and shot at by thugs. Trouble is, he's in a patrol car and they're in a helicopter. There's this scene where you think they're going to nail him, but just as Bruce is about to come out of this underground tunnel, he guns it and forces the car up the side of some concrete slab thing—as he bails out—and launches it into the air like a missile. The car smashes into the helicopter and blows it up." He turned his marshmallow over the coals. "Best exploding helicopter scene ever." He held the roasting skewer with his knees while he assembled another s'more.

Sue looked horrified. "You think he might . . .?"

"Nah, it's all special effects, Sue. Don't worry. Chaz could never do it. He gets a little wound up sometimes, but he knows the difference between reality and the movies."

"Are you sure?"

"Yep. Anyway, he'll forget all about the aircraft drills soon. I've got too much for him to do. He's my shadow, remember?" He downed the s'more in two bites, then impaled another marshmallow and aimed it at the flames.

"Okay. But if I hear reports of an aircraft getting shot down by a car, you're in big trouble."

Her lips were stretched to a broad smile. In the firelight, her cheeks glowed. She looked warm, full, and relaxed—more so than he'd seen in a long time. Just as he'd hoped for.

A trickle of relief seeped through him, easing away a little more of the earlier sting.

Sue sighed. "Actually, since you've been working with Chaz, I've seen amazing progress in him."

"Glad I could help."

"Me too. I mean . . ." Sue wiped crumbs from the corner of her mouth. "I'm really grateful for all the extra time you've put in and for all the things you've taught him. I couldn't have done all that. Thank you."

His marshmallow caught fire, sparing him from having to make eye contact. Watching the dancing flame, he told himself he was glad he could help, glad she was pleased. No. It was more than gladness—much more.

But as he blew the flame out on the charred marshmallow, a searing truth brought him to his senses: he couldn't love a woman who couldn't love him back.

CHAPTER TWENTY

Sue had read the same paragraph aloud from *Charlotte's Web* twice. Luckily for her, Daisy and Donovan didn't mind repetition.

But a nagging reminder of what she'd done to Joe would not let up. Joe's helping his ex-adopted family move into their new home—the home Joe was paying for—served as both a reminder and glaring proof of her colossal mistake up on Table Rock. Why had she panicked and said those things to him? What was wrong with her? She'd accused a man who went out of his way for others of trying to seduce her.

No, worse than seduce. Maybe she hadn't voiced it, but he knew exactly what she was accusing him of, even if she'd only entertained the idea for a few seconds.

Verbally.

Sue groaned.

"Does your tummy ache, Miss Su-san?"

"No, Daisy. I'm just tired." *And miserable.*

"You tired? Want to take a nap and read later?"

Sure. The Rip Van Winkle kind of nap.

The next several days ticked past like a countdown clock. When she flipped the calendar page to December, a renewed rush of panic hit, sending her temples pounding. A large payment was due in three weeks. She tried again to brainstorm a solution to the monthly income shortfall, but nothing came to mind.

The ranch was a sinking ship. She could no longer close her eyes and keep hoping. Maybe it was time to wave the white flag and admit defeat.

And start thinking about other living arrangements for her kids. If she could bring herself to do it.

On Thursday evening, Sue steeled herself and called Layne.

Her friend suggested they file the paperwork now, so they could get the process of finding placements for the kids rolling.

"No."

A thick pause on Layne's end. "No? I don't understand. What else were you—"

"I mean, I know we have to prepare, but I just don't want anything filed yet. Can we hold off on all that? Please?"

"Sorry, Sue. I know how hard this is."

Layne would make sure the kids were well placed when the time came. And though knowing that helped a little, nothing could ease the sting of Sue's failure.

"I'll be ready, Sue. Just say the word. Call me if there's anything else I can do."

"Thanks." She tried for an upbeat tone and almost succeeded. "Maybe you can keep your ears open for any millionaires who have a special place in their heart for unwanted kids."

After the call, Sue invited Linda and Karla into her office and told them she would be letting them go at Christmas. Might as well let them plan for the holiday, since there was a good chance the kids wouldn't be here.

Karla's eyes misted. "I've grown so attached to these kids, Miss Susan."

So have I. More than I ever thought possible. Sue suppressed the rising ache. "I know, Karla. I wish there was some other way. I really do."

Linda reached over and gave Sue's shoulder a pat. "I know how hard you've worked for this place and these kids. I'm still hoping you can—"

Chaz burst into the office screaming, "Help! Call 911!"

Sue sprang to her feet. "What's wrong?"

"It was an accident—I didn't mean to—"

Linda pulled out her cell while Chaz babbled incoherently.

"Chaz—who? Where? Show me!"

With a shaking arm, Chaz pointed out the window toward the shop, gasping between sentences. "Truck launch failed. Crushed Joe. Can't get it off him!"

Oh no. No. NO! Please, God, no! Panic froze her veins, deadening her limbs. "Call Bertie!"

243

she yelled to Karla. Then she ran outside as fast as her knee would allow, tore open the shop door, and burst inside, sick with dread.

It looked as if Joe's truck had slipped off metal ramps and plowed into the now-bent shop door.

No sign of Joe.

A herd of kids and staff poured in behind her.

Heart slamming her ribcage, Sue ran to the front end of the truck.

Pinned between the truck and door, Joe was crumpled over to one side. Not conscious. Not breathing.

She clapped a hand over her mouth. *Dead? He's dead? No, God, please . . . he can't be . . .* With a shaking hand, she touched his neck and felt for a pulse.

A faint beat.

"Linda, tell the paramedics to hurry! He's alive, but I don't know how long—"

Someone screamed.

God, what do I do? She turned to the others. "We need to move the truck. Karla, get inside and put the truck in neutral."

"No! Don't do it, Miss Susan!" Haley squealed. "I saw a movie where a truck pinned this lady against a tree and she was cut in half, but she was still alive until they moved the truck and then she died—"

"Shut up, Haley!" someone yelled.

Karla went green.

"Okay, Karla, you take Linda's phone and wait outside for the paramedics. Linda, put the truck in neutral." Sue touched Joe's neck again. Still a pulse, but she couldn't tell if he was breathing.

At least he had color, a good sign.

"Sue?" Bertie's voice, panicked.

"Bertie, help me! Go to the other side and hold him up. I'll get this side." Sue looked around at the kids. "Deeg, Edgar—get some others and push the truck back." She squeezed in between the truck and shop door and hooked Joe's left arm over her shoulders.

His weight should fall on her as soon as the truck moved.

I don't know if this is the right thing to do. God, help him, please. He loves You. If You're really there, do something. "Okay, push on three. One—two—three!" Sue readied herself to support his weight.

As the truck rolled back, the metal shop door screeched.

Joe slumped forward toward the hood.

Trembling, Sue supported his left side, while Bertie held him on the right.

Linda climbed down from the truck and went to Bertie's side. "Careful. He may have internal injuries."

Several of the girls sobbed.

"Linda, take the kids inside. Bertie?"

Sue was about to ease him down on the ground,

but Joe pulled away from the women, braced both arms on the hood, and straightened himself.

"Joe?" Sue said, barely able to breathe. "Just take it easy. Where are you hurt?"

He sucked in some air, then stood free of the truck and looked around as if getting his bearings. Wobbling slightly, he turned and stared at the dented shop door. "Aluminum."

"What?"

"Oh no, Sue. I think he has a concussion." Bertie squinted up at him. "Try counting backward from a hundred."

Sue laid a hand on his arm. "Joe, tell me where you're hurt."

He glanced around the shop, still looking dazed. "What happened?"

"You just got pulverized," Bertie said. "But between the two of you, I think your pickup got the worst of it, big guy."

Afraid of what she'd find, Sue reached over and gently felt his ribs, then his back. Nothing swollen, punctured, or bleeding. That she could see. "Hold still." She lifted his T-shirt, exposing a solid, muscular stomach.

No blood or bruising—not yet, anyway. But he could have serious internal injuries.

Trembling, she pressed fingers into his belly. "Does this hurt?"

Joe smiled weakly. "Bertie, she's just looking

for an excuse to get her hands on me." His chuckle turned into a sharp, pained cough.

"You could be critically hurt, Joe. You could've—"

Died.

The panic that had sent her running to the shop surged again like a firehouse siren. "Where are those paramedics?"

"I'm okay." Joe worked up a crooked grin. "Tell Chaz it'll take something a lot bigger than a pickup to take me down."

Fear and anger swirled and raced through her like a hot whirlwind, giving her the shakes. "That is *not* funny. I thought you were dead!"

Joe's face instantly sobered. "You did?"

"You were smashed by a truck, Joe. You don't think that could be just a *little* bit deadly?"

"I don't know, let's see." He pounded a fist on his chest a couple times and gave her a dimpled grin. "Guess not. Seriously, Sue, I'm okay. I think it just knocked the wind out of me."

But the more Joe tried to make light of the incident and reassure her he wasn't hurt, the more her panic rose, like a thunderstorm gathering strength. A storm of frightening emotions she couldn't contain.

Something huge and bad was about to hit.

She spun and dashed out the door. A blast of cold air hit and she tore up the trail as fast as she could, desperate to put distance between her and the shop, to outrun the coming meltdown. She headed for the chapel and slipped inside just as the dam burst.

Conjoining waves of relief and fear pulled sobs out of her.

What was wrong with her? Was she totally losing it? She covered her face with her hands and tried to stop crying, but the waves kept coming.

A voice from outside cut through her sobs.

Shaking and gulping air, she stumbled to the far end of the room and ducked into a corner. *Stop it. NOW.*

The door opened and someone entered the chapel.

She pressed herself deep into the corner and clapped both hands over her mouth to keep the sounds from ratting her out, her breath coming in erratic bursts. Trying in vain to be quiet, she listened for the intruder.

Joe had followed Sue up the trail, still slightly dazed. The way she'd fled set off a warning bell. He'd seen her angry, but this was odd. When he slipped inside the chapel, muffled sounds carried from the far end of the room.

The sounds of someone crying.

Following the sound he moved toward the front.

Sue quivered in the corner.

He stopped a few feet from her, less dazed but now more confused than ever. She was clearly upset and trying to hide it. Upset with him?

No, she never bothered to hide her irritation with him before.

What then? "Sue?"

A gasp, then a hiccup.

He took a step closer but hesitated. Knowing Sue, she'd probably come out of her corner swinging.

Sue moved, now visible in a small shaft of light. Her cheeks and lashes glistened, her lips trembled.

He stepped closer and kept his voice low. "Don't worry, Sue, I'll fix the—"

Something he couldn't identify mingled in the depths of her eyes. Definitely not anger. The rapid rise and fall of her chest and the way she looked at him nearly dropped him.

He swallowed hard to unlock his throat. "What's wrong?"

In one move, she reached for him and buried her face in his chest, knotting his shirt in her fists.

Stunned, he folded her into his arms.

And she let him.

His chest tightened. *Oh man . . .*

"You scared me half to death, Joe."

Her whisper sent a strange surge of hope through him. "Shh, it's okay." His heart pounded. "It's okay. Everything's fine now."

She didn't answer, just hid herself against him. She smelled sweet and clean, like breeze-dried cotton.

He held her tighter and murmured soothing sounds, cursing his hammering heart. She had to feel that.

Sue lifted her face and opened her mouth to speak, but nothing came. Her trembling lips remained parted, an easy distance from his.

Ohhh maaan . . .

A loose curl clung to her wet cheek.

With an unsteady hand, he reached up and gently stroked it away.

Her eyes drifted closed at his touch.

Lord, have mercy . . .

Heart thumping like concert speakers, he captured her mouth with his. Her lips, small but full and so soft, yielded to his, melting him instantly. He marveled at the tenderness and sweetness of her touch, the nearness of her. His hand slipped into her hair and caressed it.

A tiny sound escaped her.

It sent a ripple through him that threatened to tackle him at the knees. He cupped her face and kept kissing her, needing her warmth, needing that spark of caring he had seen in her eyes. He ached to know the tenderness he saw there, to feel it, drink it in. His mind lost everything but how amazing it felt to hold her.

At the sound of approaching sirens, her lips

murmured against his. "Joe," she whispered.

Her warm breath beside his mouth sent a pleasant tingle across his skin. Eyes closed, he touched his forehead to hers, trying to calm his raging heart and his powerful need to hold her and kiss her until she couldn't see straight.

A small shove to his chest forced him off balance.

He opened his eyes, tried to focus in the semi-dark.

Sue tugged against his embrace, her eyes flashing fiery sparks.

"Sue? What—?"

She untangled herself from his arms and jabbed his pec with a finger. "Don't do that again." Side-stepping him, she scurried away like a trapped creature that had burst free.

His pulse still raged. "Don't do what? Nearly get killed or kiss you?"

At the door, she turned. "Both!"

CHAPTER TWENTY-ONE

He's dying! God, if You're there, please help him!
Sue woke with a gasp and tried to focus on the dim corridor. She'd dozed off in the hall chair. Faint rays of dawn peeked beneath a bedroom door. She closed her eyes. The vivid nightmare of Joe being crushed to death by the truck lingered, reviving a haunting sense of dread. In her dream, she'd asked God to help Joe.

Only that part wasn't a dream. She *had* asked God to help him.

When the medics who had responded to the 911 call looked Joe over, he'd checked out fine. Completely unharmed. What were the chances a person could come through a crazy ordeal like that without a scratch?

There was a simple explanation. There had to be.

And while we're explaining things . . . There was the other incident. In the chapel. His arms surrounding her. The feeling of absolute safety. His tender, need-filled kisses.

Please tell me that was just part of the dream.
But like a homing beacon on a starry night, she

couldn't ignore the truth. That was no dream. Kissing Joe in the chapel had felt more real than anything had in a long time.

No. It was probably the combination of everything—from Joe being pinned by the truck to her panicked meltdown to Joe finding her and holding her like that, kissing her like that . . .

And not being afraid, and losing herself for a crazy moment, not wanting it to end . . .

The danger was over. So was the kiss. She needed to make absolutely sure there would be no more opportunities for *that* to happen again.

She woke the five upstairs girls, then headed downstairs and woke Daisy and Sonja, Ringo trailing her all the way. Once Daisy was dressed and ready to go, Sue went to the kitchen and started breakfast. But last night's events had jangled her nerves and left her stomach in knots.

Had she witnessed an answer to prayer? Or a freak chance of really good luck?

And what about the chapel?

No. She was *not* thinking about that.

But you kissed him.

Right after your little psycho meltdown.

KISSED him.

Sue slammed the milk on the sideboard, sloshing some out of the pitcher and onto the floor.

Ringo lapped at the milk.

You've made a mess, Sooz. How're you going to clean this up?

With a groan, Sue gathered cereal boxes and set them beside the milk.

Cori, Tatiana, and Brandi stumbled into the dining hall and started setting out bowls and tableware while the other girls arrived. The boys filed in together and took their places at the table. Hair combed, shoes tied. Not bad. Joe also smelled clean and was looking mighty—

Don't look.

Avoiding his gaze, Sue did a head count.

Eleven. One boy missing. Chaz.

She went to the study, preparing her usual speech about taking a break from schoolwork and coming in to eat breakfast.

He wasn't there.

She returned to the dining hall. "Where's Chaz?"

Joe gave her a puzzled look. "Probably getting a jump on his schoolwork."

"No, he's not there. Did you see him leave the dorm?"

"Yeah. About half an hour ago." He headed for the door. "I'll check the dorm again."

Sue did a quick search of the main house, then went out back.

Joe met her coming from the boys' dorm. "He's not there either."

She nodded and avoided the raw question

burning in his eyes. Whatever Joe wanted to discuss, she was not ready to deal with it. She hurried around the building to the front yard and then went inside the shop, averting her gaze from the crumpled shop door.

Just as she turned to leave, Chaz's head popped up from behind Joe's truck.

"Chaz? What are you doing?"

Pushing his glasses higher on his nose, he came out, clipboard in hand.

While Sue sent Joe a text saying she'd found the boy, Chaz circled the truck, tapping a pencil on the end of the clipboard in a rapid rhythm.

"Chaz?"

Muttering to himself, he stopped to scratch notes on his sheet.

She waited until the boy stopped his rounds and then laid a hand gently on his shoulder. "Whatcha doing?"

"I had it all figured out." Frowning, he pulled away from her touch and inspected the metal ramps that were knocked askew near the truck's front tires. Jotted more notes.

Joe came in, closing the side door with a soft click.

"Maybe later you and Mister Joe can work all that out. Why don't you come on inside and eat?"

Chaz hummed loudly and off-key. He circled the truck again, ignoring both adults.

"Chaz, Mister Joe can—"

The boy closed his eyes and kept humming.

Ah. Deflecting trauma.

"Chaz, listen. Mister Joe is okay. He's not hurt, he's right here. See?"

Chaz shook his head. "First, I need to figure out what went wrong. It must be in the truck's variables. I didn't have them all listed. The ramps failed . . ."

Sue turned to Joe.

He nodded. "Hey, Chaz. Let's go over all your notes together after breakfast, okay?"

The boy shook his head and paced alongside the truck, breathing short bursts from flared nostrils. He shoved his glasses higher on his nose. "Can't stay here," he muttered. "I'm gonna get sent away again."

"No, buddy. It's okay. See?" Joe held up both arms. "No harm done. Accidents happen. You don't need to go anywhere."

Chaz stopped at the front of the truck and stared at the spot where Joe had been pinned.

Sue shuddered. The horror of seeing him in that spot was still too fresh for her as well.

"The door is an aluminum alloy." Chaz lowered his clipboard to his side. He brought it up again and wrote as he spoke. "The metal is extremely pliable. Combined with J-man's weight and overall mass, the majority of the impact was absorbed by the soft metal, thus lessening the probability of damage or injury." He didn't turn around, but kept staring at the mangled door.

Poor kid. Sue's heart twisted.

Joe stepped closer to the boy. "Hey, it's okay, man. God was looking out for me. He does that. He watches over us. Even when we make mistakes."

Chaz didn't move.

"And in case you're wondering, I'm not mad. We're cool, okay?"

The boy shot a glance over his shoulder at Joe, then focused on his clipboard and nodded. He turned and darted out of the shop.

Sue allowed her gaze to drift to the door.

"Don't worry," Joe said quietly. "I can fix that."

Fix it? She could barely keep from cringing in horror at the memory of him trapped there, and all he cared about was fixing the stupid door? She wanted to close her eyes like Chaz and shut it out. *All* of it. The horror, the overwhelming relief that he was okay, the incredible sensation of kissing him, of being held for a fleeting moment like someone cherished.

But shutting her eyes and pretending it hadn't happened wouldn't make it go away.

"Joe, what happened last night in the chapel . . ."

His gaze brushed a stroke across her mouth before rising to meet her eyes.

The sound of a car motor and crunching gravel caught her attention. She went outside and Joe followed.

Layne emerged from her sedan, platinum blonde hair dazzling in the sun, dressed in her usual pencil skirt and tailored jacket.

Sue resisted the urge to look down at the baggy sweatshirt she was wearing and greeted Layne with a smile.

"Hey, Sue, look at you. I can't even tell you injured that knee." Layne smiled and then turned that gorgeous smile on Joe.

A little claw latched onto Sue's heart and twisted.

"You must be Joe. I'm Layne Stevenson." She offered her hand and he shook it. "My brother Dan talks very highly of you."

Joe shook his head. "Dan's a great guy. He's the best driller and the most dependable guy I've ever worked with. How's he doing?"

As Layne filled him in on her brother's latest business venture, she touched her hair a lot.

Did she always do that when she talked to people? Sue tried to remember.

"I'm sorry to hear about the loss of your other friend. David, wasn't it?"

"Yeah." A clouded look crossed over his face. "Dave's in a better place now."

Layne's gaze traveled up to Joe's hair. "After what you guys did for him, Dan decided he liked the shaved head look and kept it. Did you ever decide who won the bet?"

With a chuckle, Joe just shook his head, a flush creeping into his face.

"What bet?" Sue asked. This she had to hear.

Layne turned to Sue. "The way I heard it, when their friend was losing his hair to chemo, Joe bet he'd make a better looking bald guy than Dave and shaved his head for the duration of the treatment."

"You did that, Joe?"

Joe shrugged. "Something like that."

Layne examined Joe's features as if judging for herself who could win a contest of good looks. "But then Dan caught on that Joe's real plan was to make sure their friend didn't go through his hair loss alone, so Dan shaved his head too. That was really awesome of you guys to do that."

"Just guys goofing around." Joe shrugged again, the color in his face deepening.

As he struggled with Layne's praise in his quiet humility, Sue's heart sank. How typical of Joe to do something like that for a friend. And how rotten of her to make the assumptions she had when she first met him. Like the paranoid assumption she'd made on top of Table Rock. Shame ignited her cheeks. Why were rash assumptions, panicked reactions, and irrational behaviors becoming frequent occurrences?

And why did they all seem to involve Joe Paterson?

Joe locked her gaze with that same deep, questioning look she'd seen earlier.

She couldn't tear her eyes away. Suddenly, she wanted nothing more than a full-throttle ride on a long stretch of road. As far and as fast as that bike would go.

"Sue?"

Sue blinked at Layne. Apparently Layne was waiting for an answer.

"Sorry. What did you say?"

"Why don't we go into your office?"

The women left Joe and went inside. Layne took a seat on the other side of Sue's desk. "So. Let's brainstorm some income ideas."

Sue sighed. "I've exhausted every idea I could think of. What are you thinking?"

"I'm thinking you just worked your tail off to raise past due funds, but what you need are big guns for the long haul. A couple of big donors."

"Right. Big donors would be ideal. It's just that, at the moment, I'm fresh out of those." Sue eyed her friend. "Do you know of a sponsor in search of a charity to support?"

"Not specifically, but I know where you could meet some potential donors. The Children's Law Foundation Annual Benefit Dinner. It's attended by some of the state's wealthiest people."

"Benefit dinner." Sue looked down at her

sweatshirt and jeans. "No problem. I'll call my fairy godmother, change into something très chic, and crash the party."

"Or you could go with me. As district liaison, I have tickets. Perks of the job, remember? You know, you might want to consider coming back to work for the county. These connections always come in handy."

Sue tried to keep her tone light. "I may be back with the county sooner than you think if I don't find a way to save this place."

Layne leaned back in her chair. "Come to the dinner. Meet some rich, philanthropic people. What harm could it do? I mean, aside from the hives you're sure to get from wearing a dress and heels."

"Heels?"

Layne's smile put a sparkle in her eyes. "Oh, trust me. You're going to clean up hotter than Angelina Jolie. Especially with my expert help."

"Whoa, I don't—"

"But I'm thinking more of a classic look for you, like Grace Kelly."

"No. I wouldn't be comfortable all dressed up and mingling with lawyers and D.A.s and rich foundation types."

"Who said anything about comfort? If you want to gain financial support, you're going to have to work a little for it."

"Work? Getting poured into a cocktail dress

and strapping on stilettos doesn't sound like any kind of 'work' I'm interested in."

Layne clapped her hands together. "Cocktail dress! Yes! I have one that would be stunning on you. I can't wait to see you in it." She tipped her head and gazed at Sue's feet. "And if you're dead set on stilettos, I can get those too."

Fabulous. Sue leaned back in her seat and looked skyward, muttering, "These kids have no idea what I endure for them." But even as she said it, a thought pinned her beneath its weight. Nothing she'd done for them had been enough. And now the kids would be the ones paying for her failure.

Without warning, tears sprang.

"Whoa." Layne leaned forward. "Something's wrong."

Sue huffed out a laugh. "Ya think? Let's make a list."

"I know you care about these kids, Sue. And I'm going to do everything I can to help get them placed in good homes if things don't work out."

Nodding, Sue sniffed as tears continued to spring. If things didn't work out, she would have to stand back and watch these kids get torn from this place and each other and dropped into the frightening unknown. She wiped her eyes. "Thanks."

"But you seem . . . on edge or something. Like more than usual."

Sue took a long look out the window toward the shop. "Yeah, well, things are kind of chaotic right now."

"I'll bet. And how does Joe Paterson figure into that?"

Way more than he should. Sue examined the knotted hands in her lap.

"Because I'm sensing something there."

When Sue looked up, Layne's gentle, sympathetic smile offered an irresistible invitation to relieve some of the pressure building inside. "I kissed him."

Layne huffed out an incredulous laugh. "You *what?*"

"I mean—we kissed. It just happened. I don't even know how."

"A spontaneous, mutual kiss? Are you kidding me?" Layne laughed again. "Those are the best kind."

"Yeah, well, it's a major problem."

"Oh, absolutely." Layne didn't even try to suppress her amusement. "Tell me what happened." After Sue filled her in on the whole story, Layne pursed her lips. "Hmm. He came looking for you right after his near miss with death. I wonder why."

Sue stared hard at her smiling friend. "I don't know, and I don't care."

"I knew it." Layne turned her attention toward the shop. "It had to happen eventually."

Sue wasn't taking the bait. "You don't know anything. And I wish I hadn't told you. Now you're going to analyze this and try to tell me I'm—"

Layne's eyebrows shot up.

"No, see, I'm on to your game. I know what my life is. I don't need this. And I sure don't need you telling me I'm falling for a guy who's leaving in a few weeks. I don't need to feel—" There was no way to verbalize the full extent of the whirling mess her emotions were in. Or the crazy fear those feelings were stirring deep inside her. *I don't need to feel. Period.*

"I hate to say it, but I think you already do."

I can't. Fleeting moments of feeling connected, feeling loved, were always followed by long stretches of emptiness. She'd had enough of that.

"Sue, listen to me. You're just scared. You've kept men at arm's length for so long you don't know what to do when someone sweet and amazing—not to mention *insanely* gorgeous— slips past your guard and works his way into your heart."

Of course Layne would have Joe totally pegged in one meeting. But as far as Sue's heart was concerned? No. Not happening. She shook her head.

"What? You don't think I know how you are?"

"It's a lot more complicated than you know, Layne. Joe needs someone different." *Way differ-*

ent. "And my life is complicated enough without adding things I don't need. Besides, it doesn't matter. He's leaving."

"Are you sure?"

Sue eyed her friend. "Yes. He needs the income from his next oil rig job so he can support that ex-family of his. There's nothing for him here."

"Okay, have it your way. You're in control." Layne rose and leaned over the stacks of file folders on Sue's desk. "Hey, why don't you bring the staff and kids to my place for a hot tub party next Friday? They'd have a blast. Make it a sleepover. Then you and I can slip out to attend that benefit dinner. There's no risk, other than the small chance you'd have a good time."

Rising, Sue looked through the window at the compound. "Do you remember how hard it was for me to start this place, knowing the risk I was taking? Reaching blindly into the unknown? Do you know what that feels like?" Her voice wavered and she lowered it. "Well, these kids know exactly how it feels. Nothing hurts worse than reaching for something you've only dreamed of and being disappointed. There's a huge risk of being hurt."

"But without risk, you never even get a shot at your dream."

"What good is a dream that gets my kids' hopes up and then crushes them when it falls apart and leaves them empty?"

265

"Dreams give hope, Sue. Even if they're short lived. What good is life without hope?" Layne joined her at the window. "When you take a risk, at least you're alive."

Sue looked Layne in the eye.

"Besides, like I said, there's no risk in this. It's just dinner. And it's for your kids. Aren't they worth one last shot?"

Sue nodded. "Yeah. They're worth it." She heaved a sigh. "All right, get out the hairspray and heels. Let's do this."

CHAPTER TWENTY-TWO

At lights out, Sue helped Linda get the girls settled down for the night, then headed out back to her quarters. A full moon bathed the backyard in a milky glow. She paused at her doorstep.

Sweet strains of guitar music drifted across the lawn from the boys' dorm.

Sue closed her eyes and inhaled deeply, willing the crisp air to cleanse her thoughts, her agitation. But the air didn't reach deep enough. Too much had happened, disrupting order and making a mess of things. She'd never felt this way. And she couldn't keep feeling this way. She couldn't long for something she couldn't hold on to, couldn't sample fleeting joys that left her wanting more. She'd put a stop to those kinds of empty aches long ago.

And if she'd stopped it before, she could stop it now.

Heart racing, she went across the yard and knocked on the dorm door.

The music stopped.

She pressed folded arms tightly against her fluttering stomach.

What you don't want can't disappoint you.

Joe opened the door and filled the doorway, blocking most of the light coming from inside. His gaze fell to her tightly crossed arms and settled there.

"Joe, can we talk?"

"Okay." Joe glanced over his shoulder, then stepped outside, leaving the door slightly cracked.

"I want to apologize. For the incident yesterday."

"Apologize?" His brows rose. "Oh, you mean the truck thing."

Oh. Right. She probably should apologize for Chaz plowing into him with a truck. "Yes, I'm very sorry about that, of course. But I meant the *other* thing." She peeked inside the dorm and lowered her voice to a near whisper. "The kiss. That was a total mistake. I'm sorry. That won't happen again."

He couldn't have looked more surprised if Sue had said she'd just been drafted to play in the NFL.

Sue tore her gaze from the confusion on his face. Whatever was going through his mind, she didn't want to know.

Liar . . .

"Okay, just so we're clear on that. And there's something else. Since the cops don't think you'll get your stuff back, I want you to have that guitar.

268

I never use it. Take it with you when you leave here."

"What?" He shook his head. "No, Sue, I couldn't—"

"Please, Joe. Just take it." She gave him her I-mean-business look. Surely he'd seen it before and knew she had no trouble backing it up.

He searched her eyes. The moonlight lit his features and deepened the contours of his face in shadow. "All right then. Thank you."

Nodding, she turned and walked away.

"Sue?"

She quickened her pace. There was nothing more to discuss.

As her shape retreated in the glowing moonlight, a hundred thoughts clamored for Joe's attention. One rang out above the rest, relieving him of the weight that had been pressing on him all day.

She wasn't mad.

The woman who, less than a week ago, had feared an unthinkable attack from him. The same woman he'd cornered a few days later and kissed without a thought about anything but how much he wanted to.

And she wasn't mad.

And not only that, she apologized.

Like she was accepting responsibility for the kiss.

Like she'd *wanted* to kiss him.

That thought sent a rush through him. He'd spent the morning preparing to be kicked off the premises or to hear an earful from her at the very least. He spent the rest of the day in a fog because lingering sensations of her lips on his tore the air clean out of him.

Did she feel something for him too?

It took everything in his power not to sprint across the lawn and stop her.

Did she love him?

Whoa. Think, man.

He would be moving across the country soon, so if she did, did it matter? Besides, he'd been forgetting that this wasn't about him. He was here to help Sue discover she had a Father who loved her with an immeasurable, unfailing love.

Joe sank to the top step and pressed palms to his temples.

This wasn't about him.

He needed to keep his feelings out of it. She needed to know she was honored and loved more than she could possibly imagine in a way that only God could. If he didn't back off, he could sabotage the whole thing.

He needed to focus. No more getting in the way. And no more kissing.

During free time on Saturday, Joe sat across from Chaz and helped the boy work on his guitar chords while Jasmine and Vince picked out songs.

Sue passed through the foyer but stopped when she saw them. "What are you guys doing?"

"Picking songs for chapel tomorrow." Jasmine held up a stack of music.

"Chapel?" Her quizzical expression moved from Jasmine to Joe.

"Yeah," Joe said. "I was going to ask you if—"

"Can we go, Miss Susan?" Jasmine scrambled to her feet and rushed to her. "Please, please, please?"

No telling how Sue would feel about being put on the spot like this, but then again, it might work.

Sue's gaze fell to Jasmine's eager smile.

How could anyone with a beating heart turn down that sweet face?

"I guess that would be okay."

Jasmine whooped and flattened Sue with a hug, knocking her back a step. "You come too, Miss Susan. Please?"

Joe fought back a grin. He couldn't have planned this better if he'd tried. Maybe the songs and a short devotional would help her understand about God, help open her heart to Him.

Sue looked into Jasmine's eyes. "I don't think—"

"We will sing songs like when you listen outside to Papa Joe sing. It *so* good, Miss Susan. You see."

Sue went pink. Her mouth opened, but no words came.

She'd been listening? Even better. "Yeah, Sue, I'd love for you to come." *Whoa. Ease up on the L word.*

Jasmine pulled a puppy-dog look, complete with a whimper.

Sue's gaze shifted away. Excuses were probably firing off in that pretty, blonde head faster than an AK-47.

Father, help her understand how much You love her, the price You paid for her. Maybe she feels too small, too vulnerable around You. Help her know she can trust You.

The words of his own prayer suddenly hit him, snagged at his chest.

"I don't have to dress up or anything, do I?"

Grinning like a fool, Joe shook his head. "Nah, it's come as you are."

Joe was pleased to see that most of the kids participated in the singing, even if they didn't know the words. Jasmine might not have understood the lyrics, but her voice was packed with pure joy. Chaz followed Joe's fingers on the guitar without blinking.

During the worship, Joe stole occasional peeks at Sue. He couldn't help it. He did his best to focus on the Lord and on the words he was singing, but her reaction to the music caught him.

A few times, she closed her eyes and seemed to lose herself in the song. At other times, she tensed up so tightly she looked like she would bolt. The woman could go from putty one moment to a steel casing pipe the next.

But she *could* be putty . . .

No. He needed to keep his mind on the bigger picture. God wanted her heart. That was what Joe needed to keep in mind. Which wasn't easy. Whenever his gaze traveled to the corner of the room where he'd found her the other night, he remembered the look in her eyes. And the way she clung to him, how good she felt in his arms.

After the last song, he read from the third chapter in Ephesians and gave a short devotional about the length and width and height and depth of God's love. Chaz hung on every word, but Sue looked restless. Joe wrapped up the service with a prayer.

He'd barely said "amen" when Sue shot to her feet and beelined for the door.

"Sue, wait."

She hesitated as the kids filed out.

He needed to do this now, strike while the iron was hot. "I wondered if we could talk."

Sue cast a distracted glance at the kids heading back to the house with Karla. "For a minute, I guess."

"Great. Why don't we sit?"

She perched on the edge of the bench nearest the door, hands in her lap.

Taking the bench across from her, Joe cleared his throat. "So, what did you think?"

"It was nice." She swept her gaze around the small room, pausing on The Corner, now well lit with the rays of midday sun.

"Glad to hear that."

"The music is . . . different," she said slowly. "I've never heard anything like it."

"That's good—I think." He chuckled.

This shouldn't be too hard. He'd shared his faith with roughnecks and roustabouts. God had cracked some of the toughest guys Joe had ever known.

He cleared his throat again. "I just wanted to say I hope you know how much God loves you, Sue."

"Loves?"

He could almost see her thoughts churning.

"Listen, Joe, I get that you want to share your faith with me, but I still remember the answer I got when I asked God if He cared. It was a big, fat no. And you know what? It's fine. I moved on."

Wow. "Want to talk about it?"

She pinned him with her gaze. "Remember me telling you about being locked in my room as a little kid? That time, I lived with some relatives. I spent many days locked in that room. I went hungry a lot. People hurt me. It went on for so long I started to think this was normal. Then I heard somebody on TV saying Jesus loved me and wanted to save me and that all I had to do was ask. So I asked Jesus to save me." She smoothed a wrinkle in her slacks. "But nobody came. I even wrote a note that said, 'Jesus, please save me. The people here are so mean.' Then I slipped the note out under my bedroom door." She let out a wry laugh. "See, I was always thinking. Except I didn't think that one through very well." A wince crossed her face like a shadow.

Dread crept up his spine. "What happened?"

Her expression was fixed and distant, as if she was seeing an old horror flick playing in her head. "That note earned me one of the worst beatings I ever had."

What kind of sick monsters . . .?

"But it actually worked in my favor. I still had the bruises when I went to school a week later and somebody called DHS. They took me away and I rode the foster home circuit from then on." She shifted her gaze to the wooden cross on the north wall. "Maybe, in a way, God did answer my prayer."

He clasped his hands, resisting the urge to take hold of hers. "What you went through was horrible, Sue. I'm sorry."

She shrugged. "It's long past. The thing is if that's God's love, I'm better off without it. I'm no superpower, but I think I can do a *little* better than that by these kids." She frowned at her hands again. "Or at least I thought I could."

He'd been let down by people he'd trusted. He knew how pain and disappointment could burrow in and steal every last bit of hope. "God knows the pain you went through, Sue. When we suffer, so does He. But there's more to life and suffering than what we can see. He knows you and loves you more than anyone. He is good and He wants you to trust Him."

"Trust Him?"

"Yeah."

"Like you do?"

Joe nodded.

Her eyes roamed over his features. "You know, I've seen you, Joe. It seems like you really believe He's here." She looked around the room warily, as if someone would materialize from the walls. "That creeps me out."

"There's nothing scary about it. Just means I can talk to Him. So can you."

"Talk?" She glanced at the plain wooden podium at the front of the chapel. "One of the first things I learned is that talk is cheap." She rose. "Thanks, but I gotta go."

As all five foot two of her disappeared out the chapel door, Joe hissed out a sigh. Guys on the rig had been butter compared to her.

Back to square one.

Over the next few days, Sue avoided Joe as much as possible. She'd worked hard to erase the memories of the truck mishap and that kiss. Now the man had to go and throw God into the mix? She didn't need any more chaos.

Thursday afternoon, Bertie brought her crew to the barn where Sue and her group were doing critter duty. "What's the plan for getting the kids to Layne's place tomorrow night?"

The more Sue thought about Layne's benefit dinner idea, the more she let herself hope the plan might actually work. She just wished it didn't depend on her getting all dolled up and trying to make clever conversation.

Bertie cleaned her glasses on the hem of her flannel shirt. "Want me to haul a load of kids in the veedub?"

"Yeah, if you don't mind."

"So why did you give Karla and Linda the night off? Joe and I could use a couple extra hands with you gone to that fancy-schmancy dinner."

"Layne arranged for some CPS interns to come and help so they can log in some training hours. Which saves me a little on payroll. Plus, Layne's husband, Ted, will be there. He's a big guy, so with Joe and Ted acting as bouncers, I doubt the kids will try anything out of line."

"Bouncers." Bertie handed a pitchfork to Edgar and a broom to Vince. "You know, I was thinking of going into that line of work at one time."

Sue smothered a chuckle. "Yeah, I could totally see that. What changed your mind?"

"The choice between that and being a social worker was a tough call. But in the end, you gotta decide where the biggest payoff is."

"Payoff?" Sue helped Jasmine lift a bucket of goat milk and poured it into the can. "And you chose this?"

"Yep. Gotta follow the big bucks." She winked and walked away with Deeg.

What kind of a life had Bertie given up in order to work with these kids? And how much longer would she be a part of their lives?

Bertie's sharp voice rose from the other end of the barn. Ringo shot past Sue and streaked out the door, tail down.

Sue hurried in the direction the dog had come from.

Inside the last stall, Brandi stood glaring at Bertie, arms crossed tightly to her chest, while Bertie held a pitchfork upright.

"What's going on?" Sue's gaze traveled from one to the other.

Brandi's scowl shifted away from both of them.

"Let's hear it, Miss," Bertie said, voice taut.

"Nothing's going on." Brandi glowered at a cobwebby corner of the stall.

Bertie turned to Sue. "When I came in, she was threatening the dog with the pitchfork."

"That's a lie!" Brandi glared at Bertie "I was moving some hay. The stupid dog was growling at me, because he doesn't like the fork. I was just shooing him out."

Bertie's grip on the pitchfork tightened. "Shooing him out, huh?" The words came out clipped. She turned to Sue, anger seething in her eyes. "Well, my bad, I guess. It just *looked* like she had him trapped in a corner and was fixing to spear him."

Brandi's expression turned cool and impassive. "Well?"

The girl muttered something foul that Sue didn't fully catch but didn't care to hear repeated.

"Okay, since you won't be straight with me, you're off critter duty."

"Tragic. You think I care? Well, I don't. I don't care about your stinking chickens or your stupid nerdo-freak kids, and I especially don't care about this lame joke of a home."

Sue's heart sank. She counted to five, then ten. The last thing she needed was to engage in a battle with a lippy kid who was only lashing out because she thought chores were some kind of medieval torture. She didn't have the time or energy for a battle. "Fine." Bands of pain tightened across her forehead. "Since you hate it here so much, maybe you'd like to check out the hospitality at the state juvenile detention center."

Lips cinched, Brandi met Sue's gaze. *You wouldn't,* her eyes said.

Try me, Sue answered with a steady look.

Finally, the girl broke eye contact and shrugged. "Sweet. Whatever. I don't care."

"Go inside, Brandi. And stay away from Ringo."

The girl made a wide path around Bertie and left.

Bertie raised a single brow.

"I know," Sue said. "She's looking to pick a fight, but I can't deal with her attitude right now. Not with everything that's going on."

Bertie nodded and handed Sue the pitchfork. "Sure hope you know what you're doing."

That makes two of us.

CHAPTER TWENTY-THREE

"Oh. My. Word. What did I tell you?" Layne's glossy lips stretched into a broad smile. She turned Sue around to face the vanity mirror in Layne's bedroom. "Can I call it or what? You are one breathtaking blend of classic beauty and five-alarm hotness. Wow."

Sue stared at her reflection. Wow was right. *That* wasn't her. At least, not any version she recognized.

Layne had curled Sue's hair and brushed it out into a shimmering cascade of golden waves. With mascara on her lashes and a touch of black liner, her dark eyes appeared luminous and intense. Mysterious. Deep red lipstick accentuated the fullness of her lips.

"Well?" Layne leaned beside her.

"Unbelievable." Sue winced. "Where'd you find lipstick in Hooker Red?"

Layne laughed and shook her head. "It looks amazing on you. And so does that dress. Do you have any idea how insanely hot you are?"

"Great. Just what I need to gain the respect and support of wealthy philanthropists."

Layne spritzed Sue's hair with a finishing mist of hairspray.

A knock on the door came, then Bertie poked her head inside. "Layne? Your husband's calling for you."

With a worried frown, Layne stopped spraying her own French twist and set down the can. "I forgot I was going to find him some antacid. Be right back."

As she rushed out, Bertie came in and cocked an eyebrow at Sue, then spun a three-sixty and looked around the room. "Have you seen my boss around here anywhere?"

"Funny, Bert. Didn't I tell you? You're next."

That got a deep cackle out of the older woman. "Have you *seen* this place? It's enormous. And that hot tub! Even though it could float the Titanic, I don't think there'll be any water left by the time the kids get done with it."

Sue studied her reflection and resisted the urge to wipe the color from her lips. "Funny."

"No. Seriously."

Sue groaned.

With a chuckle, Bertie slipped out.

Sue stood and took one last look at herself in Layne's full-length mirror. The dress Layne had loaned her was very flattering. Black and close-fitting, it had a modest *V* in the front, a plunging *V* in the back, and a tapered skirt that some-how gave the illusion of length to her legs. Not bad. However, the strappy heels, though they looked good, were four inches of neck-breaking mayhem.

Sue went to the front room and waited for Layne.

The faint sounds of squealing and laughter carried from beyond the adjacent den.

With Joe and Ted Stevenson helping supervise, there was little chance of returning from the benefit dinner to any blood or mis-launched vehicles. She hoped.

As she admired a view of the Stevensons' front lawn through the living room window, Layne returned.

Concern creased her brow. "I was hoping it was just indigestion, but Ted is throwing up and he's in a lot of pain. I think I need to take him to the ER." Worry brewed in her eyes. "I'm sorry."

"Oh no, Layne, don't be! I just hope he's okay."

Layne went to her purse and slipped out an envelope. "Here's your ticket."

"What? No. I'm not going without you."

"Sure you are. It'll be fine. I'll call the assistant DA and make sure he introduces you to the right people. Piece of cake. You can do this."

"But I don't know anybody. And I feel ridiculous."

Layne blinked. "Are you *kidding* me? You are forty-seven kinds of gorgeous. It'll be fine, trust me. All you have to do is introduce yourself and talk about your kids."

Easy for someone to say who's beautiful, assertive, and oozing with charm. Suppressing a groan, Sue took the offered ticket.

Layne cocked her head at the other one. "I won't be needing this. Know anyone you'd like to treat to a five-course steak dinner?"

Squeals erupted from the den. Jasmine and Haley burst into the living room with towels wrapped around their swimsuits, legs dripping.

Haley saw Sue and stopped.

Jasmine crashed into Haley and gasped.

"Wow, Miss Susan!" Haley breathed. "You're beautiful."

"Like movie star!" Jasmine said, eyes wide.

"That's *really* funny, you two." Joe's voice boomed from the den. He emerged in a drenched T-shirt and soaked jeans, rubbing his hair with a towel. "Ever hear of paybacks? I'd run too, if—" He froze when his gaze fell on Sue.

The raw admiration in his eyes sent a warm tingle through her. Her cheeks ignited.

Layne touched Sue's arm. "Hey, Sue, maybe Joe could . . ." She studied Joe, her head tilted as if sizing him up. "Oh, yes. Perfect."

"Yeah." Joe's gaze was still transfixed on Sue. "Perfect."

The girls giggled.

"I'm glad you agree." Layne stepped toward him.

Joe blinked at Layne. "W-what?"

Layne tucked the extra ticket in his hand. "I hope you can eat again. You're going to be Sue's dinner date."

At the convention center, Joe held the door open for Sue.

She went inside, sneaking another peek at the tailored black dinner jacket and crisp white shirt that emphasized the breadth of his chest.

It was still hard to believe Layne's former-pro-linebacker husband had a suit that fit Joe. And even harder to believe that Joe had agreed to do this. During the chaos of Sue's instructing Layne's interns how to help Bertie, and Layne's rushed departure with her poor husband, Joe had changed clothes, run some gel through his hair, and borrowed a splash of some tantalizing cologne. In ten minutes, he'd morphed from a brawny crew boss into a stylish dinner escort.

Except Joe didn't strike her as the schmoozing-with-society type. He struck her more as—

Gorgeous. As in drop-dead.

She fanned her cheeks and scanned the crowd. Most of the guests mingled nearer the bar set up at one end of the room.

While Sue waited in the receiving area, Joe presented their tickets and got their table number. From where she stood, the cut of his jacket emphasized the contour of his shoulders and waist even more. Sue tore her gaze away and surveyed the décor.

Round banquet tables filled the center of the ballroom. The tables were dressed in black, white, and gold. Even the seats were draped in black and tied with soft, white bows in the back. Elegant, sparkling, and overwhelming.

Joe joined her. His gaze fell to her lips, then darted away. He nodded at the crowd of guests clustered at one end of the room. "I guess it's mingle time. They'll seat everyone in a while." A dimple punctuated his quirky half smile. "So, what do you think?"

I think you're about to set off every fire alarm in the place.

"I think I'd better do what I came for and get this over with," Sue said in low tones.

Joe placed a hand lightly at the small of her back, sending a tingle of warmth up her spine, and guided her through the crowd.

Sue smiled at an elegantly dressed couple, hoping her smile didn't look as phony as it felt.

Everyone had a drink in hand.

Everyone? She eyed Joe, suddenly on alert. Did he drink? Though she'd made her no-alcohol policy clear at the ranch, he might not think it applied to a function like this.

Joe escorted her toward the bar. As he surveyed the crowd, he leaned down close, giving her another whiff of that divine cologne. "So, what's

286

the attack plan?" he said in tones just loud enough for her to hear. "Want me to create a diversion while you corner the lady with the grapefruit-sized diamond?"

"Brilliant plan, Joe, really. But I think I'll stick with a covert ops plan for now. Get some more intel on the layout first."

He scanned the room, nodding. "Roger that. I'll just go check out that unsecured quadrant over there and wait for your signal."

As Joe moved toward the appetizer tables, Sue relaxed. The only controlled substance calling to Joe was the scent of hot wings and bacon-wrapped scallops.

Time to get to work, Sooz.

A sea of strange faces surrounded her, making Sue long to be anywhere but here. This was so not her element. And so not her way of doing things—presenting herself in need and asking people to help. She'd rather be dropped into a blazing forest fire to battle it solo than ask people to give her money.

But this wasn't about her. This was for the kids.

So why couldn't she shake the growing unease she'd felt over the last few days? Maybe she was just feeling conspicuous in the dress and heels. Or maybe it was the nagging threat of losing the ranch—*that* was enough to put anyone on edge.

It's just a banquet. You can do this. She smiled politely at the next person she saw.

A short, balding man in his fifties returned her smile and raised his tumbler in a salute. "Hello, young lady. Do I know you?"

And you're on. "I don't think we've met."

His moist smile widened. "You sure?" He leaned closer and raked his eyes over her dress and figure, giving her a full blast of his whiskey-tinged breath.

Revulsion knotted her stomach instantly. *Get a grip. This is an upscale benefit dinner. For at-risk kids. These people are professionals, not abusive drunks.*

He grinned—the same glassy, thick-lidded grin that often accompanied booze-saturated breath. "Yeah, I know you."

Sue read his name badge. She didn't recognize his name, but she did recognize the prestigious law firm printed in bold type beneath it. She squared her shoulders and summoned a business-like smile. "I'm Susan Quinn. I run a group home for kids from failed adoptions and kids with difficulty being placed in foster homes."

He huffed out a laugh that knocked him slightly off balance.

Staggering drunk already. Fabulous.

"Well, Suzy, has anyone ever told you . . ." His slurred words trailed off in a haze like his breath. "You look like a million bucks."

Her pulse quickened.

He's just drunk. People spew nonsense when they're drunk.

"Bet you'd like to see a mil up close, eh?" He leaned closer and whispered. "Yeah, I know your type. That's why you're here, I can tell."

With a slight shudder, she searched the sea of bodies for Joe.

A large crowd filled the receiving area in a growing cluster. A mass of elegantly clad bodies, but no sign of Joe.

"Don't worry, Suzy," the man said, his lips stretched into a slackened grin. "You'll have all the big money eating out of your hand tonight."

The skin on her arms crawled. She rubbed them. Where was Joe?

"Know how I know?"

There he was. Black and white and working his way in her direction.

She eased out a pent-up breath and faced the guy. "Excuse me. You've mistaken me for someone else."

"Nope." His glassy gaze crawled down her figure. "I know *exactly* who you are." He took a step closer and whispered, "You're Suzy Q."

Her stomach lurched.

"Get it? Susan Quinn—Suzy Q."

No. That was long ago. This wasn't him. This wasn't—

"Suzy Q, where are yooou?"

Bile rose in her throat and she spun, snagging her heel on the carpet. She pitched forward and crashed into a woman, toppling her into another man, knocking full martinis from their hands. The smell of alcohol spread like fumes. Like his breath. Like—

"Come on out, li'l Suzy Q."

She lurched backward but struggled with the angle of her heels and lost her balance. A firm grasp on her bicep yanked her upright just in time to keep her from hitting the floor.

"Sue?" Joe's voice at her ear. "You okay?"

Dozens of stunned faces stared at her. The woman she'd jostled glared, while the man with her wiped liquid from his lapel, staring her down as if trying to gauge what kind of idiot would launch herself into a crowd like that.

Perfect. Exactly the impression she wanted to make. How was she supposed to get anyone to care about her kids now?

A sickening wave of despair rolled through her. Face burning, she turned and headed for the ballroom exit.

"Sue?"

She kept going, driven by humiliation and a need to escape. Poor Joe. How embarrassing this must be for him. And the kids! She just lost her last chance to save their home because she'd reacted like a child and made a complete fool of herself. All because of some slobbering skuzzball who reminded her of ghosts long past, of being a victim.

She stopped walking. The *kids* were going to suffer for this. *They* were the victims here.

Sue turned back.

There he was, snickering with some other guy.

Sue marched toward him, vaguely aware of a renewed hush in the room. Let them whisper and gawk. She'd already blown it—she had nothing to lose now. When she reached him, she gave his shoulder a poke. "Excuse me."

The man turned and grinned at her chest. "Oopsy daisy. That was quite a—"

"Listen, creep," she said. "You just cost me my last shot at providing a normal life for some kids who have no one to care about them and nowhere else to go. I don't care what law firm you're with, you're nothing but a worm dressed in a—"

"Sue." Joe's firm hand rested gently on her shoulder.

Sue shrugged the warning hand away. Anger churned up words faster than she could spit them out. "If needy kids' success depends on guys like you, you can keep your money, you pathetic excuse for a human."

Joe moved closer. "What's going on?"

She ignored him and eyed the guy, who no longer looked amused. "Take my advice, *counselor.* Sober up and get a conscience. And a heart while you're at it." Adrenaline raging, she

291

pivoted on her heel and headed for the exit, her anger quickly turning to nausea. Trembling, she hurried out of the ballroom and sped across the tiled lobby until she reached the outer exit doors. She hurried down the steps and into the parking lot.

"Hey!" Joe called out from a few yards back.

Dread rolled through her. What had she done? She stopped between two cars, sucked in a deep breath, and closed her eyes.

You just told off a high-powered attorney in front of the state's wealthiest people. You're finished. You might as well kiss those kids good-bye right now.

"Sue?"

She stood between two cars, her back to him, shaking.

He made her face him. "What's going on? Who was that guy?"

"I blew it. I just bailed on a bunch of kids who have already been dumped on too many times." Fat tears brimmed. She closed her eyes, sending dark stripes of mascara down her cheeks.

"How? What happened?"

"I just lost any shot I had at finding a donor." Despair filled her voice.

"Start at the beginning."

"Some drunk guy was being tacky and I overreacted." She puffed out a humorless laugh.

"I know. You could never imagine me doing *that.*"

Every muscle in his body tensed. "Did he touch you?"

"No. He's just some guy who had too much to drink and not enough control of his tongue. *I'm* the idiot who panicked and knocked people over and spilled drinks on expensive suits. I'm the one who let something stupid get to me and ruin everything."

"No, Sue. It's not your fault." *But I'd love to go back inside and get my hands on the little weasel.*

"Yes, it is. I let them down. Just like everyone else has." Tears glittered in her eyes.

"Don't say that. You didn't let them down."

She wasn't convinced. In fact, she looked defeated.

Joe's anger tapered off and what replaced it was just as consuming. And increasing by the second. "You've never let them down, Sue. You fight like a tiger to protect them. You teach them to stand up for themselves. You skip meals to make sure they get enough to eat."

She shot him a sharp glance.

"You'd do anything for them. And you love them like a mother bear even though you're scared to death to admit it."

Sue stared at him, her face streaked with black, searching his eyes as if wanting to believe him but unable to. Her lips trembled.

Her soft lips . . .

No. He couldn't give in to the way he felt, not this time, not now. Especially not now.

But the heartbreak in her eyes was quickly turning his steely resolve to a heap of smoldering rubble.

CHAPTER TWENTY-FOUR

Though Joe had pulled the Suburban into Layne's driveway and killed the motor, Sue wasn't ready to face anyone. Not yet. She needed to pull herself together, shut off the suffocating river of thoughts and emotions pressing on her. How could she face her kids, knowing they would soon be separated? Sent away and dumped at another strange place—again?

Joe's expression gently questioned her. Not pushing, just waiting. Waiting for her to do what she needed to do.

Whatever that was.

"You okay?" he asked.

"I'll be fine. Listen, why don't you go on inside. I just need a minute or two." *Or three. Or several hundred.*

He looked toward the house. "Or I can hang out here for a minute. If you want."

She nodded, surprised at her relief that he was staying. She leaned against the headrest, hoping a few extra moments would scrub the gloom from her heart.

It didn't.

"Talk," she said.

Joe let out a chuckle. "Any topic in particular?"

"I don't care."

"How about oil drilling?"

She shook her head. "I have a better idea. Tell me about your girlfriends."

His face took on a slightly strained look. "That's not much of a topic."

"Good, then it won't take long."

He looked out his window at the manicured lawn. "Actually, I got a pretty late start on dating. A couple bombed attempts made me painfully shy."

"Really? *You?*"

He turned a slight frown at her. "Why do you say it like that?"

She shrugged. If the guy didn't know he was amazing *and* insanely attractive, she wasn't about to create an ego monster by telling him.

"It's been pretty quiet on that front. On the rig, when we'd have our off-shift, the guys who didn't have wives or girlfriends would go trolling for dates. I wasn't into that. I spent my time off fishing and riding with Dave." He looked out the windshield and focused on the front of the house. "I was never into the let's-try-it-on kind of relationships. Figured it wasn't fair to get involved with someone if there wasn't a real good chance of it being serious."

Sue had never heard of such a thing. "But . . .

you must have had a serious girlfriend at some point."

Joe inspected a crack in the steering wheel cover, his expression unreadable. "It's not like I didn't want that. But between work and other stuff, I guess I missed my chance to meet the right one."

Sue could see him one day finding "the right one"—some tall, pretty brunette at his side, his arm encircling her while he looked down at her with that heart-stopping smile. The picture sent a pang to her chest.

"I'm not into casual relationships." He spoke in purposeful tones. "I made a commitment to Christ as a teenager, and part of that commitment meant keeping myself pure until marriage."

Pure? Didn't that usually mean—Sue felt her face go warm as the meaning of his words sank in. *But the way he kissed me . . .*

Joe resumed his steady vigil of the house.

The temperature in the truck had dropped, but her cheeks felt like she'd gotten too close to a campfire. If Joe had made a deliberate decision to avoid casual relationships and physical intimacy, then what did he mean by kissing her like that in the chapel?

Was it just an impulse of the moment? Or something more?

In the thick silence, her thoughts raced. Every quiet act of kindness from him, every lingering look, every tender word and touch crashed over her like a giant wave of revelation, flooding her heart, mind, and soul.

What if he'd fallen in love with her?

Her heart battered her chest like a caged wild thing, startling her.

What if I'm falling in love with him?

No.

She reached for her door handle. "I'd better get inside."

"Sue, hold on."

No. I need to get away. NOW.

In spite of her fear of what she might see, she turned to face him.

With a slight frown, he cocked his head at her. "You've got some, uh . . . just a sec." He rummaged in the glove compartment and took out a burger-joint napkin. He reached over and gently wiped her cheek where her tears had dried.

She gasped at the mascara-smudged napkin and a dull weight numbed her stomach. "Oh, that's great. All this time I looked like a zombie clown. How did you keep a straight face?"

With a shrug, he kept wiping her cheek. "Didn't notice. I mean—you looked amazing tonight, but you're so beautiful without all that stuff that I—" Joe paused mid-stroke, eyes locked on hers, realization filling his face.

She couldn't move.

Joe stared at her.

Then, as if released by some silent command, she raised her hand and lightly pressed his hand against her cheek, absorbing the warmth of his skin. His expression quickly shifted, churning in a way that matched the look in his eyes. She didn't dare name it because she felt it too, a burst of something overpowering and frightening and exhilarating. Slowly, she reached up and laid her other palm on his face.

He closed his eyes, jaw muscles tensing in her hand. "Sue . . ."

The warning in his tone set off a thrill in her.

Yes, heed the warning. Unhand the man and walk away. She needed to let go but couldn't. Mesmerized by a surreal sense of boldness, she gently cupped his face in both hands.

His chest heaved as if he had a sudden need for more air than he could get. His eyes opened and a question burned in them.

She guided his face closer.

His eyes closed again. "Sue." It was a strained whisper. "I can't just—"

Her lips brushed his. Just a light stroke, but long enough to feel his quickened breath on her skin.

A low sound from his throat sent a shockwave through her.

Suddenly, his hands were in her hair, pressing her closer into a second kiss, a long, deep, lingering one that pulled her into a current, threatening to sweep her away.

She couldn't think, couldn't breathe.

Joe pulled back a fraction and looked into her eyes. Then he took her face in his warm hands and captured her lips again, this time with the same sweet, solemn longing she'd felt from him in the chapel. The way she felt that day returned, gathered strength, and flooded her with sensations she'd never known, never dared allow herself to hope for.

Oh, so this is what belonging feels like.

His lips broke free from hers and grazed her cheek, then lingered on her cheekbone with a tenderness that melted her heart.

Trembling, she pulled back. The look in his eyes made her heartbeat skip and then race to catch up.

His gaze fell to her mouth.

She closed her eyes.

But instead of another kiss, his arms encircled her and he pulled her close to him.

She savored the warmth of his embrace, the bass drum thumping in his chest, unable to think of anything but how much she wanted to stay here.

He stroked her hair, his lips brushing her forehead. He kissed her temple, then her cheekbone again. His touch sent a tingle along her skin. "I love you," he whispered.

Waves of pleasure confused her. What had he just said?

He held her tighter, so close she could feel both their hearts pounding, her own heart—

Wait—

He looked into her eyes.

I—

No.

I love—

Don't! She couldn't feel this. Couldn't want this.

Oh no . . . No . . . NO . . .

Alarm doused her senses like ice water, cutting straight through the confusion. Whatever was happening, she needed to get a grip on it.

She struggled and broke free of him, then slid across the seat. "I need to get inside."

"You're *leaving?*"

"I'm sorry. I can't be here. I need to go."

"Why?"

She looked at him but couldn't answer. The need to flee was overpowering, yet the confusion in his eyes threatened to crush her. She popped the door open.

"Did you hear what I said? I love you."

"I love you, Suzy. More than anyone else in this world, sweetie. I promise."

A gritty chill rattled through her like a bitter wind, creeping deep into her bones. "Don't say that."

"Don't *say* it?" Disbelief shadowed his features. "But I did. And I meant it."

Put it out of your mind. Just lock it out.

She slid from the truck and headed for the house. *Idiot.* How had she let something like this happen? Was she losing her mind? The entire evening was glaring proof of how out of control everything had become. She should have known better. Needing someone never resulted in anything good. Ever.

A car door slammed.

Picking up her pace, Sue glanced over her shoulder, fearing she'd have to run in those murderous heels to reach the door before he caught her.

But Joe wasn't coming after her. He was making quick time the other way.

Within minutes, Joe covered nearly a quarter mile and was only beginning to hit his stride. At this rate, he could be in Juniper Valley in no time.

Hey, don't sweat it, Sue. It's just my heart you're messing with.

He picked up the pace, feet battering the pavement, his emotions still raging. He replayed the entire evening, trying to make sense of what just happened. But the farther he walked, the less sense anything made. Thinking about it only fed his growing frustration.

After that kiss in the chapel, he'd worked hard

to keep his heart out of it. Keep everything just business. And he'd succeeded—right up until she kissed him. With that cautious, feather-light kiss that was ten times more maddening than the ones that followed.

And apparently of no significance to her.

One little kiss and she'd ripped down his defenses. Not only had he caved in, he'd chucked his brain and told her he *loved* her. To which she kindly responded by bolting like a jackrabbit.

Kiss and run. How did someone do a one-eighty like that?

But then again, she'd shown him plenty of resistance since he'd arrived at Juniper Ranch. Maybe *he* was the one with the problem. He was the bonehead who'd fallen for a woman who wanted nothing to do with him.

There's a huge boost to the ol' ego.

She hadn't only rejected him—she'd flown like hunted prey. What was it about hearing his feelings that sent her running? Did she *still* not trust him?

He stopped. That was it.

Could she ever trust him?

Cold wind whipped through his borrowed dinner jacket. If that was the case, maybe it was good this had happened now. Better now than later. Besides, he was—

Leaving.

With a groan, he turned and assessed the

distance he'd put between him and Layne's house. How had he forgotten? In a few weeks, his new life would begin thousands of miles away. He had no business falling in love with Sue, much less telling her about it.

"Father," he whispered into the night, "I screwed up. I thought I was here to introduce her to You, but after all this time, she's no more open to You than she is to me. I'm sorry. I got involved and I shouldn't have."

As a car approached, he stepped onto the shoulder to let it pass. He was leaving soon, something he should have remembered.

"No more," he whispered. "I'm done."

But even before the familiar Voice whispered to his heart, he had a good idea what he would hear.

Show her My love.

CHAPTER TWENTY-FIVE

"I love you."

Sue snapped out of her dream-fog and hoisted the mop bucket to the edge of the utility room tub. Daisy's high-pitched complaints in the dining hall drifted past her thoughts, barely registering. Sue dumped the dirty water, then set the bucket down and swiveled the faucet arm over the side to refill it.

How could three small words so thoroughly thrill and freak her out at the same time?

It didn't matter. Her life was enough of a mess without adding *that.*

She didn't want to remember the benefit dinner fiasco and what had followed, but with her trip to the bank coming up on Monday, she had no choice but to face it. She'd failed miserably to gain increased monthly support. With any luck—or more accurately, a miracle—she could hold on to the kids for a few more weeks. But at this point, it really would take a miracle for the bank to accept what she had and not demand the full amount due.

God, if You're there, let this next payment stall

the foreclosure proceedings. Just a little more time with the kids, that's all I ask.

In spite of the ranch's struggles over the past two years, perhaps she had at least helped these kids feel like they mattered, helped them move past being abandoned, past the emptiness.

Sue felt something at her feet and looked down. Water had spilled over the bucket and was shooting across the tile.

She shut off the faucet. As she slapped the mop into the pooled water and worked to sop it up, a memory lurked from the shadows. With a burst of vigor, she wrung water from the mop, pressing the wringer as hard as she could, but the memory still played on her mind's screen.

It had been dark a long time. She was hiding in a corner with the lights off so she could see the front door without being seen by anyone passing by the motel window. She had tried hard all day not to worry, but she'd read all of her chapter books from beginning to end by herself, and her mama still wasn't home. She couldn't tell time yet, but when the sky turned dark, she knew it was late. She had no idea how long her mom had been gone because when she woke up that morning, her mama still wasn't back from being out the night before. Suzy had gotten her own cereal, cleaned up the milk she'd spilled, and ate alone where people couldn't see her from the window, just like Mama had taught her. She was used to taking care of herself—it wasn't that. What scared her was that Mama said she wouldn't leave her alone like that anymore. She'd promised. Maybe something happened to her. Maybe one of those men she met downtown had taken her somewhere and wouldn't let her go.

In that dark motel, Suzy looked at the telephone, belly twisting, legs shaking. Maybe she should call the police.

But if her mama was just downtown having fun, then the police might take her to jail. Other girls' mamas didn't leave them alone for days. If Suzy got Mama in trouble with the police, Suzy would be given away to strangers again, and that scared her even more.

It turned out she hadn't hidden herself so well after all. Somebody called the police, and into another foster home she went. She never did find out how long it had taken her mama to come back that time.

It wasn't until that bogus 'reunion' weekend at the beach a few years later that she found out all her hopes were a joke. At twelve, Sue had finally wised up and realized her mom didn't give a spit wad about her. As long as there was a man nearby, Suzy would always be left out in the cold.

Sue made a last swipe across the floor and stuffed the mop in the bucket. Over the years, she'd worked hard to forget the sting of repeated abandonment and seal off the emptiness. Ironically, being single had helped. It kept things simple, disappointment-free. And that was exactly how things needed to stay.

"Did you hear what I said? I love you."

Angry tears sprang to her eyes. At least Joe hadn't added *I promise.*

But it didn't matter. Nothing good had ever come from those three words. Nothing but the whiff of a sweet fragrance on a gust of wind, no sooner here than gone. Nothing that hadn't left her feeling lonelier and emptier than if she'd never heard them to begin with.

Sue wheeled the mop bucket down the hallway and into the dining hall.

A red-faced Daisy glowered at Sonja, who was righting a tangle of dining chairs in the doorway. "My job, Sonja. Move!" Daisy plowed into the pile of chairs with her wheelchair and knocked over another one.

Sonja threw an exasperated look at Sue. "She's going to break something, Miss Susan. I'm just trying to set them back up right, so they're easier to move."

Sue heaved a tired sigh. "Let Daisy move the chairs however she wants to, Sonja."

Haley took the bucket from Sue and resumed mopping.

Jasmine entered from the kitchen with a handful of cups. "Miss Roberta looking for you."

"Thank you. Where is she?"

"Kitchen." Jasmine deposited the cups on the sideboard.

Sue went to the kitchen. The boys were busy cooking up something with garlic and basil that smelled amazing.

Bertie emerged from the pantry.

With Joe. He tensed when he saw her.

Sue directed her gaze at Bertie. "You wanted me?"

Joe took the package he was holding to the stove, where Chaz was stirring something in a stockpot in slow, steady circles.

"Not anymore," Bertie said. "Joe helped me out. I thought we were out of meat but there was a whole case in the freezer. Unmarked. Funny, I'd never seen it before. It's a meat-mystery."

Sue nodded absently as Joe walked away, then she returned to the dining hall.

Bertie followed. "Hey, what happened last night? I'm still waiting to get the full scoop."

Flushed, Sue headed for the sideboard and took out stacks of plates. Of course Bertie meant the dinner, not what happened afterward. "I didn't meet anyone who could help."

"Yeah, I gathered that much. Heard it as you stumbled past me and disappeared into your sleeping bag. I was just wondering what happened. Joe said—"

"What?" Her tone sounded like a frantic terrier. "I mean, what did he tell you?"

Bertie tilted her head, her quizzical look deepening. "He said some guy at that dinner insulted you, and you lit out early."

"It was nothing. Just a drunk slimeball with a mouth. I overreacted. Badly. I shouldn't have let it get to me, but I did, and now it's done." She wasn't going to bring up how childish it was for a grown woman to freak out and spill drinks all over rich people, then stumble out of a perfectly good banquet because of some irrational old fear. "The dinner was a great idea. Unfortunately, it didn't work out."

"So that's it then? We're shutting down?"

Heart hammering, Sue checked on the girls. Had they heard that?

Jasmine and Haley were moving the table back into place. Sonja and Daisy were moving chairs one by one.

The old woman winced. "Sorry, boss. Forgot you haven't told them yet."

"I know. I need to." Sue's gaze swept around the room and rested on Jasmine.

The girl must have felt herself being watched, because she turned to Sue and flashed a cheesy grin.

A sudden urge to hug the girl came over Sue, but with it came a fear that Jasmine would sense something wrong. Sue moved to the window facing Table Rock instead. The longer she put off telling the kids, the longer she could pretend nothing was going to change.

Bertie joined her.

Sue closed her eyes. "I'll tell them, Bert. I just need a little more time. Normal time without all the strain of—you know. Knowing they're being sent away again."

Bertie patted Sue's shoulder. "I am sorry, Sue. Truly. I wish there was some other way. Guess it would take a miracle at this point."

Sue stole a glance at Bertie. Did she believe in miracles? Sue couldn't bring herself to ask.

"So what's next?"

"That's the question, isn't it? I'm going to the bank Monday with a mortgage payment, and I'm hoping for some leniency."

"A full payment? How'd you manage that?"

"I saved a little by cutting down on payroll hours." Not to mention Joe's offer to work for just room and board.

"And you didn't take a paycheck again."

Sue shrugged.

"And you sold the Harley."

"Yeah, that helped." She winced at the reminder of another loss. "But I'm afraid it's all just money wasted."

Bertie patted Sue's shoulder, gave it a squeeze. "I know it's tough. Maybe you'll catch a break.

But if it doesn't work out, these kids will be all right. You'll see."

Sue gave Bertie a faint, less-than-genuine smile. If only she believed it.

Monday afternoon, Sue changed lanes a couple blocks before the bank and nearly wiped out a Honda Civic because she forgot to check her mirrors. She still couldn't think about that night with Joe in the Suburban without seeing that look on his face. Or how it had taken him more than an hour to return to Layne's house after storming off down the road. Or how silent he'd been ever since.

If they were going to continue working together for the time remaining, she and Joe would have to talk. Somehow, they needed to put the strain between them aside.

Sue arrived at the bank in time for her three o'clock appointment. Hand on the door, she paused. *So, God, if You really want to show off Your moves, now would be a great time.*

Inside the building, Sue was directed across the lobby to a loan officer's desk.

After introductions, Sue bit her lip and drew out the check she'd prepared—everything she had, down to her last dime—along with the last letter from the bank. "I was hoping we could talk about a way to stall the auction. Even if it's just for one month. I have this month's payment."

Nikki, the loan officer, took the check and glanced at it. "The bank is not usually in a position to alter the terms of foreclosure proceedings. However, in some circumstances, there may be a way to make an exception. Let's take a look at your account."

Was it crazy to hope this could work?

The woman turned to her computer screen and clicked away at the keyboard with lacquered nails, reading the account number on Sue's letter and typing in data. "Okay. I have your account here. Let's see. I'm pulling up the amount due by end of business today."

Sue nodded.

Nikki picked up Sue's check and read it, then looked at the screen again, this time a tiny frown creasing her smooth forehead. She set the check down and clasped her hands, still frowning.

What? Had Sue forgotten to sign it? Dated it wrong?

"This is the amount of your regular mortgage payment."

"Yes." Sue nodded.

"But this is not the amount due." She turned her monitor so Sue could see the account record. "This is."

Sue stared at the screen, shaking her head. That couldn't be right. "But that's nearly twice the payment amount."

"Bank and attorney fees incurred since the

313

last notice of default are included in the current balance." The woman touched the paper. "As stated in the letter."

Sue looked at the words without seeing them, heart sinking. "But I don't have . . ."

"I'm sorry, but the notice of default clearly states that, unless we receive the full past balance due, including all fees incurred, we must proceed with the terms of foreclosure. The property is scheduled to go to auction" —she tapped the keys some more and read her screen— "January seventh."

Sue read the calendar on the cubicle wall. Three weeks. "What about the kids—the people living there? How long do we have?"

"The property must be vacated within ten days of the sale."

So that was it. She and the kids had to be out in about thirty days.

In a fog, Sue left the bank and headed for the Suburban. A gust of icy wind knocked her back a step. It also blew away the numbness, exposing her to a bitter cold that had nothing to do with the wind. Shivering, she climbed into her car, fumbled to start it, and cranked up the heat. *Thanks, God. I guess I know where You and I stand. Again.*

No more time, no more options. She'd known this was coming, even expected it. But somehow that knowledge hadn't prepared her for the grief cutting a frozen path straight through her heart. She had no choice but to tell the kids they were going to be sent away.

How could she even tell them? She could imagine their faces, the shock. Daisy. Edgar and Chaz. Brandi.

Jasmine.

A sharp pang hit her chest at the memory of Jasmine's tiny, tear-soaked face the day she had clung so tightly to Sue, desperate to know she wasn't an unwanted freak, desperate to be loved.

These kids had been let down so much already, suffered so many broken promises. This would only prove to them no one wanted them. It was like a horrible, sick joke. Sue had been determined to make a difference in their lives, and yet all she had done was make things worse.

"What have I done?" Her heart throbbed in her throat, threatening to burst.

I've let them down.

No.

She let her forehead smack against the steering wheel, launching a torrent of tears. No, this wasn't about letting a bunch of needy kids down.

It was about losing *her* kids.

The only real family she'd ever known.

CHAPTER TWENTY-SIX

Late Monday afternoon, Joe punched off the call with the oil company manager and stowed his phone. Knowing the new rig would be operational on schedule didn't bring the satisfaction he'd expected.

Which was really weird, because the past few days, he'd wanted nothing more than to hit the road.

He surveyed the progress his guys were making on dorm cleanup.

Not bad. Anything blatantly filthy was either in the garbage or stashed out of sight, and now the dorm smelled only slightly of rank socks. Bedmaking and room-tidying had slacked off lately. Room checks hadn't exactly been a priority. His guys didn't seem to mind.

The thought of packing up and heading to Louisiana early had crossed his mind several times since Friday night. But the boys still needed a dorm counselor. And next week was Christmas. He couldn't leave the kids without any warning or a proper good-bye. Besides, the first of January would come soon enough.

A date he probably ought to mention to his current employer.

He pulled on his work jacket, put Edgar in charge, and slipped out.

Feathery snow fell, coating the valley in an endless blanket of white. Squeals of laughter came from the staff quarters out back.

Crossing the yard, he stuffed his hands in his coat pockets and followed the sound.

He'd kept busy enough on Saturday to avoid fuming over what had happened with Sue. Then he spent most of Sunday walking the desert, talking to his Father in the quiet of the frozen dunes. The miles of stillness had eased some of the sting. The rest would fade with time. Her avoidance of love probably wasn't about him. Maybe she was a prisoner, bound by her fears.

But stewing over Sue and the walls around her heart was pointless. His stay here was nearly up. Time to move on.

He rounded the end of the building and stopped.

Jasmine and Haley tossed snowballs in the air for Ringo. The dog leaped into the air, jaws snapping, and crushed the balls in one bite, sending Jasmine into a fit of giggles.

Sue stood off to one side, watching.

He trudged toward her.

Jasmine offered Ringo a snowball, but the dog licked her hand instead. Jasmine sank to her knees and hugged his furry neck.

317

As Joe drew near, Sue turned with a start. Her eyes were red and swollen, her expression hollow. As if someone had just killed her best friend.

Joe's heart twisted, right on cue. Apparently his heart hadn't gotten the rejection memo. He sighed. "Got a second?"

She swiped at her eyes. "Sure."

He moved closer and kept his voice low. "I got a call from the oil company today. They want me on deck January first. Just wanted to give you a heads-up."

"Thank you. That's good to know."

"I know things are up in the air now. Maybe you can get one of those temp ladies to stay on through January to cover me when—"

"I won't need any more help." She turned and walked to the picnic table. She swept snow off the top in brisk, even strokes.

Jasmine rushed to Joe and offered a crumbling snowball. "Throw it high, Papa Joe. Ringo love to catch."

"Does he? Let's see." Joe tossed the snowball in the air.

Ringo dashed and jumped, catching it.

"Cool trick, Jas. Did you teach him that?"

Sue brushed snow, then wiped her face with the back of a sleeve.

It's none of your business. Leave it alone.

She was upset about the ranch, understandably.

Losing her dream to give kids a place to grow up confident, equipped, ready to face the world. Losing what mattered most to her.

She doesn't want your sympathy or your help. Or anything else from you. Remember?

Yeah, he remembered. It was just that his heart was having a hard time keeping up. Joe rolled another snowball and tossed it to the dog, then went to Sue.

She cast a sideways glance at him and swiped her cheeks again.

"What's wrong, Sue?"

She shook her head. "Nothing I didn't see coming."

He shifted his stance to watch the girls and Ringo, giving Sue some space. "The ranch?"

"The auction's in three weeks." She lowered her voice. "We have to be out ten days after that."

Jasmine threw a snowball for Ringo, but it went low and hit Haley in the rear. With a squeal, Haley turned and chased a shrieking Jasmine across the yard.

As Joe watched the girls play, a dull weight settled over him. It had to be tough for Sue, knowing she was about to lose everything she'd worked for and the kids she couldn't admit she'd grown to love. And he suspected it would only get tougher in the days to come.

And there wasn't a thing he could do about it.

• • •

Tuesday, Joe trudged down the trail from the chapel to the dorm. Four days had passed since the gala disaster and not much had changed.

Sue had kept busy and quiet, and the kids still didn't know about the ranch closing.

He slipped inside the boys' empty dorm. Despite the time he'd spent in prayer, the heaviness that had driven Joe to the chapel hadn't lifted.

The boys had joined the others in the main house to watch a holiday video. He'd join them too—if he could be better company.

In spite of the recent cleaning, the dorm was more cluttered than ever. He still had a stack of junk mail to sort and toss, including a handful of letters from Jefferson-Lovett. Why the Realtor in La Pine felt he needed to know every time an owner abutting his property lobbied for new zoning was beyond him. He'd gotten newsletters in Alaska and now they'd followed him here. Maybe he'd forgo having his mail forwarded when he moved to the Gulf. He tossed the letters in the trash and kicked strewn dirty clothes into piles.

But what if the letters were something he needed to read? A couple years ago, he'd found out at tax time that his property taxes had shot up. The newsletters he'd tossed probably would've warned him of that.

Joe snagged one out of the trash and opened it. He scanned the pages, first in confusion, then a second time in disbelief. Property value in La Pine had multiplied in the last couple of years.

He read the dates of his original purchase. A bunch of Realtor lingo about an unprecedented market value upheaval. More stuff about land values spiking at a ratio of one to one hundred.

His brain wasn't computing the math. He rubbed his stubbly jaw and read the information again, then went on to the second page. His acreage was listed in a column with the original purchase price of one thousand dollars per acre. Another column showed the market value of his acres if they were listed today.

His property was worth one hundred thousand now? Incredible!

No, that wasn't right. Joe shook his head and ran through the information again.

The values listed were per *acre.*

He had twelve acres.

One hundred thousand times twelve . . .

"No way," he whispered. "That's . . ."

One point two million.

Joe slumped against the door and read the page again.

One point two *million?*

The letter also said acreage in La Pine was flying. Buyers coming out of the woodwork for prime Central Oregon property.

One point two—

He could pay for—

Wait, what's the interest on that?

With fumbling fingers, Joe pulled out his cell and called Jefferson-Lovett and got someone who could verify what he was reading and answer his questions in detail.

His figures were correct.

Joe collapsed into the armchair by the door. According to the agent's estimated figures, just the monthly interest alone on one million would be more than enough to support John and Fiona's monthly care and housekeeping. He didn't have to work in the Gulf to support them. He could work and live anywhere he wanted.

If only he could work and live here. If only the ranch weren't—

Joe raked fingers through his hair. He could pay off Sue's mortgage. Keep the kids from leaving. Keep Sue from leaving. Without a mortgage, she could make her operating budget and stay afloat with ease. He could help with that too.

He could stay on and work with the kids. He and Sue together. They could—

Whoa.

Thoughts whirling, Joe rose and paced the room.

This was too much to process at once.

He returned to the chair and fell to his knees in front of it. "Father, I don't even know how to thank You. This is a huge answer to prayer. You answered my—" Dazed, he thumbed through the back-dated letters in the trash basket, the full weight of what had occurred sinking in.

God had answered his prayers long ago. Joe just hadn't been listening.

There were so many things he could do with this kind of money. Get the ranch stocked and fully staffed. Chaz would never have to worry about being sent away again. Joe could give them stability, guidance, protection, like a—

Like a dad. A faithful, caring dad.

The thought struck like a sucker punch.

What about Sue?

Oddly enough, despite all that had happened between them, he could still see himself working alongside her, taking care of these kids, helping them gain confidence and self-respect. Raising them like a big family—together.

With all the possibilities playing in his mind, hope zinged through his veins like a gusher blowing sky high. It was an answer to prayer.

It had to be. Didn't it?

Joe closed his eyes, steeling himself for the possibility that this new dream—the dream that had been germinating in his heart from the moment he'd arrived—might not be what God had in mind.

The Lord had already done so much—paid Joe's sin debt, saved his life, healed him, showed him favor. Provided for him in more ways than he could count. Asking what God had in mind was the least Joe could do in return.

"All right, Father, I'm listening. Your way, not mine."

After an hour of pacing the dorm and praying, Joe sensed he was on the right track and strode across the lawn toward the house, about to bust yet still not sure what he was doing. He would help Sue save the place—that much he knew. He'd just go in there and tell her.

His steps slowed. Tell her what? That he was paying off her mortgage? And then what? Ask her to share her home and her kids with him? Even if she cared about him more than she let on, what made him think she wanted him here permanently? Last week, she couldn't even stick around to hear him say he loved her, much less admit any mutual feelings. What made him think she was ready to jump into a life-changing commitment?

Marriage. Family. That's what you mean. Admit it.

Right. Just march in there and propose. Great plan—if he wanted to totally scare her off.

Maybe he could save the place now, then over time, he could wear down her wall, help her conquer the fear he suspected was guarding her heart.

He stopped at the wheelchair ramp leading into the kitchen.

Who was he kidding? In the nearly two months he'd been here, he hadn't succeeded in chipping a pebble from that wall.

Joe lowered himself and sat on the ramp.

If he paid off her mortgage, she would feel beholden to him. Even obligated. He sure didn't want that. He didn't want her feeling forced. Ever. Maybe he could pay off the loan anonymously. But eventually he'd have to explain why he didn't need to leave for the Gulf. She would figure out he was the one who paid it off and feel obligated.

Or he could wait for the auction and bid on the property anonymously with someone acting as his agent. He had a lawyer friend who could help with that. But an auction could turn into a bidding war, and he couldn't take a chance on losing. Besides, if he waited until the auction, the kids would already be relocated, and he had to prevent that.

He needed a plan.

In the dining hall Wednesday morning, Sue caught a glimpse of Joe standing in the den at the front window.

He looked up and motioned her to him.

As she headed his way, he settled his gaze on the window again.

"We don't have a Christmas tree."

"I know. I wasn't planning on . . ." *Torturing the kids with a measly Christmas just before shipping them off forever.* "To be honest, I'm not much in the holiday mood."

"That's okay, you're busy, no problem. I've got errands to do in Bend today, so I'll just get one. And just so you know, I won't get back until late tonight."

Sue arched a brow. "Errands?"

The corners of his mouth fought back a smile. "Just stuff. Get a new phone for John and Fiona, shopping. Stuff."

Shopping. And stuff. Said with a merry twinkle in his eye. Sue didn't need another spin on the wheel to figure this puzzle out. She also knew asking him to not Christmas shop for the kids would be like asking him to not eat.

He left right after breakfast cleanup.

Sue rounded up all the kids and spent the day playing games, which Bertie chided her for more than once. Sue shrugged. Chores would always need to be done. If she wanted to spend her last days playing with the kids, so be it. Even so, the day passed agonizingly slow. Like a ticking clock in a quiet room, Joe's absence kept nagging at her. But it was better this way. A taste of the way things would be after he was gone.

Nothing good ever comes from longing.

Later that evening, Sue got the boys settled into their bunks for the night. By the time they were quieted down enough for her to slip out for a cup of coffee, it was half-past eleven. As she reached the house, the kitchen lights blazed.

Inside, Joe and Bertie worked to unpack groceries. A mountain of food. Turkey, stuffing, corn, rolls, onions, potatoes, whipped cream. Stacks of packages, boxes, and cans.

The scent of fresh-cut fir filled her senses and lifted her spirits.

Stubborn man. Stubborn, sweet man.

Bertie turned to Sue. "Boys all settled in? I better check on the girls before you take over bed watch. Back in a few."

As Bertie slipped out, Joe kept unpacking food and stacking it on the island, humming "It's Beginning to Look a Lot Like Christmas."

Sue started toting perishables to the fridge. On her second trip, she caught him looking at her over his shoulder.

"I'll take care of making Christmas dinner," he said. "Don't worry."

She laughed. "I'm not worried."

"No?" He lugged a turkey to the fridge. "Wow. And here I was, all prepared to argue my case."

She met him at the fridge and opened the door. "I've learned a few things since you've been here, Joe. Like getting between you and food is pointless. Possibly even dangerous."

Joe laughed and looked down at her, his dark eyes twinkling. "I'm going to spend some time on Christmas Eve with John and Fiona, but I'll be back in the evening. We can have a Christmas dinner for the kids then, if that's all right with you."

"Sounds good." Her stomach growled just thinking about it. She went to the sacks, removed more perishables, and took them to the fridge.

No one went out of his way to feed people the way Joseph Paterson did.

When she closed the fridge door, he was standing on the other side of it. He leaned back against the counter and smiled, arms folded. He seemed relaxed, happy. Too happy. Probably looking forward to moving on to the new oil rig, getting back into his regular work routine. His real life.

She tamped down a throbbing ache and turned to get more groceries. Anger rose to replace the ache, but she pushed that down too.

"Where are you planning to go? You know, after this?" Joe asked.

The question was cutting enough, but his jolly mood added to the sting.

"I'll probably stay with Layne for a little while. She wants me to move in indefinitely, but even as huge as her house is, I wouldn't feel comfortable . . ." She dismissed the rest with a wave of her hand. Joe didn't need to hear this stuff. She went back to the island to get more items for the pantry.

Joe moved nearer, his warmth radiating behind her. "Sue?" The way he said her name made it sound deep, like he had something heavy on his mind, and she was at the root of it.

"What?"

He didn't answer.

She glanced over her shoulder and met his eyes. "What if things had been different? What if you weren't losing the ranch and I weren't leaving, if I could stick around . . ."

Her heartbeat kicked up a notch. What was he doing? "That's a whole lot of *ifs,* Joe."

He nodded but didn't say anything, just held her gaze.

"A lot of *ifs* there is no point in discussing."

His eyes took on a searching look. "Right. But humor me. Let's just say . . . what if?"

The question, plus his nearness, set off an avalanche of emotions she had no power to control. Those "what ifs" had become far too easy to imagine lately—probably had something to do with Joe telling her he loved her. What if he could stay? What if she weren't losing the place? What if he could be a steady part of their lives? Part of *her* life? What would it be like to have a kind, honorable man as a companion, to feel loved?

To love?

The urge to sink into those arms threatened to do her in. She returned to the groceries. It wasn't fair. Why was he doing this?

Joe took another step, coming so close now that his breath moved the hair at the nape of her neck, sending a violent tingle through her. His voice deepened to a rumble. "I'm not imagining things, am I." It wasn't a question.

She couldn't answer.

I don't know what you imagine, but if you come one step closer, I'm going to have to either run out that door screaming or throw myself all over you.

He was cornering her. Asking her to bare her deepest fears in a way that would leave her exposed. Vulnerable.

She closed her eyes. *When you don't need anyone, no one can hurt you. It's simple. No need, no hurt.*

She mustered every bit of grit she had, then turned and faced him. "I'm not the girl for you, Joe. You can do much better. And I do better alone."

He deepened his scrutiny. "Why?"

The air between them stilled. She needed a break from that drilling look. She examined the ceiling. "It's what works best for me."

The kitchen had gotten far too warm.

She ducked around him and headed toward the foyer. "Goodnight, Joe."

As she hit the stairs, his voice trailed her. "You never did answer the question."

CHAPTER TWENTY-SEVEN

"It's time, Sue."

Sue's jaw clenched. She shouldn't have answered Layne's call. "I know."

"I have twelve case files and placement requests on my desk, all ready to go. You know the drill, it's a process. Listen, hon. I understand you're not *ready*—"

"No, I'm not." *But ready or not, there they go.*

A thick pause. "But I also know you don't want this coming down to emergency shelter care."

"Yes, you're right." Sue definitely didn't want that. Trouble was she didn't want *anything.* Actually, she wanted to chuck her phone across the kitchen and go for the kind of ride that broke all kinds of county and state laws. In a daze, she stared at the flurry of activity as the girls prepared dinner.

Totally selfish. That's what you are, Susan Quinn. You're not thinking about what's best for these kids. They're probably better off in a place where someone thinks about what they need long-term.

"And this close to Christmas, I need to get

these requests in to the judge before the holiday break."

"Okay," Sue said, rubbing her aching temples. "File the paperwork."

For the next few days, Joe was on his phone a lot, speaking in low tones. Laughing. Probably making arrangements to move and meet his new rig crew. And he was singing a lot. As if he was excited about the change, looking forward to starting his new life.

Sue kept her crew busy, sorting through clothing and deep cleaning bedrooms, even though Brandi griped about doing chores the week of Christmas. But Sue needed the activity, and the ranch needed the work. The busier, the better.

While Jasmine and Tatiana helped Daisy fold bedding, Sue took bags of garbage to the front porch and called Joe's cell to ask him to send a couple of boys to haul it down to the Dumpster. Her call went straight to voice mail.

Figured—he was probably on it again, as usual.

"Sue?" Bertie met her in the foyer, holding the office phone. "Someone calling for you. A real estate agent. I said you weren't available, but this lady says she has an offer you may want to consider."

"An offer? For the ranch?"

Bertie shrugged.

Sue took the phone and headed toward her office. "This is Susan Quinn."

"Hi, Susan. Bonnie Scott with Jefferson-Lovett Realty in La Pine. Listen, I know your property isn't listed, but I have an investor interested in a property like yours. Would you consider looking at an offer?"

"An offer? Wait—" Sue went into her office and closed the door. "The property is in foreclosure and is scheduled for auction in a couple weeks."

"Right. We get foreclosure listings. My client is interested in a short sale, which could be of benefit to you both."

Someone wanted Juniper Ranch? Why?

"How did your client hear about the property?"

"Investors also get the listings. This company is searching for an institutional-residential property like yours. Would you like to see the offer?"

Sue went to the window. The snow-dusted valley looked barren. Few people cared for the remoteness of Juniper Valley, which was one of the key reasons this place had appealed to her.

She hadn't considered listing the property, especially at this stage of the proceedings. She'd have to sell it for more than the balance of the loan, which, at this point, was higher than the market value, with all the added bank and legal fees. No one was likely to buy the property for what the bank needed, not to mention the extra she'd need for Realtor fees.

But curiosity won. "I'll take a look at it."

"Great. I'll fax it over now and await your call." Sue gave her fax number and hung up.

Bertie popped in. "Well? Legit call or crackpot?"

"I'm pretty sure that was legit. Jefferson-Lovett. Seems like I've seen that name a lot lately. She's faxing an offer now."

Bertie guffawed. "The first of many, my guess. I bet the auction listing came out today. Vultures. They'll start descending on us by the dozen now, trying to horn in before the bidding starts. Offering to take the property off your hands for pennies on the dollar."

Sue groaned. "I didn't think about that." She went to the fax machine as it picked up the call. When it spit out the first page, she read it. Bertie read over her shoulder as Sue waded through the information for details and an amount.

The buyer making the offer was an investor, from the looks of it. Montgomery Enterprises, LLC. She read until she spotted the offer.

The figure was nearly twenty thousand dollars higher than what she owed the bank.

She gasped. That couldn't be right.

Bertie whistled in her ear. "Hoo boy, not a crackpot, huh?"

Sue handed the page to Bertie. "Read it for me and find the catch. You're better at spotting sneaky stuff than I am." Sue took the remaining pages from the fax. Her eye was drawn to the comment section at the bottom.

Due to delays with other investment projects, the buyer is unable to begin renovation and preparation of the Juniper Valley property until April. If desired, the seller may remain on the property for up to ninety days, at which time the buyer will assume full possession of the property.

Bertie held up her page. "No catch that I can see. Actually sounds legit." She shook her head, lips pursed. "But I still don't buy it."

Stunned, Sue traded pages with Bertie. "Now read that." She pointed to the ninety-day comment and then read the amount again. Why would someone offer more than the place was worth? It made no sense.

"Well, here's your catch, boss. They want you to rent the place from them for ninety days. What's the rate? Probably hefty. Wonder what that's gonna run you for three months."

"I didn't see anything about a rental rate. Did you?"

Bertie sifted through all three pages of the fax. "Nope."

"Well, what should I do?"

Bertie picked up the phone and thrust it at Sue.

"If it sounds too good to be true, then it is. If it were me, I'd call that gal back and ask her what kind of imbecile does she think I am and then tell her to take a flying leap off Table Rock."

Sue could totally see Bertie doing just that. She took the phone. "I'll call and see if she can explain. It doesn't make sense, does it?"

Bertie gave her a slow, grave head shake.

Sue dialed and Bonnie answered. "I have a couple of questions if you can answer them." She looked at Bertie.

The old woman rubbed her fingertips together mouthing, "Show me the money," then slipped out, likely to check on kids.

"This may sound strange, but why are they offering more than the property is worth?"

"The property suits the buyers' needs perfectly and there are no guarantees they can win the bid if they wait for the auction."

That made sense, to some degree. Someone *really* wanted this property. Which was fine with Sue. "It also says we can stay for ninety days. What's the rental rate? Is it monthly or by the day or what?" Depending on the amount, she might actually be able to afford it.

"Sorry, that should have been included in the notes. There would be no charge for rent."

Free rent? Something was fishy. No one gave things away for free. "Are you sure?"

"Yes. The buyers made it very clear that they

will benefit from this arrangement. They don't want the property left vacant while they wait to take possession."

"But rent-free?"

"Yes. The interested parties feel that keeping the property occupied and maintained through the remaining winter months is of more value than a few months' rent."

Sue read the paper again. The figures danced as the page quivered in her hand. "I need to think about this."

"Great. You have my number. I look forward to your call."

Her heart beat faster as she read the paper again. It was a legitimate offer, as best she could tell. An offer that meant she not only pocketed a few thousand dollars to help tide the place over, but one that also allowed her and the kids to stay together longer. They would still have to leave, but not for a while.

The upside? She would have more time with the kids. And the downside? There wasn't one, was there? She was losing the place anyway. It made no difference to her whether she lost it through auction or private sale.

Sue went to her planner and flipped ahead. Depending on when the deal closed, ninety days would give her until around the first of April. She turned back to today's date. December twenty-second. Two days until Christmas Eve.

She couldn't have asked for a better Christmas gift.

But you did *ask for this. You asked God for more time with the kids.*

Her hand flew to cover a gasp. At the bank last week, when she'd asked God for more time, the bank hadn't given it. But now some investor was offering her more time—and all she had to do was accept.

"Is this Your doing, God?" she whispered. "Did You do this?" She closed her eyes. *Are You real? Do You actually care?*

Words from a song Joe often sang trickled through her heart.

> He knows my heart, the deepest part
> He feels my pain, my darkest shame
> Yet lifts me up and holds me close
> Fills me with His peace and says
> Because of My love, I call you my own.

A vibration in her pocket followed by a buzz jolted Sue out of her thoughts. She pulled out her cell and answered Layne's call.

"Sue? Sorry about the delay, but before I can send over the paperwork, I need you to double-check—"

"Wait. You haven't sent it yet? Stop. Don't send it!" Sue looked up at motion in the doorway. Bertie. Sue flashed the old woman a thumbs-up.

"Don't take my kids, Layne. We've just been given three more months."

Smiling, Joe stowed his cell and lowered the lid on the bubbling turkey broth. One day until Christmas Eve and things were coming together.

"What's up with all the calls, J-man?" Chaz wiped oniony hands on his jeans. "Got a hot girlfriend?"

"Just some details I gotta take care of."

A big grin spread across the kid's face. "Christmas-present details?"

Joe laughed. "Like I'd tell you."

Chaz grinned again. He scooped up the diced onions and flung them into the stuffing.

Joe turned down the burner on the stock. The Realtor had arranged for Joe to sign papers and visit the title company at the same time, a miracle in itself with time limited and secrecy a must. He'd spent more time on the phone the last three days than he had in his entire life. And keeping his conversations out of the boys' hearing hadn't been easy. He'd listed his property as separate lots, applied for a loan on the ranch using a couple acres as collateral, and asked the bank to prepare a down payment from his savings.

It had taken most of Monday to file for an LLC. Naming it "Montgomery Enterprises" after Chaz seemed fitting. Joe also set up the purchase offer through the LLC with the help of his new lawyer.

Luckily for Joe, Steve Weston never forgot a friend, especially one who'd saved his neck on their last climbing trek in Alaska.

And somehow Joe had managed to pick up Christmas presents for Sue and the kids. He even found some rainbow tie-dye for old Bertie.

Mr. Stewart agreed to store the gifts at his place. Mrs. Stewart had gotten teary when she saw the presents and said she was going to bake those kids something extra special for Christmas.

Just as Joe and the guys started cleaning up, Sue and some of the girls came into the kitchen.

"No girls allowed," Edgar mumbled. "We're on Christmas Eve dinner crew."

"Christmas Eve isn't until tomorrow, dork." Brandi said. "You done trashing the kitchen? We have to make tonight's dinner."

"Hey," Chaz snapped. "Us *men* are making a real Christmas dinner with all the trimmings. You might get to lick the gravy spoon. If we let you."

"We'll be out of your way in a sec." Joe grinned at Sue, then turned away. He'd have to knock that off before she got suspicious. "We're just prepping now for tomorrow night."

"You guys are fine." Sue gave Brandi a look. "We're in no hurry."

Joe turned off the broth, wiped his hands on a towel, and went to Sue. "Hope you don't mind if I spend some time with John and Fiona."

She searched his eyes. "Are you serious?

340

You've been working here for nothing but room and board. Board which usually comes out of your own pocket, if we were to get technical. Besides, they're your family. I'm glad you're going. The way you're helping them is really very . . ." She turned and brushed crumbs off the island. "You should spend more than a few hours with them, Joe. Nine days from now you'll be too far away to see them."

He bit back a smile. "Nine days? I wasn't counting."

She shot him a confused frown.

Are you going to miss me? The thought sent a warm, guilty pleasure through him. He knew exactly how many days until he was supposed to leave for Louisiana.

Except now he wasn't leaving.

"Sue, about me leaving—looks like they don't need me to be there on the first now. Is it okay if I stay a few more days?"

"Really? I mean, yeah, that's no problem."

"Thanks."

She glanced around the kitchen. Vince was spraying a soapy pot and getting more water on the counter and window than on the pot itself. Sue lowered her voice. "Joe, there's been a change in plans. Juniper Ranch isn't going to auction."

Joe raised his eyebrows to display the appropriate level of surprise.

"It's being sold to an investor. I'm signing the

papers right after Christmas. But the buyer can't take possession until April and has offered to let us stay here until then." Her face softened. "Rent-free."

The sparkle of a tear in her eye caught him off guard, set his heart pounding. He needed to be more careful. Keeping his secret might be a lot harder than he thought. "So you and the kids don't have to leave so soon now, huh? That's a plus."

She nodded and watched the teens vying to work in the same space. "It's a huge plus. And it makes me wonder if . . ." She faced him, an intense question burning in her eyes.

His pulse quickened. *Shoot. She knows.*

"I think it might have been an answer to prayer."

Sue had *prayed?* "What do you mean?"

She took hold of his wrist and pulled him toward the kitchen door, out of the kids hearing. "That day I went to the bank, I sort of asked God to give me more time with the kids. I thought He didn't answer. But this offer—it's like a gift. From out of nowhere and from a total stranger. It's probably just a coincidence, right?"

The way she searched his face kicked his pulse up three more notches. He cleared his throat. "It sounds like an answer to prayer to me."

Nodding, she blinked moist eyes. "That's what I thought."

Way to go, Father. She's beginning to open her heart to You. I didn't know she prayed for more time, and You used me to answer that prayer. He swallowed hard. "That's great, Sue. I'm glad for you."

"It's only a few months, but—" With a long look at the kids, she got quiet. "Time is precious. I'm relieved to have a little more. And grateful."

If only he could pull her into his arms and tell her she didn't ever have to leave. Instead he nodded, forced to pretend he was a surprised bystander.

"I guess I owe God and some silent investment company my thanks," she said softly.

As she left him to help with dinner, Joe fought back a smile. *That sweet heart of yours is about to bust free, and I'm going to be right there when it happens. That's worth waiting for.*

If he could stand the wait.

CHAPTER TWENTY-EIGHT

"Hey, who messed with my sequencing?" Chaz pushed his glasses higher and peered at the jumble of wires crisscrossing the back of the thin board. "Pass me that screwdriver."

Sue handed over the screwdriver and paused to stretch and look around. The den was overrun with twelve mismatched kids, three tables full of projects, and—not a partridge in a pear tree other than Sue. She hadn't intended to be the only adult on duty Christmas Eve day. Sue had given Bertie Christmas Eve and most of Christmas day off, forgetting that when she gave Linda and Karla their notice, their time was up at Christmas, not the end of the month. But Joe would be back for dinner, so she wouldn't be alone for long.

It hadn't been hard to get the kids interested in making Christmas gifts for Joe, Bertie, and the Stewarts. She helped Jasmine and Cori with their snowman by filling in the lettering on his "Let It Snow" sign with a tiny paintbrush.

The snowman for Mrs. Stewart was Jasmine's idea, after the farmer's wife delivered chocolate cream and pumpkin pies for Christmas.

"Hey, Crankypants, hand me that extension cord."

Sue snapped her head up.

The extension cord lay at Brandi's feet, but the girl either hadn't heard Chaz or hadn't bothered to respond. She'd been dozing in the corner the entire time the kids had been working.

Chaz rolled his desk chair across the floor and picked up the cord. "Got it. Don't sweat it, princess. Wouldn't want you to break a nail."

Brandi snorted and buried her face in her bent knees.

"Stupid snowman keep falling," Jasmine said. "He not stand up."

Cori frowned. "He's not stupid, he's just not fat enough. We need something in the bottom for weight. What we need is some rocks."

Jasmine jumped up. "I get rocks." She disappeared through the foyer and went out the front door, letting in a blast of cold air and the sound of Ringo barking.

Car tires crunched in the drive.

Sue frowned. Bertie wasn't supposed to come back from her sister's until tomorrow night, and Joe wasn't scheduled to return for a few more hours.

She rushed to the window to see if she needed to hide the gift makings.

A late-model sedan she'd never seen before parked near the shop. At least it wasn't Joe or Bertie.

She went to the entryway.

A tall, broad-shouldered man met Sue at the door, Jasmine at his side. His dark eyes and handsome face struck her as oddly familiar.

Ringo sniffed the man, wagging.

"Hi, can I help you?"

"I sure hope so. I'm looking for Joe Paterson." He offered a polite, dimpled smile.

Something about the man's smile quickened her pulse. Sue pulled Jasmine inside. "I'm sorry, Joe's not here right now."

"He's not?" The man's face fell. "Do you expect him back soon?"

"Maybe you could tell me who—"

"Oh, sorry. I'm Ben." He smiled again and held out his hand.

In a daze, Sue shook his hand. *Ben? As in . . .*

"Ben Jacobs. Joe's my brother."

Sue gasped, covering her mouth. "You're little Ben?"

He laughed. "I guess that would be me."

Jasmine tugged on Sue's sleeve. "Miss Susan, he need to come inside. Too cold."

"I'm so sorry. Come in, please!" Sue stepped aside for him as questions swirled through her mind like confetti at New Year's. "Does Joe know you're coming?"

346

Ben shook his head. "I was hoping to surprise him."

"Are you kidding? Yeah, this will *definitely* surprise him. He's going to be so . . ." She caught her lip in her teeth, suddenly struck by the enormity of what this would mean to Joe. "He's in Bend visiting with John and Fiona, actually."

"Is he? Good. Glad to hear that." Ben smiled.

Sue searched him for signs of animosity but didn't see any. Apparently Ben didn't have hard feelings toward the family that had discarded him. "He'll be back for dinner. You're welcome to join us."

"Well, I've waited this long. Guess I can wait a little longer." Ben smiled again, but the light in his eyes dimmed. "I'll just come back later when he's here."

"No, please, come in. Make yourself at home. Jasmine, will you introduce Ben to everyone?" As Jasmine escorted Ben into the den, Sue checked the time.

Now to wait for Joe's return.

No, this couldn't wait. He needed to come home now. She punched his number on her phone, hoping he hadn't turned his off.

"Hey, Sue," Joe answered. "Everything okay?"

"Yes, but you need to come home now. We have a surprise for you."

She could hear the confusion in his pause. "You want me to . . . come *home?*"

"Yes. As soon as you can."

He hesitated a moment. "Okay, we were just about to open presents, but—"

"Can you bring John and Fiona with you?" Sue peeked at Ben, hoping she wasn't making a mistake. "For dinner? Or would that be too hard for your family?"

A stunned silence. "I'll check, but I think they'd like that. Should be enough food."

Sue smiled. "Do you mean for you or everyone?"

"Good point. I *am* pretty hungry."

When Joe's truck lumbered up the drive, Sue sent Edgar, Deeg, and Chaz outside to help Joe with the wheelchairs. She stood in the dining hall, fighting to keep her excitement from bursting out. Her heart pounded so hard she could barely breathe. She peeked behind her at the kitchen door to make sure Ben was still out of sight.

Joe came in pushing a frail-looking man in a wheelchair, followed by a younger woman in another chair aided by the three boys.

Chaz closed the door against the chill.

Joe introduced John and Fiona to everyone.

Above the clamor, Sue met Joe's eyes. Her face probably beamed like a beacon. She didn't care; she couldn't help it.

"Merry Christmas," Joe said softly.

His smile melted her insides. "Merry Christmas, Joe."

"Merry Christmas, Joey!" boomed from behind her. Ben came into the foyer and went straight to Joe. "Been a long time, big brother," he said, voice husky. He offered a hand.

Joe stared at Ben, recognition dawning in his eyes. His chin tilted away, like he was about to ask Sue for an explanation, but his eyes stayed fastened on the younger man. *"Ben?"*

Ben smiled. "The one and only." His waiting hand stretched out further.

"Ben? Are you kidding me?" Joe took a step closer and pulled Ben into a bear hug.

Sue couldn't breathe.

The men pounded each other's backs, hugging each other hard. Voices shushed and the room fell silent.

Tears rolled down Sue's smiling cheeks.

"Missed you, little bro." Joe pulled back and examined his brother, shaking his head. "Where've you been? How'd you find me?"

As Ben told about his search, Sue watched Joe, her heart nearly overflowing.

"And then I almost had you in Alaska, but by the time I figured out what island you were based on, you'd left. It wasn't until your name turned up on the rental agreement for old man Jacobs's place that I found an address for you."

Joe gave Ben's shoulder another squeeze and

a solid pat. "Man, it's so good to see you."

"Been way too long." Ben nodded, never taking his eyes from Joe.

Kids murmured and whispered.

Sue decided to switch up the plan. She gathered a crew of kids and sent them into the kitchen to start dinner, then she gave Joe a nod and followed them.

In the kitchen, Jasmine grasped Sue's hands, giggling. "You see Papa Joe's big smile?" She giggled again. "He so happy."

"I'm very happy for him." Sue wiped her cheeks and smiled. "Okay, guys, let's see if we can whip up a Christmas Eve dinner. Um, who knows the plan?"

Armed with teamwork and a cookbook, she and the kids got things started. The turkeys Joe had popped in the oven before leaving had been roasting all day and were coming along nicely, filling the kitchen with savory smells.

Sue peeked out the door to the dining hall.

Joe strode briskly into the room—alone. He stood at the long window with his back to her, hands on his hips.

Apprehension twisted her belly. Maybe inviting the whole family here was a mistake. These were the people responsible for separating Joe from his brother.

Sue slipped out quietly and went to him. "Joe? Is something wrong?"

Joe shook his head and swiped at his eyes with a sleeve but didn't turn around.

She moved closer and touched his arm.

"No, I'm good," he said, voice choked. "This is good. Best Christmas I've ever had."

The raw emotion in his voice tugged at her heart, launching an overwhelming urge to hug him. Unsure what to do, she simply stood there, her arms hanging empty at her sides.

Joe drew a shuddery breath and flashed a glance her way. "Thanks, Sue. You have no idea what this means to me." Then he returned to the den, leaving her alone.

Loving him.

She'd never felt this stuffed in her entire life.

When the kids and Joe's family crammed into the den after dinner, Jasmine followed Sue to the crowded couch and squeezed in beside her.

Sue let out a half laugh, half groan. "Jasmine, if you squish me any tighter, I'm going to explode. And all over you, probably."

Grinning, Jasmine patted Sue's belly. "You eat too much potatoes, Mama Sue. You take seconds today. I see you."

Mama? Sue tried to focus on what Joe was telling everyone about presents, but all she could hear was what Jasmine had called her in that sweet voice of hers.

"Looks like Ben and I are sharing Santa duty."

Joe clapped his brother on the back and said something only Ben could hear.

Ben grinned and glanced at Sue. "Nobody here wants a Christmas present, do they?" Ben asked.

He was answered with shouts.

Sue talked to Fiona and John, situated to her right, as Joe passed out gifts. Sadness that she couldn't do this for the kids herself quickly disappeared, replaced with the joy of seeing Joe's eagerness. He looked more excited about the presents than the kids did. There was no way she could deny him the pleasure of treating them at Christmas.

As Ben read a name tag and asked who it belonged to, Joe took a gift to Donovan. He helped him open it, watching the boy's face as they peeled back the wrap together.

Donovan peeked into the box, then rolled his head back with a big open-mouthed grin at Joe. "Binoculars!"

Sue smiled at the boy. Watching birds was his favorite pastime.

Joe and Ben handed out more gifts to the squeals and exclamations of kids opening gifts or waiting eagerly for their turns.

Joe must have put a lot of thought into each present. And he was so good at it. It wasn't hard to imagine him being a good dad. Not hard at all. In fact . . .

A dull ache plowed through Sue, leaving a

hollow feeling. Even in a roomful of people, she was alone. Experiencing the same loneliness she'd felt as a foster kid, living in a home but not part of the family, an outsider. Or like the times she'd gone hungry so long that she no longer felt pain. Just emptiness.

Headlights in the den window stirred Sue from her thoughts.

Bertie must have cut her family visit short. But she usually parked in the lot below the shop.

Sue was wedged in so tightly between Jasmine and Sonja that it took a couple tries to get up. By the time she got free and made it to the foyer, the doorbell sounded.

A short, sixtyish woman stood on the porch wearing a fuzzy red reindeer sweater and more bling than a rapper. A blend of cloying perfume and stale nicotine knocked Sue back a step.

"Is Joey here?" The woman spied the crowded den and marched past Sue.

Sue darted around the woman and blocked her from going farther. "Why don't we start with names? I'm Susan Quinn, director of Juniper Ranch. And you are?"

The woman hitched a purse higher on her shoulder and crossed her arms over jangling necklaces. She nodded in the direction of Joe and his family.

"Leia Jacobs. I'm with them."

CHAPTER TWENTY-NINE

Sue turned to Joe.

He froze and stared at the woman in the foyer.

Ben, who was kneeling beside Fiona, looked at her too.

Another member of Joe's family? Sue turned to question the woman, but Leia was already headed for the den.

This must be the mother. Apparently Joe didn't have the same feelings of resolution with the mom as he had with the dad.

Leia eyed the gifts in John's lap. "Well, *you're* making out like a bandit." She turned to Fiona. "Fee? Got a kiss for your mama?" She bent toward the young woman.

Joe stood slowly, his lips disappearing in a thin line.

All Sue could think about was the horrible conditions in which Joe said he'd found John and Fiona. Where was Leia when they were living in filth and struggling to survive? And what did this unexpected visit mean?

Joe glanced at Ben, who also watched Leia without a word.

John Jacobs leaned back and eyeballed the woman. "Told you not to come here."

She snorted. "What kind of world is it when a mother can't even spend Christmas Eve with her own family?" She leaned close to John. "Besides, *you're* the one who told me where Joey lives."

The old man cast a hangdog look at Joe.

Fabulous. Sue shouldn't have let the woman in. She needed to pull Joe aside and ask if he wanted Leia to leave, but Joe tapped Ben and beckoned him to the tree.

Ben followed and they resumed passing out presents, ignoring the interruption.

Sue forced herself to relax.

With a huff, Leia made her way to the couch and squeezed in beside Jasmine. Beneath her dark lashes, the girl peeked at the woman's necklaces, nose wrinkling.

Cori opened her gift and squealed at a shiny, red jacket, bright scarf, and matching hat. "Thank you, J-man." She jumped up from the braided rug and gave him a side hug.

Ben read the label on another package. "To Jasmine."

Jasmine shot to her feet. "Yes! That me!"

Ben grinned and handed the gift to her.

She ripped off the paper and held up an iPod. She covered her mouth, eyes wide. "For me?"

With a huge smile, Joe nodded. "It's already loaded with a bunch of songs I think you'll like."

"Thank you, Papa Joe!"

Leia snorted. "Should've let me do the shopping. A little girl has no business with an expensive item like that. What were you thinking?"

Joe ignored her and handed a gift to Edgar, giving his shoulder a squeeze.

Actually, Sue was sort of wondering the very same thing. What *was* Joe thinking? Not that she would interfere with his desire to give the kids a nice Christmas, but the value of all these gifts combined must have cost him a mint. Even if he had a good-sized savings, how could he spend so much of his money on kids he would never—

Never see again.

Pained by the thought, Sue dragged a chair from the dining hall to the edge of the den and took a seat. *Doesn't matter. He'll be gone soon and then we'll move on. All of us.* The thought carved a void in her heart.

"Looks like I got here just in time," Leia said, craning her neck to see what else was under the tree. "Anything for me?"

Scooping up the last of the packages, Joe paused. "Heard you didn't want to be part of the family anymore." He spoke in an even tone.

The chatter in the room quieted.

Leia darted looks at Ben and Sue, then shrugged. "No harm done. You didn't know I was coming." With a quick study of Jasmine's iPod, she said, "I'll take mine in cash."

Joe froze in the center of the room and stared at Leia. "Did you say *cash?*"

Leia lifted her chin. "Why not? You shelled out a fortune on these kids, and they're not even family."

Joe turned toward the kids, who were breaking out their gifts and showing them to each other. "These kids are none of your business."

With an effort, Leia stood up and smoothed down her tangled necklaces. "I know how good those oil rigs pay. You're taking care of your family now. I'm entitled to my share."

Joe turned and handed a package to one of the kids. "No."

"Why not?"

His shoulders went rigid. "You don't want to do this here, Leia."

"I just want what they got."

Joe turned to her, eyes menacing as thunderclouds. He stepped close to her and bent over, dwarfing her with his towering frame. "Do you have any idea how I found John and Fiona?"

She leaned away from him. "Don't go twisting things around and blaming *me*. They were fine when I left. And if you're bent out of shape about ancient history, that was totally out of my hands."

"Out of your—" His words grated like metal on stone. Joe glared at the woman, nostrils flaring. "I've got nothing you want, Leia. Guarantee you that." He crossed the room to Chaz, who was showing his telescope to Daisy, and crouched beside them to look at it.

Leia's bejeweled sweater rose and fell in bursts, her face mottled shades of red. She looked around, spied Sue, and came to her. "Guess you're pretty lax about the kind of people you have working for you," she said in low tones. "Or maybe you just don't care about having a sex offender working with kids."

Sue's pulse raced. "What are you talking about?"

Leia eyed Joe and kept her voice low. "Your girl over there in the wheelchair? I wouldn't trust him alone with her for a second. He always did have a thing for the weaker ones."

Sue shook her head, mind numb. "Not Joe."

The woman shrugged, her gaze darting around the room. "Don't take my word for it. It's in the court records. When we found out what he'd been doing to Fiona and the others, the judge removed him from our home." She spied Joe and Daisy. "He was always big for his age. A bully. The judge made sure he was sent to a home where there weren't any smaller or weaker kids."

Sue's thoughts whirled. That was *not* the Joe she knew. Not the vibes she got from him.

Yet . . . sometimes vibes lied. Played tricks on a girl. Especially when a girl's silly heart got in there and confused things. Still trying to process what the woman was saying, Sue whispered,

"You said court records." She swallowed hard. "He was a minor. Those records are sealed."

Leia narrowed her eyes. "Exactly. Not the kind of thing a guy puts on his résumé, if you know what I mean."

Joe steadied the telescope for Daisy, then helped her aim it out the den window.

"Don't have to take my word for it." Leia shook her head. "Court said he was *deviant*. Fancy name for a filthy pervert. I can't even talk about what he did."

Sue couldn't listen any more. She rose and went to the foyer, needing distance from Leia.

The idea of Joe victimizing children was ridiculous. But if a court had removed him to protect other children, that pointed to potentially serious issues, even if he'd only been a kid.

Nausea crept into her stomach. She was sickened by both this news and by how desperately she hoped it wasn't true. He'd had opportunity to be alone with the boys and even some of the girls.

Had her feelings for him blinded her? Like her mom had done before her, had Sue let stupidity over a man put kids at risk?

She took a look around the crowded den. Had Joe ever been alone with Daisy? Sue held her breath and watched as Joe gave Daisy's hair a tousle and picked up another Christmas package.

And headed straight for Sue.

Joe tucked Sue's gift under his arm and made his way to her. She'd left the den and was now alone in the foyer. Good.

Leia had gone to sit with Fiona, which was even better. He didn't want to give Sue her gift in front of Leia. He also didn't want to wreck Christmas for Sue and the kids with an ugly scene. Sending Leia out the front door with a boot to her backside would probably upset the kids, so he'd resisted the powerful urge.

But very soon, when everyone else was occupied, he would escort Leia to her car and make sure she never set foot here again. Yeah, he was supposed to forgive. Didn't mean he had to look at her.

When he reached Sue, she looked up at him, expression tight.

Joe sighed. This jolly Jacobs family reunion must have been more than she'd bargained for. "Don't forget yours," he said quietly, handing her the gift. "I know. You don't do birthdays, and you probably don't do Christmas either. But everyone gets one today." He shrugged. "Nobody argues with Santa."

She took the gift absently, skimming a glance at the cluster of fancy chocolates attached with a ribbon to the outside of the package.

Joe silently thanked the girl at Macy's for that extra touch.

She opened the box and drew out the softest sweater he could find. Her gaze lingered on the pink fluff, but it seemed her mind was somewhere else. "Thank you, Joe. It's lovely." Then she lifted her gaze, eyes troubled. "I can't believe I have to ask you this," she said, her strained voice barely above a whisper. "Your adult background check cleared, but do you have a record of being a sex offender as a minor?"

"What—?" A rush of anger stole his breath.

Leia.

Heat seared his veins. "Lies. She *lies.*"

"She said there are court records. How could she lie about a thing like that?"

Because she's a cold-blooded snake. His jaw clenched until pain shot through his back teeth.

After all these years, his worth, his hard-earned credibility, was on the line again? His reputation in the hands of that woman—again?

Joe turned a narrowed gaze at Leia. No. She wasn't getting away with it. Not this time.

He spun and stormed into the den. Ben took one look at Joe's face and shot to his feet.

Joe went straight to Leia. "You're leaving."

She gawked at him.

"Now. You can walk out or we can escort you."

Leia folded her arms.

Joe grasped an elbow and hauled her to her feet.

Ben took her other elbow.

"What in the—"

"Let's go," Joe said. "You've said enough."

Together, he and Ben forced the sputtering woman to the foyer. Joe opened the door and propelled her across the porch, her feet scurrying like a fleeing insect.

Even though Ben scrambled to keep up, Joe didn't slow down but forced the wriggling, cursing woman down the steps and across the lawn to her car. At the door, he spun her to face him. "You black-hearted, lying piece of filth. You don't know me. You've got nothing to say about me and you don't deserve to share the same air as the people I care about."

"I only said what was—"

"Lies. You can't even draw breath without lying. I was just a *kid,* Leia. Remember that? A defenseless kid. And you were a monster disguised as a mother."

"Oh! How dare you—"

"How dare *you!* You made me feel like a disease. Took me a long time to figure out the disease was really you. You and your punk son, the one you threw me under the bus to protect."

"Ruben is sick and he . . . he has problems, but he's getting help now."

"Yeah, he's sick, but *you're* the sick one who turned a blind eye to the way he terrorized the kids *you* were supposed to protect. Kids you were paid to protect. You destroyed a kid to save your own skin, Leia. For money." Joe spat. What dirty money it was.

She huffed. "Destroyed? All I did was ask the judge to remove you."

"You built a case of lies against a ten-year-old kid and then left me hanging all alone with nothing but the worst kind of shame."

Ben stepped forward and stood beside Joe, arms crossed.

"I lived with the name-calling, the looks, the whispers, people shooing their kids away from me. Learned to fight the heckling. I spent years working to undo all the damage you did."

"Ben?" She turned a nervous look his way. "You were there. It wasn't like that. Tell him."

Ben shook his head. "No. You robbed me of my brother. And you let that son of yours prey on defenseless kids. You're a coward, Leia. A greedy, lying coward. You should be rotting in jail."

Leia opened the car door and scrambled into the driver's seat.

Joe grabbed the door so she couldn't shut it. He thrust a finger at her face. "Don't come back. And stay away from John and Fiona." Joe slammed the door.

The car backed around, overshot up onto the lawn, then sped down the drive, fishtailing in the snow as it left.

Ben watched the car until it disappeared, then

turned to Joe. "Wow. Never heard a closing argument like that. Ever think about going into law?"

Joe surveyed the silent, frozen valley. It felt good to finally tell her off. Good but sickening. Like he'd been chewing on garbage. He spat and turned toward the house but stopped when he saw Sue.

She held on to the porch post, looking ashen. However long she'd been standing there, it must have been long enough to witness the decades-old fury he'd unleashed on his ex-mom.

Great.

He'd left Sue with Leia's accusations ringing in her ears. He needed to explain, clear his name, prove himself above suspicion.

Again.

CHAPTER THIRTY

In the light of the front porch, the look on Joe's face was not guilt. But the fury in his voice when he sent Leia away had left Sue trembling. She barely noticed when Ben passed them and went inside, closing the door behind him. A gust of wind plastered hair across her face. She tucked a strand behind her ear and pulled her sweatshirt tighter. "Is it true that the court removed you from the Jacobses' home?"

He nodded slowly. "Yeah. I was ten. At the time, I thought it was because of something I did that I was . . . deeply ashamed of," he said. "Leia used that to cover up her gross negligence and deflect attention from Ruben, her son. By that time, Leia had me convinced I was repulsive. So, in my guilt and confusion, I confessed to things I didn't do." He met her eyes. "I didn't understand the difference between what I had done and what Leia and Ruben were saying I'd done."

Sue gave herself a moment to prepare herself for his answer before going on. "What did you do that you were ashamed of?"

Joe raised his face to the night and closed his

eyes. "I hit Fiona." He swallowed hard. "Not a day passes that I don't want to crawl into a hole for giving in and doing that."

Nausea rolled through her. The girl was mentally and physically disabled, utterly defenseless. "Why?"

Slowly, Joe met her gaze. "Leia's son was a monster. I don't know the full extent of what Ruben did to the other kids who came through the home, but I have a good idea. Sometimes he'd force me to be his lookout. I should never have done that. He threatened to beat me up if I ever told, and at first I stood up to him, because I didn't care if he hurt me. But then he threatened to hurt Ben. I was afraid I couldn't protect him, so I didn't tell. Then he started pressuring me to hurt Fiona. I refused, but he kept at it. Then he started knocking Ben around." Joe turned away and searched the evening sky. "I gave in. I shouldn't have, but I slapped her. I . . . kept at it until she cried." His voice cracked. "Ruben tried to convince me she didn't feel it. But I knew she did. He said if I ever told on him, I'd be in more trouble than anyone else because I'd . . . I'd abused a disabled kid." The last words were barely a whisper. "I remember being in the courtroom, crying and apologizing, not realizing what I was confessing to. I had no idea until a couple years later, after I'd been labeled a child sex offender." He looked at Sue, eyes filled with grief. "By then I was alone. No one believed me."

She watched him, unable to deny the sincerity in his face. But appearances could be deceiving, a lesson she'd vowed never to forget.

Leia's statements in court could have been convincing enough to have Joe removed. And it was possible that, as a child, Joe felt so guilty about hitting Fiona that he had confessed to things he didn't understand. Knowing Joe, it made sense. It also wasn't hard to believe that woman capable of lying—her character hadn't escaped Sue's notice.

But it was also possible that Sue wasn't the best judge of character. And because of that, she needed to remember her duty to protect her kids.

She pressed a palm to her churning stomach. "I need to think about all this."

"Okay." Joe nodded slowly, watching her. "Ben and I are going to take John and Fiona home. If you want, I can call you when I'm on the road, answer any more questions you have."

Rubbing her temples, she shook her head. "It's getting late. We can talk about this tomorrow." She swallowed hard. "But it would be best if you stayed in your room tonight instead of the boys' dorm."

Joe stuffed hands in his pockets. "But that means you'd be the only one on duty." He spoke quietly. "You can't do bed watch for twelve kids by yourself."

Sue shivered. "I'll manage."

Early Thursday morning, Sue headed up the stairs for one last check on the sleeping girls. Since today was Christmas Day, she'd promised to let the kids sleep in, especially the boys who had camped out in the den since she was the only one on duty and needed to keep an eye on both groups. When she returned downstairs, she crept into the kitchen, peeked out the back window at the silent staff quarters, then started a pot of coffee.

Though she was exhausted, staying awake for bed watch hadn't been hard. Her heart and mind had wrestled all night over everything that had happened.

She took her coffee into the den, stepping around the sleeping boys and over discarded gift wrappings. She sank onto a couch and sipped the steaming black brew.

Joe's explanation made sense, but it was still unsettling. Trust was too fragile a thing to give without solid proof.

She needed to know more. She knew how the system worked.

Though the events were long past, she wouldn't rest easy until she had a better understanding of who Joe really was and whether or not the courts had truly found just cause to remove him from his adoptive family. If only she could know for sure that he was telling the truth.

She rose and quietly scooped up piles of paper and cellophane, wadding them into balls.

One cluster of wrappings felt heavy. Within the discarded paper was a present. Unopened.

To Brandi, from Santa.

Sue frowned.

Brandi hadn't opened her gift from Joe. Why?

Package in hand, she climbed the stairs and tapped on Cori and Brandi's door.

No answer.

Sue slipped inside and went to Brandi's bed.

Clothes spilled from the closet and more covered the floor beside the bed. Room-cleaning and bed checks had fallen sadly behind.

All the more reason you should be trying to get these kids placed in new homes now instead of keeping them here where you can barely hold it together.

"What do you want?" A groan emerged from the dark hair covering Brandi's face. "You said we could sleep in."

Sue sat at the foot of the bed. "I'm just wondering how you're doing."

Brandi buried her face in the pillow. "Doing great—soon as I can go back to sleep."

Sue nodded. "Okay, I won't bug you. I was just curious about this is all." Sue turned the package over, revealing the tag. "Didn't you get this last night?"

The girl angled her head to see, then mumbled, "Yep," and closed her eyes.

"It hasn't been opened."

Brandi rubbed her face. "Right. Is there going to be a test on this later?"

"I wondered if it had been missed somehow. But if you got it, then . . .?"

"Then I just didn't feel like opening it. Or is that breaking another one of your rules?"

Sue glanced at Cori's sleeping frame in the other bed. "Right. Maybe it's none of my business." Or was it? Should she be concerned?

Brandi snorted and muttered.

"Is something bothering you?"

"Yeah. We're *talking* when I could be sleeping."

Sue stood. "Okay, I'll let you sleep."

The covers flew over the girl's head, obscuring her from view.

After breakfast and cleanup, Sue gathered the girls for games in the den and then headed out back to check on the guys. Joe and Ben were with the boys in the backyard at the burn barrel, burning wrappings and extra holiday trash. Ben would leave early Friday to catch his flight back home, but until then, Sue had invited him to stay at the ranch with Joe.

Joe helped Donovan lob cardboard into the fire.

Sue shivered and pulled her jacket tighter. "Joe, when you get a chance, can we talk?"

He rubbed his hands near the fire. "Sure, after we get this put out."

Sue returned to the house and headed for the den, but Brandi sprang from the foot of the stairs and stopped her.

"Miss Susan? Can I talk to you?"

"Sure." Sue peeked in on the girls and then motioned Brandi into the office.

Brandi set the unopened Christmas present on Sue's desk. "Yesterday was my birthday."

Guilt sank in her belly like a hot brick. "Oh, Brandi. We forgot. I'm so sorry!"

The girl shrugged. "Happens a lot. Everywhere I've ever lived, it's like, 'Here's a present, take your pick—Christmas or birthday.' Gets old after a while." She crossed her arms.

"I really am sorry," Sue said. "I've had a lot on my mind lately, but that's no excuse."

Brandi lifted her shoulders in another shrug. "It's not like I want to make a big deal out of it. I'm seventeen now, not a little kid. I'm the oldest one here. Sometimes I just wish I could—you know, get a break from this place. Hang out with someone my age."

It *had* been quite a while since Brandi had been with kids her age. Due in large part to her being grounded from extracurricular activities, but still . . .

"My friend Megan lives in Juniper Valley. Her parents are nice. They go to church and stuff. They came to all our soccer games and said I could come over anytime."

Of course they come to games and invite kids over. Because that's what good parents do.

"So I was wondering if I could go to Megan's for a little while. I know I'm grounded from sports and everything, but maybe just this once, for my birthday."

Wasn't it the least she could do? Sue nodded. "I'm not sure they would want visitors on Christmas. But if it's okay with her parents, and I can talk to Megan's mom, I don't see why not."

Brandi brightened. "Really? I'll call her right now. Thanks, Miss Susan."

It turned out that Megan's parents were more than happy to have Brandi over and even offered to pick her up.

Throughout the day, Sue tried to find a good time to talk to Joe, but he and his brother were still catching up, and she couldn't bring herself to interrupt that. Besides, Ben would be gone in the morning. She and Joe could talk then.

Turkey leftovers were a big hit. In the middle of dinner, Sue got a call from Brandi. She took the phone into the den, away from the noise in the dining hall.

"Miss Susan?" Brandi sounded breathless. "Thanks for letting me come, it's so much fun here. They had pizza and ice cream for my birthday. Megan invited me to spend the night. Do you think I could? Please say yes."

At least *someone* had celebrated the girl's birthday.

Before Sue could answer, Megan's mom got on the phone and offered to drive Brandi back to the ranch Friday after breakfast.

"It's very nice of you to do that, thank you." Sue gave it some quick thought. Being with people that Brandi didn't live with and hanging out with a nice, normal family might be just what the girl needed to lift her out of the funk she'd been in.

Brandi got back on the phone. "So?"

"Okay, you have my permission. Please come back right after breakfast, and don't be late." Squealing from the other end pierced her eardrum.

Brandi thanked her repeatedly and hung up.

Sue pocketed her phone and sighed. Why did the choice to trust someone always cause such a sick feeling in her gut? Would it always be that way?

But then, as far as anyone at Juniper Ranch was concerned, did it matter? Soon, she wouldn't have to worry about any of the people here.

The relief that should have given her felt more like a gaping hole.

CHAPTER THIRTY-ONE

Joe couldn't have planned the weather better. Friday turned out cold but clear and windless, perfect for launching Chaz's new remote control plane, as soon as Joe and the guys could get it assembled.

After breakfast, Ben said his good-byes and promised to get together soon, then Joe and the boys set up tables in the den to work. With Sue at the title company in La Pine signing off on the property, Bertie, who had returned late Christmas night, was in charge of everyone and gave the girls a choice of a group activity or free time. The vote for free time had been unanimous.

"Oh man," Chaz moaned. "The slot for mounting the landing gear is messed up."

Joe looked up from the wheel assembly.

Chaz frowned at the plane's undercarriage.

Joe took a closer look. "Hand me the tape measure, will ya?" He measured the space and found a misaligned slat. With a straight-edged blade, he whittled the rib to deepen the notch where the slat rested. Then he checked the clock. Again.

The stack of documents Sue had to sign would be a thick one, and she had a long drive home. But that didn't keep him from checking the time and listening for her car. He had no idea what kind of mood she would be in after signing away her property. She had been quiet when she left for town. Selling the place had to be hard, even with the extra time she believed it gave her.

Whatever her frame of mind, he needed to be ready to step in and keep everyone on task to avoid any added strain.

But Sue wasn't the only one affected by the recent turn of events. Joe was still reeling from seeing Ben and getting used to the idea of having his brother back. And then there was Leia.

He'd known he still carried bitterness toward her, but where had that sudden rage come from? Hadn't he given it over to God years ago? Obviously not, if five minutes with her had sent him right back to feeling like a terrified, betrayed kid all over again.

A ripple of anger coursed through him. Leia showing up here was bad enough, but to spew more of her filthy lies? She hadn't changed a bit.

As rough as John and Fiona had it, they were far better off without Leia in their lives.

Joe replaced the slat, measured the new space for consistency, and slid the main body back to Chaz.

The kid tested the space again with his piece

of landing gear. "Fits!" He grinned at Joe. "Manufacturer must have used a faulty die cut on that rib."

Joe nodded. "That was a really good catch, Chaz."

Chaz turned his attention to his task, cheeks blotchy.

Joe checked the time again.

How long would it take to regain her trust? Win her over to the idea of running the home together? And most important of all, to win her heart?

"Hey." Vince nudged Edgar. "We need music."

Edgar dropped an earbud from one ear and frowned.

Vince went on. "You could share, ya know."

Edgar looked around at the other guys, then back at Vince. "It's an iPod."

"J-man can provide the music," Chaz said, looking up from his task. "You should play your guitar while we work. You've just been slacking off, anyway."

Joe's brows rose. "*I'm* slacking off?"

Chaz pushed his glasses higher and snorted. "You been watching that clock the whole time. Whatcha got, a hot date or something?"

With a laugh, he shook his head. "Nope. You guys are it." He wiped dust from his hands and chucked the rag at Chaz's head. "I'll get my guitar. Be right back."

He'd left the guitar in the chapel, hadn't he?

Joe headed outside and up the trail. Hit by a sudden blast of cold, he broke into a jog. The midday sun shone high but did nothing to warm the wind cutting through his T-shirt. He opened the chapel door, but a sudden gust ripped it from his hand and slammed it against the wall.

A crash and the sound of shattering glass arrested his hand.

Animal? Or someone who didn't belong here? He stepped inside, ready to confront the intruder.

Brandi crouched in a corner as if ready to bolt, eyes wide. Between her feet lay a mess of broken brown glass and a pool of foam.

Taking a step closer, Joe smelled beer. *Oh man. Not good. At all.* "What's going on, Brandi?"

The girl peered past him at the door and moistened her lips. "Nothing, I was just—"

"Where'd you get the beer?"

"I didn't—I wasn't—" she stammered, eyes darting around the room. "I was just keeping it for my friend. You know, to hide it from her parents."

Right. "How much have you had?"

"None. I was just gonna have one, that's all. Please don't tell Miss Susan. She'll send me to that freak hospital. Please?"

Joe shook his head. "Brandi, you know you shouldn't even have beer, and especially not here."

Her look brightened. "I know, you're right. I shouldn't have agreed to hide it. I just wanted Megan and the other girls to like me. I promise it'll never ever happen again, okay?"

Joe searched the girl's pleading face. Would Sue really send the girl to an institution? Either way, he had no choice but to report the incident.

Brandi took a step closer. "You can get rid of it, and I won't do it again, I promise, J-man. Here—" She stooped and brought up another bottle, already open. She thrust it at him. "One for you and then we're even. See?" She smiled. "No harm done." Fresh blood trickled down her arm.

With a slow shake of his head, he took the bottle away from her. "No deal, kid. Come inside the house, and we can decide what you're going tell Miss Susan."

"Me?" The girl searched his face, her eyes narrowing. "You want *me* to tell her?"

Joe nodded. "She's reasonable. And she cares about you, Brandi. If you tell her the truth and take responsibility like an adult, she'll listen."

She burst out with a harsh laugh. "She won't listen. She only sees me as another nutso kid in her little spazoid collection."

A rush of wind sounded like a coyote howling.

She looked into his eyes and lowered her voice. "But *you* know I'm an adult, right?"

Apprehension prickled up his spine.

"Only one more year and I'm aged out. But if I get sent to the state place now, I could be stuck there for a really long time. All because of one beer. Don't do that to me, J-man. Please?"

"You did it to yourself, Brandi." He tossed his head toward the door. "Let's go—"

"Want to know a secret?" She took a step closer, her voice a breathless whisper. "I always thought you were so hot."

What?

"You and me, we could have a party, just this once. No one has to know about *any* of it. Our little secret. You know?" Smiling, she stepped closer and touched his chest.

Joe jerked away and stepped back.

"You think I'm pretty, don't you?"

Joe pinned her with a steady gaze. "That's enough."

She moved closer and locked eyes with his. "I can't stand that place. I'd do anything not to go there." She roped her arms around his neck and lifted her face to his.

Joe yanked her arms free. "Stop it, Brandi—"

"Don't you get it, you big idiot?" she hissed, cheeks pink.

"We're going. Now." He strode to the door. As he reached the doorway, a low roar behind him rose to a scream.

"Stupid jerk! I hate you!" She hit him like a grenade blast, rocking him off balance and sending beer spraying from the bottle as it flew out of his hand.

He spun and barely missed a blow to the jaw.

She swung again, but he caught her wrist just before it clipped his chin.

He grabbed the other wrist and held tight.

Brandi landed a sharp kick to his shin, sending him back a step. Her bloody wrist slipped out of his grasp and she took another swing at his face.

He blocked her fist, then got hold of both her biceps and held her off at arm's length.

She writhed and swore, jerking herself back and forth to get free.

He grasped tighter. *Think, man.*

Call Bertie.

Joe pushed Brandi backward and sat her down on a bench, then reached for his phone. Wasn't in his pocket. He must've left it inside. He'd have to go get Bertie and have her come here and deal with the girl. Maybe that would give Brandi a few minutes to cool off.

Joe looked the girl in the eye. "You sit right there and stay put. I'm going to get Miss Roberta. And I mean don't move an inch, you hear me?"

Brandi scowled, face scarlet, chest heaving with ragged breaths. "I'll run. You can't stop me."

"You won't get far. Don't even try it, Brandi."

Joe left the chapel and went toward the house, looking back several times to make sure the girl didn't slip out. He stopped on the front porch, where he could keep an eye on the chapel. Praying the girl wouldn't pull any more stupid stunts, he stepped inside and hollered at the guys to get Miss Roberta.

Vince threw Joe an odd look, then said maybe she and some of the girls were in the kitchen.

Joe went in, but the kitchen was deserted. He checked the utility room, then went out back. She was probably with the other kids, caring for animals in the barn.

But the barn was also empty.

Joe returned to the front yard, chilled clean through from the wind. He was shivering not only from the cold, but also from what he'd just witnessed. A girl had to be really messed up to pull something like that.

As Joe waited on the lawn, the ramifications of Brandi's behavior began to sink in. What if he'd been a different kind of guy? There were scumbags who would have taken advantage of a girl in that situation.

She's a mess, Father. She needs Your help. Her life is in a dangerous place right now.

Joe paced the length of the lawn, nearly frozen in only a beer-soaked T-shirt. Freezing and wandering around outside was ridiculous. He needed to get Bertie out there to deal with Brandi. And someone needed to call Sue.

Wait—how long had he left the chapel

unguarded? He needed to make sure Brandi was still in there before he did anything else. As he turned to go, the front door opened and Bertie stepped out onto the porch. Joe breathed a sigh of relief and bounded up the steps. "Good. I was looking for—"

"Hold it right there, Joe."

He met her at the door and stopped. "What? Why?"

The sound of shrill crying came from deep inside the house.

Joe glanced toward the chapel and then back at the house. "Is that Brandi?"

Bertie sniffed him, her lips clamped tight. "Sorry, but you're gonna have to wait out here. The police are on their way."

"Police?" Dread raced ahead of the suspicion forming in his brain, numbing him as the picture came into terrible focus. "Bertie, I don't know what she told you, but—"

"What she told me and how you both look adds up to some very serious charges."

"Charges? She's lying, Bertie." He fought to keep his voice from booming. "You *know* she lies. I can tell you exactly what hap—"

"It's out of my hands. Assault and attempted rape are capital offenses, especially in a home like this. I'm bound by law to report this. We'd be spread across every newspaper and sued ten ways to Sunday if I didn't." Bertie turned toward the girl's cry. "Best for everyone if you just stay put, Joe. Let the law do what they need to do. Sorry." She stepped inside and closed the door with a firm click.

He stared at the door.

This was just a nightmare.

It had to be.

CHAPTER THIRTY-TWO

As Sue passed the Stewart farm, another twinge gripped her chest.

Sold.

Juniper Ranch was no longer hers. The deed was signed, no turning back.

Sue reached for her phone to call Bertie, but it was dead.

Keeping her phone charged hadn't exactly been foremost on her mind last night. She turned her attention to the snow-dusted road ahead.

How had her dream come to this?

She knew *exactly* how. A blend of bad planning, trusting the wrong people, and circumstances beyond her control. But the death of her dream wasn't what tore at her.

She'd grown to love those kids. That was never part of the plan. How could anyone take in these kids and not get emotionally involved? Her heart hurt like crazy, and they weren't even gone yet. Had she really believed she could avoid this?

Rounding the last turn, the ranch came into view. From a distance, the snow-capped roofs, white and glittering in the afternoon sun, resembled a sandcastle topped with sugar. A steady wind pulled at the powder on the rooftops, tugging up bits of snow into swirling clouds that disappeared into the vast sea of white.

Nothing I love ever lasts.

Sue turned onto the ranch's road and drove toward the house.

Joe.

Sue forced his dimpled smile out of her mind. Signing over the deed felt more final than she'd expected. Juniper Ranch was history. Time to accept that she needed to put Joe and the kids behind her, just as she had everyone else she'd lost. Chalk it up to another lesson learned the hard way and move on.

Alone.

A green sheriff's cruiser was parked in the staff lot.

Apprehension nudged her on and she continued up the drive, pulse quickening. When she rounded the curve, she stopped. Another cruiser sat near the shop, two men standing beside it.

She scrambled out of the car.

High-pitched yelling from the porch sent her heart racing.

"Sue!" Bertie called down from the porch. She appeared to be restraining Brandi.

The girl sobbed as alarmed faces gaped from the window.

Sue hurried toward the house, limbs numbing

with dread, worsened because she didn't know what to fear. "What's going on?"

"He hurt me!" Brandi pointed with a shaking arm at the squad car and tried to pull away from Bertie's hold. "That monster tried to rape me!"

"What?" Sue whipped around to see the men near the deputy's car.

A uniformed officer.

And Joe.

Joe? No, oh no, it can't be true.

But his ex-mom did say—

Dread raced through her, deadening her limbs.

Joe caught her eye and mouthed her name.

"Court said he was deviant. Fancy name for a filthy pervert. I wouldn't trust him alone with her for a second."

On legs threatening to buckle, Sue stumbled toward the cop car. The officer stepped forward, but Sue skirted around him and faced Joe.

His shirt was wet and smeared with blood, and so were his hands and cheek. "Sue, I need to tell—"

"Ma'am, are you in charge here?" the officer asked.

She ignored the cop and took a step closer. "Joe? What's—" A gust of wind brought the smell of alcohol to her nostrils. Her stomach clenched. "You've been *drinking?*"

"The girl is lying, Sue. When I found her—"

She spun away as he spoke, nausea welling.

The girl is lying.

Joe's voice droned on as a decades-old memory filled her senses, chilling her again with the same realization.

You stop your lying, Suzy! You just want to ruin what I got.

She closed her eyes to shut out the sting of betrayal, of being defenseless and alone. Not again. Someone *had* to listen to the girl.

"Ms. Quinn?" the cop said.

Sue turned.

The deputy positioned himself between Sue and Joe. "A minor in your care has made charges of sex assault against your employee. Child Protective Services are on their way to collect the girl. We will be conducting an investigation and need your cooperation. Now if you'll please go inside, Officer Richards will . . ."

As he spoke, Sue looked at Joe again, dazed by a train of disjointed facts.

Sex assault. Alcohol. History of abuse. A hidden past. Accusations and lies.

Brandi broke free of Bertie's hold and ran down the porch steps, her hair a mess, her sweatshirt torn. "Look what he did to me!" She stopped in the middle of the yard and pushed up her sleeves to reveal blood and dark bruises on her upper arms. "He hurt me, Miss Susan! He was too strong, and I was so scared."

Horror shattered something deep inside. She spun around to Joe.

His face was grave. "Sue—"

"How could you?" The words were shrill and distant, like they came from far away, from someone else. "I t-trusted you."

"Ma'am?"

Trembling, Sue turned to the officer.

"Any information you have about his character or behavior would help us sort this out."

Another queasy wave rolled through her. Leia's words, the ones he'd said were lies, echoed in her mind. Sue closed her eyes. "The courts removed him from his childhood home for . . . sex abuse."

When she opened her eyes, Joe was staring at her, his face a stony mask.

The deputy nodded. "I think we're finished here for now. Mr. Paterson, this investigation will go more quickly if you cooperate. We need you to come to the station for questioning."

Joe's eyes never left Sue's as the officer opened the back door and gestured for him to take the backseat. He studied her a few more long seconds before he climbed in.

Sue watched the squad car back up. Her heart lurched.

Bertie hollered at her to come inside.

But she couldn't move. As the car retreated down the drive, her world crashed down around her.

What have I done?

Heart sinking, she squeezed her eyes shut tight, suddenly certain that the departing police car was a sign of the worst mistake of her life.

While Bertie stayed in the kitchen with the kids, Sue tried to calm the girl. But after half an hour, she still hadn't been able to get anything coherent out of her.

When two caseworkers from Child Protective Services arrived, Sue showed them to her office, and then went to get Brandi.

The girl was seated on the stairs, still a sniveling mess.

Sue had never seen her so distraught.

He was too strong, and I was so scared.

She had seen the bruises on Brandi's biceps and couldn't think about them without feeling ill, those angry purple marks and dried blood that screamed *brutal attack* across her flesh. "Brandi, the CPS women want to talk to you," Sue said quietly. "And they need to take you to the hospital for an examination."

"No. I hate hospitals. I won't go."

Sue studied the girl's fear-laced expression. "I know, but it'll be okay. It's just a routine part of this kind of investigation."

"Don't let them take me. Please?"

"I'm sorry, but you have to go with them, Brandi. I have no say in this. They need to do their job. No one is going to hurt you, I promise.'"

Sue and Brandi met the women in the office and listened as they went over the protocol. They would remove Brandi for an interview, examination, and temporary relocation.

Brandi would not like being relocated, but it wasn't up to Sue. Until the county completed their part of the investigation, the minor involved would not be allowed to stay in a home where there had been allegations of abuse. In fact, Sue could face the removal of all her kids.

As a shaken-looking Brandi left with the state workers, Sue felt a nagging need to get away and process everything, get her head on straight. But she had no time to deal with her own emotional mess. A kitchen full of disturbed teens awaited answers and reassurance.

Sue entered the kitchen and met the faces of her remaining kids.

Bertie hushed the chattering voices and raised tired brows at Sue.

"Everything's going to be okay, guys. Brandi is going to talk to the people at the hospital and get some help."

Chaz stumbled forward, eyes rimmed with red. "What about J-man?" His voice crackled. "What's going to happen to him?"

Several kids started talking at once, their voices a collective maelstrom of confusion.

How much had they seen and heard? "Listen,

guys, please." When the room stilled, Sue went on. "The police are talking to Mister Joe now, and they'll do whatever it takes to do what's right. That's all I know. The best thing for us to do is get back to our regular routines and move forward. Together. We can do that. Okay?"

Vince, Tatiana, and Haley threw glances at each other, murmuring things Sue couldn't hear.

Cori turned teary eyes at Sue. "But is he coming back?"

"What fairy tale have you been smoking?" Chaz threw Cori a glare. "Whenever things go wrong, people leave and never come back. That's how it is." His voice sounded choked. "He was the only one who ever treated me like a normal kid. J-man's like what a dad's supposed to be. He was the best one I ever had." His face reddened. "This stinks."

"Stinks," Daisy echoed.

Sue closed her eyes as the impossible heaviness pressed on her again. What she wanted to say was, *Yes, this stinks. In fact, everything about this is so wrong, so upside down, that all I want to do is curl into a ball and cry.*

The rest of the evening passed in a weighty hush, a wary silence Sue knew too well from her own days in a group home, when no one knew when another kid would be sent away or who would be next.

Sue and Bertie took their respective places on

bed watch, which now meant Sue would sleep on a cot in the girls' hall and Bertie in the boys' dorm. Bertie didn't mind running doubles—triples if she included sleeping bed watch—but running the woman 24/7 wasn't an option.

In the morning, Sue would call the temp agency for help. Though she had given Linda and Karla notice, the ranch was still in operation for ninety days. Sue needed to either bring the two women back or replace them.

Sitting on her cot in the girls' hallway, Sue stared at her phone, too wound up to sleep. She punched Layne's number, hoping it wasn't too late to call.

Layne answered and listened as Sue relayed the day's events in low tones.

"Will they do a rape kit on her?" Layne asked.

Sue winced. Talking to her friend about all this was supposed to calm the chaos in her heart, but it wasn't helping. In fact, the more she talked, the more agitated she felt. "I don't think so, Layne. She claims things didn't get to that point, that the . . . attack was interrupted when he heard something and took off."

Layne didn't respond, and in the silence, something in Sue revolted again. The scene she just described made her sick. Of course, the idea of a large, powerful man attacking a teenage girl would repulse anyone.

But that wasn't it.

"Sue?"

What kept nagging at her was how impossible it was to picture Joe hurting anyone. And yet there were those glaring bruises, reminding Sue of the lesson she had learned long ago not to trust appearances. And the alcohol was another thing Sue had a hard time imagining Joe doing. But then, experience had taught her that people were capable of hiding all kinds of things.

"Sue? Are you there?"

"Sorry, just thinking."

"Do you doubt her story? What's your gut telling you?"

"My gut?" Sue's temples thumped and her stomach churned from a steady onslaught of distress. Nothing made sense. Her instincts were in such a mess she doubted she could ever rely on them again. "Are you asking me if I think Brandi is lying?"

A long, heavy pause. "Is it possible?"

Sue closed her eyes. Of course Brandi was capable of lying—everyone knew that. But would she really lie about something this serious? "Anything's possible, Layne. But I'm not inclined to accuse a girl of lying about a thing like this."

"Ah." Layne's voice softened. "Sorry, hon, I understand."

Tears stung Sue's eyes. She rubbed them away.

"So Joe's story was off, huh?"

Joe's story?

She swallowed hard. "I didn't hear Joe's side of the story."

Silence.

A tingle of dread raced up her spine. Joe *had* tried to speak, but Sue hadn't listened to him. The man she'd come to know and trust and . . .

And . . .

The man who had followed her rules and had proven himself kind. Helpful. Generous to a fault. The man who responded to his family's abandonment and betrayal with forgiveness. Joe, who said he loved her and was now sitting in a cold sheriff's station in Lakeview being interrogated by cops.

Her chest tightened. "Layne, I gotta go. I need to make another call."

CHAPTER THIRTY-THREE

Rubbing his unshaven jaw, Joe took a seat in the sheriff station's waiting area. He'd spent a fairly sleepless night in a holding cell so he could resume questioning with another deputy at 9:00 a.m. Apparently, a couple hours of insulting questions and probing about his sex life was just a warmup for the real interrogation.

As if he hadn't already been humiliated enough when the kids saw him being hauled away in a cop car, accused of assault and attempted rape.

Of a *kid*.

That about crushed him. But the horrified kids and the invasive questions were nothing compared to the way Sue had turned on him.

She couldn't have done a better job cutting him down if she'd fired a double-barrel shotgun at point-blank range. The repulsion on her face, her disgust as she offered those accusing words—

"Mr. Paterson." Deputy Cramer came into the waiting area and pulled Joe aside. "I talked to the DA, and at this point, we don't have enough evidence to arrest, and we can't keep you any longer. But we are still conducting an investigation, so until we know more, you're not allowed to return to Juniper Ranch."

Joe shook his head slowly. "No problem. I have no intention of going back." *Ever.*

"All right, then. We have your number, and we'll be in contact. For now, you're free to go."

Outside, Joe inhaled the frigid air and waited for the sun's rays to penetrate his skin, but a steady wind stole the warmth before it could reach him. His work coat, truck, and his few belongings were sitting at the ranch ninety miles away. He could ask a neighbor to get it and meet him, or leave it behind.

Whatever. As long as he didn't have to see Sue.

When she had told the deputy about his past, he could almost feel the cold blade of betrayal slicing into his back. Just like before.

It was as if he were ten again, humiliated and alone. And once again, the people he needed the most didn't believe him. In fact, Sue wouldn't even listen to him tell his side. In one brief moment, everything he had done to earn her trust disappeared. All gone, along with the things he'd been stupid enough to hope she felt for him.

Time for a new plan. He was free. Wind at his back, no attachments. He'd gotten John and Fiona moved and had someone taking care of them. The La Pine property was listed and some decent offers were coming in. Maybe he could take a cruise. Go to Mexico. Or buzz down to Louisiana, see if the Gulf rig could still use him. They would have found another crew boss by now, but he didn't mind starting at the bottom. Sometimes he missed the hard work. Right about now, hard work and cold steel sounded pretty good.

And putting a dozen states between him and Oregon sounded even better.

After ending her call with Layne Friday night, Sue had tried to call Joe but got his voice mail. She left a message telling him she should have given him a chance to present his side and that if he wanted to tell her, she would listen. But he hadn't returned her call, and her gut churned a little more with every hour that passed. Was he under arrest and unable to call? Or unwilling to call?

Saturday morning, she agonized over whether or not to leave Joe another message. Just as she picked up her phone to try again, she got a call from the deputy investigating the case. There wasn't enough evidence to arrest at this time but the investigation was still ongoing. Joe had been released but was not allowed anywhere near the property. She was to report immediately if he violated that order.

If there wasn't enough evidence to charge him,

the case would be dismissed. If that happened, what would that mean for Joe?

Sue went back to work, letting the ranch's routines keep her from dwelling on questions she couldn't answer.

After an hour of overseeing game time in the den, a knock on the front door jolted Sue.

Had Joe ignored the police order? Heart thumping, she opened the door.

Mr. Stewart stood on the porch.

Ringo circled the farmer, sniffing his boots.

"Hello, what can I do for you?" Sue said.

He pushed the bill of his hat off his brow. "Got a call from Joe. He said to come over and get his pickup. Said he wanted me to have it." He scratched Ringo's ears. "I can always use another truck."

"He—he's giving you his truck? Why?"

"I don't know. Just said where he's going, he won't be needing it. Said the key is in his room."

"But where's he going?"

The man shrugged. "Didn't say. Just said he wanted me to have the truck."

Thoughts racing, Sue invited the man inside. "I'll get the keys. Wait here, please."

Sue went out back to Joe's quarters. Braced for what she might find, she felt cautiously in his coat, shirt, and pants pockets, being careful not to disturb his things. Things that smelled of him. Things hung over a chair or bedpost without a fuss, in a way that said Joe Paterson had nothing to hide. She straightened and looked around the room.

His keys were lying on a chair beside his cell phone. The phone he obviously didn't have—and the reason he hadn't returned her calls.

Sue returned to the main house and handed over the keys. "Did he want you to get anything for him?"

The farmer shook his head. "Nope. Said there's nothing here he wants."

Dazed, Sue sent the man on his way, then went back to overseeing the kids' activities, going through the motions without a clue what she was doing.

"There's nothing here he wants."

While everyone helped clean up from lunch, Sue called CPS to ask about Brandi, but had to leave a message, adding to her growing sense of unease. She pulled Bertie aside in the kitchen and told her about the farmer's visit.

"Joe gave the neighbor his truck?" Bertie frowned.

"Apparently. Why would he do that?"

Bertie shrugged. "Beats me."

Sue glanced at the kids, pressed by a sudden sadness she couldn't explain. She had no idea what Joe's behavior meant.

Bertie shrugged. "Maybe he just doesn't need it. He does have that job in the Gulf."

"But wouldn't he need his truck to get down there?"

Examining the toes peeking out of her Birks, Bertie said, "Maybe he doesn't want to come around here to get it." She met Sue's gaze and lowered her tone. "If you were Joe Paterson, would you want to show your face around here?"

Anxiety tingled up Sue's spine.

"What you say about Papa Joe?" Jasmine dropped her dishtowel and rushed close to Sue and Bertie, light dancing in her eyes. "He coming home now?"

Sue had to turn away from Jasmine's hope-filled face. She met Bertie's gaze and whispered, "What am I supposed to tell them?"

Bertie eyed her. "The truth is good. Especially with these kids." She shuffled over to help put dishes away.

But what *was* the truth?

Listen, kids, the man you loved like a dad was taken by the cops because Brandi claims he attacked her. And because I said he had a history of abuse. And now he's gone.

A knife twisted in her heart. She needed speed. Now. She turned to Bertie, pleading with her eyes. "Miss Roberta, I need some time to collect my thoughts. Are you guys okay here for a while?"

Bertie nodded slowly. "Careful, boss. It's slick out there."

The old woman knew her too well. "I'll be back."

The hour-long ride along snow-powdered roads hadn't done anything to relieve her anxiety or calm her thoughts. Frozen and wind-chapped, Sue killed the motor and dismounted the Harley—Joe's Harley now—and hung her helmet on the peg.

Her legs and arms were numb. Too bad her brain wasn't numb as well.

Just as she started to pull down the big shop door, she froze.

The spot beside the Harley was empty. Where was her Honda? Was it there when she left? Had someone moved it? Stolen it?

Sue hurried into the house, through the empty dining hall, and into the kitchen, but no one was there. She reached for the office phone and called Bertie's cell.

"Sue?" Bertie's voice sounded clipped.

"Yeah. Do you know—"

"Did you see Jasmine outside or in the shop?"

"What?"

"We've been searching for half an hour, Sue. We looked everywhere."

Comprehension shot fear straight to Sue's chest. "Bert, the Honda's missing. I think she might have taken it."

A quick intake of breath followed. "I'll call the sheriff."

Oh, God, please. Help us find her. "Call the police and the Stewarts and anyone else you know. I'm going to look now."

Moments later, Sue was on the road in her Suburban, flashlight on the seat beside her.

The winter sky, dark now in late afternoon, cast eerie shadows over the gray-white desert.

Sue drove slowly, scanning the road ahead and the terrain on either side, fear clenching her insides like a giant claw.

Why now? What had made Jasmine run away?

And why on a motorbike? How far did she intend to go?

I don't think I can take any more trauma, God. Are You there? Can You do something? Sue reached the Juniper Valley turnoff and pulled to a stop.

Was Jasmine on the road or trying to ride across the desert? Was she headed for town or—

Her phone chirped. Incoming call from the ranch.

"Did you find her?" Sue held her breath.

"Jasmine's been found," Bertie said. "But Sue, she's . . ."

Sue's veins turned to ice. "She's *what?*"

"Are you driving?"

Dear God. "I'm stopped." *Please, no bad news.* "What's wrong?"

"She was in an ambulance headed for Bend, but—"

"No! How bad—"

"Life Flight met the ambulance on the highway and took her in. Where are you?"

Sue gasped. *Life Flight?* Had they found Jasmine's body broken and bleeding in the snow?

"I'm . . ." She searched around her in the dark, her thoughts whirling. "At Eleven-Mile Corner."

"You okay to drive? I'll hold down the fort here."

"I can drive. I'll call you when I get there." She punched the phone off as darkness closed in. The world was spinning.

Please—don't let her die. Not Jasmine. Not my girl.

Fighting waves of panic, Sue floored it and raced to Bend.

CHAPTER THIRTY-FOUR

Fluorescent lights along the hospital corridors blinded Sue's burning eyes. She missed the ICU by a floor the first time. She gripped the handrail in the elevator, watching the digital numbers change above her. *Father—Lord—I don't even know what to call You, but if You're there, God, please don't let her die. Or suffer.*

At the ICU, the desk nurse took Sue's information and then pointed to a waiting area.

"But she's my . . . I mean, I'm her guardian, but she's . . ." Fear that they wouldn't let her see Jasmine gave her voice a frantic pitch. "Please, I need to be with her."

"I'm sorry, but no one is permitted right now. We're working to get her stabilized. We'll tell you just as soon as we know more."

Stabilized? Numb with dread, Sue went to the waiting area and sat beside a tired-looking old man. She leaned forward, head in her hands, and closed her eyes.

How had this happened? And why? What had sent Jasmine tearing off on a motorcycle?

Minutes felt like hours and days. Questions

crowded each other in her mind until she couldn't finish a thought. After an hour, she called Bertie and said she was still waiting to see Jasmine.

"Hang in there, Sue. She's a survivor. Like you."

Some survivor. Everything was falling apart—including her. Not knowing what was happening or if Jasmine would live or be permanently injured or brain dead was like a vacuum sucking the air from her lungs. Had the girl worn a helmet?

"Susan Quinn?" a woman in scrubs said. "The doctor would like to speak with you."

Sue jumped and followed on shaking legs.

A doctor waited in the hall beside a row of glass cubicles.

Sue tried to listen to his quiet, calm voice as he explained Jasmine's multiple injuries, but she had a hard time processing all the words. "Is she going to make it?"

"Because of the concussion, we're monitoring her for brain trauma. We're also watching for other internal injuries. We've treated the exhaust burns and set the broken bones. But for now, she's stable."

Stable. There was that word again. As in not fighting for her life, but not out of the woods either. Sue blinked back a rush of tears. "May I see her?"

"Yes. She's been sedated but is coming around now."

Sue entered the tiny room, struck by the cloying medicine smells, and stepped around a partitioning curtain.

Jasmine seemed so small against the hospital bed and the equipment surrounding her, hooked up to hoses and monitors and machines, the faint beeps and blinking indicators keeping mechanical rhythm. Her head was wrapped in white, closed eyes swollen, skin an odd gray. A cast encased her leg. An IV dripped into a tube running beneath her gown into her narrow chest.

So small, so vulnerable. Sue's heart lurched. She pulled a chair close to the bed and touched Jasmine's shoulder.

The girl didn't stir.

Sue reached up and stroked her cheek. "You're going to make it, baby. I know you will. You're a fighter." It wasn't right. Jasmine had spent her whole childhood fighting to survive. She shouldn't have to fight anymore.

Jasmine opened her eyes, blinked at Sue a few times, then turned her face to the far wall.

"Jasmine?"

She didn't move, only stiffened. Probably from the pain.

"Can you hear me, honey?"

The girl nodded stiffly.

"How are you feeling? Are you in pain?"

"Yes."

Sue laid a hand on Jasmine's arm. "I was worried about you, Jas. We all were." She watched the steady rise and fall of the girl's chest, unsure how to get the answers she desperately wanted. "Can you tell me what happened? Why did you leave?" *Nothing like drilling the kid while she's in pain and fighting for her life.*

Jasmine turned toward Sue, face taut. "Angry talk hurt my head. I need to ride fast."

Angry talk? Sue opened her mouth but wasn't sure what to say. "You needed to get away from someone?"

Jasmine's eyelids fluttered closed. "Need to race. Like you."

Like me?

With a gasp, Sue tried to halt the alarms going off in her head, but the reality of her own stupidity struck her like a wrecking ball.

Sue's stress-burning rides had set a dangerous example for Jasmine. The girl was simply doing as she'd been taught.

She could have died. Because of me.

Sue couldn't breathe. She forced herself to focus on what Jasmine had said. What did she mean by "angry talk"? Had Jasmine witnessed what happened between Joe and Brandi?

Sue leaned closer. "Jasmine, who was talking angry? Can you tell me?"

"*I* angry. Papa Joe gone now. He leave us all." Her voice rose, choked. "Because of *you!*"

The awful truth became clear, deadening her limbs. "Jasmine."

The girl wouldn't look at her.

"Jasmine, I only did what—"

"Brandi lies. Everyone know. You listen Brandi but not Papa Joe, and now he gone." She burst out crying.

"Shh, Jasmine, please calm down. How did you know—"

"Brandi only hurt people, but you not see. Not *listen*." Jasmine's voice rose and broke in angry sobs. "You bad mom. I hate you! I not stay with you!"

Pain twisted Sue's heart into an unbearable knot. She closed her eyes.

Jasmine was right. Sue was a terrible mom—a terrible parent. Reckless, irresponsible. Negligent. She'd set the worst kind of example. Hadn't been paying attention. She had no business caring for kids. More like damaged them all with her carelessness.

What have I done? Oh God, what have I . . .

In the sudden stillness, a strange hush had fallen.

You've built walls around your heart, but it's no home. It's just walls.

Sue looked around, pulse rising. It wasn't an audible voice, but more like the echo of a remembered voice, quiet and vaguely familiar.

"Jasmine?"

Jasmine refused to look at her.

"I'm sorry, Jas," Sue whispered. "I'm so sorry." She rose and fled the room, hurried out of the ICU, and kept going. Rounding a corner, she nearly crashed into an orderly.

Where was an exit, an elevator, any means of escape?

She found a stairwell and headed down the steps and out a door that led into another corridor. She hurried along bustling hallways.

Too many people.

She passed a small, open room containing a table with a large book open on top. A break room perhaps? Doubling back, she surveyed the room. It was empty, quiet. Stepping inside, she took in the muted décor, the empty seats, and the book, which she could now see was a Bible.

A chapel.

She reached for the box of tissues beside the Bible. She blew her nose, took a deep breath, and glanced down at the page. The words didn't make any sense. She wiped her swollen eyes and read. Turned the page and continued.

One part seemed to dance before her eyes, beckoning her to read it. *There is no fear in love . . . But perfect love drives out fear . . .*

Sue stepped back, half expecting God to appear, like a holy intervention.

Perfect love drives out fear.

A picture of Joe on Table Rock flashed in her

mind. His wounded look, his disbelief at her suspicions. Her terrible, unfounded suspicions. Then her gut reaction to the incident with Brandi, and the gnawing, sick feeling that wouldn't go away.

And now Jasmine hated her. The kid Sue so desperately wanted to help, a girl so much like herself. But no, she wasn't like Sue at all. Jasmine listened. Needed. Loved. Jasmine was so many things Sue wasn't.

Things Sue should have been.

The walls around your heart not only keep people locked out, but they also keep fear and hurt locked in.

Sue stared at the Bible. She had worked so hard to bury the past and seal off the pain others had inflicted on her, but maybe all she'd done was let pain fester, skew her judgment, keep her a prisoner.

The stunned look on Joe's face as he got into the police car kept flashing in her mind. The disbelief, the betrayal. The hurt.

What if I'm the guilty one here? Grief crushed her. All she had ever wanted was to help disadvantaged kids feel accepted and confident. Do some good.

But since when was it *good* to accuse and hurt someone who had shown her nothing but kindness?

Someone who claimed he loved her?

The full weight of shame pressed down on her. "Oh, God," she whispered, "I made a terrible mistake. I think I . . ."

Did something too cruel to say out loud, even to You.

Sue ran from the chapel, the corridors a blur. She finally found an elevator and slipped inside, repeatedly punching the button for the lobby, ignoring the stares of curious passengers. *Don't look at me. I'm a monster. All I do is hurt the people I love.*

CHAPTER THIRTY-FIVE

"Paterson!"

Crouched over a casing pipe, Joe looked up.

The crew boss made a phone gesture with a thumb and pinky.

Joe shook his head and went back to marking steel. He'd gotten several messages on the company line from Sue, each one asking him to call.

So she felt bad about the way things turned out. But this wasn't one of those I-feel-so-bad-can-we-just-forget-it-happened kind of things. This went deeper. Far deeper than it ever should have had a chance to get. He should've known better.

He shouldn't have fallen in love. With Sue *or* those kids.

Show her My love.

Joe shoved the pipe away. It clattered into another one and sent tremors rippling across the deck.

"I tried to show her," he muttered. "Didn't work. I thought I knew what You wanted from me, but I don't even know if I'm hearing You right. Probably wasn't even You."

412

Show her My love.

It was unmistakable, that whisper in his heart, that familiar Voice. The same Voice of peace and truth, counsel and comfort, that he'd long known and depended on.

Shaking his head, Joe stood, fists clenched. "I gave it everything I had, including my heart," he muttered. Aware of the looks from the crew, he clamped his lips, but the frustration continued to build. *What more do You want from me?*

Joe unclenched his fists and stared into his gloved hands, seeing not the rough leather, but the faces of Sue and the kids. A verse he'd committed to memory as a teenager came to mind.

I consider my life worth nothing to me; my only aim is to finish the race and complete the task the Lord Jesus has given me—the task of testifying to the good news of God's grace.

Joe closed his eyes, but it did nothing to keep the certainty from settling in.

God wanted him to finish what he'd started.

"This *cannot* be happening." Sue put the phone down and leaned on the kitchen counter, plastering her hands over her face.

Brandi had slipped away from a Child Protection Services worker and was now missing. CPS and law enforcement were searching for the girl and promised to keep Sue posted, but so far, no one had a clue where Brandi was.

Sue headed to the bedroom Jasmine now shared with Daisy and Sonja on the main floor while she recovered from her injuries. She peeked in at the sleeping girl and breathed a sigh of relief.

If Jasmine hated being in the same house as Sue, it didn't show on her face.

Sue watched the girl for a minute, then went to her office, collapsed into a chair, and closed her eyes. Thankfully, both Linda and Karla were available and had returned to the ranch, one blessed source of relief. But sleepless nights and a total loss of appetite were taking their toll on Sue's strength, both mentally and physically. At least she'd given Bertie a day off—that was one thing she'd managed to do right.

But there was a growing list titled *All the Things Sue Should Have Done Differently*. She should have been paying closer attention to Brandi's warning signs. She should have tried harder to form a bond with her. Should have known what was going on. That negligence may now be costing the girl her safety, her health, even her life.

She also should have listened to Joe's side of the story. She should have considered all the facts before making a judgment. Should have listened to her heart, which would have told her that Joe wasn't capable of such a vicious attack.

After several days of searching, Sue had finally

located the oil rig in Louisiana where Joe was working. She left him messages, but he didn't return her calls.

She couldn't blame him. If Joe had *not* done what Brandi—and Sue—had accused him of, then he had to be feeling angry, hurt, and humiliated.

The ache that camped around her heart tightened.

And while she was listing regrets, there were also things she should have said to Joe, things she would never be able to say now. Questions she could never ask, like how had Joe met God in this very place, the God he sang to so beautifully in that chapel on the hill.

She ached to hear those songs now.

Sue grabbed a jacket, slipped outside, and headed up the hill.

Such continuous quiet. Even when the ground wasn't frozen and covered with snow, Juniper Valley was an endless sea of calm, unlike any place she'd ever known. It was the only place she'd ever felt grounded. The deep stillness here made the city types antsy, but something about the quiet whispered to Sue's very core. Soon enough, her time here would end and she would return to the city. Alone. Being alone was all she'd known, but now it felt like a harsh prison sentence, one she'd imposed on herself.

She slipped inside the chapel and shuffled down the center aisle. Thankfully, no visible trace of the incident remained, the scene long since investigated and cleaned.

But echoes of Joe's rich voice raised in song lingered in the room, pressed on her spirit.

She eyed the corner where she'd clung to him in panicked relief, where he'd kissed her. So tender and full of—

Stop it.

Her gaze landed on the wooden bench where Joe had sat across from her and told her about God's love for her with such conviction. She went to the front of the chapel and stared up at the wooden cross.

Light poured in from the narrow side windows, warming her face and hair.

"I've hurt people," she whispered. "I damaged Joe's reputation. I betrayed him." *Just like others have done.* She waited for a sign of some kind, a whisper of agreement.

None came.

"He said he loved me and I—" *Threw it in his face. Someone finally loves me, and this is what he gets.*

Tears trailed down her cheeks.

She lowered herself to the nearest bench and wiped her face with both hands. "I was so blind. I wish I could go back to that night and tell him—" *That I love him too.*

But Joe certainly didn't want to hear that now. Too little, too late. Far too late.

There was nothing she could do.

Her tears kept falling. She looked up at the cross again.

Perhaps there *was* one thing she could do.

"God, if You can hear me, could You somehow help Joe get past all the hurt I've caused him? Can You do that? And can You please help Brandi turn up safe? Help her and Jasmine and all the kids grow up safe, strong, and confident? For their sake, not mine. I'm afraid I've messed up too much."

Perfect love casts out fear.

But what was perfect love? Was there really such a thing? She'd never even known passable love, much less perfect. Joe said God loved her. How was that even possible? How did that work, exactly? What did it involve?

What do You want from me? And will it hurt? She wasn't sure if she hoped more for silence or an audible answer. She closed her eyes. *I'm listening.*

A strange, sweet warmth stole over her. Strange but good. More than a sensation or a gust of wind, but like an actual Presence. It washed over her, saturating her inside and out. It was unlike anything she'd ever felt or experienced. Not visible, but almost touchable, like a thickening calm enveloping her.

And not creepy. Just . . . there.

"Okay, so You really are there. What do You

want from me? Am I supposed to give up control? Live under someone else's thumb? I've already been there. It crushed me, stole my spirit."

Panic bloomed in her chest, urging her to jump up and run back to the house. But to what? Emptiness? Being forever driven by fear?

Perfect love casts out fear.

Sue rose slowly and waited for the panic to escalate, but it didn't. All she felt was a giant soothing calm, a gentle beckoning. "What do You want?" she whispered to the cross. But somehow, she already knew.

Your heart.

"Why?"

The huge calm continued to spread through her like warm honey, completely saturating her like a sponge. Wrapping her in safety, surrounding her in peace. Like arms. Gentle, giant arms.

"Okay. I don't know if it's what You want, but okay," she whispered. "I give up. All my mistakes, all my irrational fears, all the stupid things I've ever done—"

Yes, all of that. And your broken heart, every last shattered piece. I want to make it whole.

Something broke inside her. Sue crumpled to her knees.

For minutes that felt like an eternity, she lay sprawled across the rough wooden bench, her heart pouring out wordlessly. But as tears flowed out, peace seeped in—first a trickle, then a stream that spread through her, filling every guarded cavity, every bereft place. It felt like—

Love.

Really?

Yes.

A flicker of hope sparked in her heart—the hope she'd refused to entertain for so long. Hope that took every last bit of courage she had. "Will You help me?" she whispered.

Yes.

Wiping her face, Sue glanced around the darkening room.

Something in the corner caught her eye.

She went closer and pulled the old sign into the light. *My Father's House.* She read the smaller words at the bottom. It was a Bible verse painted in crimson.

> Father to the fatherless, defender of widows—this is God, whose dwelling is holy. God places the lonely in families; He sets the prisoners free and gives them joy.   Psalm 68: 5-6

As she read the words *My Father's House* again, a simple truth dawned.

Her heart and her home were one and the same. She had absolutely nothing left to lose.

Sue dragged the sign out of the chapel and started down the trail toward the house, but the thing was a lot heavier than it looked. She stopped and pulled out her phone. "Hey, Linda, could you have Edgar get the ladder, and ask Chaz to grab the power drill and some heavy-duty screws? I need a couple kids to meet me out front. Thanks." She resumed dragging the sign.

God wanted her heart?

Then he would have it. Every bit of it.

CHAPTER THIRTY-SIX

Joe closed his Bible, stuffed it in his duffel, then hoisted his bag onto his shoulder and waited for the transport to shore. The first two weeks had passed in a fog, each day blending into the next until he couldn't remember how long he'd been on the sea with nothing on the horizon but water, clouds, and more water.

Being offshore where the work was hard and mindless and the pace steady had a way of forcing a guy to think. Trouble was, all he could think about were the things he wanted to forget.

Sue's disgust for him had been clear, her heart untouchable, her fears too deep. But even so— God help him—his idiot heart still wasn't getting the message.

It's ripping my heart out, but I need to let them go. Help me, Father.

After he checked into a room for his two-week off-shift, Joe called his attorney. Steve Weston was a valuable resource with his corporation and real estate expertise. Steve had called a few times since Joe had arrived at the Gulf, but he hadn't been in any mood to think about the Juniper Valley property.

Now, after some time and prayer, Joe was ready to move on. Cut his losses. And his ties.

"Are you sure about this?" Steve asked now.

"Yeah. Go ahead, just like we planned."

Joe ended the call and stared at the phone.

I don't know about this, God. But Your way, not mine.

Joe hadn't checked his La Pine listings in a few weeks. Two acres had sold and competitive offers were coming in on four more. He spent some time browsing the web for comparable listings and market value changes. Another search brought up his name on the Juniper Valley Chamber of Commerce. He laughed under his breath. He sounded like some kind of high roller. He scrolled through the local news until one article caught his eye. Frowning, he zoomed in on the picture, then zoomed in some more.

Odd. It was an old picture of Juniper Ranch, from back in the day when the My Father's House sign still hung above the entryway.

He checked the date on the photo.

Very odd. The picture had been taken less than a week ago. This was a current photo.

Who put that sign on the ranch? And why? He needed to find out without anyone knowing he was the one asking. Joe redialed Steve's number, drumming his fingers until his lawyer picked up.

• • •

As Jasmine arranged flatware on the sideboard, Sue watched the girl manage her crutches, struck again by a prickling sense of guilt.

Sue hadn't broached the subject of Jasmine's anger or her riding off on the motorcycle, because Jasmine had returned to her old self since coming back to the ranch. The girl needed time to heal physically.

Maybe Sue should just try to quietly hang on to whatever was left of their friendship for the time they had left. She headed back to the kitchen but then stopped.

Why *not* talk about it? January was already half gone. Time was precious and fleeting. Who knew what tomorrow would bring? No better time for mending rifts than the present.

"Jasmine," she said softly. "Can we talk?"

Jasmine nodded and followed her to the den. Sue offered to help her get comfortable on the couch, but Jasmine shook her head. "I not need help, Miss Susan. I take care of myself." She held herself up straight, like a tiny adult. "I have to take care of myself when I leave here."

Sue's heart clenched. "Jasmine, in the hospital, you told me you left on the motorcycle because you were angry. First, I have to say that was a dangerous way to deal with anger."

Jasmine turned to Sue with a look of disbelief.

"But before you say anything, I also need

to apologize. It's my fault you were hurt. I'm so sorry for teaching you that riding off angry was okay and for . . . a lot of things. You were absolutely right, Jas." An ache lodged in her throat. "I *have* been a terrible mom."

The girl's lashes lowered against her reddening cheeks.

"And I also want to apologize for what I did the day Papa Joe left. You were right about that too. I should've listened to him, but I didn't. I said things I never should have. I wish I could go back to that day and change things."

"You do?"

Sue nodded, unable to speak. *Oh, honey, you have no idea.*

Jasmine met Sue's gaze. "But you just doing your job. To protect kids."

"No. Joe deserved to be heard. I was afraid and stupid."

Jasmine examined her painted fingertips. Her voice dropped to a whisper. "I am sorry too. For what I say to you. You are good mom. Very good."

Tears welled in Sue's eyes, and she slipped an arm around the girl. "You deserve better."

Jasmine leaned against her. "Papa Joe say Papa God will always take care of him," she said, words slow and pensive. "So maybe Papa Joe is okay wherever he at now."

Sue smiled. "I hope so." *That's what I ask Him for. Every day.*

Jasmine looked up, her eyes glistening. "But I still miss him."

"Me too." Sue missed his silly grin, the way he interacted with the kids and made each one feel special, the way his eyes met hers from across a room. She missed his smell. His quiet strength. His gentleness—

"I wish Papa Joe come back." A tear trailed down Jasmine's cheek. "I love him."

"So do I," Sue whispered.

Jasmine studied her carefully, then put an arm around Sue and rocked her gently, shushing and making soothing sounds.

The idea of the girl trying to comfort Sue made her laugh and cry at the same time.

"Miss Susan, okay if I call you Mama Sue?"

Sue nodded, unable to speak. It would only be for a little while, but she didn't care.

"Or maybe just Mama?"

Smiling through her tears, Sue whispered, "I'd like that."

Jasmine pressed herself close to Sue's side.

Sue wrapped both arms around the girl and hugged her gently. *Father, how will I ever be able to let go when April comes?*

Later that afternoon, Bertie burst into the kitchen with the office phone in hand.

"Call for you, Sue. An *attorney*." The twist of

425

her mouth told Sue exactly what Bertie thought of lawyers.

Sue put down the cookie dough recipe she'd been trying to decipher and took the phone. "This is Susan Quinn."

"Hello, this is Steve Weston, attorney representing Montgomery Enterprises."

Probably calling to say what she feared, that the rent-free deal was too good to be true. "What can I do for you?"

"I'm calling on behalf of my client. We would like to make you an offer."

"What kind of offer?"

"My client is no longer interested in basing a facility in Juniper Valley. We understand you've successfully operated a group home there and might perhaps like to continue. If that's the case, my client is offering to sell the property back to you."

Sue's heart sank. She hoped he would say she could continue on as a renter, something she might actually be able to afford. But purchase? Not hardly.

"I appreciate the offer, but I don't have that kind of—"

"For the price of one dollar."

"—money because I don't—" Sue gasped. "What?"

"We are offering to sell the entire property back to you for one dollar."

Great, a prankster. She should have asked for credentials first. "Funny, Mr. Weston. Or whatever your name is." Sue punched off the call.

Nut job. And just plain mean. Did people really have nothing better to do with their time than make prank—

The phone rang.

Sue read the unknown number and answered. "Look, I don't know what kind of game you're—"

"Please, don't hang up. Ms. Quinn, this is a legitimate offer. I can fax it to you right now if you'll allow me."

"Your one-dollar offer."

"That's right."

Think, Sooz. What kind of gimmick is this? "Well, the obvious question is why, but this is so ridiculous that I can't even—"

"There is one condition."

Ah. The catch. "And what's that?"

"Montgomery Enterprises would like to retain the sign that is now hanging above the main building's entrance. The sign that reads *My Father's House*."

The *sign?* Sue's brain felt like cold oatmeal. "I'm sorry, I don't understand. I can buy the property for one dollar, but only if I give up the *sign?*"

"Yes." She could almost hear him checking his watch. "That's the deal."

Why on earth would the owner give the property away for nothing *and* insist on having that sign? Nothing about this made sense—*if* it was even legit.

"Can I think about the offer and call you back?"

"Of course. I'll give you my number."

She copied the number, then set the phone on the island and mowed fingers through her hair. For her, that sign was more than a piece of plywood. She'd hung it on the house as a tangible sign of her surrender, her decision to give God her heart and accept things His way. It didn't matter that the place didn't technically belong to her. As long as she was still here, her heart was here also. Everything she had and nearly everyone she loved in the world were covered beneath the banner of those words.

But no one knew that except her and God.

Think, Sooz, think.

Buying the ranch for a dollar depended on giving up the sign. A sign anyone could duplicate for fifty bucks. The deal was a no-brainer, of course. Give up the sign and the property would be hers. Debt-free.

But *why* did the deal depend on the sign?

And what kind of investor buys property for more than it's worth and then sells it for a dollar?

Sue paced the kitchen. There was a reason, and she was going to figure it out. This wasn't profitable or sound. It meant an enormous loss.

So what did the owner really hope to accomplish? Charity?

No, they would have said that up front.

She needed answers. She squinted at the scrawled phone number and began entering it on the keypad. Either the owner was a total crackpot or a cruel jokester. Or testing her maybe, to see if the sign had any special—

Sue stopped, phone in hand.

No way.

There was perhaps one person who might want to know if there was anything significant about that sign hanging above her home.

What if . . .?

No. No way. Joe couldn't be the owner. He had the Jacobs family to support. He couldn't have bought this property too.

Could he?

Sue leaned elbows on the island and mentally tallied the puzzle pieces.

Montgomery Enterprises. Because Chaz's last name was Montgomery.

Ninety extra days to stay with the kids. Rent-free.

Paying thousands more than the property was worth.

Grinning for days at Christmas.

And now handing over the property for a dollar.

But if Joe was behind this, why give it to her

now, after all that had happened, after the terrible things she'd said and done?

Her thoughts a confused jumble, she sank, face first, into her folded arms.

If she was right about Joe being the owner, why had he bought the property in the first place? What had been his original intention? Had he been making other plans for the property? Plans she ruined when she betrayed him?

Tears stung her eyes.

It was obvious. Joe was giving her back the property and walking away. Washing his hands of her.

Shame and sorrow twisted the pit of her stomach. Phone in hand, she walked outside and read the sign. If Joe *was* behind this, what did he mean by asking for the sign? Why make it a condition of the sale?

Then, with a chilling certainty, she knew. The offer was a message. A message telling her she couldn't run a home like My Father's House. He was telling her she could do whatever she wanted with the place—just as long as she didn't call it *that*.

Sue stood alone in the yard.

Joe was right. She had no clue about God's way of doing things like raising kids or running a successful group home. Or anything else for that matter. She was no Sunday-schooled, choir-singing, glory-hallelujah-shouting Christian. She didn't know the lingo or what the Bible said or how to say a proper prayer.

All she knew was that God had answered when she called and had touched her heart in an undeniable way. He'd wrapped loving-Father arms around her and she was okay with it.

But if she really *could* keep her home and her kids, then she would do things differently. She didn't know how, but she'd figure it out with God's help.

Sue keyed in the lawyer's number again, hands trembling. "Mr. Weston? This is Sue Quinn." Her voice shook. "I've made a decision."

"Yes?"

She looked up at the sign and the snow on the roof beyond it, then closed her eyes. *I'm flying totally blind here, God. All I know is that I've given my home and my heart to You and I'm hoping You'll help me do what's best. For these kids.*

"Ms. Quinn?"

She cleared her throat. "That sign is just wood, but it's very important to me. It says something that I didn't know how to say. But even though it's important to me, I can't pass up the chance to keep my home and these kids. So if your client really wants my sign, I'll let it go."

"Are you sure?" the man said.

"Yes. I accept the offer." *Father, I know it was like a promise from me to You, but I can't pass this up. I'm sorry.* She closed her eyes. *Sorry—*

"Wait, Mr. Weston?" she said in a rush. "Can you please give your client a message for me?"

A hesitation. "That's a bit unconventional. What's the message?"

"Would you please tell your client . . ." Eyes closed, she gathered her nerve. "Please tell him I believe in him. And tell him . . ."

I wish with all my heart that I could take back every hurtful thing I've ever said and done.

Her voice was about to break. She whispered, "Just tell him I'm very sorry."

Stunned silence on the other end.

Sue winced, realizing too late she was probably completely wrong in her theory about the owner. The lawyer thought he was dealing with a nutcase.

"I will deliver your message, Ms. Quinn."

"Thank you." Desperation quickened her pulse. "Can you please tell me how he's doing? Is he okay?"

Several beats of silence ticked across the line, or perhaps it was just her pulse. "My client is fine, ma'am. I'll relay your answer and your message. I'll be in touch. Thanks for your time."

Sue prayed she hadn't just made another foolish mistake.

CHAPTER THIRTY-SEVEN

In the quiet before dawn, Sue reached for the office phone she'd kept beside her during the night. Joe was the owner behind Montgomery Enterprises, LLC, she had no doubt. She stared at the phone's empty display screen.

Two days and still no calls.

She pulled out her cell.

No missed calls, no texts.

Why would he call? The lawyer was handling all the details of the sale. Joe was now free of all his ties here. His silence proved her hunch correct—he wanted nothing to do with her.

She leaned against the wall, heart throbbing.

Would the peace she had sometimes felt when talking to God come back?

"Please tell me I did the right thing," she whispered into the dark. "Please help Joe somehow get past the terrible hurt I've caused him. Give him peace like You've given me."

A warm sense of that peace surged through her.

Thank You.

Sue asked God to help Brandi, who was still missing, and prayed for the rest of the kids. Then she prayed for Joe again. She used the recurring pain in her heart as a reminder to keep asking God to help him.

How long will it hurt? And will the longing ever go away?

Sue went downstairs to the kitchen and started a pot of coffee, then headed into her office and replaced the phone. She checked the office fax and her email.

Nothing.

Back in the kitchen, she poured a mug of coffee and turned at the sound of stomping on the back step.

Bertie came in shivering, nose red. "Cold morning, boss. Hope that coffee's extra hot and extra strong."

Sue handed Bertie her mug and took down another from the cupboard. "Bertie, do you ever think about God?"

Bertie blew on her coffee, ignoring the way it steamed up her glasses. "Didn't we have this conversation yesterday?"

"Yeah, but I just wonder if—"

The office phone rang.

Sue's breath caught. She set her cup down, ran to the office and answered before the third ring. "My Father's House, this is Sue."

"Ms. Quinn? Amy Parker, Child Protective Services. Brandi Poe has been found."

"Oh, thank God. Is she hurt? Is she okay?"

"She's been on the streets the last few weeks. She's at Sacred Heart Hospital in Eugene, being treated for a number of issues. Nothing serious. She needs rehab. After that, she'll be placed at the Corvallis facility until a permanent home is available."

"Can she have calls or visitors?"

"Eventually, but for now, no. Not until we complete our investigation."

"I understand." Sue closed her eyes. "Has she said anything more about the incident? Has she changed her story at all?"

"I am not at liberty to share information we receive from a minor."

"Oh, right. Of course." Too much to hope for.

"But I *can* tell you that the allegations made against your employee have been dropped."

Sue's heart soared. "Thank you," she said, barely more than a whisper. "And thank you for calling and letting me know she's safe." Sue rushed to the kitchen and met the question in Bertie's eyes. "Brandi's been found. She's a little rough and needs rehab, but she's alive."

"I'm glad she's safe. I was fearing the worst." Bertie cocked her head. "And . . .?"

Sue ran a dishcloth over the counter in slow, even swipes. "The charges against Joe were dropped. I assume that means Brandi admitted she lied."

And if so, thank God she had, for Joe's sake.

435

If Brandi had the courage to tell the truth, then Sue was very proud of her and hoped to get a chance to tell the girl someday.

"So Joe's cleared?"

"Yes." Frowning, Sue bent low and scrubbed at a mark on the counter, mentally scolding herself again for not seeing the truth from the start. For being so quick to act on damaged instincts. *God, help me. I don't want to do that to anyone ever again.*

The older woman set down her cup and shuffled closer to Sue. "You did the best you could, Sue. You're only human. Don't forget that."

"I'm not likely to forget." Sue kept scrubbing. "We both know I made a lot of mistakes, Bert. I wish I could go back and undo them."

Because not a day passes that I don't relive every one of them.

She could keep wishing and keep trying to forget the things she'd done. Or she could forgive herself, learn from her mistakes, and move on.

"Sue, you know there's no point looking back."

She sighed. "I know. Focus my energy on avoiding future mistakes."

Bertie took off her glasses and rubbed the lenses on the hem of her new rainbow tie-dyed shirt. "Well, I'm not holding my breath. But I'll still be your sidekick anytime."

Sue shot her a faint smile. "Careful. Praise like that will go straight to my head."

436

Bertie winked. "Hey, I know what side my bread is buttered on. Speaking of which, time to wake the boys for breakfast." She headed to the back door with her coffee.

After breakfast, as the kids prepared for room checks, Sue discovered Chaz was missing. After a few minutes of hunting, she found him in the utility room.

He'd already dismantled an electric can opener and a heavy-duty flashlight and was working on the only handheld mixer that still worked.

While she was having a talk with him, Ringo galloped into the room with a bark, his shaggy coat glistening with melting snow.

"Hey! Who let the dog in like that?" Sue hollered.

Ringo shook his fur, sending droplets of water and chunks of snow flying.

"Yu-u-ck! Ringo, outside! Jasmine?" Sue shouted.

Ringo ran out, then raced back in to Sue, prancing. With another bark, he disappeared.

Goofball. Sue followed him. In the dining hall, a blast of icy air hit. The front door stood wide open, sending in more frigid gusts. She went to close the door but came to a halt at the sight of a large man standing in the middle of her front lawn.

CHAPTER THIRTY-EIGHT

Joe's heart thudded when Sue appeared in the doorway.

She didn't move. Just stood there staring at him, eyes wide.

Maybe he was wrong about her message. Maybe she didn't know the charges had been dropped and was afraid he was criminally trespassing.

But Sue wasn't looking at him with fear. In fact, the way she was looking at him wiped away his assertion that he had no more feelings for her.

Wagging like crazy, Ringo bumped Joe's hand.

Absently, he petted the dog. His gaze traveled to the sign, *My Father's House*, hanging slightly askew above the entrance. He had no idea why he was here—he had no plan. All he knew was her message needled at him until he grabbed the next flight to Portland and then drove for hours in the dark—for no other reason than to see the sign for himself.

A roar of voices brought Sonja, Deeg, and Edgar bursting out of the house, followed by Vince and Cori. They tumbled down the steps, yelling.

"J-man!"

"You came back!"

He smiled, filled with a rush of pure joy.

Chaz burst out of the house and flew down the steps, passing the others. Not slowing, he rammed Joe in the stomach with a fierce head-butt, knocking Joe back a step.

"Whoa," he said, reaching out to steady the boy. "Easy there, buddy."

Chaz jerked away and backed out of reach. He straightened his glasses, face mottled shades of pink, and glared at Joe's knees. "You didn't even say good-bye."

Crud.

"I'm sorry about that, Chaz."

Cori patted him on the back while the others came out and gathered around, high-fiving him.

Chaz stood off to one side, complexion still splotchy, arms banded across his chest.

Sue descended the steps. Behind her, a bandaged Jasmine crossed the porch on crutches.

"Papa Joe!"

What had happened to Jas?

"Hey, Joe!" Linda hollered from the doorway. "Come inside. You wanna freeze?"

Joe stole a glance at Sue, then examined each of the kids. "Chaz is right, guys. I should've said good-bye. I'm sorry about that."

"That's okay," Cori said, smiling. "You're here now."

Joe winced. "Only for a few minutes."

Sonja gasped. "What do you mean? You're not staying?"

Jasmine clunked to the edge of the steps, face puckering. "Papa Joe? You leaving us again?" She burst into tears.

Double crud. He was twenty kinds of rotten for coming here.

"*I* knew he wouldn't stay," Chaz muttered. "Everyone always leaves."

Joe winced. "Not everyone, buddy." He looked at Sue.

She stood a few yards away, eyes glistening.

"Miss Susan is staying. You guys don't have to worry about going anywhere ever again."

A murmur rippled through the crowd.

Behind Sue, Bertie emerged from the house. "All right, time to move this little reunion inside. Come on, guys, before you all turn into popsicles."

The kids filed up the steps and into the house, but Sue crossed the lawn to where Joe stood, eyes filled with confusion. "Why did you give me the property?"

He'd asked himself the same question a thousand times.

To finish what I started.

Joe glanced up at the sign. "Just something I needed to do."

Her gaze fell. When she lifted her eyes again,

grief like he'd never seen swam in their depths.

He cleared his throat. "I got your message."

Sue nodded but said nothing.

He wanted to ask his questions and leave, but the misery on her face tore at him and the words wouldn't come.

"Joe, I know this doesn't mean much now," she said. "But I want to tell you how sorry I am. I can't imagine how much I hurt you." Her voice cracked. "I don't deserve your forgiveness. But I keep remembering how you forgave your family. I know it was really hard, but you did it anyway. I wonder if someday you might find it in your heart to forgive me too." Tears streaked her cheeks, but she didn't turn away to hide them. Chin trembling, she wiped her face with shaking hands.

He swallowed hard. Seeing her broken and asking his forgiveness struck him in a way that made his heart pound.

Was it that important to her?

Forgiveness was a gift of grace, a gift he'd received himself. It wasn't something he could ever withhold from anyone who asked for it.

Joe sighed. "It's not a matter of someday, Sue." His voice softened. "I forgive you."

Her eyes closed and she wiped her cheeks again. "Thank you," she whispered. She turned toward the house. "So I guess you're here for your sign."

He frowned. Was he?

"Look," she said, voice low. "I know you don't think it belongs on my home or that I have what it takes to live up to that name, and you're probably right." Her words tumbled out in a rush. "This is all new to me. I gave my heart to God, and I hung that sign there because I needed a way to say that." Shivering, she rubbed her bare arms. "I know hanging those words on the outside won't automatically change what happens inside my home—or my heart. That will take time. The sign was just . . . a promise."

All of Sue's previous anger and fear of getting close to God came to mind. Had she really surrendered her heart to Him? Oh, the possibilities for her now were endless.

"I'm glad to hear that, Sue." Not only glad, but honored that he'd been the one to tell her about God. Which was what God had wanted from Joe all along—to show her His love.

Not to fall in love.

A shadow dampened his joy over her news. He didn't need any more reminders that he still had feelings she couldn't reciprocate.

"You probably think it was crazy to hang that sign," she said. "And maybe it was. It doesn't matter now." She spoke softly. "Your 'condition' made me realize there's no question about keeping my kids and our home." Her voice snagged on the last word. She shivered again and met his gaze. "If you want the sign, it's yours."

"I'm not going to take your sign, Sue. You keep it."

Her brow gathered in confusion. "Are you sure?"

He nodded, ashamed of himself. Anyone who'd take that sign away from her deserved to be flogged.

"So if you're not here for the sign, then why are you here?"

Good question.

"Tell him I believe in him."

Then it hit him. The evidence must have finally stacked up in Joe's favor after Brandi's confession.

"How long did it take?"

Sue frowned. "For what?"

"For Brandi to confess she lied?"

Sue's gaze fell to the center of his chest. "I don't know if she ever did," she said quietly. "I found out this morning that the charges were dropped. I can only assume she changed her story."

Joe's mind worked to add it up. It didn't. "Then . . . why the message two days ago saying you believe in me?"

She raised grief-filled eyes to meet his. "I know what kind of man you are. Kind, honorable, and more trustworthy than anyone I've ever known. I know you're not capable of hurting anyone."

Bitter words bubbled up before he could stop them. "You didn't know those things the last time I was here?"

Her chin quivered. "My heart always knew," she said. "The heart I should have been listening to."

Joe found it hard to breathe. "So you believe I'm innocent? Without even hearing my side of the story?"

She nodded, cheeks flaming. "I'm sorry for not listening to you. And for what I said that day. And for all the things I've said and all the ways I've hurt you—" Her voice choked on the last word. She looked away and wept.

His heart hammered.

"I'm so sorry," she whispered between sobs. "I can't stop thinking about all the things I said."

"You were scared."

She shook her head. "Please don't make excuses for what I did. I know I hurt you."

"Yes, you did." He blurted it without thinking.

With a sob, Sue crumpled to the ground.

Heart twisting, Joe sank to his knees in the snow and touched her arm.

She didn't look up. Her face nearly touched her knees. She gasped between sobs, as if trying to stop.

Go on, tell her again how she hurt you, jerk. "Sue, listen to me." He swallowed hard. It was a huge risk, exposing the still-tender wound. Huge.

"It broke my heart that you believed me capable of that. But only because I loved you so much."

She wept harder.

Ringo licked Sue's hand.

Joe looked toward the house. He caught movement at the den window.

Bertie peeked from between the curtains.

The front door opened, and Jasmine came outside. She clunked down the steps and crutched across the lawn. "Papa Joe?" She was shivering by the time she reached them. "Mama Sue talk to Papa God in chapel for you. Every day." She leaned on Sue and stroked her hair. "Tell him what you tell me, Mama. Tell him you love him and miss him so much."

Hope rushed through his veins and burst through his heart like an anthem.

"Mama Sue so sad for you, Papa Joe. See her bones? She not eat. Not even Miss Layne's chocolate."

But Joe didn't care about a single word after *tell him you love him.*

Sue's snow-soaked knees and legs were numb. She wiped her face and glanced up, but she couldn't meet those searching eyes, the ones that suddenly seemed to see straight through her. "Joe, you once asked me 'what if?' Well, now I want to ask you. What if I hadn't run away that night after the banquet but stayed in your arms

445

and told you I loved you too? What if I could go back and undo the terrible things I did?"

He didn't say anything.

She closed her eyes, even though she'd been crying her guts out in the middle of her lawn and had nothing left to hide. "Because I need to know what I threw away. Maybe knowing what I lost will help me never make the same mistake again."

He still didn't answer.

Sorrow shot straight through her.

Warm fingers lifted her chin. "Sue," he whispered.

She looked up.

His eyes were tender, not hateful.

Her heart hammered.

"Sue, if I knew you cared for me, even a little, I'd be here now, on my knees in the snow, unable to think straight, because you're so close I can almost hear your heart beating."

Funny, because the rumble in his voice nearly stopped her heart.

"And if I thought you loved me, then I'd pour out my heart and tell you I want nothing more than to be right here with you."

Tears welled again, blinding her.

Joe brushed a thumb over her cheek. "I'd wipe your tears and tell you how God brought me here to show you His love, but I fell in love with you along the way. I'd tell you how I . . ." He glanced at Jasmine and cleared his throat. His voice fell to a husky whisper. "How I've loved you since the moment I carried you in my arms."

The depth of his voice sent tendrils of warmth curling through her.

He turned to Jasmine. "And the worst thing is, I miss you guys so much it's wrecked my appetite. I'm so weak from malnourishment I probably can't even make it up those stairs."

Jasmine giggled.

Sue felt a smile tugging at her frozen cheeks. She cupped his face, savoring the roughness of his unshaven jaw and the raw hope in his eyes. She pulled him close and touched his lips with a tiny, trembling kiss. "I love you, Joe," she whispered against his skin. "So much."

With a sigh, he wrapped his arms around her, warming her instantly. Then he reached for Jasmine and pulled her in, engulfing them both in a suffocating bear hug.

Joy surged through her. She did not deserve this forgiveness, these kids, and certainly not Joe's love. The love that began when—

Her head snapped up. "Wait. You *carried* me? When?"

A slow smile spread across his face. "After your knee surgery. Torpedo? Sesame Street? Any of that ring a bell?"

She shook her head. "You carried me, and I *missed* it?"

Joe grinned. "Want me to do a reenactment?" He stood and scooped her up. Love shone in his eyes.

"Hey," Jasmine said. "What about me? I have broken leg!"

Joe reached for the girl.

Sue laughed. "Joe, you can't possibly—"

"What? You guys are like feathers." Joe lifted Jasmine too. With Sue in one arm and Jasmine in the other, he jogged to the porch and up the steps, Ringo trailing them.

As Jasmine bounced, her laughter sounded like bubbles on the wind.

At the door, Joe hesitated and turned to Sue. "Sweetheart, I can only go in there on one condition. You know that, right?"

She bit back a smile and raised a brow. "More conditions? But we're freezing."

He blasted out a giant, steamy puff. "You have to marry me. That's the only way I can stay."

Her heart skittered. Loving Joe, sharing this home, this family with him—

"Duh." Jasmine rolled her eyes at him, grinning. "Of course Mama will marry you, Papa."

Sue looked into his eyes. "You know the kids are part of the deal, right? All of them."

"*All* of them?" Joe turned to Jasmine in mock horror. "Even this little one here?" He jiggled her until she broke out in giggles again. He looked into Sue's eyes. Something solemn and tender radiated from his expression. "Yes, ma'am," he said softly. "I sure do."

Her heart swelled to nearly bursting. "And the guitar comes along on all of our picnics from now on."

"You drive a tough bargain." Joe heaved a sigh, eyes twinkling. "All right. So is it a deal?"

Smiling from the joy she couldn't contain, Sue nodded. "Deal."

Bertie flung the door wide, her glasses glinting from a peculiar sparkle in her eyes. "Welcome home, Joe."

ABOUT THE AUTHOR

Camille Eide is an award-winning author of faith-inspiring love stories and relational dramas for women who might like to read Karen Kingsbury, Deborah Raney, Susan Meissner, Rachel Hauck, Susan May Warren, or Robin Jones Gunn, just to name a few.

She lives near Portland, Oregon, with her handsome hero of more than 30 years. Camille is mom to three charming adults and is a proud Grammy. By day, she's a church office manager. When she's not pounding the keyboard, they let her play bass guitar and sing in the worship band. She is a fan of Harleys, Oldies Rock, Jane Austen, muscle cars, and Peanut M&Ms. She has random skills that include whipping up a pile of cinnamon rolls for a crowd of drooling young adults.

Camille blogs about God's amazing grace at Along the Banks (camilleeide.wordpress.com), reviews books and inspirational TV/Film at Extreme Keyboarding (camilleeide.blogspot.com), and writes heart-tugging tales of love, faith, and family, sprinkled with bits of wisdom and wit.

ACKNOWLEDGMENTS

Although the bulk of writing a novel falls on the novelist, it often takes multiple people to gather up all the dangling participles and bring a book to fruition. Randy Ingermanson's Columbia River Christian Writers, ACFW Genesis judges, and the "Friday Critters" have all christened this story in its early days with their helpful red pens. Thank you!

I'm deeply grateful to the dedicated, professional team at Ashberry Lane and their diligent partners for believing in my stories and in me, and for making publishing a book seem like a fun family project.

I owe more than I can say to my amazing husband, Dan, for his godly wisdom, patience, and support. And I am forever indebted to my writer friend & soul sister—the ever-gracious, immensely talented Carla Stewart.

This book would not exist if not for the hospitality of the Christmas Valley Eides who helped me envision "Juniper Valley" through decades of visits to Central Oregon's high desert, where I fell in love with its quiet, rugged beauty.

I would like to give special thanks to Megan Eide and Donnalee Velvick-Lowry for introducing me to foster group home life and to the unique kind of "family" that Hope House (Marsing, Idaho) provides, giving love to abandoned kids who would otherwise have no home to come home to.

And most of all, I owe my humblest gratitude to God for his love of story; particularly the Genesis account of how the brokenness of one turned into the blessing of many. I thank God for revealing his Father heart and unwavering love without fail.

If you would like to know more about helping a special young person become a successful, self-confident adult, visit Hope House at www.ahome2come2.com. Gifts to Hope House are tax deductible.

DISCUSSION QUESTIONS

1. Sue Quinn is a woman with old wounds and trouble with trust. How did lingering fears influence some of the choices she made?

2. What effect did her buried hurts have on the foster kids and on Joe? Have past betrayals or injuries ever skewed your choices, decisions, or reactions in a way you later regretted?

3. Sue tried to keep the kids from becoming attached to Joe. Was that wise? What would you have done in her place?

4. Joe bears a strong allegorical resemblance to a man in the book of Genesis. Who is it, and how many similarities to that story can you find in this one?

5. Joe soon finds himself falling for Sue. What is it about her that draws him? Why do you think these attributes appeal to Joe?

6. Sue claimed she expects nothing from so-called family. Did you doubt her claims?

How do the kids living at the Juniper Ranch group home meet her unacknowledged needs?

7. Several spiritual themes appear in this story. Which do you struggle with most?

   a. Though people may disappoint or even hurt us, God's love never fails.
   b. God can use bad things for a greater good (Genesis 50).
   c. With God, surrender brings freedom.

8. Sue dislikes being dependent on others, yet she agreed to give over a measure of control in order to realize her dream. In what ways, if any, have you ever had to relinquish control in order to bring about something bigger than your abilities?

9. How is Jasmine similar to Sue? How is she different?

10. What prompted Joe to "finish what he started"? Could you set aside your personal feelings or pride if it meant bringing about a greater good?

11. To whom do you relate in the story? What would you say to him or her if given a chance?

12. What fueled Sue's dream to run a group home, and what did she expect to accomplish? Were her expectations realistic?

13. If you, like Joe, had an opportunity to face people who had at one time betrayed, abandoned, or hurt you, what would you do with it?

14. What can we learn about family from this story?

Center Point Large Print
600 Brooks Road / PO Box 1
Thorndike, ME 04986-0001 USA

(207) 568-3717

US & Canada:
1 800 929-9108
www.centerpointlargeprint.com